BOUND

SJD PETERSON

Published by

DREAMSPINNER PRESS

5032 Capital Circle SW, Suite 2, PMB# 279, Tallahassee, FL 32305-7886 USA
www.dreamspinnerpress.com/

Bound
© 2016 SJD Peterson.

Cover Art
© 2016 Paul Richmond.
http://www.paulrichmondstudio.com
Cover content is for illustrative purposes only and any person depicted on the cover is a model.

ISBN: 978-1-63476-799-6
Digital ISBN: 978-1-63476-800-9
Library of Congress Control Number: 2015917569
Published March 2016
v. 1.0

Printed in the United States of America
∞
This paper meets the requirements of
ANSI/NISO Z39.48-1992 (Permanence of Paper).

Readers love the Guards of Folsom series by SJD PETERSON

Pup

"If you love BDSM, good characters, great M/M loving, strong technical writing, combined with an excellent story and plot, then I say grab *Pup* ASAP."

—On Top Down Under Reviews

"Well 24 hours after finishing, I still can't find anything I didn't like… if you are a fan of SJD 'Jo' Peterson, don't hesitate to buy this."

—Hearts on Fire

Tag Team

"…I just sat back and thought WOW! Because from the very first page my heart was bleeding… the impact took my breath away and I wasn't putting my book down for anything."

—Sinfully Gay Romance Book Reviews

Pony

"I was captivated by this third installment in the series and am now lusting after more. Thank you, again, to the incredible author, Jo Peterson, for giving voices to my guys and another beautiful love story for me to enjoy."

—Rainbow Book Reviews

Roped

"The writing is marvelous and I love these characters…"

—Love Bytes

"I found this story really intriguing."

—Joyfully Jay

By SJD Peterson

BAMF
Beyond Duty
Innocence to the Max
Leon
Masters & Boyd
My Hometown
A Night Never Forgotten
Plan B
Rival Within
With S.A. McAuley: Ruin Porn
Splintered
Tuck & Cover

GUARDS OF FOLSOM
Riveted
Pup
Tag Team
Pony
Roped
Mauled
Bound

WHISPERING PINES RANCH
Lorcan's Desire
Quinn's Need
Ty's Obsession
Conner's Courage
Jess's Journey

Published by DREAMSPINNER PRESS
www.dreamspinnerpress.com

To all those who demanded Ty get his happily ever after. It's because of you that this series was written. To Sam, who demanded I write Tek & Jamie's story.

And to Erika and Jason, the two best editors in the world. Thank you for keeping all this straight and for making me shine. I love you both!

Author's Note

Wow, what a wild ride this series has been. It all began with the Whispering Pines series and Ty's lack of a Happily Ever After. I couldn't have known when I decided to write *Riveted* (a free read for Ty & Blake) that it would lead to yet another series, but I'm so glad it did. I fell in love with the scatterbrained Micah, wept for Mason, and cheered for Aiden. Tek & Jamie? What can I say, other than I lurve them so hard. Thank you to all those who took this journey with me. I hope it was as rewarding to read as it was for me to write.

~Hugs~

Jo

Vignette from Pup

Guards of Folsom: Book One

Micah and Tackett

MICAH STOOD naked before the full-length mirror, lovingly running a finger over the soft leather of his collar—Tackett's collar—with a broad smile on his face. It hadn't been all that long since he'd forced himself into Tackett's home and heart. Yet, Micah barely remembered a life before Tackett. That's not to say he'd blocked out his past, far from it. The difference being, he'd lived his life fluttering from one thing to another, his mind on rapid fire and rarely landing long enough to truly take joy in anything.

Tackett changed that.

Micah cocked his head and really studied his reflection. He looked the same and yet felt worlds away from who he had been. He'd grown, matured, learned under Tackett's loving hands. He attempted to smooth down his hair, an impossible feat, and tugged at a wayward curl. Perhaps it was time for a haircut; present a more grown-up Micah to the world, less of a tease.

"You look beautiful, pup."

Startled, Micah's heart leapt and he jerked his head to the side to see Tackett leaning against the door with a broad smile.

"Thank you, Sir," Micah responded, returning the smile.

"You looked deep in thought. Care to share what you were thinking about?"

Micah turned back to his reflection. "I was thinking, maybe it's time for a new look, a grown-up look." He tugged another curl, watching it bounce back. "Manlier."

Tackett crossed the room in three long strides and grabbed Micah's wrist, pulling his hand away from his hair. "You are all man, pup, and if you dare cut a single curl from your head, I will deny you the right to come until they grow back."

Micah looked up at Tackett from under his long lashes, his body heating from Tackett's nearness. "Will you spank me, Sir?"

Tackett released Micah's wrist and ran his hand gently along Micah's hair, running his fingers through it. "Only if you spare the curls."

Micah slid his arm around Tackett's waist, pushing up close and nuzzling Tackett's neck. "They make me look like a kid." He brushed his lips softly over the warm skin.

"I assure you, I have never thought of you as a kid."

Micah pulled his head back and gave Tackett a disbelieving look. Tackett laughed and pecked him on the nose. "Okay, I might have referred to you as a kid when we first met."

"I do believe you asked me if I was old enough to shave, Sir." Micah started to giggle when he remembered his response. *Only my balls.*

"Yeah, well, that's because I'm an old man. I promise you, I've never thought of you as a child." He moved his hand from Micah's hair, running it along his back to his ass and squeezed. "I've always known you're all man, even when you're my boy."

"I like being your boy." Micah went back to nuzzling Tackett's neck, pushing up close and finding a little friction for his hardening cock along the soft cotton of Tackett's pants.

"Good, and my boy will have a head full of curls. Is that understood?"

"Yes, Sir, but—" He yelped when a hard slap landed on his ass.

Tackett rubbed the abused flesh. "There is no *but* except this one. Now, I do believe you were supposed to be in here getting dressed."

"I got distracted, Sir." Micah rolled his hips, rutting just a little. "Wouldn't you rather stay home tonight? I can make us a quick dinner."

"We have reservations."

"I know." Micah pouted. So much for the maturity thingy, but he was willing to use what he had.

Emboldened by the fact that Tackett wasn't releasing him but rather massaging both his ass cheeks, Micah stepped up his game. He pulled Tackett's shirt from the waistband of his pants and slid his hands beneath the material, running them along the taut muscles of Tackett's back.

"Would they be horribly upset if we were late?"

"Yes. It's a very exclusive restaurant, pup. It took weeks to get in."

Micah nipped at the exposed skin at the vee of Tackett's dress shirt and inhaled the appealing scent of Tackett's warm skin. "A quick appetizer, then?"

Tackett didn't respond, allowing Micah to rub and rut against him for a few moments until Micah was achingly hard and needing.

"What are you supposed to be doing?"

"Taking your clothes off, Sir?" He reached for Tackett's belt.

Tackett grabbed his hand, halting his movement. "Are you turned on?"

"God, yes." Micah tried to pull free of Tackett's grasp.

"Needing?" Tackett's voice was deep, husky, and seductive, sending a zing of arousal straight to Micah's balls.

"Yes," Micah huffed out. He continued to struggle, needing to free himself and get the offending pants off his man.

The hold on Micah's wrist tightened to a viselike grip, painful, but it was the snap in Tackett's voice when he said "pup" that caused Micah to go still. He knew that tone, couldn't not respond to it.

Tackett took a step back. "Display, boy."

Micah was trembling with the force of his arousal, but he locked down on his muscles, complying with his Dom's order, although not without great difficulty.

"Good boy," Tackett praised. He ran the tip of one finger along Micah's straining erection. "Very pretty."

"Thank you, Sir." He gritted his teeth, fighting the urge to thrust. Fuck, he wanted to get off so goddamn bad.

"It's a shame the restaurant requires clothes."

"We can always stay home, Sir," Micah suggested once again, silently praying Tackett would agree.

"Aww, pup, you hurt my feelings. I've been looking forward to tonight."

"Sorry, Sir," Micah responded, really not feeling all that apologetic, although the guilt did make his belly flip-flop.

"Now be a good boy and finish dressing for dinner." With that, Tackett turned on his heel and left the room, the very final click of the door engaging leaving no question as to whether Micah was done begging.

Tackett could ask him to do anything and he'd do it without question, trusting, knowing in his heart his Dom would never ask him to do anything that would harm him. Tackett rarely asked him to do much. Well, much other than to always think of Tackett's needs before his own. Something that was—most of the time—as easy as breathing. When he pleased his Dom, his own rewards were always beyond simple pleasure, they were increased tenfold.

Micah knew his place; having his day set out for him—what he wore, what he cooked, his chores, a full schedule—had done a world of good for his state of mind. Most outsiders wouldn't understand his need. Many could never imagine giving up complete control to such a degree, but Micah didn't care what others would or wouldn't do, or what they thought of him. For the first time in his life, he felt at peace. His mind was no longer the enemy. That wasn't to say he still didn't struggle with hyperactivity and an overactive mind—he looked down at his raging hard-on and sighed—or that it wasn't difficult to give up such control at times. But what he did know was he was a very happy pup and he was completely and unconditionally loved by the most amazing man in the world. Still, life was a lot more fun being naughty sometimes—like now.

Micah stood staring once again at his refection. His body was flush with arousal, hard cock ruddy and straining upward, unfulfilled. He briefly thought about relieving a little pressure. It would only take one or two hard pulls. Instead, he huffed out a frustrated breath, turned away from his image, and grabbed his pants from the pile of clothes Tackett had laid out for him. He stepped into them and winced as the soft cotton material slid across his erection, and tucking himself within the cotton, buttoning, and zipping up was torturous. Even the light touches were nearly enough to send him over the edge. He struggled to find a calm mindset, tried to push down his overwhelming need to come, focus on anything other than his body's needs.

"Fancy dinner, bah." He pulled on his shirt.

He didn't understand Tackett's need to occasionally hobnob with the well-to-do. Living in Tackett's home, Micah had grown to appreciate the finer things in life. He truly was blessed. But still, where Tackett's idea of a special night in celebration included restrictive clothing, proper manners, and bubbly, Micah's ideal evening for any occasion was a pair of comfy sweats—or better yet, being naked—curled up on the couch, popcorn, a good movie, and Tackett's warmth surrounding him.

Micah finished dressing and let out a heavy sigh. "A few hours and he'll be all yours again," Micah reminded himself. He really was being quite the selfish pup.

"Let's go, boy," Tackett yelled from the hall, followed by a quick rap on the door.

Micah slid into his loafers and ran his fingers through his curls in a futile attempted to smooth them down. He walked woodenly—appropriate with the wood in his slacks—and joined Tackett in the front room. He was just about to complain again, or perhaps beg, when he spotted Tackett buttoning up his suit coat. He snapped his mouth shut. He smiled broadly. One thing about fancy dinners was his man looked damn good all dressed up.

Micah whistled. "Looking sexy, Sir."

Tackett turned to look at Micah over his shoulder with a sly grin. "That's why I endure the stuffy clothes, to have you look at me like that."

"Apparently you haven't been paying attention to the looks I give you when you're naked. You're far more impressive with nothing at all on."

"It won't work," Tackett reprimanded. He pecked Micah on the forehead before stepping away. "Now behave, pup. We're still going out."

"I wasn't even thinking that." Hoping—yes. Confident—no. "I was being honest. You really are the sexiest when you don't hide your impressive body."

"I'm an old man," Tackett sniffed and held out Micah's coat.

Micah shrugged into his jacket with Tackett's help, then grabbed Tackett's arm before he could move away, meeting Tackett's questioning gaze with a serious one of his own. "I wish you would stop saying that. You are *not* old, only slightly seasoned and in the best possible way, I assure you."

Tackett was far from old. He had a body most twenty-year-olds would die to have. But it was the knowledge and wisdom that was only obtained through life experience and etched in each beautiful line on his face that made him all the more appealing to Micah. The laugh lines around Tackett's hazel eyes were particular favorites of Micah's.

WALKING THROUGH the door of Grand Spectacle, a contemporary French restaurant, Micah stood slightly behind Tackett, a position of comfort. While Tackett spoke to the maître d', Micah did his best not to pull at the restrictive clothes. The paradox was not lost on him. He loved to be bound, but this was different. While it was still for Tackett's pleasure and he wouldn't deny his Dom anything, in this fancy-pants world, Micah simply couldn't stop worrying that he'd somehow embarrass himself or worse, Tackett.

Grand Spectacle was opulent. White linen covered the tables, crystal wineglasses and candleholders on each. Men sat stiffly in tailored suits. Women were in dresses and dripping with diamond jewelry, an air of affluence swirling around them. Everything about the place was out of Micah's league and beyond his comfort level, but Tackett was always pushing him to expand his experiences. It wasn't just that he felt out of place in such a fancy restaurant, but that he never understood paying the high fees for such decadence. However, he trusted there was a method to Tackett's madness even if at the moment he didn't understand it.

"Right this way, Mr. Austin," the maître d' said.

Tackett laid his hand at the small of Micah's back, leading him into the restaurant. Once at the table, Tackett pulled out a chair for Micah and waited for him to sit before taking the chair next to him.

"Carlos will be right with you," the maître d' informed them. He handed them each a heavy leather-bound menu before leaving them alone.

Micah opened the menu and scanned the pages quickly before closing it and setting it aside. "I can't read French. Do they have burgers and fries?"

"No, I don't believe they do," Tackett chuckled. He put his hand on Micah's thigh, teasing his fingers along the inseam of Micah's pants. "What are you in the mood for?"

Micah looked down at the hand on his thigh and then looked up at Tackett from beneath his lashes. "It's not on the menu."

"Behave, pup. That's for dessert."

Oh yeah, he was so ready for dessert. Forcing his thoughts away from his hardening dick, he did his best to focus on getting through dinner—quickly. "I don't have a preference. How about you surprise me and order me something yummy?"

"I can do that."

The waiter came over and introduced himself as Carlos. Micah sat enthralled as Tackett spoke fluent French. There was still so much he didn't know about his Dom and lover. Carlos poured them each a glass of red wine before excusing himself.

Micah leaned over and whispered, "That was so damn sexy, Sir."

Tackett picked up his glass and brought it to his nose, sniffing it before swirling the dark liquid and taking a small sip. "Ordering dinner is sexy?"

"Jesus, that was sexy too. But yeah, ordering dinner is sexy when it's you doing it. Add in a little French and I could come in my pants."

"Don't you dare. It will ruin our dessert plans, and I'm sure you wouldn't want to deny me the pleasure of my after-dinner treats."

With the long linen tablecloth obstructing the view, Micah grabbed the hand Tackett had on his thigh and pulled it up to the hard bulge in his slacks. "I'd never deny you anything," he whispered. He pushed into Tackett's touch.

Tackett curled his fingers around Micah's cock, squeezing and causing Micah to take in a sharp breath. "You are hell-bent on driving me nuts tonight, aren't you, pup?"

"It's seems only fair, Sir." Micah bit his lip to keep back the moan Tackett's touch elicited.

Tackett squeezed Micah's dick one more time, then pulled away. "Drink your wine, boy."

"Yes, Sir." Micah pouted.

Tackett sat back in his chair, sipping his wine as he looked around the restaurant. "I told you that pout wasn't going to work on me tonight."

Micah glanced down to Tackett's lap and noticed the tent growing in his trousers and smirked. "Not even a little bit?"

"Nope. This is a nice place, isn't it?"

"It is," Micah agreed, but his gaze never left Tackett. Nothing or no one could hold Micah's focus like Tackett. It had been that way since he'd first laid eyes on the man. Sure, he'd struggled with his hyperactive brain, still did at times, probably always would. But with Tackett's help, Micah was able to control it a lot better than he used to, and every day with Tackett was a pure joy.

Carlos returned to the table and set a plate down in front of Micah. The scents of garlic, butter, and grilled steak wafted up and caused his belly to growl. "Wow, this looks and smells amazing." Micah laid his napkin across his lap before grabbing his silverware.

"Filet mignon stuffed with seasoned goat cheese," Tackett commented.

"Oh, you do know me too well."

"I simply know what you like."

Micah's mouth watered, but he held back, waiting until Tackett picked up his fork and took a bite of his pasta before digging in to his own meal. He moaned his pleasure around the first bite.

Neither Micah nor Tackett said much during the meal. The food, the setting, the company was comfortable, easy, and soon Micah was no longer feeling out of his element nor did the clothes bother him—too much.

Micah dropped his fork on his empty plate and pushed it away. "I am stuffed. I can't believe I ate all of it, but it was sooooo good," he purred.

"Did you leave room for dessert?" Tackett asked, waving over the waiter.

"Only the kind that burns calories rather than packs them on." Micah patted his belly.

"What a shame." Tackett gestured for the arriving waiter to lean down. He whispered something to Carlos, but Micah wasn't able to make out what they were saying.

"Very good, sir," Carlos said with a smile. He leaned back and picked up the dirty plates.

"What was that about?" Micah asked as soon as Carlos was out of earshot.

"Just sending a compliment to the chef."

"Uh-huh. That's a deep secret, huh?"

"That it is," Tackett said curtly.

He was up to something, Micah could tell from the smug smile on Tackett's face and the way he kept his eyes averted. It was driving him nuts. He wanted to ask what the hell but knew better. It would be futile. Tackett didn't do anything until he was ready and only on his terms, something Micah both loved and disliked about his Dom.

A few minutes passed and Micah began to shift uncomfortably in his chair when Carlos didn't return and Tackett continued to focus on everything within the restaurant but Micah. "Is he bringing the check soon?" Micah asked. He shifted again.

"Yes."

Micah wiped his mouth and set his napkin aside, picked up his empty wine glass and set it back down. He fiddled and shifted, began bouncing his leg. "Will he be here soon?"

"It's only been a couple of minutes, pup. Give the man a chance."

A couple of minutes? Damn, it felt like hours. "Really?"

"Yes, really." Tackett laid his hand back on Micah's thigh, massaging. "Take a deep breath and relax. We're in no hurry. Have nowhere to be at any set time."

"Hard to do that." Micah continued to shift and bounce his knee, scanning frantically for Carlos. "Talks of dessert and pleasure and secrets and your smug smile and—"

"My smug smile?"

Micah arched a brow at him. "Don't play coy, Sir. It doesn't work for you."

"Here we are," Carlos announced. He sat down two mugs, one a steaming cup of black coffee in front of Tackett and one that smelled like chocolate, heaping high with whipped cream and chocolate shavings. But it wasn't the amazing smelling drink that had Micah's jaw dropping, but the small blue bow tied around the teaspoon, attaching a gold ring to it.

"Is…?" Micah swallowed hard, his heart hammering. "Is that what I think it is?"

Tackett nonchalantly picked up his cup, blew the steam away, and took a small sip. "I don't know. What do you think it is?"

Micah pulled the ribbon and released the ring, picking it up and running his fingertip over the cool metal. "Well, it's either the fanciest presentation of hot chocolate or…." Micah's eyes grew wide and he gaped at Tackett. "Oh my God. Are you asking me to marry you?"

To Micah's utter surprise, Tackett took the ring from him and dropped to one knee next to Micah's chair. "You've already accepted my collar and made me a very happy and proud Dom." Tackett took Micah's hand in his. "Micah Slayde, will you now make me the happiest and proudest man by becoming my husband too?"

"Yes. Oh. My. God. Yes!" Micah squealed. He launched himself at Tackett, wrapping his arms around his neck and peppering his man's face with kisses.

Micah was scarcely aware of the applause or gasps and congrats. He only had eyes for Tackett. He swore if he loved the man any more, his damn heart would explode.

Micah thought maybe he'd drunk his hot chocolate but wasn't sure as he floated out of the restaurant. The only thing tethering him and keeping him from flying away was the firm hand holding his. *Married? I'm going to get married. To Tackett!*

"When? Should we have a big wedding, a small one, in between? Do you think we should have it in a church, justice of the peace? What about the reception? You do want to have a reception, don't you? Maybe at the club? Oh wait, maybe you'd rather have it somewhere else like a banquet hall, keep the two events separate. Oh shit, I gotta call Phillip, he's wonderful with planning events like this. He actually—"

Tackett's warm mouth covering his cut off Micah's words. His mind still reeled, flipping through one idea after another like a blinking neon sign, but then Tackett's tongue was pushing deep, swirling with his. The flavor, the feel of Tackett's slick, wet mouth sent a jolt straight to Micah's cock, and then nothing else mattered other than getting more of his man. Micah slid his hands around Tackett's waist, pulling their groins together, letting Tackett feel what he was doing to him, and moaning into the kiss when their hard cocks came in contact.

"That's better." Tackett nipped at Micah's bottom lip.

"Better than what, Sir?" Micah groaned, still trying his best to rut against Tackett.

"That I, rather than wedding plans, have your full attention."

"Wedding plans…. Oh right. Yay! I'm getting married. I—"

Tackett laid a finger over Micah's lips. "Don't you dare. We have plenty of time for that later. Now I just want to go home and have some dessert."

"Mmm, is this my dessert?" Micah thrust against Tackett.

"No, it's mine," Tackett chuckled. "But I might be inclined to share."

"Sharing is good between married folks, ya know," Micah pointed out.

"Yes, it is. Now let's go home."

Micah had to control his steps, struggled to keep them in pace with Tackett's when what he really wanted to do was break out into a run. The sooner they got home, the sooner he—they could celebrate.

The sound of "Like a Boss" playing informed Micah that Blake was calling Tackett.

Tackett pulled out his cell, looked at the display, and then arched a brow at Micah.

"What?" he responded, trying his best to sound innocent.

Tackett shook his head and answered the call. "Hey, Blake. How are you?" After a slight pause, Tackett stopped dead in his tracks. "That's horrible. What can we do to help?"

"What is it?"

Tackett held up one finger to shush him.

Micah pushed close, trying to hear what Blake was saying that would put such a concerned look on Tackett's face, but he could only hear jumbled words that made no sense. He shifted nervously from foot to foot, squeezing Tackett's hand as his dread increased. Something was very wrong.

"We'll be there within the hour." Tackett returned his cell to his pocket.

"What's going on? Be where in an hour?"

Tackett laid a hand against Micah's cheek. "We're going to have to postpone our dessert. Someone has kidnapped Jamie. We've gotta go to the club. Tek needs us."

"Poor Jamie. Oh God, poor Tek. Of course we'll be there. Let's go." Micah yanked on Tackett's hand to get him moving. There was no question. Micah could be a bit selfish at times but not when it came to his friends. He'd do, and knew Tackett would too, whatever they could to help.

Vignette from Tag Team

Guards of Folsom: Book Two

Rig, Bobby, and Mason

IN THE distance a bolt of lightning cracked, splitting the horizon. The clouds churned, gray swirling billows overtaking the robin's-egg blue of an otherwise peaceful summer sky. As if even the heavens were manifesting Mason's anger, bearing witness to Gregory's defeat and reflecting the sorrow of Charles's soul trapped in that pine box.

But not today.

Today a brilliant blue sky was above Mason as he kneeled next to the headstone of his late lover, Dom, and friend. The tears of loss and grief were the same, the hole in his heart and soul still present as it would be for the rest of his existence. Yet, as he clutched the box to his chest that contained the remains of his other lover, Dom, and friend, Mason knew this time he'd be able to make it through the agony. Once the tears stopped falling and the grief released its hold on him, he'd be able to stand again. His trembling legs might be weak, but he'd be supported by the two men who had saved him from despair and pulled him away from the edge of the abyss.

Neither Bobby nor Rig said a word as they stood over him like sentries. They couldn't protect Mason from the painful memories or the agony of loss, but with their strength and love as warm as the afternoon Florida sun, this time Mason knew he'd be okay.

I'm here, Charles, and I brought Gregory. I don't know if you can hear me. I know you weren't big on the whole heaven thing or life beyond, but just in case you can hear me, I need you to know there isn't a day I don't think about you and Gregory. I miss you both like crazy, but I'm okay now. I still grapple with guilt, you know. Sometimes I hate myself for laughing, smiling, living. But Bobby and Rig are helping me, and each day I'm getting stronger. I even have a few new friends. I know you won't believe this, but I'm actually a member of a new club and can go there, you know, around people.

Mason smiled through his tears as he thought of Micah and Ty and the rest of the amazing men within the walls of the Guards of Folsom. He turned his attention back to Charles and shrugged.

In small doses anyway. They're good to me, Charles. Bobby and Rig have immeasurable amounts of patience with me, but I'm scared. I'm still holding back. I want to have with them what we had, but....

Mason choked on a sob, felt the weight of loss crashing down on him, stealing his breath. A hand landed on each of Mason's shoulders, and then like clouds parting, revealing the sun, the storm passed and he was able to get control of himself once again. Mason blew out a steadying breath.

I realize I'm holding on to the past, that I can't truly live again, give Bobby and Rig what they need, what they deserve, until I say good-bye and let you and Gregory go. I promise I will love you both always, but I love them too and I want to make them happy, be what they want. But I need to know that's okay, Charles.

Mason tipped his head back and closed his eyes, Charles's and Gregory's smiling faces so vivid it was if they were there with him. Mason wasn't sure if it was a sign or it was Bobby and Rig, but suddenly he felt as if he'd been wrapped in big, strong arms and a peace settled into him. The tears stopped, the sun drying his damp cheeks, and he breathed deeply and steadily. A gentle breeze began to blow, and Mason knew it was time. One more deep breath and he opened his eyes. He carefully opened the small box and pushed to his feet.

With the loving arms of Bobby and Rig around him, Mason tipped the box slowly. The wind took the ashes, swirled them, some floating to the ground to cover the grave; others swirled and blew out in the direction of the ocean. Gregory would now forever be a part of the water and land he loved so much as well as with his friend and confidant.

Mason, Bobby, and Rig stood together, watching until the last of the ashes floated away. Mason looked up at first Bobby and then Rig with a smile. "I'm ready."

Bobby placed a soft kiss to Mason's temple. "So proud of you, baby."

Rig simply winked at Mason and held him a little tighter. Mason knew this was part of the healing process. Bobby and Rig had been where Mason was standing now. They understood Mason's grief, had experienced their own when they'd lost their sub. Charles might not have believed in God; Mason couldn't be sure he did either. However, he had to believe there was a higher power at work. How else could he explain how Bobby and Rig had come to him when he needed them most or that they had been in the same type of relationship he, Charles, and Gregory had and understood. Not only understood, but had lived past their own loss and had been looking for a boy to complete them.

Charles and Gregory were his past, Bobby and Rig his destiny.

The ride back to the house was quiet but not uncomfortable, each in their own thoughts yet silently strengthening each other. Mason had one last task to complete before he could go home.

"You don't have to do this right now if you're not ready," Rig said.

Mason unlocked the door to the house he'd once called home and pushed it open. "I know, but I want to."

Bobby and Rig hung back while Mason went through each room, making sure everything was clean. He was leaving behind all the furnishings but wanted to make sure he hadn't forgotten any personal items. He was glad he'd made the trip to the grave first, because as he walked through the house, it was just that, a house. One filled with wonderful memories, but still nothing more than a house. It wasn't home.

"Mason, he's here," Bobby called from the front room.

"Hi, Donavan," Mason greeted as he stepped out into the living room, extending his hand.

Donavan shook the offered hand. "Good to see you again. I can't tell you how much we appreciate your generosity."

Donavan was the director and founder of the local homeless shelter for LGBT kids. He was also the recipient of Mason's house as well as Charles's and Gregory's vehicles.

"It's my pleasure." Mason pushed into Bobby's side, wrapping an arm around his waist. "Did you bring the paperwork?"

"I did." Donavan held up his briefcase.

"Great, let's have a seat."

Rig and Bobby took the chairs on either side of Mason. Mason knew he was doing the right thing, but finalizing it on top of the visit to the graveyard had taken its toll on him. He was mentally exhausted. Rig picked up on Mason's unease and moved his chair closer and laid a hand on Mason's thigh. It was no surprise when Bobby too moved his chair closer to Mason, his hand landing on Mason's other thigh.

"I'd offer you something to drink, but I'm afraid we've already cleaned out the fridge," Bobby apologized.

"That's quite all right." Donavan pulled a file from his briefcase and slid it across the table to Mason along with a pen. "I believe you'll find everything in order. I've marked all the places we'll need your signature."

Mason signed his name to each place a colorful tab indicated without reading the document. He trusted Donavan would have everything in order and, more importantly, had the best interest of the kids in his care at heart. Mason wasn't sure how he felt at the moment. On one hand, he knew he was doing the right thing. The kids at the center needed this place. A place where they could get away, have some fun, enjoy the beach, and just be kids. Yet on the other hand, it was tough having to say a final good-bye to the last place that tied him to his lost Doms.

With a trembling hand, Mason pushed the file back across the table.

"Are you okay?" Donavan asked. "Do you need a little more time to think about this?"

Mason shook his head and grabbed hold of Bobby's and Rig's hands, entwining their fingers. Instantly, their strength surged through Mason and gave him the confidence he needed.

"No, I don't need any time to think about it. This is what I need to do. More importantly, what I want to do."

"Thank you," Donavan said sincerely. "I hope you'll come back and visit with us. I know the kids would appreciate it."

"I'll try." Mason wasn't ready to be around a bunch of kids, especially ones who would all be swarming around to thank him. Perhaps one day.

Donavan returned the file to his briefcase and stood. "I've got to get back."

"I'll get the keys," Rig offered.

Mason and Bobby stood as well and walked Donavan to the door.

"Have you given any more thought to the name?" Donavan asked.

Donavan had asked Mason to come up with a name for the house. He'd thought a lot about it, considering the place as a camp, but hadn't been able to think of anything that seemed appropriate. When he stopped thinking of it as a camp but rather a retreat for a family getaway, the name had come to him easily.

"Charles and Gregory's Sunshine House."

Donavan stared down at his feet for a brief moment and then nodded before looking up and meeting Mason's gaze. "That's beautiful and fitting."

"Thank you," Mason said sincerely.

"Here ya go." Rig handed Donavan the two sets of keys.

"Thanks, I'll be in touch again soon."

Mason, Rig, and Bobby each shook Donavan's hand and then stood together with their arms around the other and watched him leave. Mason had expected to be filled with grief and regret, at the very least a panic attack, but nothing but calmness surrounded him. He truly was ready to try to start making steps toward his future.

"Do we have enough time to walk on the beach before we have to leave for the airport?" Mason asked.

"Of course we do," Bobby responded. "Let's go."

Mason left his shoes on the porch and walked down the path, loving the way the warm sand felt between his toes. He liked living in New York with Bobby and Rig, enjoyed his time at the club, and loved the fact that, with Max's help, he was beginning to venture out and make friends for the first time. Still, he missed the beach and wasn't a fan of the cold winters. He doubted he'd ever get used to them. But perhaps one day as his confidence grew, he'd be able to take Bobby and Rig up on their offer and start doing some traveling during the colder months, as they were not big fans of the frigid temperatures either.

Mason had barely dipped his toes into the ocean when the shrill ring of Rig's cell phone sounded.

Rig pulled it from his pocket, a scowl marring his brow as he looked at it. "It's Blake." He pushed the On button and put the phone to his ear. "Hello?"

Bobby stopped abruptly. "There must be something wrong. He knows what we are doing here."

"Yes, we're coming back today, why?" Rig asked. "What's up?"

Dread spread through Mason like wildfire, and he instantly sought out Bobby's comfort. He snuggled into his Dom's side as Rig listened, his frown deepening. Whatever Blake was saying, it wasn't good.

"Okay, we'll be there. See you tonight." Rig ended the call and returned the phone to his pocket.

"What was that all about?" Bobby asked.

"It's Jamie. He's been kidnapped."

Vignette from Pony

Guards of Folsom: Book Three

Max and Aiden

KICKED BACK on the couch, feet resting on the coffee table, Aiden took a swig of his beer and looked over at Max. "My mom and dad keep asking when they are going to get to meet you."

"I'm looking forward to meeting them," Max responded without taking his eyes from the TV.

"I really think we should make plans when your schedule eases up a bit."

Max nodded. "I'm good with whatever."

Aiden turned his attention to the TV and tried to find some interest in the program, but he couldn't. He was bored. "How can you watch this crap?" he finally asked. "You're smart, educated, a man of the world, and you're watching actors run around the bush acting like outlaws. It's embarrassing."

"*Appalachian Outlaws* is reality TV. You know, like real. These are not actors."

"You're kidding me, right?" When Max didn't respond, only continued to stare at the ridiculous antics of the men defending their moonshine, Aiden added, "You can't actually think this crap is real?"

"It's entertaining to think so," Max drawled and waved a dismissive hand at the TV. "I'd love to go running around the mountains, try living off the land."

"Daniel Boone you are not. I don't think you'd last past dark," Aiden snickered.

Max clicked off the TV and tossed the remote on the coffee table before turning on the couch to better face Aiden. "Was that a jab at my manhood?"

Aiden ran his gaze appreciatively over Max's crotch and licked his lips. "I'd never jab that. Suck, kiss, stroke, absolutely. But never jab such a fine instrument."

"Quit trying to suck up, 'cause it's working. Now, stop looking at my dick and answer the question. You really don't think I would survive past dark?"

"They don't have Internet or cell service up there on a good day. I've also been in your closet. Not so much as a decent pair of walking boots or shoes. If that wasn't bad enough, your aversion to bugs makes it almost a guarantee you'll be running in search of the first luxury hotel. I'm not saying it's a bad thing. I'm just saying you're not quite made for that kind of adventure."

"And you are, Mr. Indiana?" Max countered.

"I grew up on a dairy farm. I'm conditioned for hard work and bugs. And shit, lots and lots of shit. You, on the other hand…."

"I, on the other hand, what?"

"I'm gonna get another beer. You want something?" Aiden pushed to his feet.

"On the other hand, what?" Max repeated, following behind Aiden.

Aiden pulled a beer from the fridge and refilled his mug. He stepped out of Max's swatting distance before finally admitting, "You're not cut out for labor-intensive work."

"Is that so?" Max challenged. He stepped up close and grabbed Aiden's hip, jerking him forward. "I'd say I can handle some very intense work. I'm man enough to ride your ass hard enough for you to tap out."

"Apples and oranges, Max. Apple and oranges. And may I reiterate here, no bugs when you're working me." Max was a madman when so much as a fly got inside the condo. He hated anything that swarmed, flew, or crawled if it had more than four legs. The thought of Max roughing it was pretty funny, and he couldn't hold back the snort the idea produced.

"I do believe you're laughing at me." Max's hold on Aiden's hip tightened.

The hard hold and the growl in Max's voice went straight to Aiden's groin, and he rolled his hips against Max's. "Would I do that?"

"Yes, you would, and lucky for you, I suddenly feel the urge to prove my manliness rather than spank your naughty ass."

"Oh really? And just pray tell, how do you plan to go about that?"

Max slid his free hand around Aiden's waist and grabbed his ass. Max leaned in and ran his tongue up the side of Aiden's neck to the sensitive area beneath his ear.

"Hmm, I'm thinking of pushing you down to your knees and shoving my cock down your throat." Max nipped Aiden's earlobe, causing him to shudder and arch. "Or better yet, bending you over the island and shoving my cock up your ass would be pretty damn manly, don't you think?"

Aiden tipped his head to the side, giving Max all the room he needed to lick and taste and nip. "I'm thinking both would show your manly prowess, so I'm good with either. Both suits me too."

"Both, huh?"

"Uh-huh."

"On your knees, boy."

Aiden dropped to his knees without question as Max unbuckled his pants. The instant Max exposed his beautiful hard cock, Aiden opened his mouth and it watered in anticipation.

"Greedy little slut, aren't you?"

"Only for you."

"Good answer," Max praised. He fisted his fingers in Aiden's hair, holding his head still as he guided his dick to Aiden's mouth. He ran the tip over Aiden's lips, painting them with the arousal seeping from the slit.

Aiden moaned wantonly at the delicious flavor and lapped at Max's cockhead, seeking out more of the rich, bitter taste. But Aiden wasn't the only greedy one. Max obviously wasn't satisfied with flicks and swirls of tongue if the way he pushed deep into Aiden's mouth with one hard thrust was any indication. The sudden movement triggered Aiden's gag reflex, but he recovered quickly, tilting his head back slightly and relaxing his throat.

Having an aggressive and dominant lover, Aiden had learned quickly to give up control, and he did so willingly. It still amazed Aiden that he got off on being forced to his knees and having his mouth fucked so forcefully, but he did and big-time. He loved the slight sting of pain from the tight grip Max had on his hair, the snap of his lover's hips as he pushed deep and hard because he knew Aiden could take it.

They picked up their familiar rhythm, Aiden gripping Max's lightly furred thighs, not restraining or encouraging, only holding on, loving the way the muscles flexed and rolled beneath his palms. Max began to tremble slightly, the moans and grunts growing in frequency and intensity, signaling that he was beginning to chase his orgasm and then....

Ring. Ring.

Max froze midthrust, his flared cockhead resting on Aiden's tongue. "You've got to be fucking kidding me."

Aiden pulled off Max's cock with a pop. "You're not going to answer that *now*, are you?"

Max bent and searched his pants pocket. "I have to. I'm on call."

"Seriously?" Aiden tried his best not to pout, but it was hard with Max's thick and ruddy cock just inches from his face. He briefly thought about sucking it back into his mouth, but if it was a patient in distress calling for Max, it would be selfish to demand Max's attention in such a situation. He hated to share Max, but in this case, he'd concede.

"Who is it?" Aiden asked when Max looked at the display on his cell and frowned.

"It's Blake." Max pushed the On button. "Hi, Blake. You caught me at a bad time. Can I call you back in a minute?"

"Several minutes," Aiden whispered.

Max held up a finger as he listened to whatever it was Blake was saying, a thoughtful expression on his face.

Aiden knew from the way Max rested the cell phone in the crook between cheek and shoulder while he pulled up his pants and fastened them that whatever the conversation was, his and Max's playtime was over.

"Have you called the police?"

Aiden jumped to his feet at the mention of the law and stood next to Max, trying to hear what was being said.

"Okay, yeah, I get that. Aiden and I are on our way."

"What was that about?" Aiden asked with concern.

"Tek needs our help. Apparently something about wicked scary motorcycle clubs, Feds, danger. I didn't understand it all, but from what I could decipher from the quick ramblings, Jamie has been kidnapped and they can't go to the police. They need our help."

"What can we do?"

"Don't know yet, but Blake asked us to come to the club and I told him we would be there."

Aiden didn't know the guys at the club as well, but he'd begun to build a strong relationship with Ty, and the few times he'd met Micah and Mason, he'd grown fond of them. But Max was extremely close to the other members, thought of them as his extended family. And if Max wanted Aiden there, then he'd be there and do whatever he could to help out Max's family.

BOUND

A GUARDS OF FOLSOM NOVEL

SJD PETERSON

BOUND

SJD PETERSON

Some think it's how much fun you have, your net worth, or the notches on your bedpost that define a good life. I learned at a young age that while all of those things make life both more interesting and exciting, it's how much you are loved that really matters. What I've also learned is one should never become too comfortable, for with it comes complacency, and that is where the danger lies.

I've heard many couples say "We're content" rather than "We're in love." They tend to forget the other's needs and desires, assuming the "contentment" is mutual or mistaking it for happiness. While I never lost the thrill of excitement Jamie could produce in me with just one look or the desire to fulfill each and every one of his needs and wants, I did become comfortable, lax in my duty to protect him.

Living a quiet dream, working a job I loved, and loving the man at my side, I became complacent, and for my sin, Jamie suffered.

Tek Cain

Taken

TEK'S NAME, his existence, was born of blood and violence—a daily reminder of the horrific drive-by that had caused his mother to go into early labor and taken his father's life. That vicious event had brought him into the world, and it had tied him inexplicably, inexorably, irrevocably to Jamie. Even then Jamie had been there. In a bassinet next to him in that hospital nursery.

For the two of them, there had never been any other option besides cradle to grave.

It was why they'd had no choice but to run so many years ago. To fake their deaths, leave the West Coast behind, and start anew in one of the biggest, most anonymous cities in the world. He and Jamie had fled their shared past, but they could never be completely free of it. Going witpro meant going rat, and neither of them could have done that to their club. So they did their best to just disappear—putting a continent between the two of them and their old lives.

Three thousand miles didn't feel anywhere near enough at this moment.

They found us.

Tek drove the cycle harder, pushing the engine into a determined, vengeful roar. His cell felt like lead in his jacket pocket, that cryptic text from Jamie banging around in his head, kicking up his adrenaline, each heartbeat and growling vibration of the powerful cycle alighting his every nerve. Tek was afraid, and he couldn't remember the last time he'd felt real fear.

You shouldn't have left him alone.

Tek snarled, pushed the bike harder. No matter how many years he was removed from the kid who had nearly lost his soul to protect the motorcycle club, he could go back to that darkness when he needed it. And right then—unsure of just how bad off Jamie was, but feeling, knowing, that Jamie wasn't okay—Tek let the pain and anger of remembered wrongs take him over and blacken his vision into dangerously honed focus.

If they were using any of his black poly ropes or suspension devices to cause Jamie any pain, they wouldn't survive the night.

Tek skidded to a halt inside the parking garage next to the elevator, tossing the bike aside. He stabbed the button to call the car, but when it didn't immediately arrive, he shoved through the door to the stairwell. He took the steps two at a time, mindless, his only thought, need, was to get to Jamie. How could he have been so stupid? So careless? He knew better than to ever leave Jamie alone.

It's all my fault. Stupid. Stupid. Stupid.

Tek pushed himself harder, ignoring the burn in his muscles and in his chest, one flight of stairs after another, cursing the limitations of his body. He didn't know who *they* were, the club or the Feds. What he did know was whoever it was who had Jamie would pay dearly.

At the door to the fifth floor, Tek forced himself to slow, an almost impossible feat as his mind ran through worst-case scenarios. Adrenaline surged, demanding he act, but getting himself killed before he had the chance to save Jamie would be insanity. Cautiously he pushed open the door and moved into the deserted hallway. Glock in hand, finger hovering over the trigger, he could tell from his vantage point the door to their apartment was slightly ajar. Jamie would never leave it open or unlocked. The dread spread like poisonous vines, wrapping around his chest and throat, threatening to rob him of breath. Step by cautious step, he pushed down his fear, slowed his breathing, and clamped down on his shaking muscles. He let the cold dark place within him rise up, surround him until he was enveloped within its folds.

Before entering his place, he stopped and strained to listen for any sounds from within, but it was eerily silent. Weapon at the ready and using the doorjamb as a shield, Tek pushed the door open slowly, scanning wildly for any signs of danger.

The coffee table was crushed into several pieces of splintered wood, a lamp was smashed, and papers and knickknacks were thrown about the room, but it was devoid of anyone. The kitchen area showed the same disarray—overturned stools, broken dishes—not even their sleeping area was spared from the carnage. One hell of a battle had taken place; the only thing keeping Tek sane and focused was the lack of blood or a broken body.

Satisfied he wouldn't be ambushed, Tek quietly eased the door closed behind him and set the deadbolt before moving to the last place to look—the bathroom. Heavy curtains covered the windows, keeping the room in nearly complete darkness. It took a moment for his eyes to adjust to the lack of light, but at least the covered windows would protect him from a possible attack from the next building over. He listened for sounds from within the bathroom, but the only thing he heard was the rapid beating of his own heart. Hand on the knob, Tek took a deep breath and blew it out slowly.

Please don't let him be dead.

The bathroom was dark and empty. Tek flipped on the light and fell to his knees, losing the fight against the tendrils of dread. The note taped to the mirror left no doubt as to who had Jamie. *We'll be in touch*, followed by a red eight. Crimson VIII had found them and now Jamie was in the hands of that sadistic fucker Rocco.

The air rushed back into Tek's lungs as the rage within him began to boil and spewed from him in the form of an animalistic howl. It echoed off the walls of the small room, almost shaking them.

Tek continued to cry out until his throat was raw and no sound came out. His head slumped forward and he breathed raggedly. This was his fault. He'd left Jamie alone and now they had him.

"Oh fuck! They have my Jamie," Tek groaned, fighting back the sobs that threatened to choke him.

"Think!"

Tek pushed himself to his feet. "Goddamn you, think!" He pounded his fist against his stupid skull. He'd broken his promise, failed Jamie.

He ripped the note from the mirror and crushed it in his fist, then made himself a vow. Soon it would be Rocco's throat beneath the strength of his hands. He wanted to watch the life drain from the man's eyes, the memory of Tek's face accompanying him on his journey to hell.

The shrill ring of his cell caused Tek to jerk, and he pulled it from his pocket, hitting the On button without checking the display. "If you so much as hurt a hair on his fucking head, I swear to God—"

"Tek, it's Blake."

Shit! Tek squeezed his eyes shut and shook his head. "Ah… sorry, Blake, I thought you were someone else."

"Obviously, what's going on?"

"Nothing." Tek picked up his gun from the floor and returned it to the holster at the small of his back. "Now isn't a good time."

"Too bad. Now what the hell happened to Jamie? And don't you dare say nothing. He's the only one who could elicit that kind of response. Is it the Feds or the club?"

Tek froze. Blake knew? But—

"You don't actually think I'd have made you head of security if I hadn't done my homework?" Blake asked when Tek didn't respond.

Blake was as insanely protective of Ty as Tek was of Jamie. It shouldn't surprise him that Blake had done his homework, but it did. Blake couldn't know all the things Tek had done before working at the Guards. No way. With that info, Blake wouldn't have made him head of security and damn sure wouldn't have let him within a hundred yards of Ty.

He began rummaging through the closet, looking for the Tec-9 Jamie had bought him. "No, I don't suppose you would," Tek finally admitted.

"So then talk to me. Who's got Jamie?"

Tek found the gun and checked the clip. Finding it full, he slid it back into place and set the gun on the table. He then began arming himself, strapping his knives on his wrists and calves.

"Tek, dammit, talk to me."

Tek sighed heavily. "I thought I'd seen the head of our old club in town, but like an idiot, I convinced myself I was seeing shit that wasn't there. Paranoid, ya know? I was wrong and now he has Jamie."

"What are we going to do about getting him back?"

"We? There is no we. This is on me, Blake. I'll get him back."

Once again Tek found himself stopped dead in his tracks when Blake began to laugh. "You're going to take on the entire club on your own? Don't be a fool, Tek. You need us."

"Us?" Tek asked in confusion.

"Your family here at the Guards. Now tell me what you need."

Tek sat down on the bed hard as the full weight of the situation crashed in on him. He didn't know what to do next or where to look. "I need Jamie."

"I know, son. What do you know so far?"

"Nothing," Tek informed Blake dejectedly. "They said they'd be in touch."

"Okay, I'm sending a car for you."

"No—"

"I didn't ask. They obviously have been following you and Jamie. They know where you live and work. Hell, it wouldn't surprise me if you're being watched right now. Which means I do not want you left alone."

"Fuck! Jamie's cell. I can track him."

Hope surged through Tek and he hit the End button. Dammit, what was wrong with him? Jamie needed him and he was acting like a dumbass. He fired up the app and homed in on Jamie's signal. Tek's pulse raced as his fingers swiped across the screen, expanding the map over the blinking red light.

"Hold on, Jamie."

As quickly as it had risen, the hope plummeted as he recognized the location where the blinking light was originating from. He tossed the cell aside and stood on trembling legs, scanning the area around him. A heavy, frustrated breath escaped him when he spotted Jamie's cell sitting on the kitchen counter. He ran his hands through his hair, fighting the urge to rip it from his skull. Tek's hand was shaking so bad, he had a difficult time picking up the cell and punching in the security code. The last shred of hope was ripped from him as he scrolled through the messages and e-mails and found nothing that would help him find Jamie.

With a spirit born out of soul-wrenching despair, Tek cried out and threw the cell against the far wall, smashing it into hundreds of tiny pieces.

Unable to hold back the tidal wave of grief, Tek laid his head down on the counter and sobbed.

How long he was lost in his anguish, Tek didn't know. He wept, the hopelessness pouring out of him like a tsunami, purging his heart of the cruelties he'd inflicted and in turn had been inflicted upon him and Jamie.

Neither of them had ever asked to be born into this fucked-up world of hate and intolerance. They damn sure hadn't asked to be forced into a life of blood and violence. They were now paying the price for their birthright. Tek let out a bitter snort of laughter. They'd been paying that fucking bill their whole lives.

The time between cradle to grave whooshed by, and now it seemed as if the grave was beginning to open up before them.

Tek would not live in a world without Jamie, the idea too horrible to even contemplate. How did one survive without their heart? The answer was simple—

They didn't.

A knock at the door got Tek moving, but it wasn't enough to pull him from the hopelessness he'd fallen into. Uncaring, he opened the door without pulling his weapon or checking the peephole.

"Hey, Tek. You ready?" Smitty—the newest bouncer at the Guards—asked.

"For what?"

Smitty rubbed a hand over his bald head and gave Tek a confused look. "Boss said I was to give you a ride to the club. Didn't he tell you I was coming?"

"I'm not going anywhere." What if they came back? He needed to be here. He had to take a minute and figure out what to do and how to find Jamie.

"But I got to bring you, boss's orders." Smitty looked crestfallen at the prospect of disappointing Blake. Smitty was nearly as big and meaty as he and Jamie were, but Tek wasn't convinced the man's elevator went to the top floor. Yet he was a great asset to the club. If Blake told him to watch the door, no one was coming through without permission. Smitty was completely loyal to Blake.

Tek thought about all the possibilities until his head throbbed. He seriously doubted Rocco was going to show up on his doorstep and hand Jamie back to Tek. He supposed it didn't matter if he was home or at the club. In fact, nothing mattered other than getting Jamie back. And if there was the slightest chance Blake could help.... "Yeah, I'll come with ya," he finally said to Smitty. He wasn't going to accomplish shit pacing around the apartment. He needed some fresh air, needed to clear the fog of dread out of his head and start thinking, formulate a plan.

Two years I've been running. Not only running from a town, the people within it including my family, but also from myself. I've done my best to put who I'd become when I left Chatom, California, behind me, grow above it, and God how I yearned to become a better man. Every day I struggle to forget. But no matter how hard I tried to hide from my sins, from who I was, they always seemed to find a way to slip past my defenses unexpectedly. Irony is, as much as I hated my past, it had served to keep me alert, aware, and on my toes to the dangers all around me. And then for weeks, the struggle had eased, I wasn't assaulted by memories, even dared to hope I actually had outrun my past, and me and Jamie were safe in our new-chosen home. Sadly, it was my wish to forget that allowed the dangers to come rushing in and stole the one person who mattered most to me in this fucked-up world.

I've failed Jamie, something I could never forget, never allow myself to forget. The past cannot be forgotten, changed, edited, or erased; it can only be accepted. Instead I need to learn from my past, or I am doomed to make the same mistakes.

Tek Cain

In Creeps the Past

IN THE pitch-black darkness, Jamie struggled to make sense of what the hell was going on and where he was. His thoughts were fuzzy and his mouth felt as if it had been stuffed full of putrid-tasting cotton balls. He swallowed and winced from how raw and dry his throat was. He tried lifting his hand but found he was unable. Only then did Jamie realize he was lying on his side in the fetal position, his hands bound behind his back and his feet bound at his ankles. The events of the night came rushing back.

He'd had big plans to blow Tek's mind with a little rope play, showing off the knots he'd been perfecting and then spending the rest of the night taking advantage of Tek's bound and willing body. He'd just stepped out of the bathroom after a hot shower when Rocco crashed through the door. Before Jamie had a chance to lunge for his weapon, Rocco was on him and they were rolling around the apartment. He'd gotten the upper hand on the bastard, was about to land a punishing blow to his overly smug face when he was grabbed from behind and a cloth covered his nose and mouth. He'd been an idiot and assumed Rocco was alone. He should have known better, and because of his stupidity, he was now in this situation. Kidnapped.

He was going to rip Rocco's fucking throat out when he got free.

Jamie tried unsuccessfully to free himself, but it wasn't only the bindings that were keeping him incapacitated but also the sluggishness of his mind and muscles. Whatever drug Rocco's accomplice had used to knock him out obviously hadn't worn off yet. Lying there helplessly, Jamie's thoughts turned to Tek. His heart began to race as panic wormed its way through his system. Had his captors stayed behind after he was disposed of and ambushed Tek? Was he now lying in the same miserable position, wondering where the hell he was with the same fog scrambling his brain?

Jamie's heart started to race like a runaway train, the roar of blood in his ears deafening with the rage surging through him. If they harmed

Tek, so help him God, they would pay. The anger at the thought was enough to burn off some of the drug, leaving him trembling with the force of his fury.

"Rocco!" Jamie bellowed. "Get your ass in here and cut me loose, you piece of shit!"

When there was no response, Jamie pulled on his bindings, muscles bulging, rough rope abrading the flesh of his wrists and ankles, but he continued to struggle against them. He ignored the pain, put every bit of power he had into freeing himself, but it was in vain. His screaming muscles finally gave in to exhaustion and he breathed harshly.

"Goddamn you, Rocco! If you hurt him, I swear to fuck, I'll make you suffer."

He continued to scream, curse, and threaten until his throat too gave out and he was left completely spent, drained of every ounce of strength and left with nothing but Tek's suffering to taunt him.

Jamie lay in this miserable state for an immeasurable amount of time, the complete blackness and utter silence making it all the harder. An hour, a day, two, he wasn't sure how much time had passed. Had he slept? Were the frightening images of Tek's captivity and the agony in his muscles part of the nightmare he was stuck in? Would he eventually wake and find Tek's warm body wrapped around his?

Yet the searing pain in his limbs sure felt real. His shoulders were stretched nearly to their limit, and the muscles in his legs were contracting and spasming. The pain was excruciating and began to overwhelm him. Jamie struggled to rise above it.

Blessedly an image of Tek standing before him, his body covered in a light sheen of perspiration and hard cock straining popped into Jamie's head. The look on Tek's face eased him as Tek concentrated while tying the black poly ropes into intricate knots around Jamie's limbs and chest. Jamie welcomed the vision, gave himself over to it.

Tek stepped back and smirked as he examined his rope work. "Fuck, you're hot like this," he murmured and licked his lips.

Jamie looked down his body; the black ropes stood out in sharp contrast against the pale skin of his chest. Smaller, twine-size black rope was wrapped around his cock and balls, looking obscene. His dick was throbbing painfully, but the sensation wasn't unpleasant.

The seductive grin on Tek's face as he continued to stare at his work only served to make Jamie grow harder still.

"I don't know, Tek. Seems to me you may have gotten a little carried away with your ropes."

Tek tilted his head, his brows dipping as he raked his gaze up and down Jamie's body. "I don't see a problem."

"You've roped yourself right out of getting full use of my package." Jamie chuckled.

"I kind of like seeing it all trussed up like this. It's sexy. Besides I want to hear you beg."

"I don't beg."

"You're right, normally you don't but—" Tek dropped to his knees and ran the tip of his tongue around Jamie's engorged cockhead. "—you will."

Jamie shuddered.

A loud bang and a flash of blinding light snapped Jamie out of his dream. Instinctively he tried to shield his eyes, and it was then he was snapped back to his reality. He was bound, but not by the soft ropes Tek used. Instead, they were the rough, abrasive ones of his captor. He blinked rapidly several times, trying to give his eyes a chance to adjust to the harsh light that kept going on and off.

"Say cheese," Rocco sneered.

"Where the hell is Tek?"

Rocco laughed, continuing to rapidly take photos, not allowing time for Jamie's eyes to adjust.

"Keep laughing, motherfucker. When I get my hands on you—"

"You're really in no position to make an effective threat."

"It's not a threat, it's a promise," Jamie assured him. He pulled at his bindings, itching to get his hands on Rocco, but they still didn't give.

The flashing suddenly stopped. Rocco's smug expression finally came into focus, and it caused Jamie's blood to boil. "Turn me loose and I'll prove it to you. Face me like a man, you fucking coward."

"Now, now, Junior, there is no cause for name-calling. You and Tek owe me a lot of money, and I'm simply here to collect what is rightfully mine."

"Bullshit! This is about more than some cash and you know it."

Rocco's smile turned into an ugly sneer as he stared down at Jamie. "You're right, you sick fucking faggot. I also aim to get me a pound of flesh for the embarrassment you brought on my club."

Rocco slammed the door, and Jamie was once again engulfed in blackness. He started to cry out a litany of curses and threats but at the last minute snapped his mouth shut. Screaming at Rocco, no matter how badly he wanted to, wasn't going to help him or Tek. He needed to conserve his energy, stay calm, and work on getting himself free. Only then would he tell the piece of shit exactly what he thought of him and his fucked-up club, right before he ripped the son of a bitch's head off.

Jamie closed his eyes and took deep, calming breaths. He rolled onto his other side, sighing when the pain in his muscles ebbed slightly. Instead of struggling, he rocked, flexed, and stretched his muscles as best he could while he went to work on the ropes around his wrists. This time, instead of trying to escape the pain, he focused on it. Not his own, but the pain he'd inflict on Rocco and anyone else who tried to keep him from Tek.

"HAVE THEY tried to make contact?" Blake asked as soon as Tek entered the club.

"Not yet." Tek grumbled and took a seat at the bar next to Blake.

He'd used the car ride over to get his head on straight, push the anger and grief aside. Problem was, for the life of him, he couldn't come up with a fucking thing that would help him get Jamie back, and the hopelessness kept rearing its ugly head. He was helpless until Rocco made the next move.

"Okay, bring me up to speed on exactly what we're dealing with."

"We're dealing with a psychotic motherfucker hell-bent on revenge."

"Revenge for what exactly?" Blake inquired calmly, tapping his fingers against the bar like he was asking about the weather.

Tek, once again, found himself tamping down on the anger over Blake's matter-of-fact attitude. *Focus. This is about getting Jamie back. Nothing else matters.*

"When we left, I took some money from the club," Tek told him, keeping it vague.

"How much?"

"Forty K."

"All right, so that's easy enough to return. What else—and don't you bullshit me. If we're going to get Jamie back, I need to know everything, including why you two are running from both your club and the Feds."

Tek thought about it for a moment. He respected the hell out of Blake, and the last thing Tek wanted was for Blake to find out exactly what he'd been like before escaping the Crimson VIII. That wasn't actually true. The last thing he wanted was to lose Jamie, and if telling Blake the ugly truth about his past helped get Jamie back….

"I'm going to need a drink," Tek informed him and pushed his hair behind his ears.

"Ty's putting on a pot of coffee as we speak."

"I wasn't talking about caffeine."

"You don't need alcohol. It won't help and you need to keep your head clear. How about a soda?"

Tek bristled at being told what he could or couldn't have. Blake was right, though. Alcohol would only ignite his already short fuse. "Coffee's fine," he conceded.

"It will be ready soon. So talk."

And Tek did.

"Jamie and I never asked to be born into the world we were, but we also never questioned it while growing up. It wasn't until we were teenagers when we began to realize that shit wasn't what it appeared to be. I did a lot of stuff I wasn't proud of, including killing men. But it was my own mortality that caused me to run. I'm basically a fucking coward. I could kill a man to protect my club, but when my own death was a very real possibility, I ran."

"Who wanted you dead? A rival gang?"

"That was a given," Tek sniffed. "I had a mark on my head the day I was born. You know how men lust for power. Funny thing was I would have gladly given it to them. I never asked to be the next in line to rule the club. It was forced upon me as my birthright. I would have done it, ya know. Jamie was training to be my first lieutenant and the two of us had big plans to change how things were run but…." Tek shrugged.

"But?" Blake prompted when Tek stayed silent.

"I realized I was in love with Jamie, not like another member of the Crimson VIII or a brother, but *in* love with him, and Jamie loved me too. In our world, you could run guns, rob, beat, or even kill, but faggots got an instant death sentence. Our own club would have beaten us to death if they found out."

"Is that why you ran? Your club found out?"

Tek shook his head, but before he could answer, Ty came in carrying a tray with mugs, a pot of coffee, and all the fixings.

Ty set the tray down in front of him and Blake. "Hey, Tek, how you holding up?"

"I'm a fucking wreck," he admitted honestly.

"Understandable."

"Thank you, Ty," Blake said and poured himself a cup of coffee.

He offered one to Tek, but he declined. His gut churned with the ugly memories of the past, and he doubted the coffee or anything else would sit well. "I'm good right now."

"Tek was just bringing me up to date on what's going on," Blake explained to Ty.

"I'll leave you two alone, then."

"No, it's okay. You don't have to go," Tek told him. "It's all going to come out anyway. Might as well stay and hear it firsthand."

"Tek was telling me how being gay within his motorcycle club was a death sentence."

Ty's brows shot up. "Are you kidding me? That's seriously fucked up."

"Yeah, a lot of what the club did, or does, is fucked up. Jamie and I knew the score and planned on changing shit when I eventually took over as pres. We knew we had to keep our sexuality hidden from the rest of the members, but then some crazy shit went down and the Feds got involved. They tried to get Jamie and me to turn rat. Of course we both told them to fuck off, but the sneaky bastards got some shots of Jamie and me in some pretty hot situations, and when they whipped out the photos, we about shit bricks.

"I'm sure the Feds had a ton of intel on the club. A lot of rival gang fights had gotten really ugly; bodies were turning up with extra holes. Then there was the drugs and gun running, any one of which could have landed Jamie and I rotting in prison just based on our association with the club. The Feds gave us some time to think about our choices, but really, what choice did we have? Spending the rest of our lives behind bars or going witpro, which would have gotten us killed just as surely as the release of those goddamn photos. Fate stepped in and we were presented with an opportunity, so I took $40K from the club, staged our deaths, and got out of town. We didn't stick around long enough to find out if the club or the Feds believed it, so for the past two years, we've been keeping on the down low. I guess I know the answer now. Jesus, why in the hell did we stay in one place this long? It was a stupid idea, and now Jamie is paying the price for that stupidity."

"Was it your club that took Jamie?" Ty asked.

"Yeah, and when I get my hands on them…." Tek let the threat hang in the air as he clenched his hands into fists to rein in his emotions. He closed his eyes briefly and willed his racing heart to slow as well as his rapid breath. *Gotta keep your head, man.*

"It's going to be okay," Blake said, sounding confident. He laid his hand on Tek's back. "Trust me, we will get him back."

Tek lifted his gaze and met Blake's intense dark eyes. Even his expression looked as if he truly believed what he was saying. Tek, however, didn't feel so confident. Blake didn't know Rocco like Tek did nor did he know how ruthless the son of a bitch could be.

"How can you be so sure?" Tek finally asked, wanting to believe.

"Because we will," Blake said curtly. "I've called some of the other members in—"

"Who?"

"Tackett, Micah, Max, Aiden, Bobby, Rig, and Mason, and trust me when I tell you, when we all work together, we'll be fucking unstoppable."

"Believe him," Ty added. "Blake has never lied to me, and when he tells you something, you can damn well take it to the bank."

Blake gave Ty a warm smile. "Thank you, boy."

Ty leaned over the bar and pressed his lips gently against Blake's, then turned his attention to Tek, patted his shoulder, and repeated, "To the bank."

Tek nodded, letting Blake and Ty's assurances fill him with a spark of hope. He wasn't sure he believed it yet, but it was all he had, and knowing he and Jamie had so many standing with them in their fight sure as hell felt a lot better than being alone against the world. He was beginning to understand what family really meant.

He thought he knew what it was to be part of one when he was growing up, but he was so very wrong. The Crimson VIII wasn't a family. They were a bunch of thugs who claimed to have each other's backs—a promise easily broken if someone pissed them off or there was money to be made. A family sure as hell did not kill its members simply for loving someone. The men of the Guards had given him a glimpse of what the word truly meant.

Hours upon hours I worked my muscles, whether in the gym or home, until they shook with exhaustion and I was covered in sweat. I had to prepare, keep myself strong, and endure the pain. Break down the muscles in order to rebuild them more powerfully. I understood how important it was. I was dedicated to the pain, knew with it came strength and thus a greater ability to protect what was important to me. I couldn't have known at the time that all the preparation in the world wouldn't prepare me for waiting, silence, helplessness. My body was a powerhouse, but it couldn't fight these things. Brawn can't ease a mind when each tick of the clock mocks it. Brute force is impotent against waiting.

Tek Cain

Family Feud

THE MINUTES and hours dragged on painfully slowly, Tek wavering between optimism and hopelessness in equal measures. Tackett, Micah, Max, and Aiden had joined them at the club shortly after Tek told his story to Ty and Blake. The other three would be in later that night, having gotten the news of Jamie's kidnapping while in Florida. The fact that they were rushing back to help him, especially after what Mason had to endure while donating the remnants of his past life, humbled Tek. Hell, it blew his mind that all of them were so willing to help, even put their lives on the line if need be after only knowing Jamie and him for a short time. They were truly extraordinary men.

Tek's phone rang and he jumped, all eyes suddenly on him. He pulled it out and read the display. "Restricted number," he informed them. "It's got to be Rocco."

"Take a deep breath and stay calm," Max reminded him.

Even without Max's little chat about keeping his wits being more productive than flying off the handle, Tek knew it. However, he found himself wanting to rage and scream. To demand Rocco return Jamie—it was instinct.

He was shaking with the force of keeping his anger in check when he pushed the On button. "Tek here."

"Good evening, son."

Tek gritted his teeth. *Son, my ass.* Instead he kept his voice even but deadly serious. "Where is Jamie?"

"You're going to bring me a quarter of a mil—"

"I only owe you forty," Tek spat.

"Interest, my boy. Now interrupt me again and I'll cut his fucking balls off. Understand me?"

"Tek," Max whispered, pegging Tek with an intense look. "Remember what matters."

Tek choked down his angry retort. *Jamie.* Get Rocco to tell him where Jamie was, and once his man was safe, then and only then could he dole out a little payback. Tek blew out a pent-up breath.

"Yeah, I understand. Two hundred fifty thousand. When and where do you want to meet?"

"I'll be in touch with the details. And just in case you think about pulling any kind of bullshit—" The line went dead.

"Rocco? Goddammit, what do you mean just in case? Rocco? Fuck!" Tek tightened his fist around the phone.

"Easy, Tek, you're going to need that." Max laid a hand on Tek's forearm. "Deep breath."

Tek's phone chirped, announcing a text message, and he eased his grip and stared at the display, trying to make sense of what he was seeing. His heart fell to his feet when he realized it was a picture of Jamie, his mouth open in a silent scream, eyes wide, and heavy ropes around his naked body.

"I'm going to kill him," Tek hissed. "I'm going to rip his goddamn heart out."

"What is it?" Blake asked and plucked the phone from Tek's hand. "Oh fuck."

Tek jumped to his feet, the anger and despair needing an outlet, yet he could do nothing more than pace and do his best not to puke. The sick bastard had Jamie tied up and stuffed in a closet. It only made him feel marginally better that Jamie was alive because he didn't know for how much longer. He also knew in the pit of his gut that Jamie was suffering.

While Tek continued to try to get a hold of his emotions, he heard the other guys discussing the picture. "There has to be a way to trace where the call came from," Blake theorized.

"Or maybe a way of figuring out where it is Jamie is being held. Anyone recognize the place or know where they could be holding him?" Aiden put in.

"It's a goddamn closet," Tek raged. "They have him tied up in a goddamn closet!"

Tackett stepped up in front of Tek, stopping his irate pacing, and placed a hand on Tek's shoulder. "I've been working with computers and software my whole life. I'm going to figure out where the call came from, and if I can't, I know someone who can. Give me a bit, okay?"

"How long? I have to get him out of there," Tek implored.

"As quick as I can."

Tek held Tackett's gaze, saw the conviction in the man's eyes. "Please hurry."

"I'm on it." Tackett patted Tek's shoulder. "Now you start working out what you're going to do once we know where he is."

"I'm going to kill him," Tek responded without hesitation.

"Go talk to Max and get your shit and your priorities together," Tackett encouraged. "You probably should work on a plan to get Jamie out first before you kill Rocco, yeah?"

Tek scrubbed a hand over his tired eyes and let out a frustrated breath. He was going insane, but he knew he had to find that cold place within him. Knew he could call it up when he had to, and oh fuck, how he had to.

"Yeah," he agreed.

"Good man, I'll get right on this," Tackett assured him, holding up Tek's cell phone. He then turned to Blake. "Can I use your computer?"

"Absolutely. C'mon, I'll get you signed in." Blake went to his feet. Tackett followed him to his office.

Tek slumped down into his chair, propped his elbow on the table, and hung his head in his hands. The images of Jamie's bound body flashed in his mind. His chest tightened painfully and his stomach roiled. So full of conflicting emotion, Tek didn't know if he wanted to scream, to lash out, or roll up in a ball and cry. The waiting, knowing Jamie was suffering, was going to fucking crush him.

"It's going to be okay," Micah whispered. "Tackett will be able to find him, I know he will. And did you notice Jamie's eyes? The look on his face? If you ask me, that was one pissed-off man. This Rocco dude better hope Jamie doesn't get loose."

Tek reevaluated the image that was now seared into his brain. Micah was right. Jamie didn't look hurt, he looked furious. He had been bound more than once; Jamie knew how to be still, to rise above any discomfort. The anger and worry still swirled around inside Tek, but he could at least get a grip on them. He took a deep breath, searching for his own inner strength, a strength Jamie was portraying and had brought out in Tek numerous times before. He could do this. He could keep his head and heart together and do what he needed to do.

A fire in his belly roared to life, setting determination to burn through him. He lifted his head, a small smile curling his lip. "He is one tough and stubborn bastard."

Micah returned the smile. "You know it."

The time Tackett was holed up in Blake's office was a torturous lesson in restraint. Micah had made him feel marginally better, pointing out Jamie's anger, but only slightly. With each tick of the clock, Tek's resolve didn't wane, but his patience did. So many worst-case scenarios kept playing through his mind, and no matter how hard he tried to rid himself of them, they were persistent. Taunting him. Max, Aiden, Ty, and Micah did their best to reassure Tek and take his mind off the situation, but he doubted anything would truly help until Jamie was back home where he belonged.

"I'm going to place an order. What do you like on your pizza?" Ty asked.

"I'm not hungry."

"I didn't ask if you were hungry," Ty clarified. "I asked what you liked on your pizza."

Tek stopped his pacing and cocked his head at Ty. "You sure you're a submissive? You're awful pushy."

"I'm only submissive to Blake," Ty said with a wink. "I know you may not feel hungry right now. Your gut is all messed up and you think you'd rather puke than eat. But if it's around, you might snack on it and it's not going to come back up."

"You sound like you're speaking from experience."

"I've had my fair share of stressful moments in my life," Ty said vaguely with a shrug. "But I do know that if I had someone who was on my side like Blake back then, it sure as hell would have been a lot easier. He's a good man, and he's been in your shoes. I can assure you, he will do everything within his power to bring your man home."

"He's been in my shoes? I mean, I knew Blake was a stickler for security and the safety of subs because of something that had happened in his past. But I didn't know the details."

"It's not my story to tell and you don't need the details right now. But what I will tell you is that Eli was kidnapped and killed by a very disturbed man who was obsessed with him. Blake blamed himself for years, and I think at times he still does. But he uses that guilt and loss and tries to bring some good out of it. Blake getting a chance to be an instrument in a different outcome for Jamie will go far to ease his soul even more."

Tek ran his hand over his mouth and then scratched at his unshaven jaw as he stared at Ty. "Man, I knew he was a tough son of a bitch, but I know I wouldn't ever get over losing Jamie. There is no fucking way." He shuddered at the horrible thought. "Never."

"Blake didn't get over losing Eli. He learned to live with the loss without it destroying him and you would too. But enough of this depressing shit. You're not going to have to learn to live without Jamie because we're going to get him back. So, about that pizza?"

Tek continued to battle with the despair the thought of living without Jamie had produced. Bile rose up in his throat, and he struggled to choke it down. If he allowed the misery to drown him, he wouldn't be able to make it through the next second, let alone the next hour. He couldn't afford to lose it now. One breath, one heartbeat, one minute at a time. He needed to, had to keep his shit together. Tek swallowed hard and nodded. He could do this. "Anything but anchovies."

Ty had been right. Tek not only snacked on the pizza, but before he realized it, he'd eaten two pieces. Of course then the guilt rushed in, and he was now dealing with the very real possibility of upchucking. Jamie was tied up in a fucking closet somewhere, and Tek was munching on pizza.

Tek shoved out of his chair. "What the hell is taking so long?" He stomped to the door to Blake's office. He was done waiting. He had just raised his hand to bang on the door when it opened and he nearly knocked on Blake's forehead.

Tek narrowed his eyes at Blake, not even trying to hide his irritation when he said, "I hope you're about to tell me you got a lead, 'cause I can't sit here with my thumb up my ass doing nothing a minute longer."

Blake stepped past Tek and Tackett looked up at him with a sly grin. "We got him."

"What? Where are they?" Tek demanded.

"Let's have a seat and I'll tell you what I know."

When Tackett tried to step past him, Tek blocked the path. "Fuck that. Tell me now. Where is he?"

Tackett didn't so much as flinch in the face of Tek's fury. "It's not that simple. Now are you going to sit down and listen to what we know?"

Tek was forced to follow Tackett to a table and sit when the man laid a piece of paper on it. "What is this?" Tek asked, looking at a hand-drawn map.

"We were able to get an approximate location of where the call came from and one of my colleagues was able to pin it down even further to a particular building. It's only a couple blocks from your place."

"Well, let's go get him!"

"Unfortunately it's not that easy, Tek. The building has a hundred apartments, several of which are vacant at the moment for renovations. We can't go bursting through the doors and hope like hell we get the right one. We're going to have to set up surveillance. Blake's already contacted a few members who are going to be here shortly to get the particulars."

"Fuck that, I know exactly who I'm looking for."

"And so will they," Blake interjected. "Your guy Rocco has quite the impressive rap sheet. I've got a mug shot of him from an arrest a month ago." He pulled a page from beneath the map and pushed it across the table to Tek. "Does he look the same as the last time you saw him?"

The response was instantaneous. Red-hot rage burned through Tek so quickly at seeing Rocco's face, if he hadn't been sitting, it would have knocked him on his ass. He'd despised him for a long time, but he couldn't even begin to describe the depth of his hatred now. He shoved the photo back toward Blake, not able to stand looking at the fucker's face for a second longer.

"No, he hasn't changed and I'm going."

"Tek, I'm not asking you not to go, I'm asking you to wait until we know where the guy is first. You show up sniffing around and you're going to spook them. They could end up taking it out on Jamie or moving him. Give the guys a chance to scope things out, okay?" Tackett asked. He sounded so calm and fucking reasonable, Tek wanted to scream.

"Stop and think about it," Blake added. "You know Tackett's right."

Tek met Blake's gaze. "You don't understand. I can't sit here doing nothing. It's going to crush me."

Blake held Tek's gaze a moment longer, the understanding, compassion, and sorrow evident in his dour eyes and somber expression. "I do understand, and I do know how hard it is to wait, but this is the path to take to give us the best possible chance at getting Jamie out alive. Now let's work on a game plan while the guys stake out the building. Do you know who Rocco would have with him and how many he'd bring on a job like this?"

As much as he hated to admit it, Blake and Tackett were right. He was also serious about the waiting crushing him. It felt as if his heart was being ripped out of his chest, and with each tick of the clock, the pain increased. But this wasn't about him or his pain, it was about Jamie. Once again he had to fight against his instinct to act and remind himself, this was about getting Jamie back safe and sound first and only then getting retribution.

He blew out a pent-up breath. "My guess is he'd come in quiet. Probably bring Cole, his first lieutenant. He's the only one Rocco truly trusts, at least that was the case when I left. I don't know about new members they may have added since Jamie and I skipped town, but my gut tells me, it's going to be Rocco and Cole."

"Hey, Ty? Can you bring us some drinks?" Blake met Tek's gaze. "We've got some planning to do."

Thomas Aquinas said there are three conditions that are necessary for penance: contrition, which is sorrow for sin, together with a purpose of amendment; confession of sins without any omission; and satisfaction by means of good works. If Thomas is correct and I am to stand outside the pearly gates and ask for forgiveness for killing a man, then I will surely be turned away. I feel no sorrow, no need to make amends, nor do I feel it a sin. If I am to be damned to hell for the act, then I will hold my head high, as the only regret I have is that I didn't do it sooner. My hesitation caused Jamie to suffer and he is the only one I need to seek forgiveness from.

Tek Cain

Redemption

"JAMIE!"

The sound of Tek's bloodcurdling scream and his name echoing around the dark corridor froze the blood in Jamie's veins. His steps were sluggish and his heart hammered so hard he could barely breathe, but he couldn't stop. Tek needed him.

The black labyrinth of tunnels ended in one dead end after another. Each hallway looked the same: slick, mildew-covered stone walls, a low-wattage bulb dangling from the ceiling. It seemed so hopeless and he was lost, could no longer tell which way he'd been or which way to go, he simply kept moving, had to, Tek needed him.

The one constant besides the hallways was Tek's screams. He kept calling out to Jamie, and no matter how hard he tried to get to him, Jamie was failing his man.

Jamie screamed Tek's name, trying to let him know he was there, he was coming, but the sound of his own voice mingled and mixed with Tek's, bounced off the stone walls, and echoed back in a deafening roar. Each painful step, he cursed, begged, and pleaded with the darkness that kept the way in shadows, but it refused to give up its secrets. Moving from one hall to another, Jamie's heart was shredded by Tek's torturous screams with each step.

Hurry.

Time is running out.

He's dying.

He knew it, even without the whisper of the darkness.

"Then help me, damn you!" Jamie screamed. "Tell me where he is. Help me find him!"

The darkness mocked him by leading him down yet another dead end.

Corridor after corridor, he ineffectively chased Tek's screams. Jamie's hands were raw and bleeding from leaning on the rough stone. Despair crushed down over him, making each step painful.

"Jamie! Jamie, please!"

Jamie ran his hands through his sweat-soaked hair, tugging at it in frustration. Tek's agonizing pleas overwhelmed him, robbed him of breath and strength. His legs gave out, but he couldn't give up. He didn't. Both his hands and knees bloodied, he crawled, kept moving. For how long, he wasn't sure, Tek's screams keeping him going inch after agonizing inch.

Another corner, one more, please let it be the last. "Dear God, please let me find him," *he prayed, willing to give up his life, his very soul, if he could only save Tek.*

Whether it was God or the Devil who finally answered his pleas, Jamie wasn't sure. He didn't care, but as he pulled himself up on shaking legs and rounded the corner, it opened up into a small chamber. Tek was in the center, a small light trained on his body. Black ropes were wrapped around his wrists and his arms were stretched wide as he was tied and suspended from the ceiling. The black ropes were also wrapped around both ankles, attached to metal rings in the stone floor. Tek's head was tipped back so far, Jamie couldn't see his face, but he could hear the screams, sounds echoing around the room like the howls of a wounded animal.

"Tek! I'm here."

"Good evening, Jamie." Rocco stepped out of the darkness from behind Tek.

Jamie took a step toward them.

"Not another step."

It wasn't Rocco's warning that stopped Jamie in his tracks but the light glinting off steel as the bastard pressed the blade of a knife against Tek's throat. "Let him go!"

"That will be up to you."

"Anything. Tell me what you want and it's yours."

Rocco's smile was menacing. "I want you to prove you love him."

"What?" Jamie asked, incredulous. "Of course I love him."

"I don't believe disgusting cocksuckers such as you and this piece of shit." Tek's head was pulled back impossibly farther and the screams intensified in volume.

"Stop!" Jamie had to force himself not to rush over, and he curled his hands into fists, trembling with the need to get to Tek.

"You have one minute to release him from his bindings. Your time starts now."

Jamie wasted precious seconds, staring at Rocco in confusion, before it sunk in what Rocco was asking. He rushed forward, fell to his knees, ignoring the jarring pain, and fought to untie the rope around Tek's left leg. The knot was tight, and it took every bit of strength to work it loose.

Tick. Tock.

The seconds ticking by in his head tortured Jamie as much as Tek's continued screams.

Hurry.

Time is running out.

The same voice who'd whispered to him from the darkness urged him on.

The rope on Tek's left foot gave way.

He worked at the rope on his right.

Tick. Tock.

Hurry.

Time is running out.

Jamie's heart was nearly leaping out of his chest, sweat rolling down his temples and spine.

Tick. Tock.

He scrambled with the rope on Tek's right wrist, his screams deafening, and Jamie's ears rang from the intensity. Jamie took his focus off the ropes for a second to glance at Tek's neck, willing the knife to disappear, and then up at Rocco.

"Worthless faggot, you fail," Rocco spat.

Tek's screams stopped cold as did Jamie's heart, replaced by Rocco's maniacal laughter as blood sprayed from the gaping wound in Tek's neck and covered Jamie's face.

JAMIE JERKED awake, heart pounding rapidly and drenched in a cold sweat, to find a figure crouched down, leaning against the doorframe. With the horrors of the nightmare still gripping him, it took a few beats before he was aware of where he was and able to make out Rocco's face in the dim light from the next room. He was holding up his phone, but there were no bright flashes of light. Jamie's relief at being a captive nearly made him giddy.

Just a nightmare.

"Is there anything you'd like to say to Tek?" Rocco asked.

It was only then that Jamie realized Rocco had to be videotaping him. "I...." Jamie's throat was so raw the single word came out like a croak, and he swallowed a couple of times and tried again. "I'll tell him myself."

"Aww, c'mon, Junior. Let me have a little fun here."

"Go to hell!"

"I'm quite sure I've secured my one-way ticket to the Devil's playground, but I'm not quite ready to enjoy his company just yet. However, I will be more than happy to send you to him right fucking now if you don't oblige me a little fun." When Jamie pressed his lips tight together, Rocco added the one thing guaranteed to make Jamie comply. "Perhaps I should send Tek first, then?"

"Fine. What the fuck do you want me to say?"

"That's better. How about a good-bye?"

Jamie grounded his teeth and gritted out "Good-bye." It was just a word, and Rocco was trying to get a reaction. He wasn't about to give the bastard the satisfaction.

"Wow! That's it? I'd have thought a filthy pole puffer like you would have been all tears and spewing his undying love to his bitch."

"Yeah, well, sorry to disappoint you."

"Well shit, that wasn't any fun at all," Rocco grumbled. "Hmm, I got a little time so I might as well satisfy my curiosity. What's it like?"

"What's what like?"

"Taking a dick up the ass? I mean I get why you'd want to fuck one. I've blasted plenty in my day and it feels great, especially those unwilling virgin asses. Now that's some nut-blowing stuff right there. Make your fucking toes curl, I tell ya. But I can't imagine taking it up the ass."

"You should try it sometime," Jamie spat.

"Ah, but then that would make me a sick pussy bitch like you, and I'd rather cut off my own dick than let some dude fuck me."

"Oh but raping a chick is perfectly acceptable. You've got a warped sense of right and wrong. Then again, that doesn't surprise me, considering what you stand for."

"What I stand for? You've got a lot of fucking nerve questioning me. Besides, the bitches loved it," Rocco justified. "Even if they didn't, how dare you compare it to what you've done. You dishonored your brothers, your club, and yourself. You hurt your family for a fuck?"

"Family? What the hell do you know about family?"

"Family is all about loyalty and sacrifice."

Jamie laughed at the ridiculousness of Rocco's statement. It wasn't so long ago that Jamie was part of Rocco's *family*. Those pretty little words meant dick to Rocco. They were simply used to veil a much more devious intention. Jamie shifted, and the searing pain in his shoulder caused him to cry out before he could clamp down on it. He knew exactly who Rocco was making the video for, and the last thing he wanted was for the bastard to use it as leverage against Tek. Jamie pushed down the pain, rolled slightly, and faced Rocco head-on with sheer determination.

"So why don't you cut the shit and tell me what you really want, because you and I both know I'm twice the fucking man you are, even with a dick up my ass."

The fist that shot out and connected with Jamie's mouth wasn't unexpected. Rocco had spent years trying to prove himself a tough guy, big man on campus so to speak, but he was and always would be nothing but a slime ball that had a bunch of loyal followers doing his dirty work. Jamie had never seen him go toe to toe, fist to fist with another man. No, Rocco was the type to go for the sucker punch or, just like now, hit a man he knew couldn't hit him back.

"Is that all you got?" Jamie spit out the blood that pooled in his mouth from his split lip. "Why don't you untie me and fight me like a man, or are you that afraid that this sissy faggot will kick your ass?"

Rocco's face turned a deep shade of red, but Jamie got the effect he'd been wanting when Rocco dropped his phone and lunged at him. He had to bite down on the scream that threatened when Rocco shoved him onto his back and sat over him with his arm cocked back. The pain in his arms and back caused nausea to rise up, but he swallowed it down stubbornly.

"Yeah, just like I thought," he gritted out past the pain. "You never could fight a man in a fair fight."

Suddenly, Rocco's expression morphed from pure rage to one of some sick, twisted glee. "Now, now, James," he purred and patted Jamie's cheek. "I've got plans for you, and it would fuck those plans up if I killed you now. I'd miss out on the enjoyment of watching Tek's face when you took your last breath." In a split second, the face of rage was back. "But if you push me too far, I'll just have to deny myself that one pleasure."

Pain exploded from Jamie's temple, flying outward through his head, and then nothing.

A MAN Tek didn't recognize rushed into the club dressed all in black, but it wasn't the black attire that normally was seen within the walls of the Guards of Folsom. This guy was medium in stature, head shaved, and he looked more like a member of a tactical unit, right down to the weapons on his belt, than any kind of player. He spotted Blake standing near the bar talking to Ty and made a beeline for him. So did Tek.

"Sir, we've got the intel you requested."

Definitely military or law enforcement, but the realization didn't cause Tek a shred of nervousness. "Where are they?"

Lawman raked his eyes up and down Tek, sizing him up, no doubt.

"It's okay, Nick," Blake said and pointed toward Tek. "This is Tek Cain. It's his partner that's gone missing."

"Sorry to hear that," Nick acknowledged with a nod. He then pulled out a small notebook from his pocket. "They're on the fourth floor, apartment 4012. I got a positive ID on one Rocco Lundy. There is one other male subject with—"

"Was it Cole?" Tek asked, the surge of anticipation tingling down his spine.

"The subject was not identified. Caucasian male, five feet eleven inches, approximately one hundred eighty pounds, dark hair and beard, and has sleeve tattoos, which include a skull and crossbones, dice, and the Tasmanian Devil."

"That's Cole," Tek responded with complete assuredness. He'd been about eight, maybe nine, when Cole had gotten Taz on his arm. It was the first time he'd watched someone get inked. Fuck, Jamie had been there too. Tek spun and headed for the door.

"Hey, where the hell you going?" Blake called out.

"I'm going to get Jamie," he shot back without turning around or slowing down.

At the door, his arm was grabbed, halting his movements. "What the hell, man?" he asked when he turned to face Blake. Tek jerked his arm free. "This isn't open for discussion."

"I'm not asking you not to go, I'm asking you to wait one second and think about the plan."

"I know about the fucking plan, I came up with it," Tek snapped.

"You came up with a new one you didn't share with the rest of us? Because the last time we talked, there was no mention of you rushing over there alone with guns blazing."

"Yeah, plans change. I'm not leaving him there a second longer."

"I agree with Tek," Ty offered. "I know I wouldn't be able to wait. Plus, there are more of us than there are of them."

"Not helping, Ty," Blake huffed.

"Sir, if I can interrupt here," Nick interjected. "You won't be going through the front door without announcing yourself. There is a security guard on duty. I suggest taking the service elevator they're using to take building supplies to the apartments being renovated. It's how I obtained access."

"See there, Tek, those are the kind of details we need first." Blake nodded to the bar. "Let's go work out the minute details, find out what else Nick discovered, and then *we* will go get Jamie, okay?"

Tek once again found himself hesitating when everything in his body screamed to run out that fucking door, consequences be damned, and get Jamie the hell away from Rocco. It nearly overwhelmed him, his body shaking with the need to act.

Blake didn't wait for Tek's response. "You guys go ahead and wait at the bar. I want a minute alone with Tek." As soon as the others were out of earshot, Blake faced Tek. "Listen, I trust Nick one hundred percent, but at the end of the day, friend or not, he will uphold the law, so be careful what you say around him."

"Yeah, yeah, sure," Tek responded distractedly. Jamie and getting him back were the only things he could concentrate on.

"Goddammit, Tek, I'm serious. You go off like a madman, shit's going to get out of hand. Need I remind you that your old club may not be the only people looking for you? You want to rescue Jamie only to have him sit in a federal prison? Alternatively, how about the fact that if you kill Rocco out of your need for vengeance, Nick will not be able to look the other way. Jamie will then be free to visit your ass in prison. Is that really what you want? Do you think that is what Jamie will want?"

"Fuck!" Tek ran his fingers through his hair. Blood and violence had always been his way. He grew up knowing those were the things that solved problems. It disgusted him how quickly he could fall back into his old mindset.

"We just want to be left alone. To stop looking over our shoulders and find a little peace. Is that so much to fucking ask? Dammit, Blake, tell me what to do to get my Jamie back and I'll do it. But please, please make it soon. This wait is killing me."

"I know, but it's almost over. I need you to hold on just a bit longer and we'll go get him. Can you do that?"

Tek stole a glance toward Nick. Jamie would kick Tek's ass if he had to come visit him in jail. He wouldn't even put it past the stubborn man to end up in the cell next to him for trying to break Tek out. "Yeah, I can do that."

"Good man. Now let's get the rest of the details from Nick, send him on his way, and we're out of here."

Tek struggled to keep himself from running out the door, but he forced himself to listen to Nick give them the rundown of the building and apartment. He also managed to stay while they made plans to hit the place dressed as construction workers and with the master key Nick left—he wanted no details—they were ready to go in, cool and quiet. However, when Tek's cell chirped announcing an incoming text, he was anything but cool and quiet as he stared at the screen.

"Motherfucker!" he cursed, the five-second video of Jamie crying out in obvious pain nearly enough to drive him to his knees. Instead he got moving.

"What is it?" Ty asked from where he was helping Blake into his jacket.

Tackett, Max, and Blake rushed over in alarm, but Tek turned his back and headed out the door. "We gotta go now!" This time Tek would not be stopped. "I'll explain on the way, grab your shit."

Tek pushed through the door, checking the clip on his Glock one more time and then patting his pocket to make sure the extra clip was there.

"All right, what the fuck is going on?" Tackett asked as he slid behind the wheel of the SUV.

In the passenger seat, Tek pulled his seat belt across him and secured it. "He sent me a video of Jamie screaming and a text that read Central Park."

"Central Park is huge," Blake pointed out from the backseat. "Where at in the park?"

"Who cares? We won't be going."

"You don't want to tip him off or make him suspicious. You need to reply," Max instructed.

As Tackett squealed out of the alley, Tek typed, *When and where?*

Within minutes Rocco responded. *Be sitting in a cab at midnight.* Perfect. Jamie would be home and Rocco dead by then.

"Well?" Tackett asked expectantly.

"I'm to be sitting in a cab at midnight."

"Shut it off," Tackett ordered him.

"Why? What if he calls back?" But Tek was already powering it down.

"In fact, throw it out the window," Tackett amended. "We found him easily enough through his cell, and he's obviously been watching you and Jamie. It's possible he's planted a tracking device."

Tek didn't even hesitate. His cell hit the pavement. "He could be following us right now. Step on the fucking gas."

"This is New York City." Max chuckled. "He'd only accomplish ramming into the car ahead of us."

At the traffic light, Tek considered jumping from the vehicle and going on foot. If Rocco was watching them, then it wouldn't matter if he was on foot or in a car. He was going to shake apart with the need to move, to react, to do something.

"Don't even think about it," Blake warned. He pressed his hand down on Tek's shoulder. "We go together."

Tek whipped his head back and gawked at Blake and at how the man had so easily read his thoughts. Then again, with the way he was vibrating and the fact that his hand was on the door handle, it was obvious what his intentions were.

"We stick to the plan," Blake added. He held Tek's gaze unflinchingly.

Tek stayed.

He'd always hated New York traffic, but tonight exponentially so. The only thing keeping Tek from jumping out of the car was that Tackett was one crazy motherfucker behind the wheel—probably trained the cabbies—and if they had been followed in the beginning, it was highly improbable anyone was able to keep up.

Excitement surged through Tek as Tackett pulled into the parking deck and cut the engine. He had to squeeze his eyes shut and take several deep breaths before the cold place within him began to spread out and slow his rapidly beating heart and thrumming body. He was deadly calm by the time he stepped out of the SUV.

The four of them made their way to the service elevator and to the fourth floor without a single person stopping them or questioning their presence. Tek began to doubt they were in the right place. How the hell could Rocco and Cole be hiding there—with a prisoner, no less—with the flurry of activity going on? Drywall was being hung and sanded in one hall, flooring laid in another, men going in and out of apartments, music blasting, men chatting and joking. When they turned down the next hall, it made sense. This hallway was deserted; the renovations obviously hadn't started on this section. Rocco had to have somehow gotten his hands on the work schedule, which, considering how easily four men had made their way through the building without being noticed, wasn't that surprising. Hide in plain sight.

Tek's shirt was grabbed, and he stopped.

"We get in, grab Jamie, and get out. Understood?" Blake reminded Tek.

That was the plan. Blake had warned him that if dead bodies showed up in 4012, Nick would be forced to turn over what he knew and who was involved. Regardless of what he'd told Blake, if things went bad, Tek would not hesitate to take Rocco and Cole out permanently. He wasn't worried about Nick; Tek knew how to dispose of bodies.

Still he nodded in agreement. "In and out."

With his ball cap pulled low over his eyes and key poised at the lock, Tackett looked at each of them and nodded before pushing the key in. "I can't believe they are making us start another one tonight," he complained loudly and unlocked the door.

"Job security, man," Max drawled.

"He's just cranky he ain't getting pussy tonight, 'cause his wife is going to be pissed," Blake added as they pushed through the door.

Tek hung back, listening intently.

"Who the hell are you, man?" Tek recognized Cole's familiar voice.

"Hey, this place is supposed to be empty," Tackett complained.

Glock in hand, Tek peered around the doorjamb as the conversation went back and forth. He spotted Cole, hands up, trying to get a word in edgewise as the other three men grumbled. The floor was littered with beer cans, food wrappers, and pizza boxes.

"What the fuck is going on?" Tek heard Rocco bellow from farther inside the apartment.

Satisfied Rocco wasn't going to be sneaking up behind him, he eased into the room and quietly closed the door behind him.

The guys had corralled Cole into the kitchen area, continuing to shout about restricted areas, permits, loss of overtime, blah, blah, blah. Tek tuned them out. He slowly pulled the silencer from his pocket and screwed it onto his weapon. They could stress their plans until they were blue in the face, but Tek knew there was only one way to deal with Rocco; the man had taught him well.

The volume rose steadily as all five men were talking at the same time, trying to be heard over the others until it was just a buzz of chaotic noise. Tek, on the other hand, was utterly calm, his movements slow and deliberate as he eased over to the coat closet. Tek knew there were only two closets in the place. If Jamie was in this one, he was to grab him and get back out the door. If he wasn't, Tek knew he would have to spill blood.

With a steady hand, he eased open the door and gritted his teeth. Of course it couldn't be that damn easy. It was empty.

When Tek once again peered around the corner, he caught a glint of metal, and it didn't surprise him in the least to see Rocco standing behind the other men, slowly pulling a gun from the back waistband of his jeans. Tek didn't hesitate, a single shot with only the slightest pop dropped Rocco, and before he could hit the floor, Tek was standing in the open with his weapon trained between Cole's eyes.

"You so much as fucking blink and you die," Tek warned Cole with cold fury.

Darkness serves a purpose: to show you that there is redemption through chaos. To see Jamie smile again, to see him whole and breathing, to touch and hold him was all the reasoning I needed for the violence that once again touched our lives. It was our burden, we were born to it, and through it we found a strange kind of peace, if only for a few moments. Having Jamie back validated the death, was proof my actions were justified. However, redemption has a price and darkness can linger even after the sun rises.

Tek Cain

Reunion

FOR THE first time in… Jamie wasn't sure how many hours or days it had been since he'd woken without pain in his limbs, back, and hell, his whole fucking body. He was groggy, his head swimmy, and his mouth once again felt like it was stuffed with rancid cotton balls, but he wasn't in pain. If the soft mattress beneath him and the warm, familiar body snuggled up against his back was merely part of a dream, then he had no plans on waking up anytime soon.

Jamie pushed back against the heat and reached behind him, searching for the familiar naked flesh of Tek's hip.

"Are you finally going to wake up?" Tek asked quietly, his warm lips against the back of Jamie's neck.

"No."

Tek kissed his neck, his arms tightening around Jamie. "But I missed you."

Now Jamie knew he was dreaming and refused to open his eyes for fear he'd find himself once again bound in a small dark closet and the pain would return. "I don't want to wake up." His voice was unfamiliar, husky and scratchy, and it hurt, so instead he gave up on talking and melted deeper into the soft bed and Tek's strong embrace.

Jamie should have known the dream was too good to last, because suddenly Tek was gone and, with him, his heat. Jamie shuddered, although he still refused to open his eyes, and he tensed, waiting for the pain to return, but it didn't. Instead, fingers brushed his hair out of his face and then landed gently on his cheek.

"C'mon, open them eyes. You sound like you could use this."

Hesitantly, Jamie cracked his eyes open slightly. It took a second for him to focus, but the dream had come along with him because Tek was standing over him with a glass of water in his hand. Clumsily, Jamie's limbs still not working the greatest, he slapped the water out of Tek's hand and grabbed him, pulling him back into the bed.

"Hey!" But Tek's protest was cut short, morphing into a grunt as he crashed down on Jamie.

The wind was nearly knocked out of Jamie when Tek's full weight landed on him, but it was so worth it to have Tek back in his arms. "I thought I was dreaming."

"What the fuck were you dreaming about? Tackle football?" Tek laughed.

"I don't even remember, but I like where this is going," Jamie told him. He buried his face in Tek's chest, inhaling deeply, then tightened his arms around Tek's back, keeping him close.

Tek shifted and stopped struggling, allowing Jamie to hold him, and ran his fingers through Jamie's hair. Jamie was sore as hell, thirsty, hungry, and still dealing with the effects of the drugs, not to mention he had a shit-ton of questions. The first of which was how in the hell did he get here. But for the moment, he simply held Tek, listened to his steady heartbeat, and drew strength from him.

They lay there for several moments in the silence, hands roaming gently over warm flesh and soft hair, and Jamie wasn't in any hurry for it to end.

Tek apparently wasn't as content. "C'mon, baby, you got to let me make sure you're okay," he murmured with obvious concern in his voice.

Reluctantly, Jamie released his hold on Tek and met his worry-filled gaze. "I'm okay. What happened?"

"You sound like shit. Let me get you another glass of water, and then if you're a good boy and drink it all, I'll hold you and tell you a story. Deal?"

He kissed Tek's nose, ignoring the pain in his split lip. "Deal."

Tek slid out of bed, retrieved the empty glass from the floor, and disappeared into the bathroom. Jamie sat up and only then realized where he was. They were in one of the playrooms at the Guards. The one with the big comfy king bed. Jamie looked down at the angry red raw marks around his wrists. He threw back the covers and examined the same ugly wounds on his ankles, his calves, his knees and thighs covered in bruises and scrapes. When Tek walked out of the bathroom, Jamie quickly covered his legs with the sheet.

"Thanks." He accepted the glass of water and gulped it down greedily.

Tek crawled into the bed and sat next to Jamie, watching him until he'd finished his water. "Better?"

"Oh yeah," he responded with a happy grin. The cool liquid eased his throat and he sounded more like himself. He set the glass on the bedside table and took Tek's hand.

Tek ran a single finger over the wounds on Jamie's wrists, his eyes blazing with anger.

With his free hand, Jamie reached up and laid his palm against Tek's cheek. "I'm okay, I promise. Just some bumps and bruises."

"It shouldn't have happened," Tek spat angrily. "I should have been more careful."

"Stop! This isn't on you. I let Rocco get the jump on me." Just saying the fucker's name was like acid burning his tongue and throat, but he forced himself to stay calm. Tek was barely hanging on to his anger by a thread. It wouldn't take much to ignite his rage, so Jamie considered his words carefully before he continued. "Why is it every time I get kidnapped, they got to pump me full of drugs?" Jamie asked, trying to lighten up a moment he knew was anything but. Tek was so tense it looked like he'd burst. Jamie slung his arm over Tek's shoulder, pulling him till the inch separating them was closed.

Tek looked a Jamie for a moment and then his expression softened. "That's because they know they couldn't control you without them."

"Yeah, well, the hangover is a bitch," Jamie responded with a wink. "So, you want to tell me how my knight in shining armor once again saved me?"

"What's the last thing you remember?"

He wasn't about to tell Tek about the agony of his confinement, the nightmares, or the way he'd screamed until his throat gave out when Rocco jabbed the syringe into his arm. Jamie had endured a hell of a lot more pain than Rocco had dished out. Besides, the bruises and split lip told the tale.

"I remember Rocco drugging me and there's flashes of a construction zone, screaming, but that's about it."

"I killed him."

Jamie wasn't surprised. He'd have done the same thing, but he hated that Tek had to do it. Tek would add this death—no matter how justified he was—to the notches he'd already carved on his soul. But there wasn't anything he could do about that at the moment. Tek still didn't believe he was a good man, but in time Jamie would convince him. Right then, Tek simply needed to get what happened off his chest and process it.

"Cole too?"

Tek shook his head vigorously. "No. I should have but…. No, I didn't kill him."

"Tell me what happened," Jamie encouraged. "How'd you find me?"

"That was Tackett."

"Tackett? Seriously?"

"Yeah, Jamie, Tackett figured it out. It's amazing, within an hour of your disappearance, Blake had called in the cavalry. He, Ty, Tackett, Micah, Max, and Aiden were waiting at the club by the time I got here and were all willing to help. Rig, Bobby, and Mason would have been here too but got stuck in Florida due to bad weather. They'll be here later today. I don't think I could have done it without them." Tek shook his head again, looking down at their joined hands. "I owe them, man."

"*We* owe them. They're good guys, just like you."

"Yeah well, they may have a different opinion now."

"Why's that?"

"Because I fucking killed him. I promised Blake I wouldn't, but…. Yeah, I put a bullet in Rocco's brain the first chance I got."

Jamie knew Tek and, after the pain he suffered from killing an unarmed man, was sure Tek wouldn't have killed again without reason. "Tell me what happened," Jamie asked again.

"Everything was going according to plan. The place was under construction so we dressed up like workers, and without a single blip, we were in the apartment. I was supposed to get you and get out but…." Tek ran his free hand over his face, and his brows dipped low as he remembered it. "Everyone was screaming and yelling, and then I saw Rocco's hand move back, saw the gun in his waistband and… I wasn't taking any fucking chances. I dropped him."

"I'd have done the same thing," Jamie assured him. "The guys don't know Rocco like we do. If he was given the chance, everyone would have been dead, you and me included. What about Cole? Why'd you let him live?" Jamie knew why, but he wanted to hear Tek say it. It would go a long way on the path to Tek healing from another senseless yet justified act of violence.

"I thought about it. I had the barrel of my Glock sighted in right between that fucker's eyes."

"And?" Jamie prodded when Tek went silent.

"He didn't reach for a weapon. Plus, the scared little man pissed himself. So much for being a badass lieutenant."

Jamie couldn't help but laugh. "Cole never was as violent as Rocco. I never understood why he followed Rocco so blindly."

"Yeah, well, he won't be anymore. I gave him an ultimatum. He could go back and work his balls off to make Crimson VIII the honorable club my grandpa and dad envisioned it to be, or I'd bury his sorry fucking corpse right along with Rocco's."

Jamie's smile grew, knowing he'd been right. Tek would have never killed Cole unless he had good reason. The asshole was dumb, blindly loyal, but there was good in him too. Jamie doubted Crimson VIII would ever be what it was when Tek's great-grandpa and his war veteran buddies started the club, but the blood and violence had to come to an end. Cole might just make that happen.

"I take it he took your offer?"

"Yeah and he also took Rocco back, stuffed in a large toolbox. I kept one of my promises to Blake."

"Which was?"

"No dead bodies lying around so his friend Nick won't have to throw us all in jail."

"Nick?"

"Lawman, but not important, I'll tell you the rest of the story later. What is important right now is that you're back and we need to get you something to eat and drink." He leaned over and sniffed Jamie's neck. "And a shower."

Tek started to get up, but Jamie stopped him. "Where the hell are you going?"

"I was going to go get your shower started and then rustle you up some grub."

"I'm still a bit sore," Jamie murmured, trying to sound much more hurt than he was, milking it. "I don't know if I can reach my back. Plus, you know drugs always leave me a little wobbly. I could fall in the shower if I didn't have someone there to catch me."

"I will if you stop that damn pouting," Tek chastised, but the complaint was ruined with the way his lip curled into a grin. That and the mischievous wink.

"Just wash my back, Romeo. We'll see if I'm up to anything more than that after I'm clean."

"It's not like I was fishing for a blow job or anything," Tek grumbled, following Jamie to the bathroom.

"You're always fishing for a blow job," Jamie reminded him and then rushed to the sink when he spotted what he really wanted most at that second. He held up the toothbrush. "Now for this, I'd do a hell of a lot more than a hummer."

Tek flipped on the shower. "I got it for you," he responded, sounding cheeky, and Jamie couldn't help but laugh again.

He downed a shit-ton more water, and with the putrid cotton balls replaced with minty freshness, Jamie stepped into the shower and Tek's open arms. He winced when the flow of hot water initially hit his wounds, causing them to sting, but it quickly eased and he laid his head on Tek's shoulder while the water pounded down on his back.

Jamie wrapped his arms around Tek's body and groaned. "God, this feels so fucking good."

Silently Tek washed Jamie's back and then grabbed the shampoo and scrubbed Jamie's head. "Uh, Jamie?"

"Mmmhmm," he moaned, enjoying his arms around Tek and the heat and the strong fingers along his scalp. He was totally melting.

"Is there anything I should know? I mean…. You know… any injuries I can't see?"

"I don't know. He may have rattled my brain a little. I had a wicked headache, but that could be from the drugs."

"Anything else?"

The strange tone in Tek's voice had Jamie lifting his head and meeting Tek's concern-filled gaze. "What do you mean?" Then it hit him. "Ah, I get it and the answer is no. Rocco asked me what it was like to take a dick up the ass. He was pretty affronted by the whole thing when I told him he should try it some time." He pointed to his lip. "Got this when I told him I was twice the man he was even *with* a dick up my ass."

Tek's brow dipped. "What the hell is wrong with you, taunting him like that?"

"Oh, like you wouldn't have done the same thing." He laid one hand on Tek's lower back, holding him close, and the other he ran through Tek's wet hair. "Seriously, I'm okay. A little sore, a little banged up, but I am fine. Honest."

Jamie had no doubt that once Rocco had gotten his money, he would have killed Jamie, and he also knew Rocco would have relished watching Tek's reaction to Jamie's death before he killed Tek too. Thanks to Tek and the rest of the guys, Rocco wouldn't get the chance to see his sick fantasy come true.

"Seriously?" Tek questioned with an arched brow.

"Seriously," Jamie repeated. He pressed his lips to Tek's. "Now shut up and kiss me."

Tek obliged him.

God, how he'd missed those lips, the demanding tongue, and Tek's flavor. Jamie, regardless of what he'd thought he'd be up for, found his cock beginning to swell as the kiss went on. The slight sting of pain from his sore lip didn't diminish his growing arousal in the slightest. Not with Tek's strong hands kneading his back and ass.

Unfortunately, the water cooled and that did have an effect on his desire. The way his belly growled loudly caused Tek to end the kiss and laugh, further ruining the passionate moment.

"I see where I stand on the list of priorities," Tek teased and shut off the taps. He reached out of the stall, snagged a towel, and handed it to Jamie.

Jamie grabbed Tek's hand instead of the towel and held on. "You are and will always be my number one priority."

Jamie didn't miss the well of emotions that filled Tek's eyes as he nodded or the way his voice cracked slightly when he responded, "Ditto."

Through life, people who claim to be friends come and go. Being friends isn't an announcement or a status, and in this day and age of social media, collecting friends is simply a game. However, surviving tragedy, one discovers quickly who their true friends are. For years Jamie has been my only true friend, the only person I thought I could trust with my life. It took tragedy to open my eyes, to see the hearts of those surrounding me.

Tek Cain

Homecoming

A CHORUS of "Jamie, welcome back" and "welcome home" along with hoots and clapping echoed through the small exclusive club as Jamie stepped through the door. Jamie smiled and took a bow as his cheeks heated slightly, not out of embarrassment but the warmth and good feelings his friends caused to spread through him.

"Thank you, thank you. Good to be back," he responded with a wide grin.

Blake must have closed the club, as normally even on a weeknight there would be three times as many people. As it was, there was only Tackett, Micah, Blake, Ty, Bobby, Rig, Mason, Max, and Aiden, and of course Tek, who Jamie made a beeline for. Not only because Jamie wanted to get his hands on him again, but also due to the table he stood next to, which was covered with a large spread of food. Obviously he was late for the party as everyone else had a plate of food and was already sitting at a long table draped in white linen.

Jamie accepted the plate Tek was holding out for him. "You could have warned me, I'd have worn something nicer," he whispered in Tek's ear.

"I had no clue," Tek laughed. "Surprised the shit out of me too, but who cares if we're underdressed? Check out this feast."

Jamie's mouth watered as he took in the sliced ham, turkey, fried chicken, vegetables, pasta salads, and rolls, and his stomach growled when the delicious scents wafted up to fill his nose. "Yeah, you're right. Who cares," he agreed. He heaped his plate high with a bit of everything.

"You will all have to forgive my manners. I'm glad you're here, but right now it's chow time," Jamie apologized as soon as he took his seat.

Everyone waved him off or laughed. No one seemed offended by Jamie's lack of conversation, and hopefully they'd feel the same once he was done filling his face like a pig at a trough. He was beyond starved, and manners would just have to take a backseat to the grumbling and groaning of his gut.

"What can I get you to drink?" Ty offered.

"I can get it," Jamie countered. He laid his napkin on his lap. He'd get something in a minute, but first, he picked up his fork and shoveled in a large bite of potatoes, chewing happily. It was the first food he'd had in a couple days, and the flavor was nearly orgasmic.

"I insist," Ty responded, going to his feet. "Beer, wine, whiskey, soda, you name it."

"Umm...." He considered having a beer but thought better of it with the effects of the drugs still not completely out of his system. "I'll have a soda. Thanks."

"No problem, be right back."

"I wasn't expecting this," Jamie said to Blake. He picked up a chicken leg and added, "But I'm sure glad you did it. I'm starved." The chicken was even better than the veggies. Then again, it could have been raw roadkill and he'd still have happily devoured it. The only thing that made the meal better was Tek's hand on his thigh, his reassuring presence while Jamie scarfed down his food.

Through dinner and dessert, the conversion was light. No one mentioned Rocco or the kidnapping, and by the time the plates were cleared away, Jamie sat back in his chair and patted his very full, but very happy belly.

"Wholly jumpin'," Micah commented. "I've never seen anyone eat like that. Then again, I've never met too many men your size."

"It takes a lot to maintain this mountainous figure," Jamie replied with a grin.

Micah eyed Tek, who had eaten damn near the same amount Jamie had. "You two should be in the grocery business. Or better yet, like a whole chain of grocery stores."

"Manners, pup," Tackett said, but it came out like a snort of laughter.

"I wasn't being disrespectful, Sir. I'm in awe. Between the two of them, they could eat a whole... me! And still have room for Mason for dessert."

That got everyone laughing, even the little runt Mason. Jamie smiled at him. Mason had always been extremely shy, but seeing him happy and interacting with the rest of the group, yeah, that was pretty fucking sweet.

The topic of Jamie's kidnapping didn't come up until he was standing at the bar with Tek, Tackett, and Blake.

"How are you really doing?" Blake asked.

"Tek gave me a rundown of what happened. Apparently the reason I'm doing so well is because of you guys. I really appreciate what you all did for me and Tek," Jamie said sincerely, looking each one of them in the eye. "I'm sorry you guys had to get involved in that shit. We had hoped that our past was behind us and never meant for it to put anyone in danger. Although I hate that you were dragged into this fuckery, I can't help but be thankful that you were. I don't know if we could have handled this one on our own."

Jamie hadn't told Tek everything that had happened, but he knew in his heart, had Blake and the rest of the guys not helped Tek, there was a very high probability that the outcome wouldn't have been favorable. Rocco knew Tek's only weakness was Jamie. The videos Rocco was making would have lured Tek straight to his death.

"We really didn't do anything that heroic, simply went along with your man here," Tackett replied. He pointed at Tek. "He's the real hero."

"Don't listen to him, Jamie," Tek piped up. "I was a fucking basket case. These guys kept me sane. Tackett here, the computer wizard that he is, was the one who tracked you down, and he and the rest of the guys formulated the plan. I'm just the big dumb bastard with a gun."

Jamie didn't miss the way Tek stiffened like he was ready for an angry reaction to his statement from the other men. Considering what Tek had told Jamie about shooting Rocco, he knew it was weighing heavily on Tek's mind and heart. Jamie wrapped his arm around Tek's waist, but he wasn't the only one reassuring Tek. Not one of them said anything negative about the shooting nor were they looking at Tek with disgust, anger, or worse, fear.

"You are so much more than big and dumb," Max commented.

"Wow, Tek, I do believe Max has just called you big and dumb." Blake hooted and slapped Max on the back. "That wasn't very nice, my man."

"I most certainly did n—"

"I don't know that I would have the balls to call him that," Tackett interjected with a snort. "Look at the size of the man. Jesus, Max, he's twice your size, you brave little fucker."

"That's not what I meant," Max insisted.

But obviously they were all having too much fun at Max's expense to care what he meant, and Jamie couldn't help but laugh.

"Considering his equally massive man is standing right next to him," Blake pointed out. "The two of them could turn you into a pretzel. That is, after they were done eating Micah and Mason, of course."

"Ain't no-damn-body eating my Mason," Rig said adamantly as he joined the group with Mason and Bobby right next to him.

"Our Mason," Bobby corrected.

"Nobody?" Mason asked softly, looking up at Rig. "I like it when you and Bobby feast on me."

Everyone stopped teasing and laughing and all looked at Mason with wide eyes. It was the first time Mason had ever joined the conversation in such a large group without being asked a direct question, and even then he'd be glued to one or both of his men. A few heartbeats later and Mason's cheeks pinked in color. Everyone burst out laughing.

Jamie had known in his heart no one would hold it against Tek for what he'd done. Standing in the club, surrounded by their friends, laughing and joking like nothing ever happened was the first step in proving to Tek that their friends held no animosity. Jamie couldn't think of any place he'd rather be. For the moment. Later he'd show Tek how appreciative he was that he'd done what he had to and brought them all back together again.

THE WELCOME-HOME party was dwindling down. Everyone had left early to give Jamie a chance to rest and recoup from his ordeal. Only Blake and Ty remained. Ty took Jamie into the office to apply new bandages to his wounds, while Tek sat at the bar with Blake waiting to take his man to bed and do a little reassuring of his own by wrapping himself around Jamie and listening to his heartbeat.

"Have you thought about what you're going to do next?" Blake asked.

"I don't know. Everything has happened so fast, I haven't really had a chance to think about what's next. I don't feel completely safe here anymore. I seriously doubt Cole will return or order anyone else to. However, depending on how Cole spins the tale of what happened, there may be some members who will want retribution for Rocco's death."

"I wish it hadn't had to end like that."

"I—"

"I'm not blaming you, and I'm grateful it was him rather than any of us, I was simply making the statement that it would have been easier to put this behind you."

"You don't know Rocco like I do. The minute I saw him pulling the weapon, I knew he had to die, but honestly, I think I knew he would even before we showed up at the apartment." Tek pursed his lips. "I'm not going to apologize. I'm not sorry he's dead."

"You have nothing to apologize for, and you're more than welcome to stay here," Blake offered. "No one unwanted is getting in this place. I can assure you of that."

"Thanks, but I was thinking I'd take Jamie to our cabin in the woods. Give us time to recover from the scare and figure out what we're going to do next."

"Understandable. Take all the time you need. Your job will still be here if you decide to come back."

"Thanks, Blake," Tek said sincerely and shook his hand. "I owe you."

"Nonsense, you'd do the same for me."

Other than Jamie, Tek never had anyone in his life, friend or family, who didn't expect repayment for a *favor*. But Blake and the other men he'd grown to regard as friends had opened their hearts since the first time he'd walked through the doors of the Guards of Folsom. Friendship was the only thing they expected in return. The club was a good place, filled with good people, and Tek would always be grateful for his time here even if he and Jamie decided to move on. Tek felt a twinge in his chest at the thought of leaving, a sensation he'd never experienced when he'd left Chatom. He would leave having definitely learned a lot, the most important lesson of all the kind of man he wanted to be.

"I certainly would," Tek responded past the lump that had formed in his throat.

"He's all yours," Ty announced, coming back into the club with Jamie right behind him.

"Thanks, Ty, I appreciate you playing doctor."

"Pfft, more like nurse. I only play doctor with Blake," Ty responded with a wink. He moved up next to Blake and put his arm around his Dom's shoulders. "Speaking of which, how about you and I go play a little Dr. Feelgood and let these two get some sleep?"

Blake jumped up and grabbed Ty's hand. "See you guys tomorrow," Blake announced and then yelled over his shoulder as he headed for the door with a laughing Ty in tow, "Grab the lights, will ya? I'll lock up on my way out."

"Will do," Tek responded, but Blake and Ty were already gone.

"Looks like someone was a wee bit excited for his checkup." Jamie snorted.

Tek glanced down at the bandages on Jamie's arms, his gut flip-flopping with residual guilt. He ran a finger softly over the one on Jamie's left wrist. "I'm not much of a doctor, but I do have a great bedside manner."

"I don't need a doctor," Jamie murmured. He pressed his lips to Tek's. "Just you."

"I'm all yours," Tek promised, kissing him back. "Now c'mon, you need your rest." He took Jamie's hand.

"I slept all day. I don't need rest." Jamie's statement was contradicted when he yawned.

"Mmmhmm, then you can be my big lumpy pillow while I sleep."

They'd barely gotten under the covers and laid their heads down when Jamie began making soft snuffling sounds. The next day, the day after at the latest, they'd head to their cabin and try to figure out where in the hell they went from here. For now, Tek was content to hold Jamie. He pushed up closer to him and laid his head on Jamie's chest, soaking in Jamie's heat, and let the reassuring sound of Jamie's strong, steady heartbeat lull him to sleep.

Running away seemed like something I was getting really good at. Run from my past, run from my hometown, run from the Feds, gangs, danger, clubs. Run! Run! Run! It wasn't that I was a coward, far from it. I viewed it as surviving, saving not only mine and Jamie's lives but those of others, whether they be friend or foe. And sometimes, running gave me a chance to recover, to think, to breathe. If even for a few days, hours, or moments, I found true happiness in those stolen moments when Jamie and I ran from the world.

Tek Cain

Into the Woods

JAMIE WALKED through the door, flipped on the light, and was greeted with a loud hissing sound. He spun on his heels and walked right back out, slamming the door behind him. "Dude, there is a fucking raccoon on the counter."

"So get rid of him," Tek responded, his voice muffled as he dug around in the trunk of the car.

Jamie put his hands on his hips and tapped his foot impatiently on the porch. "You do realize it's a wild animal?"

"Yeah, so?"

"So they bite if you fuck with them."

Tek stood up and looked around the car, a smirk on his lips. "Aw, is my man afraid of Rocky Raccoon? That's so cute."

"Fuck you. I'm not afraid of him"—*mostly*—"but I'd rather spend my evening banging the hell out of you rather than in the ER getting stitches and a rabies shot."

"Banging, huh?" Tek waggled his brows and stalked toward Jamie.

"Not with Rocky in there," Jamie countered and stabbed his thumb over his shoulder toward the cabin.

"Take this." Tek handed Jamie the duffel bag.

When Jamie accepted the bag, Tek pulled his gun from his coat pocket.

"What do you think you're doing with that?"

Tek gave him one of those incredulous looks that screamed *Duh*. "Making sure I get some banging," Tek responded and tried to step around Jamie, but Jamie blocked him.

"You can't shoot it. It's on the kitchen counter, for fuck's sake. I do not want critter brains splattered where we cook and eat. That's just…. No."

"So we'll scare it, and the minute it hits the floor, I'll pop it."

Once again Tek tried to step around him, but Jamie refused to budge. "You're not shooting it."

"Then how in the hell do expect me to get it out of there?"

Jamie pursed his lips and thought about it for a second. "We'll use a broom."

"What?"

"C'mon." Jamie dropped the duffel bag and slowly opened the door. The raccoon was still sitting on the counter, fat as hell—big as a medium-sized dog—munching away at whatever it had snatched from the open cupboard above it. The thing looked right at home, like he owned the place. Well fuck that, he and Tek owned this place.

"The broom is in there." Jamie pointed to the pantry.

"I know where the hell it is, but no fucking way am I going that close to Rabid Raccoon."

"I thought you had named him Rocky?"

"That's when I thought you were talking about a cute little woodland creature. That's a fucking beast."

"Aw, is my man afraid?" Jamie asked, mimicking Tek's earlier taunt. He smiled huge, totally vindicated for his fear.

Tek raised his gun.

"No! You are not shooting it. Put that damn thing down."

"I'm not chasing that thing with a broom," Tek countered, but he lowered his weapon.

The two of them stood there, backs pressed against the door, watching the beast enjoy his meal. After a few minutes, Jamie began to laugh.

"What is so damn funny?"

"I was just thinking, between the two of us, we have a good ten feet and four hundred pounds on him, and we're standing here too afraid to take our damn cabin back."

Tek glared at him and then grumbled, "That's only because you won't let me shoot it."

"Nope," Jamie chuckled. "I'm not cleaning that mess up, so we better come up with another plan, or I know two big burly men who will be sleeping in the car tonight."

"Not fucking happening," Tek said adamantly. "This is our damn place. Be right back." Tek headed back out the door.

"Where are you going?"

Tek didn't answer, and Jamie didn't turn around to see where he went, instead keeping his gaze trained on the raccoon. If it so much as moved from its perch, Jamie was so out of there.

A minute later, Tek returned with a blanket and a rake. He handed the rake to Jamie.

"What am I supposed to do with this?"

"You get his attention and I'll ease around from the back and throw the blanket over him."

"Are you out of your goddamn mind? You're going to wrestle a forty-pound raccoon with sharp claws and teeth in a blanket?"

Tek shrugged. "Like you said, we got height and weight over that bastard in spades. Not to mention brains."

Jamie had a really bad feeling about Tek's plan, but he couldn't think of a better one. He gripped the rake in both hands and held it out like a spear. "Let's do this."

The raccoon watched them with its dark beady little eyes. The growling sound got louder as Jamie inched his way closer. The raccoon must have sensed danger because it stopped eating, stood on all four legs, and backed up till its ass was against the wall. The head of the rake still feet away, it began hissing and snapping.

"On three," Tek informed him. He had the blanket in both hands stretched out. "One…. Two…. Three!"

Tek lunged, throwing the blanket, and then all hell broke loose. The animal screeched, Tek screamed, and suddenly the raccoon was charging Jamie. He did the only thing he could think of. He dropped the rake and ran like hell.

TEK STARED down at his bandaged hand. The wound throbbed with each beat of his heart. The ten stitches hurt, but nowhere near as badly as the fucking rabies shot. He rubbed his arm with his uninjured hand and scowled over at Jamie, who was driving along the back roads looking as if he didn't have a care in the world. And really he didn't. Bastard had run.

"I can't believe you ran."

"What the hell was I supposed to do? Stay and get bit too?"

"Yes."

Jamie glanced over at Tek with his brows nearly to his hairline. "You're kidding me, right?"

"Do I look like I'm kidding?" He held up his bandaged hand. "Does this look like a joke to you?"

"You got two stitches and a little needle. Besides, it was your idea to wrestle Rabid Raccoon."

Two or ten, he hadn't been counting 'cause he'd been too busy gritting his teeth to keep from screaming or crying or punching the bastard stitching him up. Jamie deserved a good jab too. Jamie, who hadn't stuck around to save him from a vicious animal and an even more sadistic doctor.

He slapped Jamie's arm. "I can't believe you ran!"

"Ow! Watch it, driving here," Jamie grumbled. "Besides, I did save you. That little fucker chased me around the damn cabin, and I barely made it back in and got the door shut without ending up with a matching wound. And need I remind you it was your idea to try to catch it with a blanket?"

Tek huffed out an irritated breath. "Just get me home. My arm hurts and I need a drink."

Jamie laid his hand on Tek's leg and gave it a squeeze. "I'll take care of your boo-boos."

"Damn right you will."

The raccoon was nowhere in sight when they arrived back at the cabin. After searching for the beast and blocking off any access into the house, Tek flopped down on the couch with an ice-cold beer and propped his feet up on the coffee table. Jamie sat next to him and draped his arm over Tek.

"We've gone up against some rough characters in our time, but Rabid Raccoon has got to be one of the toughest."

Stunned, Tek stared at Jamie. The man had been kidnapped twice in his short life, beaten, nearly killed, and he was comparing Rabid to Rocco or even the rival gang that drugged and beat him. Tek had made a big deal about the bite and subsequent stitches and shot, but he'd only been giving Jamie a hard time. He hadn't been serious, and he wondered now if Jamie was doing the same thing. Whatever his reasoning, they deserved to put the ugliness of the last week—hell, of their entire fucking past—behind them, and simply enjoy each other.

Tek downed his beer in two big gulps and set the bottle aside. "My hand really hurts," he grumbled and stuck out his bottom lip.

"You need one of those pain pills?" Jamie offered.

"Nope." Tek pushed down his sweats, exposing his cock. He wrapped his fingers around it and slowly stroked it. "Actually, I was thinking about another type of pain reliever."

"Jerking off rather than Vicodin? Hmm, I'm not sure if that's going to get rid of all your pain."

"You're right," Tek murmured. He pumped his cock a few times, increasing the pressure and enjoying his growing arousal. "I'm going to need more than just a hand job. I do believe someone mentioned banging me."

Jamie shifted, a smile curling his lips. "I said I'd rather bang than end up in ER but…."

"I'm the one who ended up in ER, and seeing as I got rid of our little problem, now you can work on my really big problem." Tek thrust his hips, pushing his erection through his fist for emphasis.

"Technically, I got rid of our little problem," Jamie corrected. He slid off the couch and went to his knees between Tek's spread legs. "I suppose I can take care of another one."

"This is far from little," Tek assured him and waved his cock at Jamie.

"Well, it is growing," Jamie teased.

Tek didn't even care about the taunt, not with Jamie lowering his head and brushing his lips over the flared head. Tek released his hold on his dick and threaded his fingers through Jamie's hair.

"C'mon, babe, make me forget all about the pain in my hand."

"I can do that," Jamie responded, his voice husky. He kissed the head of Tek's cock and then wrapped those wonderful lips around it and began sucking, his tongue teasing the slit.

"That's it. Fuck, that feels good."

Jamie took Tek deeper, bobbing his head as he ran his hands up and down Tek's thighs, fingers digging in a little.

Tek scooched his ass forward, leaned back a little, and gave Jamie full access to his groin. He then fisted his hand in Jamie's hair, encouraging him to take more, to move faster.

"Deeper," he groaned and snapped his hips.

Jamie obliged him, humming his agreement before taking Tek balls-deep.

"Fuck yeah, that's it," Tek praised.

Jamie pulled back slightly at the same time Tek thrust up hard, causing Jamie to gag. Jamie let Tek's cock slip from his mouth and sat back on his calves. "Easy there, tough guy."

"Your fault. If your mouth didn't feel so fucking good…." Tek wrapped his fist around his wet cock. "Get back here. I wasn't done with you yet."

"Not only a tough guy but a pushy one," Jamie teased.

"Like I said—"

"I know, my fault. I can live with that." Jamie yanked Tek's sweatpants down his legs. "For what I have planned, you're going to need to get rid of these." He pulled Tek's pants off completely and tossed them behind him.

Tek didn't even care. He kept stroking himself, tightening his grip and pulling from base to tip, rubbing his thumb over the flared head on each pass. He was so fucking horny, and if Jamie didn't hurry the hell up, Tek was going to end up blowing before he got Jamie's mouth back on him.

"This too," Jamie ordered and yanked at Tek's T-shirt. He tried pulling it up, but it got caught on Tek's arms when he refused to let go of his dick.

"Can you just bend over a bit and open that big mouth of yours?" Tek groaned.

Jamie grabbed Tek's hand and pulled it away. "Not so fast."

Tek tried to pull free, but Jamie refused to release him. "C'mon, man. You can't stop at half a blow job." He started to grab his cock in his other hand, but the bandage got in the way.

"Am I going to have to tie your hands down?"

"You can't. I have an owie," Tek grumbled. he held up his bandaged hand again. "You're supposed to be taking care of me, you know. Easing my pain, but you're not. You're making it worse."

Jamie pulled off Tek's shirt, being careful of Tek's wounds when he slid it over his injured hand. "How am I making it worse?"

"'Cause not only does my arm and hand hurt, now something else hurts too. You should kiss it and make it all better."

"Here?" Jamie asked. He kissed Tek's knee. Then he brushed his lips across the center of his thigh. "Or here?"

"Dammit, Jamie, stop being mean. You know exactly where I'm aching."

"I know, and I promise to make it worth the wait." Jamie removed his shirt and tossed it in the same direction as Tek's clothes. He ran his hands down Tek's lightly furred chest and across the ridges of his hard stomach before grabbing the waistband of his own jeans.

"You gonna do a little striptease for me?" Tek spread his legs farther, and resumed stroking his cock.

"Only if you turn that loose." Jamie nodded toward Tek's crotch. When Tek only stared up at him, licked his lips, and stroked faster, Jamie slapped his hand away. "Hands behind your head. Your hand is supposed to be elevated anyway."

"That's not going to help what is hurting the most at the moment," Tek assured him, but he did as Jamie instructed. Jamie could be a stubborn shit when he had a plan, and if Tek wanted his dick to get a little action, he was going to have to let Jamie have his way. This time. "All right, now get those pants off and get back to the spit and shine, will ya?"

Jamie bowed his head and stared at Tek from heavy-lidded eyes as Jamie popped the button on his jeans and eased down the zipper. Tek's mouth watered when Jamie pulled back the flaps on his jeans and exposed his hard cock.

"That's what I'm talking about. I'll do you if you do me."

"Oh, you're going to do me all right." Jamie pulled a lube packet from his pocket along with a condom before pushing his pants down and stepping out of them, kicking them away.

"What was all that hype about banging me?"

"Later."

Tek groaned in frustration.

Ignoring Tek's growly complaint, Jamie tore the condom packet with his teeth and took the rubber out, then tossed the wrapper aside and held it up while waggling his brows seductively. Tek wasn't complaining but rather moaning in delight when Jamie rolled the condom down Tek's shaft. Even the brush of latex sent of sparks of heat and a tingling sensation down to his balls. His pleasure rocketed when Jamie squeezed out a good amount of lube and then reached around. Tek couldn't see

Jamie's hand, but from the small grunt before he bit his lip, Tek didn't need to be a rocket scientist to figure out what Jamie was doing.

"Turn around. I want to see."

Jamie kept working his finger, his eyes fluttering shut.

"Better yet, let me help." He reached out, grabbed Jamie's arm, and spun him.

"Hey, watch what you're doing. This is a very delicate procedure."

"Lucky for you I'm an expert. Bend over and grab your ass cheeks." Tek moved to the edge of the couch. He ran his index finger down Jamie's slick crack and teased the tip around his hole. "Fuck, you've got a sweet ass."

Jamie wiggled the ass in question. "Get me lubed 'cause it's going to be even sweeter when I'm lowering it down over your cock."

Tek slapped his ass cheek. "Then be still."

Jamie pulled his cheeks farther apart and bent in half, his ass on perfect display for Tek. Tek's cock twitched in response and his pulse sped in anticipation. He eased the tip of his finger into Jamie's tight hole, moving it in a small circle. When he pushed it in to the first knuckle, the deep husky moan he got in response was satisfying. After Tek had worked his finger all the way in, he pumped it in and out of Jamie's hole and then added another finger in alongside the first. He then leaned in and ran his jaw over Jamie's ass cheek.

"That tickles," Jamie murmured. He was pushing his ass back, thrusting a little, and that hard, taut ass was too much of a temptation. Tek bit it, just a little love bite really, but enough that it made Jamie jerk forward, dislodging Tek's fingers.

"No biting the goods," Jamie chastised and turned around. "Sit back on the couch."

Who was Tek to argue such an inviting prospect, knowing what was coming next? He pushed back, spread his legs, and ran his fingers over his sheathed cock, slicking up the condom. He then wrapped his hand around the base, holding it upright when Jamie crawled onto the couch and straddled him. Jamie laid his hands on Tek's chest, fingers splayed over his pecs.

"You ready for me?"

"Dumb question, Jamie," Tek groaned. "Now ride me before I force my dick up your ass."

"Might be a little hard for you to force anything on me. You know, in your weakened state," Jamie teased, sliding his ass back and forth over the head of Tek's cock, the muscles in Jamie's legs flexing and bulging as he moved.

"Don't make me prove it." Tek tried to sound tough, but his growl came out more like a groan. Jamie's slick ass teased the head and nearly drove Tek mad with need. "God, Jamie. C'mon, you don't know how bad I need this. Don't make me beg."

Jamie lowered his head and brushed his lips over Tek's ear. "I like it when you beg."

Tek shivered when Jamie licked the shell of his ear. "Fine, pretty please with sugar on top?"

"Oh, I think you can do better than that." Jamie lowered himself slowly on Tek's cock, but before Tek could thrust up, Jamie lifted up again, coming all the way off Tek's cock.

"Jamie," Tek said warningly.

"Yes, baby?" Jamie lowered himself down, but once again, just as the head breached his tight ass, he lifted up again.

Tek gritted his teeth to keep in the curse that wanted out, or maybe it was begging. Either way, it wasn't happening, and he huffed out a breath instead.

"Aw, my poor abused man," Jamie cooed and pressed his lips against Tek's. He licked at Tek's bottom lip until Tek opened, and he pushed his tongue in. Tek was thrumming with need as the kiss went on and on, and Jamie continued to sway, teasing the tip of Tek's cock with his slick crease.

The kiss was hot and passionate, but it wasn't all-consuming— that was Jamie's ass. Tek released his cock when Jamie once again lowered just enough for the head to breach his hole. Tek didn't waste any time. He wouldn't be denied again. He grabbed Jamie's hips in both his hands, ignoring the sting of pain from the wound, and pushed Jamie down at the same time he thrust up, hard.

"Oh fuck!" Jamie cried out as Tek impaled him on his cock.

"I'm done with the teasing," Tek grunted, then held tight and rolled his hips.

Jamie didn't respond, at least not with words, but the moaning and rapid breathing was evidence he was done with the teasing as well. Jamie tipped his head back, shifted his knees, and slid his hands up to Tek's shoulders.

Tek returned his hands to the position above his head. Now that he was balls-deep in Jamie's tight ass, he didn't have a problem giving up a bit of the control and allowing Jamie to set the pace. "That's it, baby, ride me," he encouraged.

The new submissive position was all the urging Jamie needed. He grabbed Tek's wrists, holding them as he moved and swayed, his hard cock straining upward, bobbing against Tek's muscular stomach with each movement.

"God, I love your cock," he murmured. "Love how it burns, stretches… fills me."

Tek's pulse raced, his breathing coming in short pants as his orgasm built. He'd been so fucking ready to blow when Jamie's lips were wrapped around his shaft, but now he didn't want it to end. He struggled to slow his breathing, to get his out-of-control libido reined in. But the way Jamie's tight passage was clamping down on his dick, the slick heat engulfing him, he knew he wouldn't be able to hold back for long.

He tried pulling his good hand free, but Jamie tightened his grip. "I'm not going to last long. Want to bring you with me," he murmured and tugged again. This time Jamie released him and returned his hands to Tek's shoulders, never missing a thrust. They became even more forceful when Tek wrapped his hand around Jamie's straining cock and pumped it hard and fast.

"Ah fuck!" Jamie called out, tipping his head back farther. "I'm… I…. Fuck, Tek. Needed this so bad, can't hold back. I'm sorry."

"No apologies needed. Come with me," Tek moaned. A knot formed at the base of his spine and his balls drew up. Jamie's ass clamped down hard as Jamie's body went bowstring tight.

"Tek!" Jamie cried out as the first blast of his release shot out and landed on Tek's chest. It and the way Jamie's ass squeezed his cock was all it took, and Tek let go and filled the condom deep in Jamie's ass, Jamie's name on his lips.

Jamie slumped forward, burying his face in Tek's neck and breathing harshly. Tek wrapped his arms around him, held him. The past week was forgotten—the battle with the rabid raccoon, the whole world—while he held Jamie, so fucking thankful he could.

No matter how much we wish otherwise, we being the common folks of the world, real life always calls and fucks up vacations. I wished I'd been born rich, then my life could have been one long vacation. Then I realized, as hard as things were at times for Jamie and me, everything we'd experienced was for a reason. It certainly tightened our bond, and more importantly, it taught us to dream. To look beyond the here, plan for the future, and to set goals. To hope.

Tek Cain

Looking toward the Future

THE MORNING sun streaming through the drapes lit up the cabin in red, gold, and yellow. Although he'd been awake for quite some time and his bladder was screaming at him to get up, Jamie was too warm and content, stretched out with Tek cuddled up against him. Tek was obviously in no hurry to get up either because he'd been awake before Jamie. The random patterns he'd been drawing on Jamie's chest were the first thing Jamie had been aware of when he opened his eyes.

Tek propped himself up on his elbow and looked down at Jamie. "Want to draw straws to see who has to make the coffee?"

"No, I'll do it. I've got to piss." Jamie started to slip from bed, but Tek refused to release his hold on him. Jamie gave him a questioning look. "I thought you wanted coffee?"

"I do, but I don't want to get up."

"Then lay here. I'll get up," Jamie retorted.

"But I want you to stay with me."

"Well, now we have a bit of a problem, don't we? I can't very well make coffee or piss from here." Jamie flopped back down on the bed. He really didn't want to get up either. He could hold it.

"Five more minutes," Tek murmured. He pushed up close, then laid his head on Jamie's chest.

Jamie ran his fingers through Tek's hair, enjoying the quiet and warmth for a few more moments. "How's your hand feeling?"

"Hurts."

"Bad?"

"Nah, just aches a bit, but I forgive you."

"For what? I didn't bite you nor was it my plan to try to wrestle a raccoon with a blanket."

"You could have stopped me or come up with a better plan or at least some suggestions."

Jamie busted out laughing. "I could have stopped you? Seriously, Tek, you get shit in your head and look out. Besides, I did offer an alternative."

Tek threw his leg over Jamie. "Aren't you glad we didn't go with your plan? It's kind of hard to fuck, let alone snuggle, in the car."

The weight of Tek's leg across his groin smashed Jamie's morning wood and, worse, put pressure on his overly full bladder. He quickly extricated himself from Tek and made a mad dash for the john.

"I wasn't done snuggling," Tek called out behind him.

Jamie didn't respond till he blew out a relieved breath once he was pissing. "It was either end your snuggle session or you were getting a golden shower."

"It would have been worth it."

Jamie flushed and washed his hands, drying them as he leaned against the door frame and gave Tek an incredulous look. "Yeah, until you had to clean the mattress. Besides, I want coffee." He tossed the hand towel behind him in the general direction of the sink.

Jamie found the coffee can unmolested by their unwanted guest and got a pot brewing while Tek took care of his morning business. Soon enough the two of them were taking their mugs of steaming coffee and heading out to the porch. They sat on the top step, shoulder to shoulder.

"So what do you want to do today?" Jamie asked as he sipped his coffee.

"Absolutely nothing," Tek said immediately. "I am officially on vacation. I deserve it."

"And I don't?" Jamie asked with a single brow arched.

Jamie hadn't been making a reference to what he'd been through or how he was dealing with it, but he could tell by the way Tek's gaze cut to Jamie's wrists, that was where his thoughts immediately went.

"How you doing?" Tek inquired.

"I'm fine. The scrapes and bruises are nearly healed and it damn sure didn't hurt that I lost a couple pounds." He chuckled and patted his gut.

"It's not funny," Tek grumbled.

"It wasn't at the time, you're right, but fuck, Tek, we need to talk about this shit and move on. Nothing we can do to change it. I choose to laugh at it rather than let it destroy me." Jamie nodded his head. "Yeah, I guess we should talk about what happened."

"I don't want to right now. The only thing we need to figure out at the moment is where we go from here. You think we should head back to the Guards?"

"Yeah, eventually we'll have to. We're broke. We'll work our asses off, bank some cash, and head back here. We could totally be mountain men. We got the look." Jamie ran his free hand through his week's worth of growth on his jaw.

Tek turned his head from side to side, staring out at the landscape with a doubtful expression. "Umm, one problem, Jamie, no mountains around here."

"Ass," Jamie cursed and slapped Tek on the back. "You know what I meant."

"Any chance you have a long-lost relative I don't know about who's going to leave you a fortune in his will?"

"Nope."

"Up for robbing a bank?"

Jamie cocked his head and gave Tek a disapproving look. He wasn't even going to dignify that stupid question with an answer.

"Then yeah, I guess our only other option is to head back into the city. Hide out at the Guards till the heat dies down. Maybe Blake's friend Nick can look into finding out if the Feds are still looking for us or if they believed our ruse. I seriously doubt Rocco and the rest of the MC had become buddies with them since we left or tipped them off to where we were, so we may be good there."

"But we can't know when, where, or if the Eights will show up unannounced."

"And therein lies the crux of our problem," Tek said with a nod.

"You think maybe Blake's friend could do intel on the club? Or maybe Blake or Tackett know some way we can get surveillance on the Eights to see if Cole takes your threat to heart."

"Maybe." Tek shrugged. "We could ask, but either way we are going to have to stay on our toes and be extremely careful from here on out."

"Makes my fucking head hurt thinking about it," Jamie complained.

"I know, but the only option we have at the moment is to take Blake up on his offer to stay at the club. It will drive me nuts not being able to go out or have our own place, but at least it won't be as bad as a pine box or a six by eight."

"Agreed. So how about we worry about it later and enjoy a little peace and quiet at our own place while we still can."

"I'm with you on that." Tek held out his mug.

Jamie clinked his against it. "I do have a few good ideas every now and then."

"As long as it doesn't involve raccoons," Tek mumbled under his breath, but Jamie heard him.

"Yeah, well, speaking of which, we need to change your bandage, and I need another cup of coffee." Jamie pushed to his feet and held his hand out for Tek.

Tek took the offered hand and followed Jamie into the cabin. "Okay, but after you play nurse, I'm spending the rest of the morning on the porch in the old rocker with my feet propped up."

"Sounds like a hell of a plan to me," Jamie agreed.

DRESSED IN nothing but a pair of briefs, Tek sprawled out on the blanket next to the pond, shades pulled over his eyes and giving not a single fuck. He'd been just as lazy all morning, keeping to his plan and spending it kicked back on the porch. After lunch, the only exertion was splashing around in the pond with Jamie, but even that was totally laid-back and relaxing.

Tek flipped over, folded his arms, and propped his chin on them. "Get my back, will ya?"

"Sure." Jamie sat up, grabbed the suntan oil, and poured out a good amount in his palm, and even though he'd rubbed his hands together to warm it, Tek still jerked when the cold oil hit his heated skin. Jamie rubbed his slick hands over Tek's back, fingers digging in a little as he kneaded the muscles, and then moved down to his thighs and calves.

"Damn, I wish we didn't have to go back. I could get used to this," Tek drawled sleepily.

"I think that should be our goal, then. Work our asses off for a few years, save up some cash, and spend the rest of our lives right here. Just you and me."

"We could grow a garden, get us some cows, a few chickens. Hell we could be totally self-sufficient. We wouldn't ever have to leave our little spread of land. Be total hermits."

"I don't know if I'd go that far. I said mountain men, not Farmer Pete." Jamie laughed. He laid down next to Tek in nearly the exact same position, arms folded with his cheek resting on them. "I think you'd get tired of me being your only companion."

"I don't think so. You were my only true companion growing up, the only one I ever wanted to be with." The smile that curled Jamie's lips caused Tek's stomach to flutter and his heart to melt.

"You're awful mushy for a guy who can eat a sub for dinner and another for dessert. They must have been talking about Subway subs," Jamie teased. "You're not sounding very badass at the moment."

In one deft move, Tek landed on Jamie, had his arms pinned, and was lying on him chest to back, thigh to thigh. "Am I going to have to prove to you once again how badass I really am?" Tek growled in Jamie's ear.

Jamie pushed his ass up into Tek's groin. "I'm hearing a lot of talk but little action."

"You're really fucking asking for it," Tek warned.

"Still just talking."

Tek released his hold on Jamie's forearms, grabbed his shorts, and retrieved a condom from the pocket. He shoved his briefs down and rolled the condom down his shaft. Jamie taunted him by swaying and rocking. Tek yanked down Jamie's underwear and briefly considered spanking Jamie's ass, but he had a better idea. Oh there would be slapping involved, but it would be from him slamming into Jamie. Tek snatched the bottle of oil, poured some down the crease of Jamie's ass, and then ran his cock up and down it.

"Does this feel like just talk?"

Jamie moaned, lifting his hips slightly. "Feels good, but you're still not proving your badassery," he taunted.

"You're going to pay for your teasing ways, I assure you," Tek promised as he continued to slick up his sheathed dick in the crease of Jamie's ass with short thrusting movements.

"Talk, talk, talk, talk. I'm beginning to think that's all you can do is talk, talk, talk, but you can't walk the walk."

Tek knew what Jamie was doing, and for fuck's sake, he was going to give him exactly what he was asking for. He gripped Jamie's briefs on either side and ripped them from his body and, seconds later went to his knees between Jamie's legs and pulled the taunting bastard's hips up till he was on his hand and knees.

"You'll be the one who won't be walking," Tek promised and pushed the head of his cock against Jamie's hole. With short, steady thrusts, Tek worked at Jamie's ass until he opened up and Tek was able to drive himself home in one long, slow, steady stroke. He had no desire to damage Jamie. Tek forced himself to remain still, despite the shaking in his limbs and the ground teeth it cost him. Tek slid his hand around Jamie's hip and pressed against his hard shaft. Rubbing his palm back and forth, he soothed and aroused at the same time he gave Jamie a moment to adjust to Tek's sizable girth, enjoying the way Jamie's ass contracted around his cock. Tek's pleasure increased with each movement of that perfect slick, tight heat.

It took a moment before the shock of Tek's sudden intrusion wore off, and slowly oh so fucking slowly, Jamie's body yielded to him. Tek leaned over and licked a path from between Jamie's broad shoulder to the back of his neck, tasting clean sweat and sunshine on Jamie's skin.

"You ready for more?" he asked against the base of Jamie's skull.

"Would you shut the hell up and fuck me." Jamie shoved his ass back hard, taking Tek balls-deep.

Tek pulled all the way back till just the head of his cock was still buried in Jamie's ass. He then grabbed Jamie's hips in both his hands, holding him in a bruising grip, and yanked Jamie back at the same time he snapped his groin forward.

Over and over Tek plowed into Jamie's sweet ass, Jamie meeting each hard thrust, rocking back, demanding more and more with his powerful body. Tek slowly pulled back, watching his oil-slicked cock slide from Jamie's body until the flared head was stretching that tight ass before plunging in again. Slow to fast, gentle to hard, hot to cool, the dueling sensations made Tek's balls ache with need and his blood boil.

All too soon Tek's cock seemed to swell further and Jamie's ass tighten, and he knew his release was imminent. Fuck, Jamie felt good, too good, but he'd be damned if he'd blow before Jamie got his fill, before he was sure the taunting bastard walked with a hitch in his step when it was over. Tek gritted his teeth, clamped down on his own need, and redoubled his efforts, pounding into Jamie at a brutal pace.

Jamie's groans became pleas, then pleas became shouts, and still Tek fucked him with single-minded determination. Sweat poured down his neck, trickling along his spine, and he was breathing like a thoroughbred racing for the finish line. It was inevitable; he couldn't stop the steamroller. He was going to fucking come. He barely managed to hold off until Jamie threw his head back, as he exploded into orgasm.

Tek continued to thrust into Jamie through his orgasm. Again… again. Jamie's shouts louder, Tek's name echoing through the forest. Blood roared. Heart hammering. Accelerated. Pounding. Desperate.

Then, red-hot heat engulfed him, singed his entire being. The sweet burn rushed down his spine. He held his breath, muscles tense, and in the next instant he burst wide open. He erupted deep inside Jamie's body, flooding it with every drop of his passion.

Jamie's arms gave out, and he collapsed on the blanket, breathing harshly. Too zapped to move, Tek lay on top of Jamie, panting and tingling and feeling so fucking good that if he had the energy, he'd shout or laugh or…. Didn't matter. He wasn't moving, even if he could.

Jamie didn't seem to mind—he was as limp beneath Tek as Tek felt. He closed his eyes, breathing in Jamie's scent, a slight smile on his face as he thought, *So going to be walking with a limp.*

Tek was a total badass, and he didn't have to prove it. He knew it.

We are always planning for it, yearning for it. Saying things will be better in the future.

But what is the future, really? The next day? The next moment? The future is what we make of it.

Stop waiting for tomorrow, for it may never come.

Live your life.

Tek Cain

Reality Interrupts a Dream

SPOTTING JAMIE sitting on the hood of the car, his back against the windshield, head down, Tek tromped down the stairs with two cold sodas in hand. "What ya doing?" Tek asked as he handed one of the sodas to Jamie.

"Doodling."

Tek climbed up on the car next to Jamie, stretched his long legs out, and checked out the notebook on Jamie's lap. It was a damn fine drawing of the cabin, only he'd added on to the small dwelling, added a full wraparound porch, shutters, and had even sketched a walkway and gardens.

"Jesus, that's awesome. I didn't know you could draw like that."

Jamie flipped the notebook over. "It's just a doodle," he said nonchalantly and tipped back his drink.

"The hell it is," Tek challenged. He snatched the notebook, held it up, and studied the drawing. Jamie often scribbled silly cartoon characters or random peace symbols and graffiti-style fonts, but he'd never seen him create something so lifelike, so beautiful. "This is amazing!"

He snatched the sketch back. "Stop teasing me," Jamie grumbled.

Tek cocked his head and glared at Jamie. "Don't make me beat you." Jamie started to open his mouth, but Tek pointed a finger at him in warning, shutting him up before adding, "I'm not lying. I said it's awesome, so it is."

"Oh really?" Jamie said skeptically. "You make all the rules on art?"

"In this case, yup. I think we should frame it."

"What?" Jamie squawked. "I've always known you had some weird decorating ideas, but this has got to be the worst. We are so not framing it."

Tek grabbed the notebook and hopped down off the car before Jamie got it in his head to crumble it or worse, tear it up. "I'm not saying we need to use it for decoration—which by the way, fuck you, I'm a great interior designer, thank you very much—but as a reminder of what we're working for. Our dream home. We should set it right next to our piggy bank."

Jamie snorted nearly, choking on his soda. "You're such a dork. We don't have a piggy bank."

"We'll get one. A great big pink one."

"All right, fine, you can frame the drawing, but we are so totally not getting a big pink piggy bank."

Tek opened the car door and tossed the notebook on the seat. "Yup, one with a little crown and everything."

"You're done," Jamie announced. He stomped off toward the house, laughing.

"I haven't even started," Tek countered and followed Jamie into the cabin. When he stepped inside, he was hit in the chest with a duffel bag.

"You're right. You haven't. You have to finish loading the car."

Tek frowned. He didn't want to head back to the city, not yet. Yes, he was excited about their plan, and the sooner they made some money, the sooner they could start on their dream home, but reality was waiting for them in the city. They still had to deal with what happened and be prepared for any backlash that might fall upon them. But he didn't have to like it.

Tek held the bag to his chest. "I think we should stay one more day," he suggested hopefully.

Jamie grabbed the other bags. "Can't. You already told Blake you'd be back to work tomorrow morning."

"We could say we broke down."

Jamie met his gaze, and Tek could see the same desire to stay as Tek felt, but Jamie also had an expression of determination or maybe it was resolve. He gave Tek a small smile. "Do you really want to do that?"

"Yes, but I'm not going to. Doesn't mean I can't wish."

"I know, but it's time."

Tek held Jamie's gaze a moment longer and then nodded. "I know," he agreed softly.

WITH THE cabin closed up and steps taken to assure Rocky and his friends could no longer crash their pad while they were gone, Jamie and Tek headed back to the city. Jamie laid his head against the window, staring out at the landscape rushing by, but he wasn't seeing it, lost in his own thoughts. Surprisingly, with everything that had happened, he wasn't dwelling on it or even thinking about it. Instead, he was planning renovations, thinking about jobs, money, goals. He wasn't sure if he was subconsciously blocking out what had happened with Rocco, but he was glad for the distraction. Square footage, floor plans, and landscaping filled his thoughts as Jamie dozed off.

"Jamie. We're here."

Jamie jerked awake, dazed and unsure of where he was for a few seconds. "Wow, I could have sworn we just got in the car." He stretched, rolled his head to work out the kink that had settled in his neck, and yawned.

"That doesn't surprise me, since you were snoring within ten minutes."

"Seriously?"

"Pretty much." Tek patted Jamie's thigh.

"Man, I'm really sorry I didn't keep you entertained."

"No worries. I found a great classic rock station and the time flew by."

Jamie looked up at the building and realized they were outside the club. "It's late. Aren't we going home?"

Tek tilted his head and stared at him with a strange expression before saying, "We can't. It may not be safe."

"Oh right." Jamie shook his head, his brain not firing on all cylinders yet. He reached for the door, but Tek grabbed his arm.

"You okay?"

"Yeah, it was just a simple mistake. I must have been sleeping harder than I thought." Tek didn't look convinced. "Knock it off, you damn worrywart. I'm half-asleep. I simply forgot." Jamie opened the door and stepped out. It wasn't a lie. Even though he'd rather not think about what happened, it didn't mean he wasn't aware of it. He was simply choosing not to if he could help it. "Pop the trunk, will you?"

Reality came rushing back in a flash when Tek joined him at the back of the car, Glock in hand. Jamie glanced at it and then looked up at Tek with a questioning expression.

"We can't be too careful," Tek responded, his gaze darting around to the dark beyond the lighted parking lot.

Fucking reality. Jamie huffed out a frustrated breath and angrily snatched two bags that contained their clothes and personal items and then slammed the trunk. "We'll get the rest of the shit in the morning."

Without taking his gaze from the shadows, body tense, Tek nodded. The car alarm beeped, causing Jamie to jump, his own tension ratcheting up. He made his way to the back door and stood next to the wall, giving Tek access to the locks.

"Hold this." Tek held out the gun.

Jamie hesitated for only a heartbeat before taking it and kept a watchful eye while Tek worked on the digital locks. The shrill alarm blared and Jamie jerked again. Fucking hell. All the calm he'd found while hiding away in the forest was gone, and his movements were stiff when he followed Tek inside, pulled the door behind them, and checked to make sure the locks engaged while Tek went to punch in the code. He then waved at the camera, letting whoever was manning the security booth that night know that all was well before taking his weapon back. He engaged the safety and returned it to the holster at the small of his back.

When they made it to the playroom they'd be calling home for a while, Jamie was still tense, and since he'd slept the entire ride home, he wouldn't be getting to sleep without a little help.

Jamie dropped the bags on the bed and pushed his fingers through his hair, slicking back his bangs. "Think Blake would mind if I snatched a bottle of whiskey from the bar?"

"Whiskey?"

"Yeah, reality has a way of making me want to drink."

"How about you go take a hot shower and I'll go get us some drinks? You hungry?"

Jamie sat down on the edge of the bed and untied his boots, then pulled them and his socks off. "No, and you're the one who drove. I'll get the booze while you take a shower."

Tek pursed his lips and scanned the room with an intense expression. Even safely behind the locked doors, Tek was still on guard and Jamie hated that it had to be this way but also knew he couldn't change it.

Obviously satisfied or maybe realizing how ridiculous he was being, Tek finally gave in. "Bring a couple beers back for me, will ya?"

"You got it."

Jamie walked across the dimly lit club to the bar. He snatched a bottle of Jack Daniels off the shelf and opened it. He poured a shot and threw it back, savoring the burn, knowing with enough of them, the tension of being back would fade.

He poured another one and held it up. "Fuck you, reality," he grumbled and downed it in one big gulp. He grabbed a six-pack of Budweiser out of the cooler and took it and his bottle back to the room.

AFTER A hot shower, half a bottle of booze, and Tek banging the tension out of him, Jamie finally slept. More like passed out, he realized as he sat up and took in the silent room around him. Tek's bag was open, the contents scattered around as if he'd been rummaging through it, the bathroom light off. Apparently Tek had gone to work, and when Jamie glanced over at the clock, it was confirmed. It was nearly noon. Jamie sighed in relief when, next to the clock, he noticed the glass of water and two aspirin. He popped them in his mouth and washed them down with the entire glass, then leaned back against the headboard, in no hurry to pull his sorry ass from the comfort of his bed.

There was so much he needed to think about, to start planning for, but with the current drumbeat banging inside his head, it was the last thing he wanted to do. Besides, looking toward the future seemed kind of silly until they worked on what was standing between them in the here and now. And whether they talked about it, set it on the back burner, or ignored the elephant in the room, until they found the same calm they had before Rocco's bullshit, they couldn't move on.

Throwing off his covers, Jamie slid from the bed and walked on heavy legs to the bathroom, the pounding in his brain intensifying with each step. Another thing he was going to have to work on. Alcohol was not the answer for tension. Fuck, if he'd grabbed a bottle every time his life had thrown him a curveball, he'd already be in need of a twelve-step program.

He flipped on the light and caught his reflection in the mirror. His hair was disheveled and standing on end, he had dark circles under his eyes, and his cheeks were flushed. "Serves you right, you dumbass, drinking like that." *No more booze to excess, ever*, he vowed.

A hot shower, teeth brushed, a couple more glasses of water, and he still felt like shit, which served to solidify his conviction. The hangovers simply weren't worth it. And neither was ignoring his problems. Some clean clothes, a little breakfast, and he was sure he'd be at least able to function without the fucking drumline. Maybe then he could decide what the next step toward recovering their calm should be.

Sometimes living hurts worse than death.

Tek Cain

Freak-out

IT TOOK two days after his overindulgence to finally figure out what the hell to do next. Tek was working long hours, and when he wasn't, he wanted to spend all their time in the club with the rest of the gang. Which on most days would have been fine, but Jamie missed the time alone they'd shared at the cabin, and he missed the crazy and wild kinks they had been exploring. That night he had plans to rectify both.

Tek had the night off and Jamie wasn't about to share his man with anyone. He'd seen Tek unrolling and rolling his black poly ropes with a longing look on his face, but he hadn't offered to tie Jamie up since before the kidnapping. Jamie knew it was a kink Tek enjoyed immensely. Hell, he enjoyed it too, and he wasn't about to let Rocco take it away from them. Tonight, he'd be the one in charge.

Jamie finished drying off from his recent shower, brushed his hair and teeth, and then called out to Tek in the main room, "Hey, do you mind going to the bar and grabbing us a couple of drinks?"

"Sure, what do you want?" Tek called back.

"I'd like a beer. Will go perfectly with the movie and popcorn." Jamie winked at his reflection and smiled. He had no plans to kick back and watch a movie, and Tek would be tied up. Literally. Jamie snickered at the pun.

"Okay, be right back."

Jamie waited until he heard the door close and rushed to the closet where Tek kept his ropes. He pulled down four from the shelf and then grabbed another for good measure. He quickly secured ropes to the four posters of the bed, and by the time Tek returned, he was sitting on the mattress, bare-ass naked, running the strand of the fifth rope through his fingers.

"What the hell is going on?" Tek asked and set a tray with glasses, ice, whiskey, and beer on the dresser. "I thought we were kicking back and watching a movie?"

"I lied," Jamie responded unapologetically. "Now strip."

"What if I wanted to watch a movie?" Tek questioned, but Jamie knew it was bullshit because Tek was already unbuttoning his jeans.

"You can watch it later." Jamie stood up, the long soft strand of the rope tickling across his hard cock. "If you have the energy, that is."

Jamie was riveted to the sight of Tek's muscular thighs as he pushed down his jeans and kicked them away. Each movement caused the thick muscles to bulge and flex. Tek obviously noticed Jamie's appreciative expression because he slowly ran his hands over his thighs to the hem of his T-shirt, then pulled it up, inch by painfully slow inch, exposing the hard ridges of his stomach, his pinkie grazing along the line of hair that went from the waistband of his briefs to his navel. Jamie wanted to follow with his lips and tongue, but he stayed where he was. He'd feast on every inch of Tek once he was bound to the bed and at Jamie's mercy.

"You're a good little cocktease, aren't you?" Jamie drawled, slowly winding the rope around his hand.

"It's only a tease if I don't plan on putting out." Tek glanced at the ropes around the bed. "And from the looks of it, you're already assuming I do."

"Damn right you will," Jamie responded with utter conviction.

Tek pulled off his shirt, throwing it haphazardly to the floor, and then ran his fingers through his hair, resting his hands on the back of his head, showing off his impressive arms and chest. Oh and they were very, very impressive, but it was the large bulge tenting Tek's briefs that kept Jamie's attention.

"Now the briefs."

In true Tek fashion, always needing to hold on to his control as long as possible, he hesitated, a smug smile on his face. Fucker knew exactly what effect he was having on Jamie, and he was going to draw it out, set the pace—at least until he was secured to the bed. Instead of instantly dropping his underwear as Jamie had instructed, he slid his hands down each side of his neck, across his collarbone, and to his pecs. He pinched each nipple several times, causing them to get hard, before inching his fingers toward his waistband.

"You do realize I'm going to have to punish you for this, don't you?" Jamie asked, his voice deep and husky with need.

"I'm counting on it," Tek said with a wicked grin.

Jamie stood tall, unwound the rope, and gripped it in both hands, stretching it. "Then drop your fucking drawers, or I'll be the only one coming tonight."

Tek stared at him, no doubt trying to assess if Jamie was serious. Jamie didn't flinch, just met his gaze with a hard one of his own. Apparently Tek seen the conviction in Jamie's eyes. Tek instantly shoved his briefs down and stepped out of them.

"Smart man," Jamie praised. He grabbed one of Tek's swollen nipples, squeezing it until Tek grunted. "However, I'm still not convinced you deserve to come, but I suppose you can try to prove to me that you do."

"I'll do my best."

"I'm sure you will." Jamie took Tek's mouth in a blistering kiss, dropping one end of the rope and fisting his hand in Tek's hair, taking complete control. Tek didn't even try to fight him, he simply opened his mouth wider and let Jamie set the pace.

They were both a little breathless and hard as granite when Jamie finally ended the kiss. He stared at Tek for a moment longer, enjoying the sensation of their cocks rubbing against one another, loving the way little sparks of electricity zinged up his spine from the intimate contact. Reluctantly he stepped back before he could say fuck it to his plans, throw Tek down on the floor right then and there, and drive himself home in Tek's tight ass. He clamped down on the desire and took another step back.

"On the bed. Lie face up, legs spread and arms over your head."

Tek got into the position Jamie had instructed and Jamie stood next to the bed, admiring his man all laid out like a feast. Tek's hard cock strained up from his body, bobbing slightly as it pulsed and throbbed, taunting him. It was one temptation Jamie wouldn't deny himself. He bent, wrapped his lips around the flared head, and sucked hard.

"Oh fuck!" Tek pushed up into Jamie's mouth. Jamie allowed Tek to thrust a few times as he savored the feeling of Tek's cock stretching his lips, his bitter and musky flavor on his tongue. He took Tek's cock into his throat and swallowed around it, causing Tek to cry out in pleasure. Satisfied with the needy sounds he'd produced, Jamie leaned back and let Tek's cock slip from his lips. Jamie then moved to the foot of the bed and gathered up the rope tied to the post.

"And you call *me* a cocktease," Tek huffed.

"Yeah, but I'm really fucking good at it," Jamie shot back and wound the black rope around Tek's left ankle, securing it before moving around the other side of the bed and stabilizing Tek's other leg in the same fashion.

"How's that feel? Not too tight, are they?" Jamie asked.

Tek tugged on his restraints, then shifted his position a little and went still, his only movement the steady rise and fall of his chest. "Feels good," he murmured, his eyes dark with lust as he stared up at Jamie.

Jamie trailed his fingers along Tek's calf and thigh, smiling when Tek shivered at the light, teasing touch. Silently he secured both of Tek's arms over his head and slightly stretched out from his body. The entire time he worked, he could feel Tek's eyes on him, watching him. It was like a kiss to his tingling flesh, ramping up his desire all the more.

Jamie picked up the fifth rope from the floor, then once again stood over Tek, examining his handiwork. The dark ropes stood out in sharp contrast to Tek's skin. The light sheen of perspiration on Tek's body made it appear as if it were glowing beneath the overhead light. Without taking his eyes off Tek's impressive form, Jamie set the extra rope on the mattress, pulled open the bedside table drawer, and pulled out a black scarf he'd put there in anticipation of the evening.

He held it over Tek's cock, letting the soft silky material tease Tek's groin, over his stomach and across his breastbone, causing Tek to shudder again. Jamie then folded it and laid it over Tek's eyes.

"Lift your head." Tek did, and Jamie secured it into place. "Can you see anything?"

"Nope, which is a shame."

"Why is that?" Jamie inquired.

"Because I was really enjoying the way your cock was bobbing and weeping as you moved."

"Sorry to disappoint you," he said without a shred of sincerity. He could tease Tek to madness and from experience knew the loss of sight would only heighten Tek's pleasure. As Tek settled into the mattress without worry, the trust he showed in Jamie caused Jamie's heart to swell.

He hadn't planned on it, but since Tek had brought ice into the room, he seized the opportunity to grab a couple of cubes. He held one loosely in his fist, letting it melt, the first drop landing on Tek's erect nipple and causing him to jerk.

"Shit, that's cold." He tried squirming away as the droplets continued to fall on his chest, but his restraints kept him in place.

"Colder than this?" Jamie asked, then laid the cube on Tek's other nipple and covered it with his palm.

"Jesus!"

Tek continued to squirm as Jamie ran the cube around first one, then the other nipple, and finally ran it down Tek's breastbone before tossing it away. He then bent and followed the trail of water with this tongue, warming each nipple between his lips, sucking gently until Tek was no longer trying to get away but was pushing up into Jamie's mouth.

"You like that, do you?" Jamie asked against Tek's flesh.

"Fuck yeah," Tek moaned.

Jamie brushed his lips across each of Tek's erect nubs, then moved down Tek's body, placing soft nips on his way to Tek's cock. He kissed the flared head and ran the other ice cube along the shaft.

Tek's back bowed off the bed. "Holy shit, Jamie! That's fucking cold."

"Of course it is. It's ice." Jamie laughed and continued to run it up and down Tek's length.

Tek's jerking and squirming intensified as Jamie continued to tease him, and he nearly came off the bed when Jamie slid the ice down to his balls. "Whoa! No! Stop! Fucking hell, Jamie!"

Jamie took pity on him, but only slightly. He popped what was left of the ice in his mouth and then wrapped his lips around Tek's cock, giving him sensations of both hot and cold. Tek still squirmed, but he was no longer shouting, and soon enough his movements morphed to thrusting.

Jamie continued to suck on Tek's cock, making loud slurping sounds and letting the excess water run from the corner of his mouth, bathing Tek's balls.

"Christ, you keep that up much longer and I'm going to blow a nut." Tek wantonly pumped his hips.

Jamie instantly he released Tek's cock. "Ah-ah-ah. No, you don't." Jamie wrapped his fist around the base of Tek's dick, putting pressure on it. The head was a deep ruddy color and the shaft pulsed against his palm.

"Fucker," Tek groaned, his body tense. He was breathing heavily, no doubt battling with the need to come and the pain from Jamie's tight grip.

"Not yet, but I will be soon," Jamie assured him.

Once Tek's panting slowed and he blew out a heavy breath, Jamie released Tek's cock. He picked up the unused rope and studied it, then Tek's tense muscles. Jamie had obviously pushed Tek too close and it would be very difficult to wrap the rope around Tek's chest in his current position and state. He should have planned better. Shaking his head at himself and smirking, he threw the rope on the floor and instead pulled open the drawer again, this time retrieving the lube and a condom. As quietly as he could, he opened the condom, rolled it on, and squeezed a dollop of lube into his palm before setting the tube back in the drawer. He slicked up the condom and his fingers, then simply stood over Tek, silently watching the rise and fall of his chest and his flushed skin, letting the quiet surround them and giving Tek more time to get himself under control.

After a few more minutes, Tek turned his head back and forth as if he was trying to sense Jamie's presence. Jamie didn't move.

"What are you doing?" Tek asked, sounding hesitant.

"Watching you."

"What fun is that when you could be touching all this studliness," Tek countered.

"It's lots of fun, especially with the way my dick feels in my hand."

Tek frowned and tilted his head as if trying to see beneath the blindfold. "Are you jerking off?"

"Yes," Jamie lied, glad Tek couldn't see his grin.

"I want to see."

"You've seen me jerk off before. It's nothing new."

"Dammit, Jamie, that's cruel, man," Tek grumbled.

"Don't you like knowing the sight of you all tied up makes me hard as fucking steel?"

"Yeah, I like it, but I'd love it if I could see you, or better yet, let me jerk you off."

"That would be difficult in your current predicament," Jamie teased.

"I said it once and I'll say it again. That's cruel, man."

"My poor abused stud," Jamie cooed and ran the tip of his lubed finger down Tek's shaft, then teased his balls with it.

Tek raised his hips. "I know somewhere else you could put that slick finger."

"This is my show. I'll decide where my digits are going."

Tek pursed his lips, and Jamie couldn't help but laugh.

"That's not very Dom-like," Tek reminded him. "You're not supposed to be laughing at my suffering."

"Hmm, let me see if I can prove just how Dom-like I am," Jamie countered. He climbed up on the bed and straddled Tek's hips. Hand on his thighs, he nudged Tek's sac with the head of his sheathed cock. His gaze landed on the ropes around Tek's wrists and an image from his nightmare flashed in Jamie's mind, causing his breath to hitch. He shook his head to dispel it, instead focusing on the here and now. He looked down at Tek's cock, the way it was bobbing as Jamie continued to tease his balls, and the sight was enough to rid himself of the awful memory but his pulse was still a little fast.

He pushed back a little farther, shifted slightly, and with one hand, lifted Tek's balls. With the other, he guided the head of his dick to Tek's hole.

"Oh fuck yeah." Tek tried to push down on Jamie's cock, but his restraints didn't allow him to do any more than squirm.

Restraints.

Dark.

Screams.

Jamie's pulse kicked into overdrive as the images from his nightmares flashed rapidly in his mind's eye. He squeezed his eyes closed, but it only made the visions more vivid and he opened them again. He tensed and he couldn't look away from the ropes binding Tek's wrists. *What the fuck is wrong with me?* He didn't understand why those unwanted dreams were coming back to him now? And why in the fuck was his heart practically thumping out of his chest? Only he didn't have time to figure it out because suddenly his lungs seized and he couldn't take a breath.

"Jamie?"

Jamie continued to stare at the ropes as he struggled to breathe. *Ropes.* He had to get those fucking ropes off Tek.

"Jamie, what's going on?" Tek asked in alarm.

Jamie tried to open his mouth to say something, but he couldn't get in any air to form so much as a grunt. He…. He…. Fuck, he had to get those fucking ropes off Tek before he passed out.

Hurry.

Time is running out.

He's dying.

Jamie lunged forward and scrambled to release Tek's wrist, but his hands were shaking so badly he was having difficulty with the task.

"Jamie, goddammit! Fucking talk to me."

He could hear Tek screaming at him over the loud rush of blood in his ears, but he couldn't respond even if he wanted to. His only thought, his complete focus was on saving Tek, getting him free.

Jamie worked at Tek's bindings as Tek continued to scream, but the sound was muffled, as if Jamie were hearing him from under water. But it didn't matter. All that mattered was freeing Tek. Time was running out, the darkness closing in on his vision. When it finally overwhelmed him, the last thing he heard was Rocco's maniacal laughter before the blackness took him.

I have stared down the barrel of a gun, the man wielding it wanting nothing more than to end my life. I've sat in a six by eight, my fate in the hands of others. I have even watched those who I considered brothers die, held them as they took their last breath. But I have never felt as helpless as I did in the face of Jamie's panic. The look of horror on his face is something that is seared into my soul. It is him and only him that matters. Even above my own life, Jamie matters most.

Tek Cain

True Fear

WHAT THE hell was happening? Tek was doing his best not to let his panic overwhelm him, but being bound with his eyes covered, he was helpless and Jamie wasn't responding. He could feel Jamie working the binds on his wrist like a crazed man. In his struggle, Tek's blindfold was dislodged and he'd seen pure terror on Jamie's face as he undid Tek's right hand.

"Jamie, talk to me. What's going on?"

Jamie ignored him, still scrambling to free Tek's left wrist. Then, without warning, he froze and his eyes rolled back in his head.

"Jamie!" Tek screamed and watched in horror as Jamie fell to the floor.

Tek quickly finished removing the ropes from his ankles and scrambled off the bed. Jamie had landed in an awkward position, his face obscured by his long hair and partially hidden beneath the bed. With his heart leaping out of his chest and his hands shaking, Tek carefully rolled Jamie till he was lying on his back. He pressed two fingers against Jamie's neck and relief surged through him when he felt the strong and rapid pulse.

"Jamie, baby, please wake up," Tek pleaded. He shook Jamie's shoulders. Nothing. "Jamie, dammit, wake up."

Jamie didn't respond, and Tek's panic ramped up a notch. He jumped to his feet and rushed out of the room.

He spotted Max sitting at the bar and he hurried to him, screaming, "Max! I need help. It's Jamie."

Everyone in the club turned and stared at him in shock, but Tek didn't so much as give them a thought.

"What is it?" Max asked in alarm, already off his barstool and making his way to Tek, Aiden and Blake right behind him.

"It's Jamie. I don't know what happened. One minute we were having a good time, and the next he went nuts," Tek explained as quickly as he could, heading back into the room.

Max pushed past him as soon as he cleared the door and went to his knees next to Jamie. "Did he hit his head?"

"Umm… no, I don't think so. I was blindfolded and he was straddling me on the bed, then suddenly he went quiet and, a moment later, he was frantically pulling on my binds. He knocked off my blindfold and he had… he…." Tek had to swallow hard past his constricted throat. "He looked so scared. Is he going to be okay?"

"He's got a strong heartbeat and his breathing is steady." Max lifted each one of Jamie's eyelids, examining them.

"Here ya go," Aiden said quietly. Tek glanced over and found Aiden holding out a pair of sweatpants toward him. "In case we have to take him to the hospital."

"Thank you," Tek responded and quickly pulled them on.

"Do I need to call an ambulance?" Blake asked.

"Not yet, I think he's coming around. But keep everyone out of here," Max said, pointing to the crowd that was forming at the door. He then laid the back of his hand against Jamie's forehead and against his cheek. "Jamie, can you hear me?"

Tek fell to his knees next to Max in time to see Jamie's eyes flutter open. He looked dazed as he stared up at them. "That's it, baby, wake up for me," Tek encouraged and took Jamie's hand in his.

"What the hell happened?" Jamie asked, sounding and looking confused.

"You tell me."

Jamie continued to stare at them as if they were speaking in tongues. Then he shook his head and sat up. He ran his hand over his face, and Max and Tek were forced to move when Jamie shifted and sat back against the side of the bed. He had a look of concentration, as if he were trying to piece the events together.

"Does anything hurt?" Max asked.

Jamie shook his head.

"Do you feel light-headed, nauseated? Any strange sensations?" Max questioned further.

Again Jamie shook his head. Tek scrambled over to Jamie's side and took his hand, squeezing it, silently reassuring him. Tek then looked at Aiden. "Could you grab me a towel out of the bathroom, please?"

Aiden rushed to the bathroom and brought one to him. Tek took it and laid it across Jamie's lap, knowing Jamie would feel silly sitting there with a condom on his dick while being examined by Max.

"Do you remember what happened before you passed out?" Max asked.

"It was weird," Jamie said with a frown as he wiped the sweat from his brow. "I started getting these weird images from the nightmare I had the other night, then my heart started pounding out of my chest and I couldn't breathe. Never experienced anything like that, and it will be too fucking soon if I ever experience it again. It was the oddest thing. I had no control over myself and all I knew was I had to get Tek free." Jamie whipped his head around and met Tek's gaze, a horrified look on his face. "I didn't hurt you, did I?"

"No, but you scared the shit out me." Tek squeezed Jamie's hand again.

"Sorry, I don't know what the hell that was all about."

"Sounds like a panic attack. Have you ever experienced them in the past?" Max inquired.

"Nope, and I would have remembered. That was some freaky shit right there. It was like part of me knew Tek was safe, but I had this overwhelming and completely irrational need to get those fucking ropes off him."

"You didn't tell me you were having nightmares." Tek ran his hand soothingly over Jamie's forearm.

"I didn't think it was a big deal. It's not like they were reoccurring or anything. I only had it twice."

"It's obviously bothering you more than you thought," Max surmised. "We should get together and talk about it later this week."

"You saying I need a shrink?" Jamie asked with a scowl.

"Well, you are nuts," Tek teased, the tension in him finally dissipating.

Jamie laughed. "You have a point."

"Okay, I'll let you two get back to"—Max stood up and nodded toward the bed—"whatever it was you were doing."

"Thanks for helping us out." Tek went to his feet as well and shook Max's hand, then Aiden's. "Both of you."

"Anytime," Max responded. Aiden simply smiled as he followed Max out the door and closed it behind him.

Tek held out his hand for Jamie. "Let's get up off the floor."

JAMIE PUSHED up off the floor and sat on the edge of the mattress. Guilt assaulted him when Tek continued to stare at him with a concerned expression. "Would you sit down? You're making me nervous."

"You— Jesus, Jamie, you scared the fuck out of me."

"I'm sorry. I didn't mean to. Hell, I'm not even sure what just happened or why."

Tek sat down next to him and bumped his shoulder against Jamie's. "I know it wasn't your fault, but fuck, do you mind not doing that again?"

"Yeah, I'll see what I can do," he told Tek, but he honestly had no idea how he could prevent it from happening again since he wasn't sure what the hell had triggered it. He'd had plenty of nightmares in his life, some horrifying ones, and they had never caused him to freak the fuck out like he just had. The scariest part was, not only was it able to override his arousal, but it caused him to black out.

"You doing okay now?"

Jamie grabbed the towel, wiped the sweat from his brow, then noticed the condom on his limp dick and groaned before snatching it off. "Yeah, but I feel like a total tool. I'm really sorry I fucked up your orgasm and your evening, or rather didn't fuck it up but…. Well, you know what I mean," he huffed and fisted the condom.

"Stop apologizing, will ya? It's not your fault. So you want to talk about the nightmare?"

"It's just a nightmare."

"Bullshit, it's obviously bothering you a lot more than you're admitting for it to cause you to freak out like that."

"Yeah, I guess." Jamie shrugged.

"So talk," Tek urged.

Jamie shrugged again. "Like I said, it was just a nightmare. I had it the first time when Rocco had me drugged up so I didn't really think too much about it. I mean, yeah, it scared me, especially waking up and being in the dark and disoriented from the drugs, but I didn't really remember much of it, only flashes of you being tied up, screaming for me while Rocco....” The image of Rocco's evil grin as he put the blade to Tek's throat and the look on Tek's face when his scream went silent, when Rocco slit his throat from ear to ear, flashed in Jamie's mind. The sound of Rocco's maniacal laughter filled his ears, and he had to swallow down his fear and pain.

“While Rocco did what?” Tek asked quietly.

“Killed you,” Jamie admitted. Tek was right there, safe and sound, but saying it aloud caused Jamie's chest to constrict.

“Hey, I'm right here, and Rocco can't hurt me or anyone else ever again.” Tek ran a soothing hand up and down Jamie's back.

“Yeah, I know, and that's why I didn't think it was a big deal when I had the dream again. At least the next time, I woke up and you were warm, alive, and asleep next to me. Knowing it was a dream and that you were there and safe, instead of the unknown when I had the dream the first time, went a long way in making me feel better. I don't know why it came rushing back tonight.”

He was about to apologize again when he remembered Tek's warning and amended it. “Totally ruined my boner, man, and I'm sure it did the same thing for you.”

“Pfft, ain't no big thing.” Tek looked down at his lap and then back up at Jamie with a big smile. “Well, at least it's not right at this moment.”

Jamie reached over and squeezed Tek's cock. “Biggest one I've ever had, even soft.”

“Only fucking dick you have ever had.” Tek shot a hard glare at him. “Only dick you'll ever touch besides your own if you know what's good for you.”

“I do know what's good for me,” he assured Tek and pecked him on the cheek. “Another thing that's good for me is a drink. My throat is dry as the Sahara Desert.” Relieved the tension and worry that was marring Tek's brow was finally gone, Jamie went to his feet. He wrapped the towel around his hips, and tossed the condom in the wastebasket on his way to the dresser and the tray of booze Tek had set there earlier.

He grabbed a beer, popped the top, and tipped it back, letting the cool liquid soothe his throat and the alcohol settle his still-frayed nerves. He set the empty back on the tray, wiped his hand over his mouth, and grabbed another one.

"Hey, slow down there, cowboy," Tek cautioned. "You were just passed out on the floor, and I'd rather not find you there again tonight. Or any night, for that matter."

"We should have gone with your plan," Jamie muttered and popped the top on the other beer, but he did heed Tek's warning and sipped it rather than guzzling it down.

"What was that?" Tek asked as he dropped some ice in a cocktail glass and added a good amount of whiskey.

"Popcorn and a movie," Jamie reminded him.

"See, you really should listen to me more often. I do know a thing or two about a thing or two."

Tek had warned him about it being too soon for rope play, considering what he'd endured with Rocco, but Jamie wouldn't listen. He simply wanted to put Rocco and his bullshit behind them and move on with their lives. Get back to where they were before and that included enjoying their kinks.

Tek obviously noticed the anger that flared up in Jamie at the thought of Rocco once again being able to affect their lives even from the grave, because he stepped up to Jamie and took Jamie's face in his hands.

"It will be okay. It's going to take time, but we'll put him and the bullshit in our past behind us."

"I hate it, you know. That the bastard is worm bait and he's still fucking with us."

"I know." Tek laid his forehead against Jamie's, holding his gaze. "But he's gone and in time we'll... well, we won't forget and we shouldn't, but he and the rest of the Crimson VIII will lose their power over us. We have to stick together and keep putting one foot in front of the other toward our goals and dreams."

"When the hell did you get so smart?" Jamie wrapped his arms around Tek's waist, pulling him closer.

"I've always been smart, but you were too busy watching my ass while we were growing up to notice."

"Not only when we were growing up. But it is an ass worth staring at."

"Yes, it is. So how about you show me how much you like it while sprawled out in that bed over there?" Tek nodded toward the bed in question.

"Yeah, you going to give me another shot at this ass?" Jamie patted the taut, muscular globes in question.

"Hell yeah, I am." Tek arched a single brow. "But no ropes, deal?"

The anger flared fast and furious in Jamie's gut. *Fucking Rocco.* But with Tek's gentle gaze on him, it dissipated just as quickly. Tek was right. He usually was. The ropes were a bad idea tonight, but they would be addressing this again. Perhaps if it was Tek tying him up next time, it would have a different outcome. It was certainly worth a try.

"Okay," he finally conceded. "No ropes."

"Don't look so disappointed. I thought it was my ass you liked, not the ropes."

"I like both, but if I had to choose, your ass would win out every time," Jamie confessed.

"Good answer." Tek pecked Jamie on the cheek. "Now come on, find yourself another condom and let's pick up where we left off."

"I'm already ahead of you," Jamie told him as he set the beer on the nightstand and snatched another condom out of the drawer.

"But first, let's get rid of these." Tek took one of the ropes off the bed and wound it up. "I'm not letting anything interfere with getting my nut this time."

Jamie helped Tek remove the ropes and store them back on the shelf in the closet. Tek grabbed Jamie's hand and stopped him on the way to the bed. "We'll try it again when we're both ready. Tonight I just need you to love me and I need to know we're okay."

Once again, Tek was right. It wasn't the kink or Rocco or anything else that mattered. Jamie grabbed Tek's hips, spun him, and licked a path from the crook between Tek's shoulder and neck up to his ear as he steered him to the bed.

"There isn't anything I'd rather do than show you how much I love you." Jamie pushed Tek down on the bed and covered his body with his own. "You may not walk for a couple of days, because holy fuck do I love you a lot."

Jamie took in Tek's laughter as he covered Tek's mouth with his own. Letting go of everything but the man beneath him, Jamie proved just how much he loved him.

Life flies by, and it's easy to get lost in the blur. In adolescence, it's "How do I fit in?" In your 20s, it's "What do I want to do?" In your 30s, "Is this what I'm meant to be?" I think the trick is living the questions. Not worrying so much about what's ahead but rather sitting in the gray area—being OK with where you are.

Tek Cain

Fragile—Handle with Care

FRIDAY NIGHTS were a security nightmare, but for Jamie, it was a blessing. Since his freak-out or panic attack, whatever the hell it had been, Tek had been… smothering. It wasn't exactly the right word, because when it came to sex, it was far from smothering—it was nonexistent—but the rest of the time, yeah, smothering, and it was starting to get on Jamie's nerves. He loved the fact that Tek was worried about him, and he understood. If the roles were reversed, he would probably act the same way, but damn, a man needed to fucking breathe once in a while without feeling as if everything he did was being analyzed. Tek was making him feel as if he was emotionally fragile and would crack at any minute. He could only imagine how much worse it would be if he told Tek the nightmares happened far more often than twice. That was one tidbit he planned on keeping to himself.

"Hey, Jamie, how you doing tonight?" Max asked.

Jamie took the empty barstool next to Max and waved at Aiden on the other side of Max before answering. "I'm going crazy, and before you ask, it has nothing to do with my freak-out the other night."

"So I take it no more panic attacks?"

"Not even so much as a jump in pulse," Jamie assured him.

"If you ever want to talk about it…."

"I don't!" Jamie snapped, then instantly regretted it. He pulled his growing beard through his fingers and hung his head. "I'm sorry, I'm just frustrated, but I shouldn't have snapped at you."

"It's understandable. You're frustrated. You've been through a lot."

"I just want to put it all behind me. But Tek's making it difficult with the way he's treating me like I'm some delicate thing that needs to be handled with care."

"It scared him," Max reminded him.

Like he needed reminding. Hell, it had scared the shit out of him too, but it didn't mean he was going to let it change who they were. "I know. It did me too," he finally admitted.

Max patted Jamie on the back. "Give it time. You two are solid in your relationship, and it's obvious you both love each other very much. It will work out and my offer stands. If you ever need someone to snap at, I'm your guy."

"Thanks, Max, I appreciate it."

"What can I get you, my big ol' growly bear," Micah asked with a flirty smile.

"A beer might help the growly."

"I like growly." Micah batted his lashes before sashaying away.

Max's and Jamie's gazes met and they both shook their heads. It did no good to comment on Micah's flirting. He meant nothing by it, and it only proved what a saint Tackett was. If Tek flirted like that…. Yeah, not happening. Jamie would be way beyond growly.

When Micah moved away, Jamie turned his attention back to Max. "There is one thing you can help me with."

"Name it."

"Any suggestions for handling cabin fever? As much as I love this place, being here 24-7 is driving me fucking nuts. Tek doesn't think it's safe to go back to the apartment—not that we could afford it anymore without me working. Which is another thing that's driving me batty. I'm starting to feel like a complete loser not being able to contribute financially."

"You need money?"

Yeah, he did, so they could get back to the cabin where they wanted to be. But he shook his head. "No," Jamie said adamantly. He was not going to take money from Max or anyone else. "I just need to figure out how the hell to make cash and still have Tek attached to my hip."

Micah set a beer down in front of Jamie. "You should talk to Tackett. He works with me attached to his hip all the time."

"Not the same." Jamie laughed as Micah winked and headed down the bar.

"He actually makes a good point," Aiden said. "The wave of the future is people working from home. Hell, even school is going online. Tackett would certainly be able to steer you in the right direction."

"I'm computer illiterate," Jamie confessed.

"So am I," Max laughed. He clinked his beer against Jamie's before taking a gulp. "But Tackett is amazing with computers. I bet he'd be willing to help. Just think about it."

"Yeah, I will," Jamie replied and tipped up his beer. He didn't know a thing about computers. There, he'd thought about it. He'd have to try to think of something. Hmm, maybe one of those webcam gay porn sites. He could…. *Tek would fucking kill you.* Yeah, that's even a worse idea than the interactive whatever. He took another big gulp.

THE PROSPECT of a job with computers apparently wasn't as impossible as Jamie believed it was. Micah or Max must have said something because two days later, Tackett approached Jamie. By that point he was climbing the walls and was willing to do just about anything.

"Honestly, Tackett, you're wasting your time. I don't know the first thing about computers, but I really do appreciate the offer."

"You don't need to have any experience. I'll teach you everything you need to know. In fact, I'd prefer it. You won't be acting like a know-it-all geek like some of these little fuckers coming out of MIT."

Jamie pulled the dart back, aimed, and bull's-eye! He smiled, feeling a bit cocky as he went and pulled the dart, marked his score, and stepped aside. No way was Tackett going to get two bull's-eyes in a row.

"I don't know, Tackett, I've never been one to learn a new skill easily. Bit of a slow learner."

Tackett stepped up to the line, aimed, and—bull's-eye. He threw another—bull's-eye. The third dart landed in the center of his name on the corkboard, having won the game. "I used to suck at this game, took me years before I could do that." Tackett nodded toward the board and effectively wiped the grin right off Jamie's face. "It simply took practice."

Jamie gawked at Tackett's back as he headed to the table, took a seat, propped his feet up, and picked up his glass in a toast toward Jamie.

"You sandbagger," Jamie grumbled and joined him. Tackett must have let Jamie win the first one, because he'd totally kicked Jamie's ass the next two, and the final game, Jamie was sure Tackett had been showing off, letting him think he actually had a chance. He glared at the bastard.

"Oh, don't be a spoilsport. I was merely driving my point home. You can do this, and make a decent salary. I'm not asking you to build a computer or even a program. Just fire up the laptop and *click click click*."

"*Click click click*, huh?" Jamie asked suspiciously.

"Okay, there's a little more to it than that, but seriously. I know you can handle it. I'll get you everything you need. The software will already be loaded into the laptop. You'll have some test scripts to follow, and then all you have to do is click around and try to randomly break shit."

"Well, I can certainly break shit. I've always been like a bull in a china shop," Jamie chuckled. "A software tester, huh?"

"Yes." Tackett finished his drink and set the glass aside before standing. "C'mon, I've got a laptop in my car."

"What? We're going to start now?" Jamie asked, scurrying to catch up.

"No time like the present, my boy."

TEK WALKED through the door and did a double take. "Now there's a sight you don't see every day."

Jamie looked up from the laptop he was working on. "I've used a laptop before."

"Yeah, but it's the first time I've seen you on one where you weren't kicked back with your dick in your hand and some hot man-on-man action heating up the screen." Tek leaned over Jamie's shoulder and looked at the screen, clueless as to what he was looking at. "What is that?"

Jamie spun around in his chair, crossed his arms over his chest, and smiled. "I have a new job."

Tek glanced at the screen and then at Jamie in confusion. "A job?"

"Yup. You are looking at TTS's newest software tester."

Tek gawked at him. "TTS? What does that stand for?"

"It's tech talk. You wouldn't understand."

"I speak very clearly, thank you very fucking much. How can I not understand myself?"

Jamie stood shaking his head and snickered. "Tech, you know short for technology?" Jamie reached over and cupped Tek's dick. "And this Tek, yeah, there is nothing short about him."

"Damn right." Tek smirked and kissed Jamie. "I need a shower. I smell like smoke and beer."

"Want some company?"

"I'd love it." He stripped on the way to the bathroom, dropping his clothes. "Seriously, though, you got a job? How the hell did that happen?"

"I'm working for Tackett, well, actually one of his old companies." Jamie pulled off his shirt and pants and tossed them aside before turning his back on Tek to set the shower taps.

Tek briefly forgot what he'd asked as he took a moment to appreciate his man's impressive body. Even the ink held him rapt as Jamie's muscles flexed and rolled. Tek should hate the symbol, but he did not. He no longer wanted to forget his past but embrace it. It was a reminder of where they began, where they were now, and where they wanted to be in the future. Forgetting the past doomed him to making the same mistakes, and he'd learned his lesson. He brushed his fingers along Jamie's back. *Truth & Knowledge.*

Poised at the shower door, Jamie looked over his shoulder. "I got something on me?"

"Me." Tek pushed Jamie into the shower. He crowded Jamie beneath the warm flow of water. "A working stiff, huh?"

Jamie poured out some shampoo into his palm, set the bottle aside, and scrubbed Tek's hair. "Yup, you're not the only one bringing in the cash now."

Tek closed his eyes and groaned, Jamie's fingers and the suds making his scalp tingle. "Really?"

Jamie maneuvered Tek's head until it was beneath the spray, rinsing away the suds. "Yup. Turn around and I'll do your back."

"Enough we can start saving for those cows and chickens?"

"What the hell is it with you and livestock?" Jamie asked, those blunt fingertips now lathering up Tek's back and easing the tension in his muscles. "I should never have mentioned the mountain-man thing."

"Especially when there are no mou—Ow!" Tek jerked when his right ass cheek was pinched, hard. He rubbed at the abused flesh. "What the hell was that for?"

"You know what that was for. Besides, I don't really know what I'm going to be making, but we might want to think about getting us a new place first. Maybe one with a little less seventies flair?"

"I decorated it that way."

"I know."

Before Tek could respond to Jamie's slight, he was pushed under the spray and was too busy spitting and sputtering. "Bastard," he finally got out.

"Once we get a new apartment," Jamie continued without missing a beat or even acknowledging Tek's curse. "We should probably remodel the cabin first before we start arguing over animals. I think we should get some updates and modern conveniences to make our lives a little easier before we start worrying about housing for critters."

Tek turned and grabbed Jamie in a hug. "When the hell did you get so grown up?"

"Started working on it right after I got rid of the diapers." Jamie laughed.

Tek's smile and the teasing reply faded away as he stared into Jamie's eyes. "We're going to be okay, aren't we?"

"We're going to be more than okay. We're going to be great. We have each other."

Tek pressed his lips against Jamie's, feeling better about their future than he had in a long time. Even before Rocco, they had merely existed. Sure, they were happy, growing, learning, but still had no real plan or direction. They had simply been taking their lives one day at a time. Now, the excitement and passion he felt was poured into the kiss, letting Jamie soothe his heart and soul.

Jamie ended the kiss and laid his head against Tek's forehead, his breathing just a little faster, causing Tek to smirk. He loved having such an effect on Jamie with a simple kiss.

"Do me one more favor," Jamie whispered softly.

"Anything."

"Don't let what Rocco did take away our pleasure."

"Never," Tek swore.

"Then promise me you won't let what happened the other night stop us from exploring what we enjoy."

"Jamie—"

Jamie laid a finger over Tek's lips. "I'm not asking you to right now, but don't let what happened stop us from enjoying it. Max said it could be a onetime thing, so let's just try, okay?"

The image of Jamie, his eyes wide with terror as he tried to release Tek from his binds, flashed in his mind, and he had to swallow down the bile that rose up in his throat. He never wanted to see that look on his lover's face again, nor did he ever want to feel so helpless.

"Just say you'll try." Jamie held Tek's gaze, his green eyes pleading.

Never one to deny Jamie anything, Tek nodded. "I'll try," he promised.

"Thank you, that's all I can ask."

Tek's gut was still roiling with the idea of what could happen, but he promised. If Jamie needed this, then dammit, he could at least set aside his own reservations and unease and help Jamie—hell, help himself—overcome this obstacle. They could do it.

We will do it.

He kissed Jamie again.

I hope.

Fear can take hold of a man, dig its claws in, and never let go. Memories fade and life goes on. But the fear never leaves. It simply lays dormant, waiting to pounce. We may not be able to erase it or remove it, but that doesn't mean we have to give in to it. We must learn to live with it and not allow it to cripple us. In fact, we can use it as a catalyst to propel us to better things, to make us stronger.

Tek Cain

Catalyst

TEK'S HANDS were trembling so much he was having a difficult time getting Jamie's wrist bound. He removed the rope, gritted his teeth, and tried again. This time each soft section of his poly rope laid perfectly next to the other, six deep before he looped the end through the iron ring and secured it.

"How's that feel?"

Jamie wriggled his fingers. "Feels good."

Tek took a step back and ran a critical eye over his lover. Jamie was naked, standing in the center of the playroom, his feet shoulder width apart, his cock thick, but Tek only gave it a passing glance, focusing instead on the rise and fall of Jamie's chest—slow and steady. Next he looked for any signs of perspiration, trembling, anything that would clue Tek in to Jamie's distress. He found none. But he had to be sure.

"The beard's looking good." He ran his palm over Jamie's jaw and then pressed his lips to the side of his neck, relieved to feel the rhythmic pulse.

"Yeah?"

"Oh yeah," Tek assured him. He placed one last kiss to Jamie's neck before stepping back.

The second he picked up the second rope, his hands began to tremble again. The skin had mended around Jamie's wrists, but the ugly yellowish tint to his flesh was a reminder of the injuries he'd suffered at Rocco's hands. Tek rubbed his thumb over the discoloration. No wonder Jamie had panicked when….

Tek jerked his gaze from Jamie's wrist to his chest—steady rise and fall.

"Tek? You okay?"

Still watching Jamie's breathing, Tek did his best to swallow down his reservations and nodded. "Your nipples keep distracting me," he lied and then, to make it more convincing, leaned down and nipped the erect nub.

"Hey! Watch those teeth."

"These ones?" Tek grazed his teeth over the other nipple.

Jamie snaked out his free hand, grabbed Tek's hair before he could pull back all the way, and pushed his face back into Jamie's chest. "Do it like you mean it."

Happy to have the distraction, Tek mouthed Jamie's chest, licking and tasting before sinking his teeth into the muscular pec. It wasn't enough to break the skin, but it was enough to cause Jamie to go up on his tiptoes and grunt. Tek continued to assault Jamie's chest, pulling the soft hairs through his teeth, kissing, licking, tasting until some of the tension had eased from his body and Jamie was moaning softly.

Tek continued his assault up toward Jamie's collarbone, sucking on it for a few seconds before doing the same on the side of his neck, pulling the blood to the surface and leaving his mark.

"Damn, I guess you do mean it," Jamie groaned, big body swaying.

"Any more requests, or can I carry on now?"

"I'm all yours. Do with me what you will," Jamie said slyly. The mischievous look in Jamie's eyes sent a thrill down Tek's spine.

He ran the rope through his fingers, his arousal renewed, but the instant he took Jamie's wrist into his hand and made the first loop with the rope, the thrill morphed into an uneasy prickling sensation. *Son of a bitch.* Why the hell couldn't he calm the fuck down and give Jamie what he needed?

Even though his arousal was waning, Tek ground his teeth, determined to make this good for Jamie. He wound the rope around his wrist, taking care not to wrap it too tightly, and loosely secured it to the opposite iron ring with a slipknot. By the time he had both Jamie's arms secured, Tek's mouth was dry and he was trembling. Every few seconds, he'd steal a glance at Jamie, checking on his well-being, his reaction, rather than the bindings.

"Just a second." He walked stiffly across the room and grabbed a bottle of water. He gulped down a large amount, soothing his dry throat, but it did nothing to help with the tension knotting his muscles. *Get a fucking grip, Tek.* He shook his head, trying to dispel the images of Jamie lying lifeless on the floor, but it was impossible. Not only did they linger, but they were interrupted by flashes of Jamie's panic-stricken face as he scrambled to remove Tek's bindings.

After one last gulp and a few deep breaths, Tek squared his shoulders and turned around. Jamie was looking at him with an expression somewhere between thoughtful and concerned. "We don't have to do this," he offered softly.

"We are fucking doing this," he spat and, with his hands balled into fists, stormed across the room and snatched up a rope.

"Tek, it's not important. Let's try again another time."

"The fuck it's not! You want this, I want this, we are fucking doing this," Tek shouted, his anger, rather than any kind of arousal, burning within him. He angrily clutched Jamie's ankle. Jamie stumbled but didn't fall.

"Stop!"

They were fucking doing this. Fuck Rocco and his bullshit. He was dead. Jamie was fine. Jamie wanted this. They were fucking doing this. He wound the rope tightly around Jamie's ankle, his movements jerky.

In a flash Jamie's foot connected with Tek's chest and sent him flying backward. He landed on his ass. He instantly jumped to his feet, breathing harshly. "What the hell was that for?"

"I told you to fucking stop! Look at yourself. You're practically foaming at the mouth, and if you tremble any harder, you'll shake apart. This is supposed to be about arousal, sex. It's supposed to be hot. Watching you have a meltdown is none of those things."

"Meltdown? That's rich coming from you. If you hadn't freaked the fuck out, I wouldn't be so goddamn worried," he screamed in rage and frustration.

Like two Brahma bulls facing off, both he and Jamie panted, nostrils flaring as they stared at each other. The tension in the room was thick, nearly palpable, and the bitterness of it burned Tek's nose and throat.

Jamie squeezed his eyes shut, took a deep breath, and when he opened them once again, there was no longer any anger, only sadness. "Look at us. This isn't how it's supposed to be. This isn't us."

Tek's guilt, rage, and sorrow swirled around in his gut, caused his chest to ache, and he hung his head, hiding his face in his hands. "I'm so sorry," he whispered.

"Don't you dare apologize. I'm the one that pushed you to do something you weren't ready for. You can't help the way you feel, and I get it. Hell, I've experienced it. We'll just try again another time."

Tek scrubbed his hand over his face and rubbed at his burning eyes. "Yeah, okay." Dejected, he removed the rope from Jamie's wrists without meeting his gaze.

"Hey," Jamie said gently and pulled Tek into a hug. "It will be okay, honest."

Tek laid his head on Jamie's shoulder, letting himself be held, absorbing his heat and strength. Jamie's strong arms and nearness instantly soothed Tek's frayed nerves. "I didn't mean to snap at you. I'm just tense and can't seem to relax."

"We've had a hell of a scare, a threat that may still be lurking. It's totally reasonable that we'd be tense. We'll get through this. No matter what life has thrown at us, we always get through it together, right?"

Jamie was right. They'd faced some heavy shit in their day. But for Tek, this last one left a deep mark on him, especially with the way Jamie had reacted. It was as if with each bad thing that happened, another piece of their souls was damaged. How many fucking hits would it take before it became irreparable?

"Yeah, we always do," he admitted. *But at what cost?*

TEK STOOD outside Max and Aiden's door, wringing his hands. He'd never put a lot of stock in shrinks, but if Max could help, Tek was willing to try anything. A month had passed, two more attempts at rope play, and they had both been disastrous. The crazy thing was, it had been Jamie who had been tied up and tortured, and yet it was Tek who couldn't seem to let it go. For all his boisterous posturing, it was Jamie who was the stronger of the two of them.

"Tek," Max greeted and held the door open for him. "Good to see you."

"You too, Max. Sorry to bother you at home, but I really need your opinion on something." Tek glanced around the posh living room, looking and then listening for sounds of Aiden's presence. He hoped to talk to Max alone, but on such short notice, he'd pour his heart out to Aiden too if need be.

"You're never a bother. Come on in." He waved toward the dark, rich leather sofa. "Have a seat. Can I get you something to drink?"

Tek sat on the edge of the couch, resting his forearms on his thighs. "No, I'm good. Is Aiden home?"

"No, he had some errands to run. I would have thought you'd be moving into your new apartment today."

"We are, this afternoon. We don't really have much stuff." Tek grinned. "Jamie won't let me decorate this one."

"From what I've heard, that's not a bad thing." Max chuckled. He took the seat across from Tek. "So what did you want to talk about?"

Tek took one deep breath and then another. He pursed his lips and met Max's gaze. "I'm failing him again," Tek admitted.

"Why do you say that?"

"I've tried everything to get us back to where we were, and no matter what I do, I can't seem to help him find pleasure in stuff we used to enjoy. He freaks out if he ties me up. I can't relax nor get aroused when I tie him up. Hell, since I can't seem to give him what he needs, I offered to let him do rope play with someone else and he went off. Pissed as hell. I don't know what else to try."

"What has Jamie's response been?"

"Other than his reaction to my suggestion of tying someone else up, he's patient with me, keeps telling me it's not important."

"So maybe you should listen to him. Just because you're not finding any pleasure in the act now doesn't mean you won't in the future, and it doesn't mean you're failing him."

"Yeah well, I sure as hell feel like a failure. Tackett helped Micah with his focusing issues, and Bobby and Rig were able to help Mason with his depression, but I can't even help Jamie or myself get back to enjoying a simple kink since this shit with Rocco went down."

"You're comparing apples to oranges there, Tek. Those guys didn't use BDSM to deal with their issues; they simply looked for ways to overcome such obstacles within the world they already lived in. Micah and Mason were fully integrated into the lifestyle when they met their current Doms. Micah struggled with ADHD for years. It was the combination of Tackett's methods as a Dom as well as the love and trust between them that has been most successful for them. I stress, *them*. It's a very personal journey. Take Mason, for example. He has suffered from social anxiety and depression and always will. His previous Doms, no matter how much they loved him, were unable to help him, so they sheltered him. Several psychiatrists tried to help, but they blamed his problems on the fact he was gay, his lifestyle choices, or both. It took Bobby and Rig to recognize that Mason didn't need discipline and punishment but rather a very strict and structured life as well as a lot of patience."

"So which approach should I take with Jamie?"

"Neither."

"But—"

"The BDSM lifestyle isn't a cure-all, Tek. You're talking about men dedicated to a lifestyle, who found ways in which to help their submissives deal with personal issues within the way they choose to live their lives. You and Jamie have kinks that you enjoyed exploring and may one day enjoy again. But willingness to *play* a role as a submissive or a dominant is not the same as being one. My advice: just be you and let Jamie be him. Stop worrying about what's not happening and focus on what is. Enjoy being together."

"You make it all sound so simple."

Max laughed, then leaned forward and patted Tek on the knee. "Life is never easy. You of all people should know that."

"Boy, do I know it," Tek agreed.

"But you've also been gifted with something very rare. You two have a very powerful love and absolute commitment to the other. That's what matters most. The small details will work out in time."

Tek took a moment to let Max's words sink in. He was right. Whatever they did sexually was satisfying as hell whether it was raw and animalistic or slow and passionate. What did it matter if they ever used another rope again?

"Yeah," Tek said with a nod and a huge smile. "The small details will work out."

"Yes, they will. Mind if I ask you a personal question?"

"Sure."

"Do you think that perhaps you make life harder than it needs to be at times?"

Tek stiffened. "What's that supposed to mean?"

"It wasn't an accusation, simply a question. While most couples look out for each other, I can't help but notice you seem to have taken it to the extreme in your belief that you are somehow responsible for Jamie."

"Considering we were born into an extreme world, I don't find it all that unusual. And Jamie *is* my responsibility."

"Don't you mean the two of you are responsible for each other?"

Tek shook his head. "Jamie is my responsibility, not the other way around. It's been that way since my birth. I was born to lead."

Max sat back and tapped a finger against his chin as he stared at Tek.

Tek shifted in his seat, feeling uneasy with the intense way Max was looking at him. Finally, he couldn't stand it a second longer. "What?"

"I was just thinking what a heavy burden was placed on you at such a young age."

"Jamie's not a burden."

"I didn't mean it like that, Tek. Growing up knowing you were to take over the motorcycle club and thus rule the other members put a lot on you at a very young age. It must have been rough."

"I guess, but I don't think I thought about it as necessarily something bad when I was young. The older I got, the more I realized that many of the things the club did weren't right, and being naive, I thought I would be able to change it once I took over. But you can't change people like the Eights."

"And yet you sent Cole back with the threat to clean it up or else?" Max questioned.

"Yeah, like I said, I was naive and perhaps I still am. I hope he'll clean it up, but at the end of the day, if they leave Jamie and I alone, I don't really care what they do with the club. It's not my responsibility anymore."

"And neither is Jamie."

"I—"

Max held up his hand. "I only mean that it's okay to take a bit of the weight off your shoulders. All the bad things that happen in life are not your fault. Jamie is your best friend, lover, and equal. Take a breather and enjoy that special bond."

"I'll try, but some things are hard to let go of." He pushed to his feet and held out his hand. "Thank you."

"I know, but sometimes letting go is exactly what you need to find true peace." Max stood, looked at the offered hand and, instead of accepting it, gave Tek a hug and patted him on the back. "You're a very lucky man, as is Jamie. I did nothing but point that out. Now go help your man pack before he throws out all your decorations."

Tek laughed and hugged him back. "Maybe I can salvage the curtains! See you later."

He had a lot to think about. Tek doubted he'd ever stop feeling responsible for Jamie. It was too ingrained. Still, he did feel better than he had in months, Tek whistled as he closed the door behind him. His—no, their future looked very bright.

How many times have I heard bad things happen to good people? Well, ya know what? They happen to bad people too. It may not be fair that the good and the bad must suffer the same fate at times. We don't always understand the why and we'll drive ourselves fucking crazy trying. My advice: simply shrug and say, eh, it happens, deal with it. I've lived by that philosophy the whole of my life. It's not the events that define me but how I respond to them, the good and the bad that determines the quality of my life. Do I have doubts? Hell yeah, everyone does, but I refuse to wallow in sadness, to give in to my fears. I choose to rise above them and count my blessings, enjoy the gift I've been given—Jamie.

Tek Cain

Gifts

WALKING DOWN the hall of the posh apartment building, Jamie knew this place was way out of their league and, damn sure, way out of their price range. At apartment 1320, he set the box down and fished the key from his pocket. Opening the door and taking in the beautiful travertine floor tiles, the open floor plan, granite countertops, high-end stainless steel appliances, and the spectacular view of the city skyline from the wall of glass doors that led to their private balcony, just how far out of their league they were was hammered home. He picked up the box off the floor and shut the door. He started to set it down on the polished granite, then thought better of it and set it on the floor. This place was way too fancy for him, and he doubted he'd ever get used to it. More than likely, he'd always feel like a faker stepping past the doorman and pretending he belonged there.

As badly as he and Tek wanted out of the club, they weren't about to take handouts. Their pride wouldn't allow such things. However, they also couldn't afford a decent place and still save money, and there were the security concerns in the run-down tenements they could afford. Until they were sure the MC wasn't going to seek retribution, they'd always be looking over their shoulders. Hell, they probably always would be. Blake found a way around their determination to do things on their own by insisting the apartment was part of Tek's salary package as head of security. He and Tek knew it was bullshit, but it was either take Blake's offer or continue to live in a playroom at the club.

Jamie flipped on the light in the master bathroom and whistled in appreciation. The large walk-in shower, sunken jetted tub, and marble countertops on the double vanity made him rethink the possibilities of getting used to this place. They were definitely luxuries he would never tire of, and he knew they'd made the right choice.

"Hey, Jamie, you here?" Tek's voice came to him from the other room.

"In here!" he called back.

"Holy shit! Will you get a look at this place?"

Tek walked through the bedroom door with a box in his hand, and Jamie cocked his head and pursed his lips. "If that contains what I think it does, you can take it right on over to the garbage chute."

"What? You don't think my retro décor will go with this place? The seventies look is back in style."

"Yes, but reproduction, not stinky secondhand store finds." Jamie waved dismissively.

Tek dropped the box on the floor and grabbed Jamie's wrist before he could step out of the room. "I was worried about that."

"What?" Jamie asked in confusion.

"This fancy-pants place would go to your head. Do I have to remind you we are still just poor white trash?" Tek said teasingly.

"Yes, but we are poor white trash with some swanky digs," Jamie countered. "Have you checked out this place? You've got to see the bathroom. If you ever can't find me, look there first."

Jamie instantly regretted what he said when he saw Tek's smile fall. It hadn't been all that long ago that Tek had stepped into another apartment and found Jamie gone. "I'm sorry. I shouldn't have said it like that. I only mean—"

"I know what you meant," Tek replied, recovering quickly. "Let's see that bathroom."

Jamie rolled his neck, releasing some of the tension, and followed Tek, standing at the doorway while Tek inspected the room. Thankfully the smile that returned to Tek's face when he turned around was genuine.

"I won't have to come looking for you. I'll be in that tub right along with you. Damn, this place is something."

Glad the morose reminder had passed quickly, Jamie reminded himself to be more careful with his word choices in the future. "Let's go explore the rest of this place together." Which really meant a half bath they hadn't checked out, since besides the master bedroom and bath, the place was open. The modern white leather furniture with chrome accents and matching chrome tables would have seemed sparse and uninspired, but the splashes of blue in the décor, with pillows and a rug, gave the place an inviting feel. Within a few minutes, they found themselves on the balcony. Tek sprawled out on the oversized chaise lounge and Jamie nestled between his spread legs, his back resting against Tek's chest.

For long moments they were silent as they took in the view of the city, a cool breeze blowing with a hint of coming rain. "I've changed my mind. It's not only the master bath that I'll be spending a lot of time in. Fuck, this is gorgeous," Jamie commented, completely awestruck at how beautiful the city was from this level.

"Yeah and lucky you, you'll get to enjoy this while you work, Mr. Stay-at-Home Man."

"Only as much as you do. What was it you said about working hours? Something about I better get my shit done before you head over to the club because I'll be going with?"

"That gives you plenty of time to play with your laptop, or you can bring it with you." Tek shrugged, completely unapologetic. "I'm not letting you out of my sight any time soon."

"You do realize eventually you're going to have to stop being so overly protective, don't you?"

"Why?"

"Well...." Jamie thought about it for a moment, trying to come up with a good answer, but he knew Tek well enough to know that his protectiveness wasn't born from one instance but a lifetime of believing Jamie was his responsibility. Jamie had been raised to believe the reason he'd been put on this earth was to protect Tek with his very life. "Never mind, it was a stupid question."

"It wasn't stupid, but I can't change the way I am any more than you can." Tek tightened his hold on Jamie and kissed the side of his head. "We're stuck with each other and our quirky ways."

"I could think of worse things to be stuck with." Jamie laughed. "So where did you run off to this afternoon?"

"I went and saw Max."

"Yeah, what for?" Jamie inquired. He had a sneaking suspicion he knew what it was about, and hopefully Max clued him in about panic attacks.

"He said we were hopeless."

"I could have told you that." Jamie snorted. Jamie sat up and turned around, sitting Indian style at the end of the chaise. "But seriously, you do realize that it's going to take time. We had a hell of a scare, and honestly, anyone would have some lingering doubts and fears."

Tek raised a brow. "Have you been talking to Max?"

"No, not really. It's just an observation. I think we're trying too hard, ya know? But I'm not a professional. What did Max have to say?"

"Pretty much what you did. I hope you don't mind, but I told him about the problems I was having with the whole rope thing, that I felt like I was letting you down."

"Tek—"

Tek held up his hand. "I know what you're going to say, and you were right. I was trying too hard too quickly, but it took Max to make me realize it. He said that the BDSM lifestyle wasn't a cure-all. I was comparing you and me with men who had dedicated themselves to a lifestyle we only play in. It was stupid of me to think what worked for Tackett and Micah, and Bobby, Rig, and Mason would work for us. It took Max to point out that, yeah, we like some kinky stuff, but it isn't the same as what those guys have." He shrugged. "Our relationship has nothing to do with who is dominant or submissive or what we do or don't do. That I needed to stop worrying about shit like that and focus on us. Enjoy being together."

Jamie leaned in and pressed his lips softly against Tek's, kissing him before saying, "That Max is a smart man. What we do isn't important. That we are together while doing it is." He kissed Tek again.

"Why in the hell didn't you say that?" Tek asked with a sly grin. "Would have saved me a lot of grief, ya know."

It was Jamie's turn to shake his head. He didn't even need to answer. They both knew Tek was the most stubborn man on the planet, and Jamie ran a close second. He simply kissed him once again and then stood. "Let's go enjoy being together while we bring up more boxes."

"Sounds like a great plan. The faster we get this stuff up here, the sooner we can go check out that sweet tub."

Jamie held open the door for Tek and then closed and locked it behind them. "And it won't take long, since you are not allowed to bring up anything but your clothes."

"Not even the curtains?" Tek tossed over his shoulder.

"Especially those," Jamie laughed.

IT ONLY took them a couple hours to clean out their old place, make a quick stop at the Goodwill dumpster, another at the grocery store, and they were back at their new place. Seeing as the apartment was furnished, had every amenity they could ever need in the kitchen— even the linen closet was stocked—they simply needed to unload their clothes into the dresser and hang up the rest in the closet. Done and done. Moving was a breeze. Cooking, on the other hand? Not so much. Tek waved a towel in front of the screeching smoke detector.

Jamie rushed into the room, water dripping down his body, a towel around his waist, and a panicked look on his face. "What the hell is going on? Where's the fire?"

"I burned the macaroni and cheese."

"How in the hell did you burn the macaroni and cheese? All you had to do was boil some water and add the noodles." Jamie went to the stove and lifted the lid on the stinky pot and wrinkled his nose. He cocked his head and stared at Tek, dumbfounded. "Why is the cheese burnt?"

"I think there is something wrong with the stove," Tek said in his defense. Thankfully the blaring alarm shut the hell up.

"Couldn't be the cook?"

"No."

Jamie snatched the empty box from the counter and thrust it in Tek's face. "Remove from heat, add milk and cheese, and stir. Which part of that do you think you may have neglected?" Jamie bit his lip, no doubt trying to hold in his laughter, but it didn't matter. The shaking of his big body tipped Tek off.

Tek glanced back and forth between the box and Jamie, searching for a good excuse. Coming up empty, he tossed the towel aside, threw his hands up, and stomped out of the kitchen.

"Where are you going, Betty Crocker?" Jamie didn't even try to hold back his hoots of laughter as he followed Tek into the bedroom.

"I was going to make you a nice dinner in celebration of the first night in our new home, but now I don't want to." He kept his back to Jamie as he dug out his cell phone from his dirty jeans.

"That was so sweet. I'm sorry. I won't laugh at you. It's the thought that counts, right?"

"Nope, you hurt my feelings." He discreetly dialed the number he'd looked up earlier just in case this very thing happened.

"Tek, c'mon, I said I was sorry."

"How are you going to make it up to me?"

"Name it." He ran his hand down Tek's back in a soothing manner. Tek turned and met Jamie's gaze. "Drop the towel."

Jamie instantly did, and Tek hit the Send button and brought the phone to his ear. He kept his gaze riveted to Jamie's crotch.

"What the hell are you doing?" Jamie whispered, his hands on his hips.

"Play with yourself?"

"What? Who the hell are you calling?"

Tek stepped up and pumped Jamie's soft cock a couple times while the phone rang. When someone answered, Tek stepped back, nodded toward Jamie's dick, and mouthed "Do it" before turning his attention to the phone call.

"Yes, this is Tek Cain. I called you earlier. Could you have my order delivered?"

"Who are you talking to?" Jamie repeated, except this time, instead of his hands on his hips, he had one tugging on his balls and the other stroking his shaft.

"Appetizer? No, thank you, I have my own."

"We'll have it delivered in fifteen minutes."

He licked his lips. "Make it thirty." He ended the call, and in a flash, the phone hit the floor and Jamie hit the bed. Tek dropped to his knees between Jamie's spread legs. "Chinese with a little Jamie appetizer is a much better way to celebrate our new place than boxed mac and cheese," he said slyly before swallowing Jamie to the hilt.

JAMIE KICKED back on the couch and rubbed his belly, stuffed to the gills. The kung pao and General Tso's chicken had been delicious, even if it was cold. Thirty minutes hadn't been nearly enough time for "appetizers," and it was closer to an hour before Tek ran down and picked it up from the front desk.

"Damn, I love having a dishwasher, makes cleanup so much easier," Tek announced as he flopped down next to Jamie and propped his feet up on the coffee table. "You ready for dessert? I bought a box of chocolate cupcakes."

"Nah, between the appetizer and dinner, I'm stuffed."

"In more ways than one," Tek snorted.

Jamie shifted, enjoying the ache in his ass as much as the full feeling in his gut. "I'm not even complaining. I'm a happy boy."

"One hell of a successful housewarming party if you ask me."

"Oh, which reminds me—" Jamie pushed off the couch and hurried to the bedroom to retrieve the box he'd stored in the closet.

"Dammit, Jamie, can't we just kick back and relax? I don't want to unpack anything else," Tek grumbled.

Jamie ignored Tek's whining and set the box on the corner of the coffee table, then used it to shove Tek's feet off. He left it sitting there in the center of the table as he sat back down next to Tek and grabbed the remote. Without a word, he clicked on the TV.

Tek glanced back and forth between Jamie and the box. "What is it?"

"Nothing. You said you don't want to unpack another box tonight so you can open it tomorrow. What do you want to watch? Ohhh, look. *The Big Bang Theory* is on. I love this show. Sheldon is a fucking riot."

"Yeah, yeah, so are you," Tek shot back, then grabbed the box and shook it. "What is it?"

Jamie took the box from Tek and set it down on the table again—worried he would break it. "You can find out tomorrow." He sat back, working hard to appear nonchalant when he wanted to burst out laughing at the irritated look on Tek's face.

"You really can be an ass sometimes." Tek jumped to his feet, snatched up the box, and took it to the island like a little kid worried someone was going to take his shiny new toy.

Jamie quietly followed, standing behind Tek as he opened the box.

"Are you fucking kidding me!" Tek hooted. He pulled out the giant pink piggy bank, sparkly gold crown and all. "Where did you find this?"

"It's amazing what you can find on the Internet."

"I know exactly where to put this." Tek clutched the pig to his chest and headed to the bedroom—thank God it wouldn't be part of the living room décor.

Tek set it on one side of the dresser and then went to the closet and returned with an 8x10 frame and set it next to the pig. He stood back with a big satisfied smile on his face. "Perfect."

"I can't believe you did that. It's nearly as tacky as the damn pig." Jamie laughed.

Tek pulled him into a hug. "Now it's the perfect welcome-home celebration." He kissed Jamie, his happiness like little sparks on Jamie's tongue.

They were truly blessed to have such an amazing place to call home, even with the stupid pig and the silly doodle of a cabin. It really was perfect.

Abraham Lincoln said, "You cannot escape the responsibility of tomorrow by evading it today." I never evade it and it was futile to think I would ever stop feeling responsible for Jamie, no more than he could stop feeling the same about me. And really, is that such a bad thing? I do however, desperately want us to find a sense of security and a measure of peace. In order to do that, I knew I had to step back from tomorrow and deal with the responsibility I had left behind me.

Tek Cain

Dealing in the Past

PAPERWORK WAS one of Tek's least favorite aspects of his job. The incident in the club last night was really nothing more than two wannabe submissives, rivaling for the same Dom, bitch slapping each other. However, the report had to be typed and filed. Tek sat back in his chair and shook his hands out. "I should have taken a typing class."

"They have software programs that can teach you."

Tek looked up to find Blake standing at the door to Tek's office. "Would it require me to spend more time on the computer?"

"Afraid so," Blake chuckled.

"Yeah well, in that case I think I'll stick to the ol' peck and find method. So to what do I owe this surprise visit?"

"I'm not interrupting anything am I? I can come back later—"

"Nonsense." Tek gestured toward the chair on the other side of his desk. "My fingers could use the break."

Blake slid into the chair and pulled an envelope from the inside pocket of his jacket. "I was worried what Nick would find when he ran your real names. For the most part, Nick is a very honest man, but if the warrants were active, he wouldn't have been able to ignore them." He slid the envelope across the desk. "He signed me on to his computer and then turned his head for five minutes."

Tek stared at it for a moment, a sickening feeling settling in to his gut. So many things he'd done in his past he wasn't proud of. Things he doubted Blake would be able to forgive him for. Was this the end of his time at the Guards? Tek couldn't bring himself to pick up the envelope, afraid of what it contained and yet knowing he had to look.

"It's not going to bite you, Tek."

Tek raised his head and met Blake's eyes. "Did you read it?"

"Who do you think printed it?"

The smile on Blake's face eased some of Tek's worry, and he picked up the envelope. He flipped open the flap, pulled out the paper, and unfolded it. He scanned the report, trying to make sense of what he was seeing. *No Active Warrants.* "You sure you typed in the right names?"

"Yes and I checked twice, both in the Federal and California State databases."

Tek laid the report out on his desk and pulled his beard through his fingers without taking his eyes from the paper. How in the hell was that possible? "It has to be a mistake."

"I don't think so. I found active warrants on Rocco and about half a dozen other members of your old club, but whatever the Feds were investigating, apparently it wasn't tied to you or Jamie."

Tek sat back in his chair and blew out a long breath. Those fuckers were willing to get him and Jamie killed to make their case against the Eights. Still, it amazed him that they hadn't gotten the dirt on him, considering what went down at the Banger's warehouse and the number of bodies left in the wake of the madness. Whatever. He wasn't about to question the gift.

Tek tapped his finger against the report. "Thank you for this. I really appreciate it. You have made my day."

"It was my pleasure." Blake pushed to his feet. "Now get back to work and let me know if you want that typing program. I'm sure I can find you one."

Tek held up his hands and wiggled his fingers. "These things have a mind of their own, but thanks anyway."

After Blake left, Tek picked up the report and read it again with a big smile on his face. "Well, I'll be damned." Now all he needed to do was check what was going on with the Eights and maybe he and Jamie might find that peace after all.

THE SOUNDS of Flogging Molly emitted from the overhead speakers, and Jamie swayed to the rhythm as he banged away at his laptop. He'd always had a competitive streak and could be a bit stubborn, so he loved the challenge of trying to break the program. Who would have thought he'd actually get paid to break shit?

He downed the rest of his soda and crunched on a piece of ice while glancing around the club. It was still early so only one table in the exclusive members-only area was occupied. Jamie didn't recognize the silver-haired gentleman with the finely tailored suit or the younger man sitting with Blake. More than likely another prospective new member. There seemed to be quite a few joining lately.

Jamie started to get back to work when he spotted Tek walking through the door. Only then did Jamie glance at the clock and realize it was dinnertime. He closed his laptop and sat back in his seat.

"Hey, hot stuff, you ready for dinner?"

Tek slid into the seat next to him and raked his eyes up and down Jamie's body. "I am if you're on the menu."

Jamie leaned over and pressed a soft kiss to Tek's lips. "For what I'm packing, it would take far longer than the thirty minutes you have."

Tek glanced over to where Blake was sitting and then turned back to Jamie with a sly grin on his face. "Boss looks busy. How about we have dinner in my office? It's been awhile since I had you spread out on my desk and feasted on this luscious body." He laid his hand on Jamie's thigh, fingers teasing the inner seam of Jamie's jeans as he moved his hand up.

Heat rushed to Jamie's groin, his cock hardening with the memory of Tek banging him over his desk. That had been after Tek had gotten off—literally—after work. Jamie knew Tek was only teasing him. The man was too dedicated to his job and to Blake to actually jeopardize his position. Jamie laid his hand on Tek's, halting his movement. "You're a fucking tease."

"Pfft, you love it," Tek chuckled.

Jamie shoved Tek's hand off his thigh. "Not when it means I'm going to be suffering from blue balls for the next four hours."

Tek laid a folded piece of paper on the bar next to Jamie's laptop. "Maybe this will make you feel better."

Jamie picked it up, unfolded it, and read the typed words. He looked up and gawked at Tek. "Dude, that's not even funny."

Tek draped his arm over Jamie's shoulder and pulled him closer. "It's not a joke. Neither of us have any active warrants with the Feds."

Jamie looked between the paper and Tek. "If this is real, then I'll totally let you do me over your desk."

Tek whooped, then grabbed Jamie's hand and yanked him out of his chair. "Hot damn! I'm about to get me a feast for dinner."

Jamie laughed but allowed Tek to manhandle him. "Seriously?"

"Yup," Tek responded, sounding sure. "Totally going glutton."

"That's not what I meant." No way was that report legit. He and Tek had to have had active warrants. The shit they'd done….

"Oh, yeah, the report is correct too," Tek pointed out as he continued to lead Jamie out of the club.

"No fucking way!"

Tek stopped in the hallway and pulled Jamie into a tight embrace. "Same thing I thought but it's real. With Rocco gone, no one is hunting us. No Eights, no Feds. We're free, baby."

Jamie stared at Tek, trying to process the ramifications of the news. They'd been on the run and looking over their shoulder for so long. And now, for it to be over. That they could actually stop running and start working toward the future they'd hoped for. Damn! It seemed too good to be true.

"Pinch me," Jamie requested, still holding Tek's gaze.

Pain radiated out across Jamie's left ass check. "Hey, what the hell?"

"You told me to pinch you," Tek responded, sounding completely unapologetic. "You're not dreaming, babe. The Feds aren't after us, and now with Rocco dead…."

"But what about the rest of the Eights?"

"Way to be a Debbie Downer. Just for that we're having cold sandwiches and chips for dinner." He pinched Jamie's ass again, harder this time before he headed down the hall.

Jamie rubbed the abused cheek and followed Tek into his office.

Tek set his lunch bag on his desk and pulled out a sandwich. After checking it to make sure it was the right one, he handed it to Jamie and pulled out his ham and cheese. Since they'd returned from the cabin, they'd been serious about saving every dime possible. Blake never charged either of them for eating at the Guards, but neither he nor Tek was going to take advantage of Blake. He already was doing way too much for them.

Jamie took the chair across from Tek, propped his feet on the desk, and unwrapped his PB&J. "I don't mean to be a downer. I guess I'm just used to the other shoe falling."

"Maybe it won't this time."

Jamie's brows hit his hair line. "Wow, how the roles have reversed. I'm usually the dreamer."

"It's my New Year's resolution."

"It's only November," Jamie pointed out around a big bite of his PB&J. There was something missing. *Ah!* He snatched a bag of chips, opened them, and added them to his sandwich.

Tek wrinkled his nose. "That's gross."

Jamie responded by taking another big bite, crunching happily.

"Seriously, it's not that I'm a dreamer, I'll leave that to you," Tek said with a wink. "But I figured we were due some good news. I plan on making sure Cole and the Eights stay out of our lives."

"How do you plan on doing that?"

Tek sat back in his chair with a wide grin stretching across his face. "We may not be on the Feds' radar, but the Eights are. I figured with an anonymous tip pointing them in the direction of a couple graves, the Eights will be far too busy with their own shit to be worrying about coming after us."

"You are an evil, evil man and I love you," Jamie responded, returning the smile.

It was a great plan. Cole may or may not take Tek's advice to turn around the club. However, with the dirt Jamie and Tek had on them, it guaranteed they'd be far too busy with their own shit to bother with him and Tek.

Their future was looking brighter and brighter.

There are moments in life during which we understand what it truly means to live. It's not getting up every morning and trudging off to work, the hours you put in, or the paycheck at the end of the long week. It's the people that you allow into it. Letting people into our lives wasn't something I was sure about. There was this ingrained fear and mistrust of anyone who wasn't Jamie. But with each passing day, without even realizing it, the men at the Guards of Folsom have wormed their way in, and suddenly I am surrounded by friends, not just any type of friend but men I trust with not only my, life but the life of what is most precious to me—Jamie. They have a place in my heart and have touched my soul, and when I am with them, I feel completely alive.

Tek Cain

Wee Willies and Tushies

THE MONTHS after moving to the apartment were some of the best since coming to live in the city. Thoughts of Rocco and retribution were beginning to fade. Not that Tek or Jamie would ever forget—they couldn't—but they were settling into their new lives and each day was a gift. Falling asleep with Jamie in his arms and waking up next to him, even if a little chilled because Jamie was a blanket hog, was something he would never get tired of or take for granted.

Whether Tek had to work the day or night shift at the club, Jamie adjusted his schedule with ease. Jamie was getting pretty damn good with a computer, and even within the walls of the noisy club, because Tek still couldn't bear to leave Jamie alone, Jamie was able to block out the external stimuli and was proving to be a hell of a software tester. He was also making damn good money at it, and the pink piggy might have to find her twin in the very near future.

Neither of them had mentioned the ropes. They were still wrapped with care and sitting on the shelf in the bedroom closet, but they were no longer the enemy. Their sex life was off-the-charts hot. The large walk-in shower and the jetted tub were becoming two favorite play areas. Jamie's skill with the computer also uncovered some interesting sites, and their collection of plugs, clamps, and other toys was growing.

Growing at an even faster rate were the friendships and closeness between them and the rest of the guys from the Guards of Folsom. That night they were hosting their first dinner party, and what better way to do it than with those who had come to mean the world to them?

Tek pulled open the oven door and checked the mini quiches. He'd set the timer and it still had a good ten minutes, but he didn't trust this beast. It had a way of flaring up and burning shit randomly. At least that was his story and he was sticking to it.

"Damn, it smells good in here," Jamie yelled from the bathroom. "How much longer on the timer?"

"Ten minutes."

"Stop opening the oven door and don't you dare turn it off or, God forbid, turn it up. I'll be out before the timer goes off, just going to shave real quick."

Tek jerked his head in the direction of the bathroom. "Don't you fucking dare!" He'd always loved Jamie's beard and had hated to see it go when they'd left California. Now, not only was it hot as hell to see his man looking like the big bear he was, but it was also a reminder of the fact they were getting back to being who they always were and, more importantly, who they wanted to be, without fear of being recognized.

"Calm down, I'm not shaving off the beard, just cleaning up my neck. Now hush and make sure the table is set, will ya?"

Tek couldn't help it. He had to pull open the beast one more time, just to be sure it wasn't getting all pissy, then quietly closed it. He made a few final touches to the table, wiped fingerprints from a glass— fucking lead crystal, who would have thought—and replaced the linen napkin he'd used. He took one last look, satisfied everything looked perfect when Jamie appeared. His hair was damp and slicked back, and the beard Tek loved to run his hands over was still there. He wore black dress slacks, a silver belt, and a pale blue button-up dress shirt.

"Looks good."

Tek raked his gaze up and down Jamie's body. "It most certainly does."

"This old thing?" Jamie snickered and stepped into the kitchen area. He pulled out a drawer, from which he retrieved a spoon and dipped it into the cheese sauce that was in the warmer. "We could probably go ahead and pour the chips into a bowl," he said, lifting the spoon to his lips.

Tek stared in awe at Jamie as he moved easily around the kitchen, tasting and checking to make sure everything was just right. Tek finally shook his head. "When in the hell did you get so good in the kitchen?"

"You simply have to read the directions, Tek. It's really not that hard."

Like the way he took to the computer, Jamie had taken to cooking with ease. Although their bills were next to nothing, thanks to Blake and his sneaky ways, Jamie refused to allow them to eat out or order takeout very often. He claimed he could do it just as well and for half the cost. Tek didn't know if Jamie could compare himself to the chef at the Guards or Tek's favorite Chinese restaurant, but he was pretty damn good at it. The weight of the pink piggy was proof he was also right about the money they would save by eating at home. Good thing Jamie took up the cooking because Tek was sure the kitchen was conspiring against him.

"It is if the oven hates you," he muttered lowly.

"What was that?"

"Nothing. Which bowl do you want me to use?"

"Get the bright blue one from the top of the cupboard over there." Jamie pointed to the cupboard he was talking about and then pulled the oven door open as the timer began to chime.

Tek found the bowl and filled it with tortilla chips, his only contribution to the meal. "You cook, you clean, and you make great money. I gotta wonder why in the hell you keep me around."

Jamie grabbed a pot holder, pulled the quiche from the oven, and set them in the warmer. He tossed the pot holders on the counter and ran a soothing hand down Tek's back to his ass, then patted it.

"Right here, baby."

"You keep me around for my ass? Seriously?"

Jamie patted his ass again and then pecked his cheek. "No, because you *are* an ass." He spun out of Tek's reach. Before Tek could go after him, the buzzer rang.

"Oh look, I do believe our guests have arrived." Jamie laughed and headed to the door.

They'd given Howard the names of their guests, and anyone not on the list wasn't getting past the doorman. Tek still hadn't figured out if Howard was simply that loyal at keeping the residents safe or he feared Blake. Since Howard wouldn't even let Blake, who owned the place, up unannounced, Tek figured it was probably the former, but the latter drove it home.

Jamie opened the door to Micah's smiling face. He was carrying a covered dish. "I told you, you didn't have to bring anything."

Micah waved him off and then crooked his finger. Knowing the routine, Jamie bent down and allowed Micah to peck his cheek. "I know, you yummy-smelling bear, but it gave me an excuse to have sugar. I made brownies. Tek!"

Micah crooked his finger at him as well, and Tek bent to accept the kiss.

"I told him it wasn't necessary, but he insisted," Tackett explained and then shrugged. "It's his ass."

"I'm not supposed to have too many sweets. I get a sugar buzz." He laid a single finger over his lips. "But it's soooo worth it."

Micah might have gestured for him to be quiet, like it was some big secret, but the man didn't even try to lower his voice. Tek met Tackett's gaze. "Sounds like someone needs a spanking."

"Daily." Tackett laughed.

Micah was in full party mode. Tek knew very well Micah could be still. He'd seen a huge change in the hyper submissive since he'd first met him. However, what hadn't changed, thank goodness, was Micah's infectious smile and his fun and flirty ways. Micah made Tek smile simply by being in the same room.

THE FOOD was a huge hit, and Jamie couldn't help but swell with pride. It was his and Tek's first dinner party, but if he had anything to say about it, it certainly wouldn't be their last. If anyone would have told him while he was growing up that one day he'd live in a posh apartment in a ritzy high-rise, having dinner parties with real china and lead crystal, he'd have told him they were out of their fucking minds. This was far removed from the kind of parties they used to attend at the Crimson VIII's clubhouse. Not only were the surroundings completely different, the people he now shared drinks and food with were on a whole different plane than those he'd partied with in his past. The best thing was, the conversations didn't revolve around booze, sex, drugs, violence, and death as those he'd heard while growing up. Rather, with these men whom so many looked down on, accused of being sick and depraved, the talk was about life, love, dreams, and the future. And laughter. So much laughter and happiness.

After all the compliments, plenty of seconds, and even thirds of the meal he'd prepared, Jamie couldn't help but smile, feeling a wee bit cocky.

It was a nice group, small enough everyone could talk intimately and relax without the craziness or stricter rules of the club. Jamie was a people watcher, always had been, and he prided himself on being able to read people. Even in this relaxed environment outside the Guards, Jamie could easily read the telltale signs of Mason's and Micah's submissive natures still shining through in the way they cared for their Doms and always made sure their needs were met, their plates filled, and their glasses never dry. Jamie looked over to where Micah was talking animatedly with Tek. It appeared to be a hot and heavy conversation that had been going on for a while as evidenced by the dazed look on Tek's face—Micah often had that effect on people when he was on a roll. Still, Jamie didn't miss the way that Micah's gaze very often shifted to Tackett, who was chatting with Bobby in the kitchen. Micah always knew where the man was.

"This is an awesome party," Rig complimented. "I'm going to have to get on to Bobby for slacking in his entertaining skills. He used to love throwing parties."

"You two have been pretty busy with Mason. How's your boy doing, by the way? In all the craziness, I never got the chance to ask you how the trip to Florida went."

"You had a lot on your mind," Rig pointed out. "It was good, sad of course, but I think it went a long way in helping Mason say good-bye and finding at least a little good out of the tragedy. He's really proud of the work they are doing at the Sunshine House."

"Sunshine House?" Jamie asked in confusion and then remembered what Mason had done. "Oh right, the beach house for homeless LGBTQ kids. He should be very proud, and I can tell by the look in your eyes, you are too."

"I am. I'm truly blessed to have him in my life."

Jamie cut a quick glance to where Mason was standing on the patio, a big smile on his face as he talked with Ty and Aiden. He was relaxed, happy, and enjoying the party without being wrapped around one of his Doms or hiding that brilliant smile. Remembering the unsure and frightened man he'd met the first time, it was obvious Mason had bloomed under the watchful and loving care of Bobby and Rig.

He clapped his hand on Rig's shoulder. "It looks like he could say the same thing about you and Bobby." Jamie noticed Tek gesturing to him with a wave. "I think my cohost needs me. Can I bring you back anything?"

"No, I'm good, but thanks. I think I'll go give Bobby a hard time for his slacking."

As soon as Jamie approached, the dazed look on Tek's face cleared and he said to Micah, "Hold that thought. Jamie needs my help."

"Take your time. I'm going to go sneak another brownie, but don't tell Tackett." Micah giggled.

Jamie was taken aback, confused, as Tek grabbed his arm and pulled him toward their bedroom. He didn't say a word until the door was shut behind them.

"Oh my fucking God, can that boy talk." Tek ran his fingers through his hair and then scrubbed them across his face. "I know why he's not allowed to have sugar. The man is cray-cray when he's buzzing."

"Aww, I think he's cute." Jamie laughed.

"Oh, he's cute all right, fucking adorable even, but seriously, Jamie, I don't think he took a single breath in twenty minutes. I was exhausted just listening to him." Tek cocked his head. "Did you know there are things called Manx?"

"Never heard of them."

"Well, apparently they are like Spanx but for men."

"Still not sure what they are."

"Man girdles. They lift, shape, and flatten. You can even get them with padded tushies and enhancements for wee willies."

"Tushies and wee willies?" Jamie questioned with a smirk.

"Oh God! He's rubbing off on me. Now do you see why I needed rescuing? I should not know about tushies and wee willies, Jamie! It's just… just…." Tek threw up his hands. "I need to go scrub my brain. You go talk to him."

Jamie burst out laughing as Tek went into the bathroom and closed the door behind him. But it was the distinct sound of the lock engaging that had Jamie wheezing and snorting. Tek really was afraid of a sweet little man with sparkly love and a sugar buzz.

Tackett obviously had realized Micah was dipping into the sugar a bit too much because when Jamie stepped back out of the bedroom, Tackett had his arms around a vibrating Micah, head bowed as if he was speaking near his ear.

Jamie grabbed a beer, popped the top off, and settled on the couch next to Blake. "Having a good time?"

"I am. Thank you for inviting us." He nodded in the direction of Tackett and Micah with a big smile on his face. "Micah's been having a great time too, I see."

"Yeah, well, I bet they have an even better time later."

"You and Tek have a birthday coming up soon. You planning another party?"

"Whew. I haven't even thought about it. One party at a time." He chuckled. It was coming up in three weeks. He'd have to decide what to do for Tek soon. Considering how good this party was, maybe he would consider having another one here.

"You're more than welcome to have it at the club. I know you and Tek aren't really into the scene, but a BDSM-themed party can be a whole lot of fun. Plus, no cleanup afterward."

"Oh, I do like that idea. Maybe a surprise party," he contemplated out loud. The more he thought about it, Tek in leather and dancing and the scenes around them would make for a great time. Oh fuck, they could play clip the tail on the pony. Aiden and Max would fucking love that.

"Let me know and I'll be sure to clear the schedule for whichever night you'd like."

"I wouldn't want you to close the club on our account. You already have done so much for us. I wouldn't feel right about you losing a night of revenue."

"You didn't ask, I offered. Just think about it." Blake held up his empty wineglass. "I think I need a refill."

"Oh fuck, sorry, what a crappy host. I'll get it." He held out his hand to take Blake's glass.

Blake patted Jamie's thigh. "That's okay. I want to see if Ty needs anything too. Plus, looks like Tek has recovered sufficiently from his chat with Micah." He nodded toward the bedroom door where Tek was standing. "We'll talk again later."

The rest of the evening, Tek stayed glued to Jamie's side. It had really very little to do with Micah. That had been an excuse. Jamie knew it was for another reason by the way Tek kept massaging his ass and kissing the side of Jamie's neck. He was horny and sleepy. Jamie was feeling both as well, and as he shut the door on the last of their guests, he leaned against it and sighed in relief.

Tek stood next to him shoulder to shoulder and leaned his head back against the door. "I'd call that one hell of a successful first party."

Jamie looked around their apartment: everything in place, not a single beer can crushed on the floor, no cigarette burn holes on the furniture, no passed-out dude lying in his own puke or strange naked chick spread out on the couch. Instead, the dishes were done, leftover food wrapped and put away, the place as clean as it had been before their first guest arrived. Damn, they really had changed their notion of a successful party.

"You notice anything strange?" Jamie asked.

"Yeah, we're standing here next to the door instead of lying naked on the bed."

"No… well, I mean, yeah that, but look how clean this place is."

Tek laughed. "You noticed that too? We sure have come a long way, huh?"

"I'd say so." Jamie turned his head and met Tek's gaze. "You think we're out of our league here? You know, acting like posers?"

"I don't know, Jamie. I guess sometimes." He grabbed Jamie's hand and pulled him toward the bedroom. "But I don't want to think about it right now."

"Let me guess, you want to think about me putting my wee willy in your tushie."

Tek stopped at the doorway to gawk at Jamie for a few seconds. "Are you out of your damn mind! It's my whopping willy that will be tickling your tushie."

They were still laughing when they landed on the bed.

What is that saying? Something about give a man enough rope and he'll hang himself? Yeah well, Jamie never did do things the conventional way. Give that man enough rope and I was the one hung.

Tek Cain

One Step Closer

FOR MONTHS, Jamie and Tek had spent every chance they had to escape the city at the cabin. Neither of them had much experience in construction, but it was a damn good thing they were quick studies. They had to be, since not only was money tight, but they were tight wads. This weekend was no different. Not that it was a hardship—hard work, yes—but Jamie couldn't think of another place on earth he'd want to spend his time off.

"Damn, this is looking amazing," Tek complimented.

Jamie jerked, flailing momentarily as he tripped over the paint can. Thankfully he caught it at the last second before more than a few drops landed on the tarp.

"Oh shit, sorry. Didn't mean to startle you," Tek said, then walked over and turned down the CD player.

"Give a man a heart attack, why don't ya?" Jamie grumbled.

"I stood near the door watching you for like the last five minutes, waiting for you to finish bellowing," Tek teased.

"It's called singing," Jamie informed Tek and then flipped him off.

Jamie had been lost in the rhythmic guitar of George Lynch and doing his damndest to sing louder than Don Dokken as he belted out "Breaking the Chains" while painting the new drywall they'd finished the day before. He and Tek planned on doing as much of the work on the cabin as they could. Since the plans called for the living room to remain virtually the same with the additional rooms added on either side, they started there.

They'd removed all of the god-awful paneling, added additional insulation, sealed the windows, and hung new drywall from ceiling to floor. Neither of them had ever done drywall work before, and there had been a lot of cursing and sweat. Mistakes were made, but in the end, they'd actually done a damn fine job and there were only a few spots where the seams and mud were visible. The chair rail they planned to install later would cover up that little imperfection.

They finished closing up the paint cans, wrapped the brushes to keep them from drying out—one more coat after this one dried would do it. They then stood side by side to admire the work they'd accomplished.

"I can't wait to see this finished," Tek commented.

"What? You already complaining about a little hard work?" Jamie teased. "I think this is half the fun. Plus, we'll appreciate it a lot more knowing we did it ourselves."

"I agree, but it will still be nice to sit back with a bottle of cold beer, easing our aching hands and making a toast to mission complete."

"I can see that, but not for many, many, many years," Jamie smirked.

He wiped the sweat from his brow with the back of his forearm and only then noticed the big glob of paint smeared across his arm and no doubt now across his head and hair. He huffed out an exasperated breath and went to the sink to wash up.

"Yeah, you're right. I guess I better get used to spending my days off and vacations with a hammer or a paintbrush in my hand. Especially since we'll be working on the barn as soon as this place is completed."

"I swear. I think you've bumped your head one too many times there, Farmer Pete," Jamie laughed.

"Hey, at least something good will come out of all those knots and bruises," Tek countered.

It had started out as a joke, but the more Tek talked about wanting animals, the more Jamie was beginning to think the man was actually serious. He stared at Tek while drying his hands, and no matter how hard he tried, he simply couldn't see Tek wearing cowboy boots and a hat and shoveling shit. Nope, couldn't picture it.

"How about we grab a quick lunch and then you can help me finish this up?" Jamie suggested.

"Wouldn't you rather just spend the day hanging out by the pond?"

"Sure I would, but then this room wouldn't get painted." He stepped up to Tek and leaned in to run his tongue up the side of Tek's neck, tasting the sweat and spice of his skin. "And if you're a good little helper, I'll give you a big surprise later."

Tek shuddered. "I like big surprises." He grabbed the bulge in Jamie's shorts and squeezed. "Especially big hard surprises."

"Fucking horndog. You've got a one-track mind," Jamie accused.

"Yeah and your point is?"

Jamie just shook his head and went to the fridge to pull out a couple bottles of water. It was a good thing he knew Tek so well and shared that one track most of the time. By nightfall they should both be very happy, very satisfied horndogs.

TEK WALKED into the darkened living room; only a single low light shone from outside the back window. The room still had the lingering stench of paint, but the cool breeze blowing through the open windows was helping to clear the air. After his hot shower, the cooler temperatures in the room felt good.

"Jamie?" Tek called out. He threaded his fingers through his damp hair and tucked the long strands behind his ears.

"Out here," Jamie called from outside.

Jamie had promised him a big surprise, and Tek was already hard in anticipation. He'd been working a lot of overtime lately, as had Jamie, and their sex life had suffered over the last week. Tek planned to rectify that problem.

Tek slipped on his flip-flops before he walked out the front door and around the side of the house to the backyard. A full moon was shining high in the sky, the illumination filtering down through the trees, lighting up the yard.

"Hey—" Whatever else Tek might have been going to say was forgotten as he spotted Jamie leaning against a tree near the small fire he had going in the burn pit. He was dressed in a pair of loose-fitting jeans and nothing else. Wrapped around his left wrist was a thick black poly rope while he was stroking the other end with his right hand. Tek licked his lips at the sight of his man dressed like that, the red and gold of the flames dancing across all those luscious muscles. But his gaze kept returning to the ropes, and the sight of them was what kicked up Tek's pulse.

"I figured it was time we finally took back what was ours, and what better place to do it than here." Jamie waved his hand around, indicating their little piece of hidden heaven.

Whether the effects of Jamie's kidnapping were finally behind them or had faded sufficiently enough, Tek didn't care. He wasn't the least bit hesitant when he stalked toward Jamie.

"This is your big surprise, huh?" Tek asked, his tone low and seductive.

"Well, it's part of the surprise, but not the big part." Jamie grabbed his crotch, emphasizing his meaning.

Tek eyed the ropes hanging from the branch above Jamie's head and then the fire. "Romantic."

"I got it in spades." Jamie ran his hand along the rope once again.

"Yes, you do. That and so much more," Tek murmured.

Jamie pushed out his chest, preening a little. "So how about you get rid of that shirt and come play with me?"

Fuck, it had been so long since they'd played this game. A game he'd thought they would never play again. A thrill raced down his spine at the chance. For the first time in what seemed like forever, he didn't feel a single sliver of reservation about what was happening. Hell, he wouldn't even be opposed to being the one doing the tying. And oh the things he wanted to do to Jamie while he was bound. Naughty things. Things that would drive his lover out of his mind with lust. He hadn't been dwelling on it, or even worrying about it. The ropes had remained in their closet, and as time passed they became nothing more than that—ropes. But he was ready, knew it, felt it in the pit of his soul. Rocco had no more control over them, and this would prove it once and for all. Seeing Jamie with the black rope in his hands and the seductive smile on his face, obviously Jamie was ready too. Tek was hard and his skin tingled with the anticipation of taking back their lives in the hottest way possible.

Tek pulled his shirt off. After scanning the area and seeing nowhere to put it, he let it drop to the ground. "From the way you're stroking that rope, I'm going to guess your plans don't include me being the one doing the tying up."

"Nope."

"I didn't think so," Tek confirmed. "So what are you going to do with me now?"

"Hmm, I'm still thinking about how I'm going to go about this," Jamie was now playing with the rope much like the way Tek had seen him stroke his cock—long, slow pulls, his fingers in a loose circle around the rope, back and forth, back and forth.

"How long you plan on torturing me with waiting?"

"Are you hard?" Jamie asked, ignoring Tek's question.

"Yes. I popped wood the second I saw what you were up to."

"Let me see. In fact, why don't you just get rid of those pants altogether?"

Without taking his gaze from Jamie's, Tek slowly slid out of his pants and boxers. The cool breeze that blew and rustled the trees was offset by the warmth of the fire. He was so fucking horny, and as much as he realized this was Jamie's show, Tek couldn't help but wonder how he could take control and get Jamie to stop staring and stalling, and out of his pants. Shouldn't be too hard. He was very, very good at distracting Jamie. After knowing him since birth, Tek was aware of all Jamie's weaknesses.

He ran his hands down his chest to his stomach. "Now that you have me all nekkid, what ya plan on doing with me?" He thrust his hips and rolled them a little, his erect cock bobbing with each movement. Trolling.

"It's not going to work." Jamie twirled the rope in his hand, holding Tek's gaze.

"What? I'm not doing anything," he responded innocently, as he continued to sway his hips and teased his cockhead with the tip of one finger.

"Uh-huh. Sure you're not. You forget, I know you probably better than you know yourself, and I damn sure recognize that sneaky look in your eyes."

"How can you see my eyes from way over there?" Tek moaned with the first hard pull on his shaft.

"I don't need to see them. I know. Now come here and turn around. And for fuck's sake, let go of your dick. That's mine. In fact, keep your hands behind your back. I don't trust you."

"You wound me, baby. How can you not trust me?" Tek pushed his bottom lip out in a mock pout.

Jamie didn't respond, but Tek didn't miss the disbelieving expression as Jamie continued to twirl the rope. Tek shrugged. It had been worth a try. He clasped his hands behind his back and moved to a position directly beneath the ropes dangling from the branch. As he passed, he made sure to brush his shoulder against Jamie and put a little wiggle in his walk, making his dick dance with each step.

Tek had no sooner turned around when Jamie grabbed Tek's hands and leaned in close to his ear. "If you don't want to do this, say so now. It's the only chance you'll get."

When Jamie pulled back, Tek held his gaze for several heartbeats, searching for any hint of hesitation on Jamie's part. There was none. The only thing in Jamie's eyes and in his expression was determination and lust.

"I want to," he finally replied with utter conviction.

"Thank fuck," Jamie said against the side of Tek's neck and then kissed the sensitive spot just below it.

Tek started to utter a snappy comeback, but Jamie smashed their lips together and short-circuited Tek's brain with a blistering kiss. Tek moaned into Jamie's mouth as his hard shaft came in contact with Jamie's groin. He thrust his hips, looking for more of the tantalizing friction.

"Damn, you're needy, aren't you?" Jamie asked against Tek's lips.

"You've been neglecting me," Tek pointed out, panting a little from the intensity of the kiss.

"May I remind you, you're the one who's been working crazy hours? I've only been doing it because you were." Jamie wound the rope around Tek's wrists. "How does that feel? Not too tight?"

Tek didn't even care anymore who was at fault. He was focused on the way Jamie's fingers felt against his flesh as he worked the soft ropes. Tek opened and closed his hand a couple of times, testing the rope. It was secure, felt good against his skin.

He shook his head. "No," he said, voice thick with growing arousal.

Jamie pressed his chest to Tek's and ran his hands up Tek's arms as he lifted them over Tek's head. Tek took the opportunity of Jamie's nearness to enjoy more of the delicious friction along his dick by rolling his hips. With Jamie's head tipped back as he secured the ropes to the branch, Tek gave in to the temptation right there and sucked up a mark on Jamie's neck, tasting his appealing skin.

Jamie shuddered, then stepped back and shook his head. "That made me all tingly."

"Get back over here, and I'll do more than make you tingle."

"Oh, you'll get your chance. How's that feel?" Jamie asked, nodding toward Tek's bound hands.

Once again, Tek opened and closed his hands, tested the strength of the ropes. "Makes me fucking hard as nails."

Jamie's gaze settled on Tek's dick, and he licked his lips. "Too bad you won't be hammering those nails. That's my job."

"Oh my God, that was the worst pun ever." Tek snorted. But he wasn't laughing when Jamie went to his knees in front of him and licked the head of Tek's cock.

Tek couldn't help but thrust, had to, begging with his body for Jamie to wrap those lips around his dick as he had so many times before. Tek would never get tired of that warm mouth and talented tongue.

Jamie denied him what he wanted. Instead he took another rope, tied it to Tek's left ankle, then wound it around Tek's leg, a section of it tickling Tek's balls when Jamie wrapped it around Tek's waist. He created the same pattern, the same tickling sensation on the other side of Tek's body, ending it by tying it to Tek's right ankle.

"Now that's what I call a work of art." Jamie sat back on his calves as he took in Tek's body with an appreciative look on his face.

The ropes around his lower half didn't restrain him, but the feel of them against his flesh were like a tight hug, each movement increasing the tickling on either side of his balls and sending sparks of warmth to spread through him, quickening his pulse and making his dick throb.

It was a compromise, a brilliant one at that. Tek could still move, would be able to free himself easily, and yet he felt completely bound, rooted to the ground, unwilling to move. The last hint of hesitation drained from Tek in the face of his growing desire.

Jamie stroked his knuckles up and down Tek's thigh and then leaned in and pressed his lips to it, placing warm kisses to Tek's skin in between the strands of ropes. Goose bumps bloomed across Tek's skin as the tingling sensation from Jamie's warm breath and soft lips rushed through him.

Jamie slid his palm over Tek's other thigh before kissing it as well. "You can't come until I tell you."

"I… I'll try not to," Tek moaned.

"This will help." Jamie pulled a small black string the size of a shoelace from his pocket and held it up.

Tek studied the lace and gave Jamie a nod. Jamie had used it before, and while Tek knew from experience it wouldn't completely stop his orgasm, it definitely helped stave it off a little longer than he could without it.

"Just hurry, please. Fuck, I want you so goddamn bad. Been too long," he said, his limbs already shaking slightly in excitement.

"Too long," Jamie repeated. He kissed the head of Tek's cock. He lapped at the precum seeping from the slit.

Tek watched Jamie eagerly lick at the engorged head as he gently wound the string around Tek's sac snugly and then around the base of his cock. "Damn that feels good."

"Yes, you do," Jamie murmured, his lips brushing along the length of Tek's cock as he spoke. "I'm going to make you feel a whole lot better." He followed the same path that his lips had taken down his cock, only using his tongue for the return trip.

Tek stared, rapt at the sight of Jamie's mouth on him. He also liked the way the string caused his erection to grow impossibly harder, the deep ruddy color of the flared head glistening in the light of the red and yellow flames. Heat rivaling that of the fire burning in the pit flared through him and ignited his nerve endings. He rocked his hips, the pleasure intensifying.

"God, Jamie. Suck me," Tek moaned as the throbbing increased. "Stop teasing."

Jamie looked up at Tek, his green eyes full of lust mingling with a hint of mischief as he swirled his tongue around the head of Tek's cock. "I'm not teasing. I'm building the anticipation," he corrected. "You always said it was half the fun."

Tek shifted in his restraints. *Shit!* He wanted to grab Jamie's hair and force his head down on Tek's straining erection. The ropes were both stimulating and frustrating as hell in equal measures. Instead, he could only stand there as Jamie continued to lightly lick at Tek's cock, and moan as he tried to find a balance with the conflicting sensations and needs. For long moments, Tek's voice was too thick, brain too scattered to form proper words. And then he didn't need words, didn't need to beg or complain because Jamie was swallowing him down, his throat contracting around Tek's dick.

"Ah fuck! That's it, Jamie. Just like that," Tek praised.

Tek thrust gently against Jamie. It was impossible to not move as Jamie began to suck him in earnest. His dark head bobbed as moaning and slurping sounds poured from Jamie and he feasted on Tek's cock. All the while, those blazing eyes never left Tek's face. Seeing Jamie like this only added to the eroticism, and Tek thrust harder, wanting, needing more as the fire within his belly raged to an inferno.

"Damn, I love to watch you suck me off," Tek said huskily. "Almost as much as I love feeling it."

Tek gasped as Jamie took him deep into his throat again, swallowing around the head several times until Tek felt his orgasm rush down his spine. "Ja—oh fuck…. Jamie, I'm gonna—"

Jamie jerked back and fisted Tek's cock, making him whimper with the near painful grip. "Not yet," Jamie growled, his voice sounding raw.

"Shit!" Tek began to tremble all over as the need to come overwhelmed him, yet he couldn't with the viselike grip on his cock. For long torturous seconds, Tek stood teetering on the edge, unable to leap off into orgasm nor step back and catch his breath.

"Deep breaths," Jamie encouraged as he nuzzled Tek's hip.

Tek hung his head, eyes squeezed tightly shut and his jaw clenched until the immediate need began to subside. The rush of blood in his ears drowned out the sounds of the crackling fire and rustling of the trees.

"That was mean," he grumbled, working to slow his labored breathing and pounding heart.

"Aww. Let me make it up to you." Jamie went to his feet and pecked Tek on the lips.

"I don't think that is going to make up for it," Tek huffed. Christ, his nuts were so tight they ached with the demanding need to empty them. "C'mon, man," Tek pleaded. "I need to come. Like right-fucking-now before my sac bursts."

Jamie soothed his hand over Tek's rapidly rising and falling chest, then kissed him again. "Soon," he promised and stepped back.

"Hey! Why are you stopping? I just need… fuck, just a little more and I was there," Tek complained pitifully as he looked down at his engorged cock and cringed. The black string looked obscene against the deep red color. "Jamie, dammit, finish it. Make me come," he demanded, the sound coming out suspiciously like a whine.

"Keep your shirt on," Jamie sniffed.

"I would," Tek grumbled. "But you made me take the damn thing off."

He was wound up tighter than a forty-year-old virgin in a whorehouse. His muscles were bowstring tight and trembled with the exertion. And damn, he wanted to come so fucking bad. Tek was on the verge of begging, pleading, sobbing if he had to. Tek loved foreplay— hours of it—but their foreplay generally meant taking the edge off before the real heat was fired up. This was just torture after being too busy for sex for the past week, and dammit, he deserved to get off. Needed to like he needed his next fucking breath. He pulled against his restraints, the movement causing his throbbing cock to bob painfully.

Jamie stood in front of Tek with a sly smile curling his lip. He was enjoying Tek's discomfort a wee bit too much. Tek ground his molars and squeezed his eyes shut. He wasn't going to beg, dammit. He wasn't. After several deep breaths, the immediate need to come waned, but he knew it was still lurking just beneath the surface. If he opened his eyes and looked at Jamie or received one touch, he would blow like a fucking fountain.

"Aren't you going to look at me?"

"Nope." Tek shook his head vigorously. He couldn't.

"Aren't you just the least bit curious about what I'm doing?"

Tek knew what Jamie was doing. He was standing there in those damn jeans that hung just below his cum gutters. Tracks he wanted to fill, to lick, to…. No. No. No. He took several deep breaths.

"Give me a minute, will you?" He did his best to think of the foulest, disgusting things he could. It took several moments before he felt he was in better control of himself, but still he kept his eyes closed.

"Fine, be a brat." Jamie laughed.

The suspense was killing him, but Tek didn't dare open his eyes. He pulled at his restraints, the ropes cutting in a bit, binding him, serving to remind him he was at Jamie's mercy. Suddenly there was warmth against his back and the sound of fabric rustling, and Tek smiled to himself. Jamie's pants were falling away and soon he wouldn't have to rein in his orgasm, but would be shouting Jamie's name to the forest.

"I should keep you tied to this damn tree and make you listen to me come," Jamie murmured from behind him.

Tek opened his eyes and watched the fire dance in front of him. "But you won't."

Jamie wasn't touching him, but he was close enough that the heat radiating between them was evidence of just where Jamie was, and Jamie's breath was warm against Tek's back as he spoke.

"How can you be so sure? I think it would be fun to taunt and tease you until you can beg convincingly."

Tek's smile grew wider when he heard the crinkle of a wrapper and, shortly thereafter, the sound of a cap being snapped open. "Hmm, I don't know, Jamie. I think it would put an interesting twist on things if you tried to fuck me till I begged you to stop. We haven't ever tried that one."

"I bet I could." Jamie ran his finger down Tek's spine to the crease of his ass. "But not tonight."

"Not up to the challenge, huh?"

"Oh, trust me. I'm up all right," Jamie countered. He emphasized his statement by pressing his cock against Tek's ass. "It's the fact you've denied me a good O the last week that has me hesitating to accept your challenge." Jamie splayed his hand on Tek's stomach as he rutted against Tek's ass.

Tek swallowed hard. Jamie's warm hands on him caused Tek's nerve endings to zing. "Jamie," Tek whimpered, no longer in the mood to taunt his man further.

Jamie continued to rut against Tek, licking and kissing Tek's shoulders and neck with his hot mouth. His husky words were incomprehensible as Jamie spoke and moaned against Tek's skin. The hand on his stomach rubbed up and down, each downward pass teasing the head of Tek's cock. Tek widened his stance. He was breathless and thankful for the ropes or he'd be on his ass with how weak his knees were. When Jamie's cock pressed against his hole, Tek bent as far as the ropes would allow and held his breath. The forest around them grew dead silent as if it too were holding its breath in anticipation.

Tek pressed his ass back against Jamie's cock, greedy to have Jamie buried balls-deep inside him. Jamie was rocking his hips back and forth, back and forth, not putting any real strength in his thrust, teasing, until Tek thought he'd go mad. When Jamie moved his hips forward, Tek anticipated the movement and shoved back with all his might. They both hissed at the sudden invasion. Jamie instantly went still and gave Tek time to adjust to the intrusion, but Tek wasn't having it. His body was thrumming. He needed Jamie to move, to plow into him. He wanted to feel the burn. He wriggled in Jamie's firm grip, then contracted and clenched his ass over and over until Jamie let out a low rumbling moan and started to move.

"Damn you, Tek," Jamie groaned. "You know exactly how to strip me of every ounce of control."

Buried deep inside Tek's body, Jamie held Tek's stomach with one hand. He splayed the other hand over Tek's heart and pulled him to his full height as he rolled his hips.

"Ah…. Damn," Tek panted, pulling harder against his restraints as his toes curled. He adjusted his stance and the slight change forced Jamie deeper still.

"Does that feel good, baby? You like my cock deep inside you, don't you?"

"Oh yeah," Tek gritted out between harsh breaths. "I like it slamming into me too. C'mon, Jamie, fuck me."

The hand on Tek's stomach moved down, those nimble fingers releasing the binding on Tek's cock before tightening around it in almost a painful grip. Jamie rubbed his thumb over the head, massaging the precum seeping from his slit into the sensitive flesh. Jamie buried his face in Tek's damp and tangled hair, his panting breath hot on Tek's skull as he moved his hips faster, harder, yet still held Tek close.

All conscious thought fled, need and passion spiraling out of control, and Tek gave himself over to Jamie completely. The hand on his cock tightened and sped up, working it at the same fast pace as the dick stabbing into him. Jamie worked his ass like a man possessed, and Tek welcomed every hard thrust, every stroke along his length, moaning his pleasure to the night sky.

It had been too long; they'd known it wouldn't last long, couldn't. After a couple harder thrusts, Jamie was screaming Tek's name, his cock swelling impossibly harder, stretching Tek to the brink, and ripping the orgasm from him without warning. Tek came longer and harder than he'd ever experienced. His head spun as everything in his body went tight, shut down, in the face of unimaginable ecstasy.

Finally, as the last drop of seed pulsed from his body, Tek gasped, panting for breath, with Jamie still buried deep inside him. Tek trembled with the exertion it took to keep himself upright, thankful for the strength of the binds.

After several minutes, Jamie finally shifted, sliding out of Tek's body with a moan, and removed the restraints around Tek's wrists. Jamie held him and eased him down to the ground. They lay on their sides, Jamie's chest against his back, on the jumble of clothing before the waning fire.

Jamie rubbed his thumb over Tek's wrist. "You okay?"

Tek was boneless, his brain scattered, his body completely satisfied. "I'm so much better than okay. Jesus, that was… yeah."

"What?" Jamie chuckled.

"I have no words for just how fucking good that felt."

Jamie was silent for a moment, then kissed the side of Tek's head before whispering, "You don't know how happy I am right this second."

Tek stared at the burning embers that were keeping the front of him just as warm as the big body pressed against his back. In his happy, contented state, he could now admit that he'd been worried something would go wrong, but it hadn't.

"I think I do," Tek whispered and then amended it to "No, I know I do. This world keeps throwing shit at us and we just keep knocking down each and every obstacle."

"That's 'cause we have each other," Jamie said softly.

"Always."

During idle times, I admit my thoughts will run away from me. Having too much time on my hands has never been a good thing, and my mind can easily become my own worst enemy. Doubt begins to settle in and with it that dormant fear rears its ugly head. Will I continue to suffer from such things—yup, always. But when doubt starts clouding my mind and fear grips me, an easy solution is to get my ass up and get busy. A busy mind and body doesn't have time to dwell.

Tek Cain

Happy Birthday

LEANING AGAINST the railing, Tek stared out over the skyline of the city. This had quickly become his favorite place to hang out and think when he was home. The vastness of the city beyond reminded him just how small he was in the grand scheme of things. Since their party, Tek had been contemplating Jamie's question: *You know, acting like posers?* Were they? Tek still didn't have the answer. People like him and Jamie didn't live in posh apartments; they didn't have vacation homes in the woods, doormen, and they damn sure didn't have a piggy bank full of money unless they'd stolen it. People like them didn't work for it, they took what they wanted. And wasn't that what they were doing by living in such a nice place? Taking from Blake without working for it.

Propping his elbow on the railing, he leaned his cheek against his palm and, with his other hand, ran the long strands of his goatee through his thumb and index finger, looking to the landscape for the answers but finding none. It hadn't been all that long ago they'd arrived in this city, broke and desperate, and now at twenty-five, they were living in grandeur without earning it. Everything seemed too easy. Just like the non-fallout from killing Rocco. *Too damn easy.* They didn't deserve this place. Fuck, they *were* posers. The proverbial other shoe would eventually fall. It had to. It always did. Life never was this damn easy for anyone, especially for people like them.

"Hey, you're supposed to be getting ready," Jamie informed him as he joined Tek on the balcony.

"I don't know if I want to go out," he replied without taking his gaze from the view.

Jamie ran his hand down Tek's back, pushing up close. "What's the matter?"

"Remember the night of our dinner party, you asked me if we were posers. I just realized we are. We don't deserve this." He waved his hand toward the city. "None of this."

"Where the hell is this coming from?"

Tek stood straight and placed his hands on the railing, squeezing it tight. "What have we done to deserve this? We certainly haven't worked for it."

"We survived," Jamie said softly. "That's what we did to deserve this. We survived and against all the odds we didn't let the violence define us, but rather we let it catapult us to reach for a better life."

Tek turned his head. "You don't get to live like this simply by surviving, Jamie. People endure worse shit than we did every day and they don't get this. We're kidding ourselves. No one kills the president of a dangerous motorcycle gang and just walks away. There has to be retribution. You have to pay the fucking price. That's how it goes, Jamie. You gotta pay the fucking price." His voice rose until he was shouting and anger and dread were churning in his gut.

Jamie didn't so much as flinch in the face of Tek's anger. Instead, he laid his palm against Tek's cheek, his expression gentle and his voice calm when he said, "We paid the price, Tek. We paid in blood, sweat, and tears from the moment we were born. Twenty-five years we've been paying for our violent births. It's time to reap some of those rewards."

Tek was breathing harshly, staring at Jamie, and trying his best to comprehend what Jamie was saying despite his fury and despair.

"C'mon, Tek, deep breaths." Jamie pulled him into a tight embrace. "I've never lied to you, so trust me when I tell you, you deserve everything we have and so much more."

Tek laid his forehead on Jamie's shoulder and tried to remember how to breathe.

They held each other for a long while, Tek clutching Jamie to him like a lifeline until the rage and despair began to seep from him.

"That's it. I got ya. You gotta believe me," Jamie murmured as he stroked his hand over Tek's head.

Finally, after what seemed like an eternity, the tension in Tek's body released its tight grip on his muscles and he could take a full breath. He lifted his head and rolled his neck.

"If I'm like this on my twenty-fifth birthday, can you imagine what I'm going to be like on my fortieth?"

"And I'll be right there to hold you until it passes."

"God, I love you," Tek whispered. He pressed his lips to Jamie's, letting the last of all the ill feelings go.

"I love you too," Jamie said and kissed him back. "You okay now?"

"Yeah, I think so."

"We don't have to go to the club tonight if you'd rather just stay home. We can curl up on the couch and I can spend the evening doing my best to show you just how much you deserve."

"No, I'm better. I don't want to ruin our birthday by being a raging crazy man."

"Well, you are a crazy man. I mean seriously, look who you picked for a partner." Jamie chuckled.

Tek wasn't laughing. "That's not crazy, that's the one sane thing I did in my life. Smartest too." He kissed Jamie one more time and then ran his fingers through his hair, smoothing down the tangled mess. "You know, I'm not sure what brought all that on tonight. I got to be more careful of thinking too deeply."

"I think you're always going to have bouts of doubt and anger. Hell, I know I will. But I also think they'll happen less and less often as time goes on."

"I hope you're right."

"I am," Jamie replied, sounding completely sure of himself. He patted Tek on the arm. "Let's go get dressed. We have a celebration to attend, yeah?"

"Yeah."

"JAMIE! TEK! Happy birthday," Micah screeched and then gave them both a peck on the cheek.

"Thank you," they both replied.

"I was just coming to get more bubbly. The bar in the back is seriously lacking in party favors."

Jamie wrinkled his nose. "Don't get any on my account. I don't like champagne and Tek here don't either."

Micah gave a dramatic sigh. "It's not about the taste. It's about how you look while holding it and the way it tickles your nose."

"You're hopeless. You do realize that, don't you?" Tek chuckled.

"Completely," Micah responded with a wink and then waved them on. "Now you two yummy birthday bears go get a drink. Everyone is waiting for you."

They both watched Micah swish and sway to the back room. Only when he disappeared did they turn to look at each other and begin laughing. "I really love that little shit. C'mon, yummy bear, let's go get this party started."

"Right behind ya."

They stepped into the members-only area, which was closed for their private party, and immediately everyone went silent for a heartbeat and then a chorus of "Happy Birthday" filled the air. The club was decorated with blue, red, yellow, and green streamers and balloons. At the far end of the bar, a table was stacked with brightly wrapped boxes and colorful bags. Next to it was another table with a large birthday cake, complete with a shit-ton of candles, no doubt twenty-five for each of them.

Jamie grabbed Tek's hand, entwined their fingers, and headed to the bar with a big goofy grin on his face.

"Happy birthday," Blake said and shook each of their hands. "What can I get you two to drink?"

"I'll have a draft," Tek said.

"Not me. It's my birthday. I want one of those fruity drinks with a little umbrella and lots and lots of alcohol in it."

Tek's brows nearly disappeared into his hairline as he stared at Jamie.

Jamie started laughing. "That's what happens when the first person to greet us is Micah. He's rubbing off on me. Beer is fine."

"He does have a way of doing that," Ty said and waved over Phillip.

Phillip was a part-time bartender in the main club. Jamie was glad to see Micah and Ty would have the night off. Phillip wished them a happy birthday as he set two drafts down in front of them. There was a stir in the crowd that drew Jamie's attention.

"Have a seat," Blake told them. "The entertainment is starting."

Jamie and Tek stared at Blake and then each other. Jamie shrugged. "Boss's orders."

They started for an empty table, but Jamie caught sight of Max and Aiden waving them over from a table near the stage. Only then did he notice the rest of their gang. The music was thumping through the club, the lights flashing on the dancers on the stage as they snapped and popped in a hip-hop fashion.

Jamie slid into an empty chair and waved at the guys, the music too loud to talk over. Tek took the other empty chair next to him. They sat shoulder to shoulder, Tek's hand on his thigh as they enjoyed the choreographed routine on the stage. The men were dressed in tight black leather shorts, strips of wide leather in the shape of an X across their torsos, and heavy soled boots. They moved in perfect sync, and before long Jamie found himself tapping his foot along to the beat, enjoying the way the men moved. He'd never been much of a dancer, hadn't really had the opportunity to learn. Hell, he'd never even been to a dance, but he enjoyed watching it.

Jamie sipped on his beer, head bobbing in between drinks. Tek was getting into the groove and was swaying and tapping his hand on Jamie's thigh. When the song ended, the crowd cheered and clapped. Jamie set his beer on the table and brought his fingers to his mouth and whistled.

One of the dancers broke formation and took a microphone someone from behind the curtain held out to him. "I understand we have not one, but two birthdays to celebrate tonight. How about the birthday boys come join us in a little bump-and-grind action?"

"Uh-oh," Jamie heard Tek mutter. *My thoughts exactly.* Jamie waved his hand side to side and shook his head. No way was he getting up there and bumpin' anything.

"Everyone, let's give Tek and Jamie a little encouragement, shall we?"

The crowd began to applaud, whistle, and cheer.

"C'mon, guys, go show them how it's done," Bobby encouraged and gave Jamie's shoulder a little shove.

"Shake it, yummy bears," Micah added.

The rest of the table tried their best to entice him and Tek to get on the stage, but they both stayed rooted to their seats.

"I'm so going to kick Blake's ass," Tek muttered against Jamie's ear.

"I'll hold him down."

Suddenly the dancers all rushed off the stage and grabbed Jamie's and Tek's arms, pulling them out of their chairs. Jamie had no doubt he could have fought them off if he'd had the notion, but what the hell. He'd just stand up on the stage and watch the dancers.

They had another idea.

A strange version of "Happy Birthday" blasted through the speakers, and halfway through the song, Jamie unbelievably was following along with the simple steps of a line dance and Tek—Jesus, Tek was shaking and gyrating. By the end of the song, Jamie was running into the other dancers, stepping on toes, and his cheeks were damp from laughing so damn hard.

He was still laughing, his arm slung over Tek's shoulder as they made it back to their chairs. He picked up his drink in a toast as everyone applauded and cheered, then downed his beer. Dancing? Who would have ever thought he'd be up on a stage dancing, and even more shocking was how much fun he'd had. He and Tek should go out dancing more often.

Jamie leaned over and placed a big sloppy kiss to Tek's cheek. "You definitely got the moves."

His glass to his lips, Tek winked at him. "It's all in the hips. Just like fucking." That got everyone cheering and clapping again.

Phillip rolled over a cart filled with bottles of champagne and glass flutes. He poured a glass for each member of their table. Micah winked at him when Jamie held the delicate glass in his big hands. Once everyone was served, Blake stood and raised his glass.

"I'd like to make a toast in honor of Jamie and Tek. The day I met you two, it was like welcoming in old friends. You both have become important to the club as well as to those who enjoy it. I am honored to have you in my life and hope to for many, many years to come. Happy birthday, my friends."

"Hear, hear!"

Jamie raised his glass and nodded in Blake's direction. He brought the glass to his lips but had a difficult time swallowing past the lump that had formed in his throat. Blake wasn't the only one who felt honored. This had to be one of the best birthdays of his life, and with the bright future he and Tek had ahead of them, as well as the friends who would be a part of it, he had no doubt that this was just a hint of what was to come.

The night was filled with warm wishes, hugs, and laughs. The cake cut and gifts opened, Jamie took Tek's hand and took him to the center of the small area cleared of tables being used as a dance floor. As a slow song played, Jamie held Tek in his arms and swayed to the mellow rhythm.

"I almost wish we would have had the party at home," Tek whispered sleepily.

"You know, our old room is right over there, and I do believe it's not occupied at the moment."

Tek pulled back slightly and met Jamie's gaze with a smile. "We wouldn't have to say good-bye."

"Nope," Jamie agreed, returning the grin. "They'd simply think we were going in to get a little birthday nookie."

Tek pulled out of Jamie's arms. "We *are* going in to get a little nookie. Let's go."

Jamie laughed and followed Tek to the room. Just as they stepped through the door, Tek cursed. "Be right back."

"Where are you going?"

Instead of answering, Tek called out behind him, "Don't start without me."

He leaned against the wall and shoved his hands in his pants pocket to keep from doing just that. His fingers brushed against the smooth metal. He had planned on giving it to Tek when they got home but.... He pulled out the ring and closed his hand around it. He then sat on the edge of the bed and kicked off his shoes.

Tek entered the room with a small flat box with a silver bow wrapped around it. He closed the door and locked it before saying, "You didn't think I'd forget your birthday, did ya?"

"I would hope not since it's the same day as yours."

Tek sat down next to him. "I had the hardest time coming up with a good idea for a gift. Everything seemed... I don't know, impersonal. So... here." He handed Jamie the box. "I hope you don't think it's stupid."

"I'm sure I won't." Jamie pulled the ribbon off and lifted the lid on the box. An old tattered notebook lay inside, the same one he'd seen Tek writing in for years. His journal. Jamie looked up at Tek in confusion.

"I've been writing in it since I was little. It's the story of my life, of our lives."

"I can't take this. This is your private thoughts."

"I want you to have it. Hell, it's all about you anyway and I don't have anything to hide from you."

Jamie's chest ached with the trust Tek was putting in his hands. He wasn't just giving him a journal, but sharing his most intimate thoughts and secrets.

Jamie's eyes burned with unshed tears. "Tek, I don't know what to say."

"Then don't say anything." He leaned over and pressed his lips to Jamie's. "I'm sure you can come up with another way to say thank you."

Jamie opened his hand and held the ring out.

Tek looked down at it and then back up at Jamie. "That's not exactly what I had in mind." But he was smiling as he took it out of Jamie's hand. He held it between his fingers and, with his other hand, ran his index finger over the thick band of white gold. "Is this what I think it is?"

"Well, I figured after twenty-five years together, it was time I made an honest man out of you."

Tek took the box from Jamie and set it on the bedside table and laid the ring on top of it. He kissed Jamie again, sliding his hand under Jamie's shirt to stroke the small of his back. "Hmm, now I think it's time I say thank you." He moved his hand higher and kissed a trail along Jamie's jaw.

Jamie moaned and lifted his chin, giving Tek free access to his neck while he unbuttoned Tek's shirt and ran his hands over the warm skin of Tek's stomach and ribs and through the soft hair on his chest.

Tek mouthed at Jamie's neck, sucking up a mark. He stopped kissing Jamie only long enough to pull his shirt up and off before turning them and easing Jamie down onto the mattress. He moaned again, arching a little when Tek moved down his neck to his collarbone, then lower still. He teased one of Jamie's nipples with the tip of his tongue as he ran his hands over Jamie's stomach.

"I still can't believe this is going to be all mine," Tek murmured.

"It always has been," Jamie assured him, threading his fingers through the soft strands of Tek's hair.

Tek bit lightly, dragging his teeth over Jamie's other erect nub. Jamie's breath caught, and he released it, the air coming out as a rumbling sound of approval when Tek began sucking on the nipple, flicking his tongue over the sensitive flesh. Tek teased at Jamie's waistband with his free hand, one of his fingers dipping below it to brush ever so slightly over the head of Jamie's cock.

"God, that feels good." Jamie arched into Tek's touch.

"Going to make you feel even better." Tek moved back up Jamie's body, covering him and taking his mouth in a deep kiss. He unfastened Jamie's pants, freeing his straining erection.

Jamie slid his hand around to the back of Tek's head, fisting it in his hair, deepening the kiss as he thrust up against Tek's palm.

Tek ended the kiss, breathing harshly. "These have got to go." He tugged on Jamie's pants.

Jamie lifted his hips, making it easier for Tek to pull off his pants. Tek kissed him again, slower this time, more intense. Without taking his mouth from Jamie's, Tek somehow managed to wriggle out of his slacks. Jamie closed his eyes and sighed into Tek's mouth as Tek's shaft slid across his hip.

Jamie snaked his hand beneath the pillow. *Thank you, Blake, and your attention to detail.* He took the lube he found there and pressed it into Tek's hand. "Want you," Jamie whispered against Tek's lips, his voice deep and husky. "Want to feel you inside me."

"Want that too," Tek groaned and wedged himself between Jamie's spread legs, then bent low for another passionate kiss.

Pulse roaring in his ears, his cock throbbing with need, he wantonly spread his legs wider, still thrusting hard against Tek's groin. Jamie slid his hands over Tek's back, pressing down, encouraging him to move, fingers digging in.

"Do it. Need you."

A cool, lube-slick finger pressed against Jamie's hole, and his eyes fluttered shut as Tek pushed the tip of his finger inside.

"Damn, I love how tight your ass is. The way it clamps down on my finger." He worked it in a little farther, sliding it back and forth so damn slowly and carefully, but Jamie needed more.

He clutched Tek's arms and bore down hard. "Don't tease me."

Tek slid his finger deeper, working it hard and fast, then added a second. "This what you want?"

Jamie shook his head, thrusting in earnest. He tried to speak, to tell Tek what he wanted, but his throat was dry and his words came out thick, more of a groan. But Tek understood, knew what Jamie needed, and he pulled his hand away. Before Jamie could miss it, the wide head of Tek's cock was pushing in, stretching him, and filling him.

"God, Jamie, your ass." Tek plunged deep. "I can feel it squeezing me, stroking me like a tight wet fist."

"Fuck, you make me burn." He leaned up and nipped at Tek's kiss-swollen bottom lip and then cried out when Tek pinched his nipple, twisting it as delicious sparks of pain skittered along his nerve endings.

Tek slid his arms beneath Jamie's legs, lifting them up and out, nearly bending Jamie in half when he planted his hands on the mattress and fucked Jamie hard and deep. Jamie slid his hand between their bodies and grabbed his cock, squeezing it and stroking in time with Tek's fast pace.

Their grunts and moans of pleasure echoed around the room, and the headboard banged against the wall as Tek rammed into Jamie's ass again and again. The look of bliss on Tek's face, his lust-filled eyes, and the perfect stretch and burn as Tek continued to thrust was sensory overload. The intensity pushed Jamie closer and closer to the edge.

"Not going to last…. Fuck… Tek… I—" Jamie's babbling caught in his throat and he gasped as his orgasm washed over him.

During each pulse of his release, Tek rocked into him with stuttering thrusts. His muscles coiled with tension, and he held on until the last drop seeped from Jamie's body. Only then did he close his eyes, holding his breath for a second longer, then moaned softly as he came deep inside Jamie's body.

His legs were released and they fell heavily to the mattress. Jamie laid his slick hand over his chest, felt the rapid beat of his heart beneath his palm, his breath harsh.

Tek collapsed on top of him, burying his face in the side of Jamie's neck, his breathing just as fast as Jamie's, his rapid heartbeat thumping against the back of Jamie's hand. They were in no hurry to move, Tek melting into Jamie, and he welcomed the heavy weight and warmth.

Jamie skated his fingers along the damp skin of Tek's back, content and boneless. Completely relaxed, he barely noticed when Tek shifted them, pulled Jamie closer, and covered them with the soft cotton sheet.

Jamie supposed he should get up and clean them, but he had no desire to move at the moment or put a fraction of an inch between them. For the moment, he lay in Tek's warm embrace, enjoying the last minutes of his birthday, happy knowing by the next one he'd be married to this amazing man. He had no doubt that he deserved a happily ever after and not a single shred of doubt that Tek deserved one too.

I've read each word within this journal a hundred times, maybe even a thousand. Ran my fingers over each page, each doodle and smudge. I've added my own tears to the remnants of yours. I lived each and every one of the events written here, but to read about my life through your eyes was the greatest gift I've ever been given. Each time I read it, I would come to this blank page and it mocked me, the story unfinished. But perhaps that was the point. Our story didn't end the day you gave me your journal. It was simply yet to be written.

Today will be the last time I read your words. The book of our past will be secured away until the book of our future has been written.

The second greatest gift you gave me was the day you said "I do." You made a vow before our friends to love me till the end of time. I'm holding you to that, and if you're reading this, then you kept your word. Just like I always knew you would.

Happy twenty-fifth anniversary.

Forever yours,
Jamie Cain

A Dream Come True

THE GRAY light of dawn crept through the curtains. In the distance, a rooster crowed, welcoming the sun.

Jamie rolled over, buried his head beneath the covers, and nudged Tek. "It's your turn."

"I don't want to. Sleeping here," Tek grumbled. He pulled his pillow over his head.

Jamie nudged him again. "You have to. It's your turn."

In the warmth of his blanket cocoon, Jamie started to drift off, only the soft snores coming from Tek preventing him from getting back to sleep. "C'mon, Tek. I let you sleep in yesterday. You gotta get up. Besides this was your idea."

"Why didn't you talk me out of it?" Tek asked, his voice muffled by the pillow.

"I tried, but you're so goddamn stubborn you wouldn't listen. I wanted to be a mountain man."

"We don't have any mountains around here," Tek reminded him.

Knowing it was futile to get back to sleep, Jamie huffed, threw off his covers, and sat up. "Fine, forest man. Now get up, Farmer Pete." He jerked Tek's pillow away from him and threw it across the room.

Tek rubbed his eyes and then stared up at Jamie sleepily. "Can't I have just thirty more minutes? Pretty, pretty please. I'm tired."

"Nope, not unless you want impatient cows busting the fence and helping themselves to breakfast again?"

"Ugh! No, I don't feel like mending fences today." Finally seeing reason, Tek sat up and leaned against the headboard. He yawned and scratched his belly. "Want to help?"

"Nope." Jamie pecked Tek's cheek and slid from the bed. "I have to start lunch."

"Lunch? But we haven't even had breakfast yet," Tek called out behind him as Jamie headed to the kitchen to put on a pot of coffee. First things first.

Jamie grabbed the pot, took it to the sink, and flipped on the tap. "Yeah, I know, but feeding eleven men takes some major prep work."

There was silence from the bedroom as Jamie got the coffee brewing, but he knew the second it hit Tek when he heard him shout "Fuck!" followed by his feet hitting the floor and the bathroom door slamming.

Since renovations were completed the previous year and they'd moved to the cabin full-time, Tek had often lost track of what day it was. Jamie still working—albeit from home—he had become the one to organize everything, pay bills, order stock, and keep Tek informed of the day of the week. Tek's argument—and a logical one—was that since Jamie had to be on the computer most days anyway, it would be easier than teaching Tek how to use the budget program. While Tek was comfortable with computers, he really wasn't a fan of technology. Now, if Jamie could just find a logical excuse not to help with morning chores, he'd be golden.

Dammit, why did those baby chicks and those calves with their big brown eyes have to have been so damn cute anyway? Better question was, why in the hell did he promise to help if Tek bought them all? Jamie shrugged. Oh well, once the kittens were born, he'd be making more promises in order to keep them all as well. He was such a glutton for punishment.

Jamie looked up from the mugs of coffee he'd just poured to see Tek walk in the kitchen wearing a light blue T-shirt stretched tight across his chest and a pair of loose-fitting Wranglers that hung low on his hips. Damn, country living sure as hell agreed with Tek.

Jamie brought the mugs to the table, whistling. "I gotta say, Farmer Pete, you are one damn fine-looking man. Must be all that fresh air and good country living you're doing."

Tek took a seat at the table with a big smile, making him all the more handsome. He flexed his biceps. "Amazing what a little hoeing and shoveling shit can do for the guns."

"All right, all right, put your weapons away before you hurt yourself."

"Yeah, whatever. You love them," Tek said smugly and took a sip of his coffee.

Jamie also loved the way Tek was always relaxed with a laid-back attitude, even when working hard. He loved the way constantly being outdoors had lightened Tek's hair and tanned his skin. And yeah, he definitely loved the way the hard labor-filled days had strengthened Tek's body in ways a gym never could duplicate. Fuck, who was he kidding? Jamie loved everything about the man he was lucky enough to have as his friend and lover.

"That I do, babe." Jamie snatched a bag of muffins he'd picked up at the local bakery and set them on the table before taking a seat and sipping on his own very much-needed caffeine.

"What time's everyone getting in?" Tek asked around a big bite of muffin.

"Two. I'm really looking forward to seeing the guys and getting a chance to show off what we've gotten done around here. I can't believe it's been a year since we've all been together." He and Tek had been to the club a couple of times, but it was hard getting away with the animals, and both times someone from the group had been missing.

"Right, and I'm curious as hell what Ty's big announcement is. I hate surprises. Don't know why they couldn't just tell us over the phone."

"Because they know you are worse than a kid on Christmas Eve, and they like torturing you."

"Well, it's working," Tek huffed.

"And you should be too. Drink your coffee and I'll pour you another in a to-go cup. The sooner you get your chores done, the sooner you can help me with lunch."

"I don't cook." Tek finished the last of his muffin.

"That's 'cause you suck at it, but you can help me with something that doesn't involve the stove."

"It's not the only thing I suck at," Tek said and waggled his brows.

"That's why I keep you around," Jamie teased. "Now go feed the critters before I change my mind."

Tek washed down his muffin with the rest of his coffee, then pushed out of his chair and leaned down close, his lips nearly touching Jamie's. "Like you would ever change your mind. You love me too much." Tek then kissed him and wiped the smart reply right off Jamie's tongue. "And lucky for you, I love you too much to ever leave."

Tek sauntered out the door, leaving Jamie a little dazed and feeling really, really fucking lucky.

"THE PLACE looks amazing," Bobby complimented. "Thanks for giving us the grand tour."

"My pleasure. Jamie and I are pretty proud of the old place."

"Old place?" Tackett snorted. "Looks like you've remodeled every square inch. I hardly recognize it."

"Well, considering it's gone from a one-room shack to a two-bedroom, two-bath shack, it doesn't surprise me," Tek countered. "We're adding on to the barn in the fall. Jamie can't seem to say no to strays."

"Lucky for you, huh," Ty teased.

Tek pointed a finger at him. "You're not allowed to talk to me unless it's to tell me your big secret."

"Mmm, smell that? Smells like Jamie's burgers are about ready. We should head out back." Ty made a hasty retreat out the back door.

Tek frowned at Ty's disappearing form.

"He can be an irritating little shit, can't he?" Blake patted Tek on the back.

Tek's frowned deepened. "You know what this big announcement is, don't you?"

"Oh wow, I just got a whiff of those burgers. Better get out there before Ty eats them all," Blake said without acknowledging Tek's question and followed his boy out the door.

"He's not the only one who's an irritating little shit," Tek called out.

Bobby laughed and Mason giggled. Tek rounded on them. "Do you know?"

Bobby held up his hands, and Mason, still laughing, stepped behind his Dom. "We know as much as you do. But may I suggest we go after them, you hold them down, and Mason and I will beat it out of them."

"Sounds like a plan."

On the back deck, Max, Aiden, and Rig were already sitting at the table with their plates full, Blake and Ty in the process of filling theirs. "Change of plans," Tek told Bobby in a stage-whisper. "Burgers first, then we beat 'em. Deal?" He held out his fist.

"Deal," Bobby agreed and bumped his fist.

Tek continued to hold out his fist. "C'mon, little man, don't leave me hanging."

"Deal," Mason responded and bumped Tek's fist.

"Who's getting beat?" Jamie asked when Tek stepped up and accepted the offered plate.

"Ty and Blake."

"Are they teasing you again, the big ol' meanies?"

"I never said a word," Ty called out.

"I really dislike him," Tek grumbled. "I think Blake's been slacking on his Dom duties."

"Trust me, I haven't been slacking. He simply responds only to true dominance," Blake countered.

"Ooh, burn!" Micah snickered.

"You all can leave now." Tek plopped down at the table with his plate. "I don't know why I invited any of you."

"You didn't. I did," Jamie corrected and took the seat next to him.

"You can leave with them," Tek grumbled, snatched a beer from the bucket, and popped the top. He took a long pull while everyone at the table laughed.

"I think you should tell him," Bobby said to Blake. "I think you've made him suffer enough."

Tek gawked at Bobby. "You knew," he accused.

Bobby simply smiled and took a big bite of his burger.

"You're on the to-be-beaten list too." Tek then pointed at a very guilty-looking Mason. "You too."

"I think we've had enough fun at Tek's expense," Blake announced. "But honestly I didn't want to say anything until we were a hundred percent sure the deal went through."

"What deal?" Jamie asked, the same question Tek was wondering.

"We've sold the club."

"What!" both he and Jamie said at the same time. Their eyes met, Jamie's expression as shocked as Tek felt.

"Why would you do that?" Tek asked.

"It's time. Ty and I have decided we don't want our child growing up in the city, so we're moving back to Oklahoma."

"Oklahoma?" *Oklahoma?* What the hell. Blake hated the country, the ranch life, the smell of shit. *Why in the—? Wait a minute....* "Child?"

Ty's smile was brilliant, lighting up his entire face. "Yeah, Blake's mom has been bugging us for years. We finally gave in and hired a surrogate. We're going to be dads!"

"What...? When...? Oh hell, congratulations!" Jamie hooted and jumped to his feet. He hugged Blake and then Ty.

Tek ran his hand through his hair, still stunned. Blake and Ty were going to be dads? In Oklahoma? Wow, he certainly wouldn't have seen that coming. How did that even work? Who cared how it worked? It was fucking awesome. Tek hugged them both as well.

"So, Oklahoma, huh?"

"Yup," Blake said with a nod. "I figured a kid could do worse than growing up on a ranch."

"And you all knew about this?" Tek asked, looking at the rest of the gang.

"We're going too," Max announced.

"My brother has been trying to get me to move there for years," Aiden explained. "I figure with Blake and Ty moving back to Pegasus, it was finally time to take Lorcan and Quinn up on their offer."

"And you're okay with this?" Tek asked Max. "What about your practice?"

"I'll be traveling back and forth between the two cities for a while until I can get someone to take over my patients, but yeah, I'm totally okay with this. Aiden can be very convincing."

"What about the rest of you? Are you all moving to Oklahoma too?"

"Oh, honey, not me and Tackett," Micah announced. "I'd go simply mad in a little town. I like shopping too much, but we're going to visit and play cowboy. Maybe even a little pony. Ain't that right, Aiden?"

"Shut up," Aiden huffed, his cheeks turning pink.

"And what about you guys?" Jamie asked, looking in the direction of Bobby, Rig, and Mason.

"Nope, we're sticking around and making sure the new owners don't fuck everything up," Rig said. "Plus, we love our place, but like Micah and Tackett, plan on going cowboy-up every now and then."

Tek sat back in his chair, stunned, as his friends, his family, talked about all the changes that were happening in their lives. While

Tek was happy for all of them, he couldn't help but feel a twinge of sadness. He and Jamie had run from their past and right into the arms of a true family, something he and Jamie had never experienced until they'd come to New York, and now it felt as if it were all ending. Sure, he and Jamie were no longer there every day, but they knew they'd always be welcomed back home and their family would always be there. And now….

"So that's it? No more Guards of Folsom?" he asked, the sadness in his heart causing his chest to ache.

"No."

Tek looked up and met Blake's gaze. "But you just said—"

"I sold the building, but we are the Guards of Folsom." Blake waved his hand around to each man sitting at the table, including Tek and Jamie. "We'll always be there for each other, no matter where we live. We're simply writing the next chapter of our lives."

Jamie put his arm around Tek's shoulders and hugged him. He kissed Tek's cheek and then nuzzled his neck. "Just like us, Farmer Pete, and what a chapter it will be."

Keep reading!

Riveted

A Whispering Pines Ranch
A Guards of Folsom story

By SJD Peterson

When Ty left Pegasus for New York, he knew he was falling for Blake but wasn't sure he could trust him. Blake didn't know whether he could be vulnerable enough to take on another boy. Since the move to the Big Apple, Blake and Ty have learned how to live with each other. Now they need to let go of their pasts and take the next steps outside the playroom.

To all those who demanded Ty and Blake's Happily Ever After,
this book is for you.

Chapter 1

THE OLDER man sitting on the other side of the bar with a predatory gaze wandering down Ty's body was nothing new. Tyler Callahan, better known as Ty, had seen that same look in many eyes as he stood behind the bar, slinging suds and hearing a variety of propositions. He'd heard them all, everything from the simplistic—"Wanna fuck?"—all the way up to ridiculous descriptions of how they would have him on his knees, begging to breathe. That one had left him snickering and blowing nothing more than his tip. While Ty was flattered and more than a little appreciative of the tips shoved in his pants, shirt, and tip jar, not a single one of the men who'd left them even so much as tempted him.

This newest man, while attractive with his salt-and-pepper hair, short-trimmed beard, muscular body, and an air of authority swirling around him, was no different.

"C'mon, boy. I can make all your naughty dreams come true."

Ty cringed hearing the word "boy" spoken by this man but plastered a smile on his face and set the beer the stranger had ordered down in front of him. "I'm not your boy and I seriously doubt you could handle my dreams," he responded with confidence.

Ty started to step back but the man grabbed his arm in a vise-like grip, not allowing him to move. "Oh trust me, no matter how kinky, dangerous, or bizarre, I'll leave you satisfied like no one else ever could."

"Take your hand off what's mine and you might survive to make someone else's dreams come true," Blake warned.

Ty looked up to see Blake standing behind the large man, his hands resting on the stranger's shoulders. The grip on Ty's forearm remained as the stranger leisurely ran his gaze down Ty's form again, then calmly turned his head back to meet Blake's gaze. "This is a private conversation. I don't see any mark of ownership."

"I'm going to ask you one more time to take your hand off what is mine—the next time I won't be quite so nice about it."

A shudder went through Ty. He could easily shove off the hand on his arm, but there was something about Blake, his quiet confidence, possessiveness, and strength that caused Ty to hesitate and let his lover deal with it. It warmed not only his heart to see Blake like this but also his groin. A one-two punch of sexy.

In the year that Ty had been working at Folsom, he'd seen Blake in this same situation numerous times, and his record was perfect. Either the aggressive Dom found himself on his ass on the concrete sidewalk outside the club, or he was smart and followed Blake's request.

Ty held his breath for the tense moment the stranger and Blake continued to stare and size each other up. He let it out when he felt the hand on his forearm fall away. Smart man.

"He's not collared, so I assumed he was available. I meant no disrespect." The man held out his hand to Blake.

Blake accepted the offered hand, shook it, but did not release it. "You're new here so I'll forgive your disrespect this time. In this club you do not put your hands on a sub without his or his Dom's permission." Blake's voice was hard and brooked no argument. He then released the man's hand and took the stool next to him rather than his usual stool at the end of the bar. Ty's man was definitely putting his ownership on full display.

"Could I convince *my* boy to get me a bottle of water?"

Fuck, Blake was hot when he got all badass Dom, then turned loving eyes on him. Another shudder shook Ty to his core. "You can convince me to do anything, Sir."

Ty pulled a bottle from the cooler, opened it, and set it down in front of Blake. He wanted to lean across the bar and kiss him senseless but he knew better. When they were in the club, Blake called the shots.

Blake studied the water bottle for a moment and then looked up at Ty, a brilliant smile on his handsome face. "Perhaps I should have ordered champagne instead."

Ty knew exactly what that self-satisfied smile on his lover's face meant.

Blake had hated the fact that Ty had gone to work at the club, but Ty refused to be a kept man and he simply wouldn't have stayed with Blake if he couldn't support himself. The amount he made was pennies compared to Blake's wealth, but it wasn't about the money so much as his peace of mind. Maybe it was his need for an out just in case things didn't work out, or perhaps even his pride. Much to Blake's frustration, he hadn't been able to change Ty's mind, so instead of continuing an impossible-to-win argument, Blake had been in negotiations with the owners to buy the club. Ty and Blake had had more than a few heated words over it, but in the end, Ty understood Blake's almost obsessive need to protect, given what had happened to Eli. If he was completely honest with himself, he liked it. For the first time in his life, someone actually cared enough to want him around long-term.

"I take it your meeting was a success then, Sir?"

"That is was, boy."

"Will I now be sleeping with the boss, Sir?" Ty asked teasingly.

Blake stood, leaned over the bar, grabbed the collar of Ty's T-shirt in his fist, and pulled him close, their lips practically touching. "That's later. For now I'll settle for a kiss."

Heat infused Ty, the intensity increasing when Blake smashed their mouths together, demanding entrance. Ty gave himself over to the possessive kiss. He had no doubt this was for the benefit of the stranger who had dared touch what Blake deemed as his rather than for himself. Whatever the reason, Ty gave up control completely, letting Blake explore his mouth until he had his fill and left Ty breathless and hard as nails when it ended.

Blake sat back on his stool and gave the man next to him a wide, cocksure smile.

The older man nodded. "Now he does look truly owned."

Blake's smile grew impossibly wider.

"I couldn't help but overhear your conversation. You must be Blake Henderson." The man held out his hand again. "I do believe you're the reason I'm here. I'm Bobby's friend and how-to-hide-all-that-money advisor, Tackett Austin."

Blake accepted the hand and shook it again, this time without the challenging glare in his eyes. "Right, right, Bobby has told me a lot of good things about you. Nice to finally meet you."

"Well, hopefully that will help make up for my less-than-stellar first impression."

"I'm a little possessive of my boy," Blake said unapologetically.

"As you should be. You're a very lucky man, Mr. Henderson, he's quite lovely. May I?" Tackett asked, indicating his intentions with a nod of his head toward Ty.

"That I am," Blake said confidently. "Be my guest."

Tackett held out his hand. "Tackett Austin."

Ty accepted the hand and shook it. "Ty Callahan."

"Nice to meet you, Ty."

"Likewise, Sir."

Blake winked at Ty and then turned his attentions to Tackett. The two of them began discussing the sale of Folsom; Ty took the opportunity to check on his other customers and service the new ones who were beginning to stream in. Friday nights were always crazy busy, the club beginning to fill up shortly after five when the work day ended and becoming completely full by nine.

Ty had just handed out a couple of bottles of water to one of the regular subs when he looked up and spotted Micah, another bartender he often worked with, stepping up behind the bar. That took Ty aback. Micah wasn't on the schedule; Ty had checked and didn't expect Caleb, his suds-slinging buddy for the night, until seven.

"Hey, Micah. Did you forget what day of the week it was again?"

Micah was a beautiful man, with thick dark curls and the palest baby-blues Ty had ever seen. He had started working at the club right around the same time Ty had, coming from another club called The Whip. During the first two weeks Micah, had shown up three times on his day off. He'd been so used to working his schedule at the other club that it had taken him a while to get used to the new one. Ty still loved teasing him about it.

"Ha ha ha. Bitch, please." Micah scoffed. "Your Dom was doing the begging for a change."

Ty looked back over his shoulder toward Blake, who was still chatting with Tackett. "I take back what I said about you," Ty said, unfazed. "If you got Blake to beg, then you're a better man than I am."

That made Micah laugh. "Yeah, he begged me to cover your shift tonight. You know he would only beg for you, you smug bastard." Micah froze, eyes going wide. "Oh sweet Jesus. Now *there* is someone I'd love to beg for."

Ty followed Micah's gaze. It was directed toward where Blake sat. "You mean Tackett?" he asked.

"Tackett," Micah echoed.

"He's like twice your age," Ty said incredulously.

"Spank me, daddy!"

Ty nudged him with an elbow. "It's official. You're even more perverted than I am."

Micah shrugged. "I can live with that. So introduce me."

"I will if you tell me why Blake has you covering my shift. What's he up to?"

"Don't know, but I'll make something up if I have to." Micah never took his gaze from Tackett.

"Lot of help you are. C'mon." Ty huffed and handed Micah a towel. "Here, sop up the drool from your chin."

Micah grabbed the towel from him, tossed it aside, and shoved Ty toward the end of the bar where the two men sat.

"Pushy bastard," Ty grumbled. "You sure you don't have any dominant tendencies?"

"Why don't you bend over and find out."

Ty just shook his head at Micah's antics. Once he reached the bar where Tackett and Blake sat, he stopped and waited for Blake to address him. He could feel Micah vibrating behind him. Ty had seen many men come and go, but he'd never seen his friend so affected before. Ty had begun to suspect that Micah wasn't really into the scene at all. Micah knew all the proper ways to address the Doms with respect, eyes lowered, flirting and teasing them, but Ty had never seen Micah go any further than that. As far as he knew, Micah wasn't seeing anyone so maybe he was just picky. Tackett certainly was a step above most men in the looks department.

Blake met Ty's gaze and waggled his brows. "Hey, you sexy beast! Got any plans for the night?"

"Well, Sir, I'm not really sure. Apparently, my new boss has just given me the night off."

Micah tugged on the back of his shirt.

"Sounds like you owe your boss a really big thank you," Blake said with a sly grin.

Tackett chuckled, and Ty bit his lip to keep from joining him. "Do you have any suggestions for a suitable 'thank you' gift I could give him?"

Micah's tugging grew in strength and speed.

"I do," Blake said confidently. "But I think we should discuss this in private. It's a very, very *special* kind of gift."

The hungry look in Blake's gaze sent a tingling sensation racing down Ty's spine and made heat pool in his groin. "Then it's a good thing I'm off work so we can privately *discuss* this gift."

"Micah, could you call and ask Thomas to bring the car around?"

The club employed a driver and provided a black sedan for taking home patrons unable to drive either because they were too drunk or, because they were too exhausted and/or sedated. But he and Blake never used the car. Blake didn't drink and, while they occasionally played at the club, his lover preferred their own home. Ty found it odd that Blake was asking for the car, but he didn't comment on it.

Micah didn't respond either, just continued to stare at Tackett and kept up his insistent, irritating tugging.

"Micah," Blake said louder, making Micah jump and the hand on Ty's shirt halt.

"What?" Micah snapped and then turned red when he realized how he'd responded to Blake. He glanced quickly between Tackett, Blake, and Ty, the color in his cheeks deepening when he realized he'd been standing there, zoned out with his mouth gaping.

"Sorry, Sir," Micah said, lowering his eyes and releasing Ty's T-shirt. "What was it you asked?"

Blake barely contained his laughter when he once again asked Micah to call for the car. Micah gave Ty a panicked look before answering, "Yes, Sir."

Ty took pity on him.

"Mr. Austin, Sir. This is Micah Slayde," Ty said, pointing a thumb toward Micah. "He'll be replacing me as your server. Just let him know if you need anything." Ty arched a brow at Micah. "I'm sure he'll be more than happy to provide it for you."

Micah nodded vigorously. "Anything, Sir."

"Thank you, Micah. I'll keep that in mind."

After Micah finally pried his gaze from the older Dom and went to call for the car, Ty and Blake said their good-byes to Tackett and headed to grab their coats. When they stepped out of the club, a bitterly cold wind caused Ty to shiver. He was never going to get used to the winters in New York. The snow was pretty in pictures or to look out at from inside a warm home, but being out in it was brutal on a southern boy. Blake tightened the arm he had around him, pulled him close, and held him tight as they hurried to the waiting car.

Thank God the heat was already blasting from the vents. Ty brushed the snow from his coat and shook it from his hair. "Jesus, it's cold. I'm not sure I'll ever get used to this."

"I love winter," Blake responded, wiping the snow from his own coat. "Or rather, I love getting to warm you up. C'mere."

Ty climbed onto Blake's lap, straddling his thighs. "Are we going to discuss that special gift now, Sir?"

Blake grabbed Ty's hips and pulled him forward, causing Ty to moan when their groins came in contact. "I'm thinking talk is overrated, don't you?"

"Mmm hmm." Ty gripped the back of the seat, one hand on each side of Blake's head, and began to rock his hips, cock swelling. "I'm definitely more of a hands-on kind of guy."

Blake licked and nibbled at Ty's bottom lip, teasing. "And I'm definitely better at showing rather than telling."

Ty continued to grind against the growing bulge in Blake's slacks as the kiss deepened, groaning when Blake found his erection, cupped it in his hand and squeezed

"Oh yeah, much better at hands on," Blake murmured against his lips. "Lean back."

He sat back, and Blake popped the button on Ty's jeans and eased down the zipper. Ty arched his back, pushing hard into the hand Blake wrapped around his erection.

"You're so hard for me," Blake murmured, his hand speeding up, stroking Ty's cock in a firm grip.

Dick throbbing with need, a tingling sensation tickling at the base of his spine, Ty thrust into that tight grip. God, he was so close already.

Just as the car came to a stop, so did the hand on his prick and then Blake wrapped a band of leather around the base, pulled it tight, and snapped it.

"Dammit," Ty grumbled. "I should have known I wouldn't get to come so easily."

"You love it." Blake's finger swiped across the head of Ty's cock, spreading the liquid seeping from the slit before bringing it to his mouth and sucking the digit inside. "And so do I."

Ty whimpered when Blake tucked his erection back into his jeans and carefully zipped and buttoned them.

"My poor denied boy," Blake consoled, the smug look on his face ruining the effect. Ty huffed, causing Blake to chuckle. The Dom then opened the door. "I promise to make it worth your while."

Excited to see what his lover had in store for him, Ty scrambled off Blake's lap and stepped out of the car. He groaned when he heard Blake behind him say, "*If* you're a very good boy."

Chapter 2

BLAKE STOPPED with his hand on the doorknob, head cocked as if he were listening to a noise from within. "You may want to keep your coat on for a bit."

Ty stopped with his coat halfway down his arms. "Why? Didn't you pay the heating bill?"

With his free hand, Blake reached out and stroked the prominent bulge in Ty's jeans. "We have company." With that, Blake opened the door.

The scent of basil, tomato, and warm yeast wafted out of the apartment, and Ty quickly shrugged his coat back on, fumbling to button it up. He'd recognize that scent anywhere. "Your mom?" he hissed. Keeping his voice low, Ty grumbled, "You got me hard as fucking nails and your *mom* is here?" Ty shook his head. "I say this with the utmost respect, Sir, you are one mean bastard."

Blake laughed, then gave Ty a chaste kiss. "She isn't staying. C'mon." He grabbed Ty's hand and pulled him toward the kitchen.

Ty got a brief look at the dining room table as they passed: crystal and china dinnerware, white tapers burning in silver holders, and a matching bucket filled with ice and champagne. A single red rose in a silver vase completed the romantic look, set for two—thank God.

"Ah, there you two are. You're just in time," Martha said as she pulled a loaf of bread from the oven. "Everything is ready; you just need to slice the bread."

"I've got it, Mom." He kissed her on the cheek and took the potholders from her. "Everything looks and smells great. Thank you."

"You're welcome," she said sincerely, hugging her son. "It's a special night, yes?"

"Very special," Blake assured her.

Martha went up on tiptoes and whispered something in Blake's ear, to which Blake replied with a shake of his head. Ty's gut rolled. He hated surprises, and he could tell by the look on their faces that they were cooking up something—and it wasn't just Martha's famous lasagna.

Martha Drover was a petite, beautiful woman, and it was easy to see where Blake got his good looks from. They both had the same deep brown eyes, smooth olive skin, and dark hair, although Martha's was now streaked with silver. More importantly, she was just as beautiful on the inside and had accepted Ty as the man in her son's life from day one. But while she had gone out of her way to make Ty feel like a part of their small family, he still held a part of himself back. Martha seemed to know when he was taking a step back and would smile, pat his hand, and ease off, but she tried harder the next time. The guilt ate at him some days, but he just couldn't silence the small voice in his head that kept whispering this would all end one day.

"Ty, you look a little flushed. Are you getting sick?" Martha hugged him, then reached up to feel his forehead.

"I'm fine," he assured her, wrapping his coat a little tighter. *Nope, not sick. I'm in pain, my balls ache, and it's your son's fault with his obsession with cock rings, but really, I'm fine.* "Good seeing you and wow, it smells good in here. Lasagna?" he added, trying to shift the attention away from his discomfort.

Martha gave him a suspicious look but nodded. "I know it's your favorite. Here, let me have your coat. I'll hang it up on my way out."

Ty shot a panicked look toward Blake and clutched his coat. Thankfully, Blake took pity on him—*bastard should since it's his fault.*

"Mom," Blake said, coming up and wrapping his arm around Martha before nudging her toward the front door. "I've got this. Thank you for cooking for us. It's the perfect way to celebrate." Blake helped her with her coat and gave her a hug. "I'll call you later, okay?"

"I'm heading out to meet some friends for drinks. Call me tomorrow," she said with a wave of a hand. "I don't expect to be home early."

"Hot date?" Ty asked, waggling his brows.

"Hmm, perhaps," she demurred, but the smile that curled her lips was telling. She reached to give Ty a hug; he accepted it but was careful to keep his lower body away from her. He winced when he bent, since the forward motion pulled on his groin and strangled his bound cock further. Before releasing him she tilted her head and studied him carefully again. "You sure you're feeling okay?"

"He's fine, Mom," Blake said. "You know I take good care of him, and if he were sick I'd already have the chicken noodle soup heating and him tucked in bed."

Martha continued to stare at Ty. God he was going to kill Blake. He did his best to give her a convincing smile. "I know," she said, finally releasing Ty and patting Blake on the arm as she pulled her gloves from her coat pocket. "You're very good to him. Speaking of which, when are you two going to finally settle down and give me some grandbabies?" She arched a brow at Ty.

That stopped him short and he coughed to cover up his shock. "Uh, don't look at me," he sputtered. "I've got the wrong plumbing."

Blake laughed, shaking his head as he opened the door. "Good night, Mom."

"Good night, boys."

Martha stopped just outside the door and started to say something, but Blake interrupted her. "Love you, Mom. Call you tomorrow."

"What the hell was that all about?" Ty demanded when Blake shut the door. "Grandkids?" Ty's gut rolled at the thought.

"She's been on this kick ever since Ricky Martin adopted those twins," Blake said easily and helped Ty with his coat. "It will pass."

"It better," Ty grumbled. "I don't want any kids. Does she realize I'm a very needy man and don't share my attention well?"

"I know, boy," Blake said, his dark eyes sparkling. He was undeniably amused at Ty's rant. He pressed his palm to the front of Ty's jeans. "*Very* needy of my attentions."

Ty moaned and pushed into his hand. Then he remembered he was supposed to be angry at Blake and narrowed his eyes. "I can't believe you got me all worked up and your mom, Jesus, your *mom* was here!"

Blake wrapped his arms around Ty, leaning in and nuzzling his neck. "Will you forgive me if I promise to make it up to you?"

"I don't know," he muttered, at the same time turning his head to the side to give the man more room in which to work. "It was pretty mean." His complaint turned to a moan when Blake began nipping and licking along Ty's neck.

Blake snickered. "Okay, I admit it was mean, but in my defense I thought she'd be gone by the time we got home."

"Oh please," Ty said with a snort. "She takes every opportunity to see you these days. I think she's a little jealous of the amount of time you spend with me at work."

"Speaking of which," Blake said excitedly, clapping his hands together and rubbing them. "Let's eat and pop the cork. We're supposed to be celebrating." He leaned in and gave Ty one last kiss. "Then I'll do a little ass kissing when you're naked and on the bed," he promised, pulling Ty along to the kitchen.

Once they had set the lasagna and fresh bread on the table, Ty arched a brow at him before taking his seat. "I'm going to hold you to that, you know."

"What, the ass kissing?"

Ty nodded and filled his plate.

"Oh trust me, I'm planning on it," Blake said with a soft laugh, pulling the cork from the champagne bottle and then pouring them each a glass. He handed one to Ty. "Here's to new business ventures."

Ty clinked his glass against Blake's. "Here's to your promotion, going from a guard at Folsom to warden." He took a sip, the bubbles tickling his nose.

When Ty lowered his glass, Blake was staring at him with an odd expression on his face. "What?" he asked, setting down his glass and picking up his fork, Martha's pasta calling his name.

"I like it," Blake said, nodding with a thoughtful look. He filled his own plate, still nodding and seeming to get more excited. "Actually, I think it's a perfect name."

"What, 'Warden'?" Ty asked absently. He shoveled in a large bite of lasagna and chewed happily.

"No. Guards of Folsom."

"And we all know how you guard the place," Ty drawled with a smirk. "You're right, it is perfect."

Blake fell silent for a moment, watching him before speaking again. His voice was sincere when he said, "It's not the club I guard, it's you. As should every Dom guard and protect their sub."

"You sure showed your ownership of your sub with Mr. Austin tonight."

"I don't own you, Ty, and you're much more than my sub," Blake said quietly.

I've never been worth owning. Fuck, that was his truth. He'd been a throwaway his whole life. It didn't matter how hard he wished otherwise, it always ended. A lump formed in Ty's throat and he reached for his glass, wrinkling his nose at the champagne. "I'm going to get a glass of water," he said, pushing away from the table. "Would you like some?"

"Yes, please."

With shaking hands Ty filled two glasses with ice and went to the sink. He hated when his past came creeping up on him. No rhyme or reason, his insecurities just seemed to attack whenever they had a mind to. He'd had a great day, got the night off, was having a great dinner, and Blake had gotten his club, so why the hell was he shaking so goddamn badly inside and out? It felt like he was suffocating.

He filled one glass and downed the water, which did little to help with the lump in his throat and only managed to cause the churning in his gut to intensify. He refilled it and the glass for Blake, then set them aside. After shutting off the tap, Ty clutched the counter and closed his eyes, then took a deep breath and blew it out slowly. Tonight was about celebrating Blake acquiring the club, not about him. *Live in the moment. Enjoy what you have now*, he reminded himself. The mantra was getting harder and harder to say and even harder to believe. He'd been cast aside his whole life by people who always tired of him, so he should be used to it. But this time, with Blake, Ty knew it was different. He wouldn't only be losing another home or a Dom, but his whole world.

Forcing away those thoughts, Ty took one last deep breath and grabbed the glasses of water. He plastered on a happy expression before heading back to the dining room. Blake deserved this celebration.

Setting one glass down next to his plate as he passed, he went and held the other out for Blake. Blake stared up at him, those dark eyes burrowing into him, looking past the fake smile and into Ty's very soul. Ty averted his gaze, clamping down on the tremor that threatened, but it was too late. Blake had already seen the lie.

Taking the glass, Blake set it aside and pulled Ty onto his lap. Blake pressed his hand against Ty's cheek, thumb tracing his bottom lip. "I hate these fake smiles," he murmured. "What do I have to do to win your trust?"

"I do—" Blake silenced him by pressing his thumb over Ty's mouth.

"Do you remember the first time I called you my boy?"

Christ, yes, he remembered it. It hadn't come during a scene or because of a chore well done, but during one those rare, special moments when their passion turned to slow lovemaking rather than fucking. *"My boy,"* Blake had whispered against Ty's neck as they both came down from their orgasmic high. The memory was seared into his brain, causing him both elation and dread.

Ty nodded, not trusting his voice.

"When I said it, I meant it," Blake said with genuine warmth in his eyes. "You *are* my boy, my lover, and the most important thing in my life. I need you to believe that."

He wanted to. More than anything else he wanted to believe that this time would be different. He could say he did, but Blake would know that the words were only to pacify him and not heartfelt. Instead, he nodded again and said quietly, "I know." Because he did know that Blake was trying; it was his own ghosts that haunted him.

"I'm also a very patient man, Ty. I'm not going to give up until you believe me. Maybe this will help." Blake pulled an envelope from his pocket and handed it to him.

"What is it?" he asked, eyeing the letter suspiciously.

"It's not going to bite you. Just read it," he encouraged, pushing the envelope into Ty's hand.

Ty glanced at Blake and narrowed his eyes. The thick envelope contained numerous pages of paper clipped together. As soon as he unfolded them, he recognized them as legal documents pertaining to the purchase of the club. Ty glanced back up at him and shrugged. "I know you bought Folsom. Isn't that what the champagne was for?"

Blake took the papers and flipped the papers to the last page, a huge smile on his face when he handed the pile back to Ty.

Ty scanned the page, his heart stopping in his chest when he read, "Owner Blake Henderson, Co-owner Tyler Callahan." He shoved the papers back at Blake. "No!" He tried to get up but Blake held him around the waist.

"What do you mean, 'no'?" Blake's brow creased.

"I'm not taking handouts from you." Ty scrubbed a hand across his face, trying to get his irritation under control before he spoke again. "Blake, we've talked about this," he said and met Blake's eyes.

"It's not a handout. It's a sound business decision," Blake responded calmly. "You're smart, good with the customers, and will bring a lot to the club to help make it successful."

Ty still wasn't comfortable with the idea and Blake must have picked up on his discomfort because he added, "I'll tell you what. If it will set your mind at ease, we'll set up a payment plan to take a percentage of your profits until half of the down payment has been paid. Fifty-fifty partnership."

Searching Blake's face, Ty tried to find any deceit in Blake's eyes or expression. He wasn't as good at reading the man as Blake seemed to be at reading him, but he knew Blake well enough to know when he was being sincere or just pacifying Ty.

Ty sighed and relaxed again. "You'll have the payment plan drawn up?"

Blake shook his head, posture falling in dejection. "There you go, not trusting me again," he said sadly.

The sorrow in Blake's dark brown eyes tore at Ty's heart. His need to comfort was automatic and he shifted, straddling Blake's lap and wrapping his arms around him. "I'm sorry. It's not that I don't trust you with this, I swear. I just don't want you feeling as if you have to take care of me or that I can't do it for myself."

"Goddammit, Ty," Blake growled, grabbing Ty's biceps in a tight grip and shoving him back. "Don't you fucking get it? I don't have to take care of you—I *want* to take care of you, and I want you to take care of me." He crumpled the contract in his fist, a fiery light burning in his eyes. "Fine, don't take my word for it that I want you around." He shoved the papers into Ty's chest. "This is your written guarantee that I want you around, and not just today but long-term, that you're my partner in every sense of the word."

The fight seemed to drain out of Blake, and he dropped the papers in Ty's lap, then slumped back against his chair. "Tell me what I need to do to prove it to you, Ty, and I'll do it."

Ty once again wrapped himself around Blake, pressing his face into Blake's neck. "Don't leave me" slipped out before he could bite down on his tongue to keep the words from passing his lips. Fuck, he was a goddamn grown man and he sounded like a pathetic child. He wished he could pull the words back into his fucked-up head where they belonged.

But it was too late—Blake had heard them. To Ty's surprise, Blake didn't mock him or shove him away in disgust for the weakness he'd just shown. Blake just wrapped his arms tightly around Ty and kissed the top of his head. "All I can do is promise you I won't, but only time will prove it to you." He stroked Ty's hair soothingly. "I know our pasts have left their scars on us. I'm much more protective and possessive of you than I was with Eli and I know I can be a little smothering; it's my scar." Blake's soft touch in Ty's hair tightened and he eased Ty's head back until their eyes met. "I buried Eli and opened myself up to you. I need you to bury your past and do the same for me. Trust me to handle your scars."

"I'm trying," Ty said sincerely. He blinked back the tears that threatened, refusing to let them fall or to show any more weakness. "I don't know why I get so freaked out. It's like it pops up when I'm happiest and fucking chokes me. Most of the time I can push it away, but sometimes…." He shook his head in disgust. "It's not you, Blake. You and your mom have done nothing but try to make me feel at home since day one. But sometimes I'm too fucking weak to deal with my childish abandonment issues and I end up doing shit that's going to make them become real."

Blake took his hand out of Ty's hair and soothed it down his back as he chewed on his bottom lip, deep in thought. After a long moment of silence, Blake's despairing expression melted away as a new gleam started to light up his eyes. He grabbed Ty's hair again to force Ty to look into his eyes. "Okay, here's the deal. You trust me with your finances, right?"

"What little I have is yours. You know that."

Blake's lip twitched, but he held back the smile, keeping his expression neutral and his tone of voice professional. "So, as long as I provide you with the proper legal documents and repayment plan, you'll be my business partner?" The thought of owning Folsom caused Ty's gut to flutter, but in a good way. Him, no-fucking-body Tyler Callahan, owner of a club. Christ, he hadn't seen that one coming. "Yes," he said seriously, although he could not help feeling a little giddy.

Blake slid his eyes up and down Ty's torso, then licked his lips. "You trust me with your body, right?"

"It's yours," Ty said without hesitation. Hell, there wasn't much Blake hadn't done to his body. Bound it, beaten it, fucked it, and loved it. The answer to that question was a no-brainer. In all their time together, Ty had never once had to use his safeword. That didn't mean that Blake didn't push Ty's limits. Christ, the man could push them right to the edge where Ty was hanging on by the tips of his fingers and barely keeping a grip on his sanity. However, Blake could also read Ty like a book and always knew when to back off.

His bound cock was grabbed and massaged. Between the thoughts of Blake pushing his limits, the hand on his dick, and the tongue that demanded entrance into his mouth, Ty's eyes rolled back in his head. He gave himself over to Blake and let the stress and unease that had gripped him earlier flow from his body.

When Blake pulled back from the kiss, he leaned his forehead against Ty's as they breathed each other in for a moment. "Don't you see? You already *are* my boy and my business partner. Trust me that we can work on your scars together."

"Yeah, I can do that," he said, chasing those smiling lips, wanting more.

Blake laughed into another kiss, the vibration tickling along Ty's tongue, and Ty pulled Blake's happiness into himself, giving his own tongue back.

"Now that *that* is settled," Blake announced and gently gave Ty a shove, encouraging him to get up. As soon as Ty got to his feet, Blake was on his and grabbing his hand. "Time for that ass kissing I promised."

Hell yeah! He hadn't completely ruined the celebration. He was getting another chance and this time Ty was going to make damn sure it ended in one hell of a bang. Laughing, he followed Blake to their bedroom.

Chapter 3

As Blake pulled Ty into their bedroom he couldn't help but think that his boy was going to drive him out of his ever-lovin' mind one of these days, he just knew it. One day he'd be laced into a straightjacket and his mom would be visiting him in his no-sharp-objects-allowed padded room and wiping the drool from his chin.

He loved the man; the good Lord knew he did. Every inch of the infuriating bastard, the good, the sexy, even the flawed parts, and he had no doubt Ty loved him back. Ty may not have ever said the words out loud, always hemming and hawing or distracting Blake when he'd tell Ty he loved him, but Blake still knew it.

Didn't matter, really—love wasn't words, love was actions and that's all he needed from Ty.

Still, the man drove him loco.

He understood why Ty couldn't completely trust him yet. Hell, it hadn't been so long ago he hadn't trusted Ty. And really, their issues were pretty much the same. Ty was afraid he'd leave him, and he in turn was scared shitless someone would take Ty away. He'd spent many a night having private conversations with Eli as Ty slept next to him, trying to walk an impossible line of living in the past and looking toward the future.

It wasn't until Eli's ghost nudged him—or maybe it was the way he felt when he looked at Ty while he slept—that he reached the turning point. Either way he knew, had their fates been reversed, he'd want nothing more than for Eli to find someone he could snuggle up to at night who made him feel secure while he slept. He knew beyond the shadow of a doubt Eli would want him to be happy being security for someone.

Closing the door behind them, Blake flipped the switch to illuminate the bedside table lamp. There was a soft smile on Ty's face as he looked up at him, but the events of the night—the elation, arousal, falling into anger and guilt—left their telltale signs as weariness in Ty's eyes and the small crease in his brow. The emotional highs and lows also left him pliable in Blake's hands, and he easily allowed Blake to lay him across their king-sized bed without any resistance or words.

Everything about Ty fascinated him. Blake let his eyes roam leisurely along the short, stocky man with his muscular, powerhouse body. Sometimes the man was so cocksure he demanded respect and control of his world, yet other times, he was that eight-year-old little boy being abandoned in a small office of a courthouse and shedding tears for a little chicken he'd named Charlie.

He loved everything about Ty, even if some aspects of his personality were more difficult to deal with than others, but this side of Ty—this submissive side, laid out before him to do whatever Blake wanted, trusting him completely—was the side that called most to Blake. It appealed to both his dominant side and his need-to-nurture protective side.

Popping the button on Ty's jeans and easing down the zipper, Blake held Ty's gaze as those pale-blue eyes focused on each move Blake made. He was thrilled at the notion that a simple touch could command the sole focus of that fascinating mind.

Silently, Blake pulled the denim and silk away from Ty's bound cock, eased both garments down his muscular legs, and tossed them away. Ty's cock was flushed deep in color, straining obscenely upward from the black leather band secured around the base. His bound balls shone with a purplish-red glow.

"Christ, you're sexy," Blake murmured, swirling a finger around the wet tip of the flared cockhead.

Ty took in a sharp breath but remained silent, waiting. He wouldn't speak until either Blake asked him a question or he was ready to beg. Here, behind closed doors, everything was easy. Ty didn't have to think. There was no past, present, or future, only his Master's pleasure. The anticipation of what Blake had planned for him was evident in the slight trembling of Ty's muscles and the excitement gleaming in his blue eyes.

Pushing up Ty's T-shirt, Blake's gaze feasted on the ridges of muscle running across Ty's belly; continuing to push the cotton material up farther revealed the thick muscles of his chest, the little gold rings in Ty's nipples catching Blake's attention. A temptation too great to ignore, Blake leaned in and sucked one of the pierced nubs into his mouth, tongue flicking the ring back and forth until Ty moaned. Blake kissed his way across Ty's breastbone to give the other nipple the same attention, only this time adding a scrape of teeth.

"Ah God," Ty moaned, back arching.

Ty's nipples were extremely sensitive: with a twist to the gold, a bite of pain to the pleasure, Blake could make his boy come from just the ministrations of his lips, tongue, and teeth to the little nubs.

But not tonight.

Blake leaned farther over Ty and pulled the T-shirt up and over his head as he pressed his denim-covered groin against Ty's cock, the abrasive material causing Ty to hiss. Blake covered his mouth, taking the sound in. He dominated the kiss, tongue thrusting deep, teeth threatening, but Ty gave as good as he got. They devoured each other, feasting until they were both breathless and grinning when it ended.

"I do believe I made you a promise, didn't I?" Blake asked, grinding his hips into Ty, rubbing their erections together.

"Yes, Sir," Ty moaned, ass coming up off the bed seeking out even more friction.

Straightening, Blake slapped Ty's thigh. "Hands and knees, boy."

Ty nodded, his voice a little strained. "Yes, Sir." He flipped over, knees on the edge of the bed with his feet dangling over the side, and planted his hands on the mattress.

Blake took a minute to enjoy the sight of his boy on display for him. Ty's summer tan had faded, his skin now a light cream color over all those strong, luscious muscles. *All mine.* The thought made his cock throb.

Blake ran his hands lightly over each cheek of that perfect ass, squeezing the meaty globes and pulling a grunt from Ty, the sound morphing into a moan when Blake leaned down and pressed his mouth to Ty's lower back. He moved downward, teasing from the top to Ty's crease with lips and tongue, kissing each ass cheek before spreading them wide.

"I always keep my promises," Blake whispered before teasing the tip of his tongue slowly around Ty's hole. "Don't come, boy."

"Ahh, I-I won't, Sir," Ty panted.

Blake explored his boy's ass painstakingly slowly, alternating between kissing and biting at the muscular mounds and licking from the top of his crease down to the delicate sac and back up to tease at Ty's tight little hole.

"Oh fuck." Ty groaned and pulled away a bit when Blake pushed his tongue into him.

Blake curled his fingers around Ty's hips, holding him and not allowing him to move away as he dove in with his tongue, fucking Ty's ass. Ty gasped, body tensing as he moaned and began babbling incoherent nonsense while Blake went at his ass with single-minded determination.

"No!" Ty howled, pulling away when Blake slipped a finger deep inside him. "Ca-can't. Jesus, I'm going to come," he said harshly, head dropping between his arms, chest heaving as he tried to get himself back under control.

"Just breathe," Blake said, instantly stopping all stimulation and rubbing at Ty's lower back. He wasn't holding Ty's orgasm back to be mean or to punish. He wanted to keep his promise yet be buried deep in his boy when they came. "I got ya, deep breaths," he encouraged as he popped the button on his own jeans and pushed them down his hips. "Wait for me, boy."

"Oh… yeah, okay," he gasped. Ty took a couple more deep breaths, then seemed to relax his body slightly, though the muscles still continued to tremble and a fine sheen of perspiration covered his body. "Damn, that was close," he chuckled and blew out another long breath.

There was no way Ty was going to last long. Hell, with the gorgeous body spread out before him, the needy sounds pouring from his boy, and the taste of Ty on his tongue, Blake doubted *he'd* last very long. They needed to take the edge off, and then he'd spend the rest of the night showing Ty just how much he loved him.

"Over the bed," he instructed, pulling at Ty's hip to encourage him to place his feet on the floor while he spread the pre-come oozing from his own slit down his shaft. Lining up his slick cock at Ty's entrance, he whispered, "Ready for me, boy?"

"God, yes," Ty moaned pitifully. "Need you so fucking bad."

"I know, I need you too," he murmured, nudging at Ty's wet hole. Ty opened up for him, accepting the invasion with a sigh and a moan. Slowly, gently, Blake slid into him until he was fully buried in Ty's body.

Blake stretched out, pressed his chest against Ty's back, and wrapped his arms around him. "Love how tight your ass is," he praised, one hand splayed out over Ty's chest, the other lightly stroking Ty's cock as they began to rock together. "Love how you feel around me, against me—" He inhaled against Ty's neck, taking the musky scent deep into his lungs. "—the way you smell."

Ty moaned. "Need to be everything for you. Everything. Always. Oh God," Ty babbled. His words were disjointed as he began to rock harder.

Blake's slow, languid thrusts sped, the tight heat around his cock demanding. "You are, Ty," he whispered as he moved a little faster. "You're everything I need. You're my beautiful boy, my lover, my breath. Everything I could ever want." Blake's fingers curled against Ty's chest, feeling his rapid heart rate. With his free hand Blake tugged at the leather, releasing the band around Ty's cock and balls and letting it fall to the floor.

"Yes… so close." Ty clutched the bedding in a white-knuckled grip and threw his head back, back arching. "Please, please, please! Love me, Sir." Ty's voice broke on a sob.

"Always," Blake growled and slammed into Ty faster, wrapping his fist around Ty's cock. "I'll always love you. So fucking beautiful. God, Ty, let me be your everything," he panted. His climax built, moving through him; his pulse roared in his ears, heart pounding.

"Yes! Oh fuck!" Ty's body went completely rigid, mouth wide in a silent scream, and cock throbbing hard in Blake's hand.

His boy was beyond the point of no return, already beginning to fall into bliss. One more hard thrust, and Blake whispered, "Come for me." The wet heat fountained over Blake's fist before the last word was even out of his mouth.

"Ah! Yes, oh God." Ty's words were barely distinguishable, flowing into a deep, satisfying moan, as his body swayed and trembled, in constant motion as he rode his orgasm.

Blake stayed buried in Ty's ass, holding back his own need by pure fucking orneriness, refusing to give in until every drop was pulled from Ty's body. The contractions around his dick caused his legs to weaken and he locked his knees to keep from falling.

One last thrust, the sounds of Ty's whimpers, the smell of sex, and the vise grip around his cock all finally stripped Blake of his control and he came deep inside Ty, shooting pulse after pulse, a growl filling the air. "Mine."

Ty's arms gave out and they both collapsed to the bed. Ty grunted as Blake covered him with his full weight, but he sighed and melted into the mattress, breathing hard. They stayed like that for long, silent moments as they each basked in the euphoria, Blake still buried deep in Ty's body.

He was sated and boneless and he didn't want to move. But with his pants around his legs and his knees about to give out, Blake finally pressed a kiss to the side of Ty's neck and forced himself to rise.

"Hey," Ty protested as Blake's cock slipped out and he lost the heat of Blake's body covering his own.

Blake smiled and swatted him playfully on the ass. "You'll thank me later. Up into the bed," he ordered and kicked off his jeans. Ty complied and Blake pulled off his shirt, throwing it haphazardly behind him, and then turned out the light before he crawled beneath the covers next to Ty.

"You were right," Ty mumbled, pushing up close to throw a leg over Blake's hip and an arm over his waist.

"I usually am," Blake chuckled, kissing Ty's nose. "But what was I right about this time?"

"This is way better than hanging off the bed with a nearly two-hundred-pound man crushing me. Although," Ty said with regret, shifting his hips until their softening cocks came in contact, "I do miss certain crushing parts, Sir."

"If you can get it up again, it's all yours, boy." Blake replied seriously. Part of him hoped Ty would take the challenge, but it was a small part. The majority of him hoped Ty would just snuggle close and enjoy a little post-fuck basking, at least for a few minutes anyway.

Ty laughed and kissed him. "I'll give you a few minutes to bask."

Oh yeah, his boy knew him very well. Blake relaxed further, his body and mind content. "You're so good to me," he said, cradling Ty close.

"That works both ways, Sir." Ty sighed.

"Yes it does," Blake said, kissing the top of Ty's head.

They lay together for a long while, just listening to each other breathe, hands gently caressing backs and chests. If Blake ever had a shred of doubt creep into his mind about whether he and Ty belonged together, they were completely erased in moments like this. He knew Ty felt it too.

Only one last obstacle stood in the way of them being completely whole and secure in each other, and Blake would go to the ends of the earth to remove it.

Chapter 4

"I WANT to remind you once again, the chafing can be avoided by regular care. I'd suggest making it part of your daily routine."

Phone between his ear and shoulder, Blake scribbled more notes in the margin of the instructions in front of him. "Morning and night like clockwork, I can assure you. I've got some last-minute errands to run so I won't be at the club when you drop it off, but Bobby is expecting you."

"Let Bobby know I'll be there at noon."

"Shall do. Oh, and Jason?"

"Yeah?"

"Thank you. This means the world to me," Blake said sincerely.

"You're welcome. See you tonight."

Blake ended the call and folded the instructions, slid them into the folder, and returned it to the desk drawer. Leaning back in his office chair, he scrubbed a hand over his jaw. Damn, he was nervous. Tonight was a night of celebration with a few of their closest friends. He tried to convince himself there wasn't a damn thing to be anxious about, but his queasy gut and jittery heart obviously weren't getting the memo.

Pushing back from his desk, Blake went in search of his boy. Ty wasn't the only one who would benefit from a day of heavy submission.

TY SAT silently in the passenger seat, eyes straight ahead, looking out the front window as they headed to the club. Blake doubted Ty was seeing the bright lights and commotion of the city as the car crept along the busy streets.

He had kept Ty in heavy bondage, helping him find his headspace, and in turn it had helped Blake find his own. Ty's brow had creased when Blake dressed him for the evening, but he never asked about the new harness. The heavily studded leather straps came over Ty's shoulders in a V, connecting to a large O-ring, which in turn connected to the strap that encircled his muscular chest just below his pierced nipples. Another studded strap ran downward to another large O-ring that anchored the strap around Ty's waist, and still another strap ran down to Ty's groin, affixed to a heavy metal cock ring.

God, Ty was magnificent in nothing but leather and silver studs, his heavy cock bound.

It had taken every bit of Blake's self-restraint to help Ty into his black dress slacks and silk dress shirt when all he wanted to do was throw his beautiful boy down on the bed and fuck him senseless.

Soon. First they had an announcement to make to their staff.

Blake pulled up behind the club and put the car in park before turning to Ty. "Tonight is a big night for us, boy. Anything you want to say before we go in?"

Ty smiled at him and shook his head. "I just plan to follow your lead, Sir."

Blake leaned over and pressed a kiss to Ty's lips. "I plan to flaunt my business partner's… assets, among other things," he teased and kissed his boy again before turning serious. "I'm proud to have you at my side tonight."

"Thank you, Sir. I'm proud to be there."

Blake smiled and stepped out of the car, then hurried around to open the door for Ty. As soon as Ty was out, Blake entwined their fingers. "Our public awaits, boy."

TY WAS relieved when the bulk of the staff finally left, leaving behind what Blake would consider his closest friends. The nice intimate group meant he could finally sit back and relax. Everyone had been great upon hearing the club's transfer of ownership, and Ty and Blake spent most of the night shaking hands and being congratulated. Luckily for him, Blake had given the speech and laid out their vision for the club, so he'd only had to stand at Blake's side and smile. He still wasn't quite used to the idea of being an owner, but he had to admit the idea was growing on him.

He'd just opened a bottle of water and taken a long pull, relaxing onto one of the leather stools next to Micah, when Blake approached him. Blake gave a curt nod to Micah before saying, "Follow me, boy."

The authoritative tone in Blake's voice had him jumping to his feet. Ty stole a glance toward Micah, who had a wide grin on his face. Obviously his friend was privy to information Ty wasn't, and he had to fight the urge to stick his tongue out at the smiling bastard as he hurried to follow Blake.

Ty could easily read Blake's body language. His back was straight, head held high, and his steps were measured. Ty fell back on his training and walked to heel behind his Dom, posture perfect and eyes low.

Blake led him to the center of the stage in front of a leather-bound bench. "Strip and kneel, boy," Blake ordered without turning away from their small audience.

Ty's eyes went wide, and he hesitated as the shock of Blake's words hit him. He recovered quickly, however, keeping his eyes low as he unbuttoned his shirt and dropped it while kicking off his shoes. A tendril of unease and excitement trickled down Ty's spine. Seldom did he and Blake play in public. It wasn't that either one of them was modest— far from it. But Blake's possessiveness ran deep and unless the situation demanded it, he rarely put Ty's body on display in front of others.

Removing his pants and socks, Ty swallowed down his confusion, put his complete trust in Blake, and went silently to his knees, careful to ensure his posture was flawless.

"Today was a very special day for me and my boy," Blake said, addressing their friends. "It means a great deal to us that you are here and were able to share in our good news."

Out of his peripheral vision, Ty watched Blake nod and a man he'd only just met tonight, Jason, got to his feet. Carrying a wooden box just slightly smaller than a shirt box, Jason joined them on stage and handed the box to Blake. "Thank you."

Jason nodded and then moved past his line of vision, his footsteps sounding behind Ty a few strides and then stopping, before Blake spoke again. "Today is special for another reason. In the last year, my boy and I have had to face many obstacles, but we've overcome them together. I'm so proud of him and before anyone can ever question who he belongs to again, I'm collaring him."

Wait.

What?

The word "collaring" was like a bomb strike Ty hadn't seen coming and his head started to lift, reeling from the shock, but he caught himself at the last moment and kept his position. Holy fuck, he couldn't have heard Blake correctly.

The few times Blake had fastened a leather collar around his neck, he'd loved the way it felt. Not in the physical sense so much, but more in the way its presence made him feel. The collars he'd worn in the past were for show, accessories to complement the outfit Blake had chosen for him, but with even those small bands of belonging around his neck, Ty had walked a little straighter, a little prouder. The feelings the collar brought out in him, he could only assume, were like those caused by a wedding ring—an outward sign of the commitment made to another person.

Ty's skin prickled as goose bumps covered his body, and he fought to keep his breathing even when Blake moved to stand before him. "So proud of you, boy," Blake whispered, running his hand through Ty's hair, and then he did something that shocked Ty even more than the statement of collaring. Blake dropped to his knees in front of Ty, placed a finger beneath Ty's chin, and lifted his head until their eyes met.

Blake smiled at him, a hopeful gleam in his dark-brown eyes, and held out a silver collar. "This is more than a sign of ownership, boy," Blake whispered for Ty's ears only. "It's a symbol of my commitment to you and yours to me."

Forcing his gaze away from those soft brown eyes, Ty looked down and accepted the collar. The silver-colored metal was heavy and cool beneath his fingers as he ran them along the polished surface, but it warmed quickly in his hand. When he turned it the lights reflected off the gold that covered the inside of the collar. Ty's breath hitched when he read the inscription.

Alongside their entwined initials were the words: Forever His.

"Before you say yes, know that once it's riveted on, it won't come off." Blake ran his fingers gently over Ty's where he held the collar. "It's permanent and indestructible, Ty, just like my commitment to you."

Ty took a deep breath and wiped his eyes before meeting Blake's gaze once again. "Scars and all?"

"Scars and all," Blake echoed with a soft smile on his handsome face.

Blake then helped Ty to his feet. He was a little off-balance with the swell of emotions surging through him, but Blake steadied him and took the collar. "Jason, if you'd be so kind," Blake said, holding the collar out. "My boy has accepted."

The applause, shouts, and whistles from their friends snapped Ty back to where they were and his cheeks heated. The embarrassment of having an audience for such a private moment was quickly forgotten, however, as Blake ushered him over to where Jason stood next to a small table.

"Display," Blake ordered before he walked to the table and picked up a small silver band.

Ty's hands went behind his back, and he shifted his feet slightly until his position and posture were perfect. His body responded to the elation of what was about to happen, his flesh warming and his cock hardening.

Blake brought the band over and showed it to Ty. It was almost identical in design to Ty's collar, the same silver metal with gold lining, only smaller in size. Blake tilted it and moved it closer so Ty could read the inscription. It was identical to his.

"It works both ways," Blake said softly.

Ty swallowed hard and nodded. Everything just seemed so surreal, or maybe he was just dreaming. The last year had certainly been a fantasy. Blake coming into his life, moving to New York City, he was a club owner for God's sake, and now a commitment not just as Blake's submissive but as his partner in every sense of the word. Damn, he didn't know if he wanted to laugh or cry.

Both emotions battled for supremacy and as an effect, Ty stood there trembling with his heart in his throat. He more than likely looked like a complete and utter fool since he was also aroused as hell, watching as Blake sat down in a chair next to the table where Jason had his tools laid out.

Blake, however, looked completely composed and sure of himself as he rolled up the right sleeve of his dress shirt, winking at Ty as he laid his exposed forearm on the table. "You don't think I would allow anyone to do something to you I hadn't tested out first, do you?"

"No, Sir," Ty responded hesitantly.

His hesitation had nothing to do with the question. He knew Blake would never do anything to him that wasn't completely safe, but he was confused as to why attaching a collar would be dangerous or something that would need to be tested first. A trickle of unease seeped into him as he watched Jason run a thick strip of leather and a wide piece of metal between Blake's wrist and the bracelet. Blake's entire forearm and hand, except a small section of the metal around his wrist, was then covered with some kind of heavy material.

Ty's brow furrowed, his anxiety level rising, as he observed Jason reach into what he'd thought was an ornate fire for decoration with a pair of tongs and pull out a red hot piece of metal. Unable to keep his eyes lowered, Ty looked to Blake in alarm. Blake, who could read Ty so well, smiled and said soothingly, "It's okay, focus right here on me."

There was a loud sound of metal hitting metal and Blake winced. Ty shot a look toward Jason and glared.

"Ty." Blake's voice was like the snap of a whip, one that couldn't be ignored, and Ty focused his eyes back on Blake's.

Clenching his fists where they rested against the small of his back, Ty forced himself to keep his eyes locked with his Dom's. As much as he tried, he couldn't completely ignore the sound or the steam billowing up as Jason poured water over Blake's wrist to cool the metal before setting the next rivet. Ty took a deep breath and held it. The effort it took to keep still caused his tense muscles to vibrate. He'd endure anything for Blake, any amount of pain—hell, he craved, often begged, for the erotic pain his lover could inflict. The thought of Blake being hurt, however, almost made him physically ill.

Jason was quick and when he patted Blake on the shoulder and said, "All done," Ty let out the breath he'd been holding.

Blake muttered his thanks to Jason, already moving toward Ty to stand behind him. "I'm officially yours, Ty. Are you ready to be mine?" he whispered, brushing his lips against Ty's ear.

"I already am, Sir," Ty answered without hesitation, meaning every word. He was Blake's in every sense of the word.

"Then let's make it official."

Ty allowed Blake to lead him to the leather bench and help him lie out in the proper position. The back of his head, neck, and shoulders were draped in heavy leather, but Ty was barely aware of what Jason was doing. Blake had gone to his knees in front of him, those dark eyes holding his as the Dom caressed Ty's cheek. Through the entire riveting process Ty felt no pain, none of the heat. He wasn't even aware of Jason or anyone else in the club as he lost himself in Blake's eyes and soothing touch.

He'd spent his entire life yearning to belong, to be wanted and loved. Even when he'd lost all hope of ever having a family, convincing himself he didn't need one and people weren't worthy of trust, on some level he'd never stopped dreaming, hoping.

Blake loved him, protected him, and brought so much happiness to his life. Wasn't that what family did? As he continued to stare at Blake, his eyes so warm, his expression one of pure bliss as Ty lay there accepting his symbol of commitment, it occurred to Ty that it didn't matter what kind of family you grew up in—the one you made was what was important.

Ty tried to blink back his tears, but one escaped and rolled down his cheek as he came to the realization that Blake and Martha had made him part of theirs.

Blake wiped the salty droplet from Ty's cheek and whispered, "I love you."

And Ty knew it, felt it in the center of his being that Blake loved him, and he in return loved Blake with everything he was. But he couldn't say it, afraid he would lose it and break down and weep like a baby. Instead he swallowed hard, keeping his teeth clenched, and nodded.

When the covering was pulled away and barrier between his neck and collar removed, Blake helped him to his feet and Ty nearly collapsed. There had been no pain, no physical hardship to endure; it was the full weight of the commitment behind the metal circling his throat that nearly drove him to his knees. He didn't fall, however, but stood in the center of the stage; with Blake at his back and in front of those gathered, Ty puffed out his chest and proudly displayed Blake's collar.

"Although this collar represents Ty's submission to me," Blake announced, "it's also a symbol of my devotion and commitment to him and his to me. It, as well as the band around my wrist, is a constant reminder of the promise we made to each other. It is the promise of forever, and I'll work every day to be worthy of him."

As everyone stood and applauded, whistling and calling out congratulations, Ty reached up and lovingly stroked the collar. *Forever.* Ty gave in to the overwhelming emotions, throwing his arms around Blake and burying his face in Blake's neck as the tears started to blur his vision.

Blake held him tightly, giving him a minute to get his emotions under control before pulling back slightly and lifting Ty's chin. "Go show it off so I can take you home."

Ty sniffed and grinned as he wiped at his damp cheeks. "Yes, Sir."

He started to pull away, but Blake stopped him and leaned in close, speaking against Ty's ear. "And when we get there, I'm going to fuck my beautiful boy through the mattress."

A shudder went through Ty at the harsh growl in Blake's voice, and he groaned loudly when his cock was grabbed in a tight fist and pumped a couple of times. Ty practically ran off the stage. The sooner he accepted the congratulations from their friends, the quicker they could go home.

BLAKE HAD seduced his mind and demanded his focus, and in return Ty had given him his body to command. Yet in the end, Blake had found his soul and given him the home and family he was always missing, and Ty was his forever.

Keep reading!

Mauled

Beyond Duty: Book Two
A Guards of Folsom story

By SJD Peterson

Gunther Duchene, aka "Gunny", and Macalister Jones, aka "Mac", have overcome the obstacles of coming out and retiring after serving more than twenty years as Marines. Their exit ceremony is behind them, their wedding vows are made, and now it's time for the honeymoon. What better way to kick off their marriage than enjoying the retirement gift Mac gave Gunny? With the leather pants and collar packed, it's off to New York City and the Guards of Folsom club to celebrate—BDSM style.

To all who wanted more Mac & Gunny, this is for you.

Prologue

MAC WATCHED Gunny's face closely as he lifted the lid and frowned as he pushed aside the tissue paper and pulled out the gift. He brought the folded pair of black leather pants to his nose and inhaled deeply. His smile was crooked when he lowered the pants and looked at Mac.

"Next adventure?"

"You said you wanted to start exploring the leather-daddy clubs," Mac said easily. "Figured you'd need to be dressed appropriately."

"In just leather pants?" Gunny teased.

"Keep digging," Mac said and pointed toward the box. He could hear the growl in his voice at the thought of Gunny going in one of those clubs in nothing but a pair of leather pants. Mac would be up on charges of assault soon after arrival.

Gunny folded the pants and set them on the dresser next to the box. He ran a hand lovingly over the leather before he rummaged further. He pulled away more tissue paper and removed another garment. He carefully unfolded it and held the black leather long-sleeve shirt up to his chest.

Gunny tilted his head. "Um, Mac. The subs usually wear a harness."

"And you'll be wearing that," Mac pointed out resolutely. "And it will be buttoned to the top."

"But—"

"This is not open for discussion, Gunny. Keep digging," Mac grumbled and crossed his arms over his chest.

"And you thought I'm cute when I'm jealous," Gunny chuckled under his breath.

Mac grunted in response as he watched Gunny fold the shirt in the same careful manner and set it on top of the pants.

Gunny pulled out the last gift and unwrapped it. He held the collar in both hands, the tissue paper fluttering to the floor. He ran his thumb over the leather, flicking the large silver O-ring. The look on Gunny's face was hard to read. Mac had expected what? Turned-on? Excitement? But what he saw looked like reverence, confusion, tenderness. Mac hadn't expected those emotions.

Mac hefted himself off the bed and ran his hand down Gunny's back. "You okay?"

"I sometimes have these dreams," Gunny said softly, still looking at the collar. "I'm in this club, and there is this huge crowd standing around me all trying to get my attention. I'm not sure whom to pick. They are all screaming, and it's this jumble of noise so I can't understand them. I'm so fucking confused, but I know I can't be there without someone." Gunny turned over the collar in his hand and shook his head. "Then you push your way through the crowd, walk right up to me, and put a collar around my neck, and everyone knows who I belong to."

"That's why I'd never let you in one of those clubs alone." He wrapped his arms around Gunny's waist and kissed the back of his neck. "Everyone would try to take you from me."

Gunny set the collar aside and turned in Mac's arms. "They could try," he said and pulled Mac in closer.

Chapter 1

"HEY, GUNNY! You're never going to guess who I was just talking to." Mac stopped dead in his tracks when he entered their home gym. Gunny was standing near the weight bench doing overhead military presses in nothing but a pair of nylon shorts. His muscles were bulging from the effort, sweat rolling down his impressive chest.

"Who?" Gunny grunted, still working the weights.

"Doesn't matter," Mac groaned. And it didn't. Hell, the world didn't matter, not when Gunny looked like that. Mac stepped up to Gunny as he extended his arms over his head. "Hold that pose."

"What?" Gunny asked, sounding confused, but he held still.

Perhaps it was the lust Gunny had to see in Mac's eyes or the fact that Mac was leaning in to chase a droplet down Gunny's chest that made him smile knowingly.

"You're interrupting my workout."

"Oh hell, I'm about to work you out all right," Mac assured him and ran the palms of his hands over Gunny's hard pecs, across his shoulders, and along his biceps. He then gripped the bar, helping to hold it as he nipped at Gunny's chin.

"Promise?" Gunny chased Mac's lips as he brushed them along Gunny's cheek.

"It's a guaran-fucking-tee." Mac pressed their mouths together, demanding entrance with his tongue. Gunny opened to him. He never denied Mac.

The kiss went on, hot and wet and so damn good, until their arms began to tremble and they were breathless. Mac ended the kiss, licking the last of Gunny's flavor from his lips, then helped him set the bar on its brace.

"I guess I better shower, then," Gunny suggested and shook out his arms.

Mac grabbed a towel from a hook and tossed it at Gunny. He caught it easily and swiped it across his damp face.

"That's cleaned up enough," Mac murmured and snatched the towel away. He slid his arm around Gunny's slick back, stepping close once again. "I like you like this. Remember that time we snuck off from morning PT?" Mac released Gunny and stepped back. "Oh shit, that reminds me. I came in to tell you about the phone call I got before you distracted me."

Gunny flexed his biceps. "Yeah, totally my fault. It's the guns."

"Stop that," Mac grumbled and swatted playfully at Gunny's impressive artillery. "So as I was saying, Captain Walker called. He wants us to go to DC. A lot of shit's been going down since the repeal. He wants us to come and speak at a conference."

"Speak about what?"

"Do you not ever listen to me? The repeal. You know, how I can tap your ass and still take out an enemy from two thousand yards."

"I'm pretty sure that isn't exactly what the brass had in mind," Gunny chuckled.

"Maybe not exactly those words, but same meaning."

Gunny froze, his eyes going wide. "Did you say we?"

"Yup."

"Oh hell no! I am not talking in front of a bunch of strangers. You're the chatty one—you do it."

"No prob. All you have to do is stand there and look purty."

"Yeah, well, I'm not real good at that either, not with this mug."

Mac rolled his eyes at just how ridiculous Gunny could be. But it was one of the things he loved about the man. Gunny had no clue how incredibly sexy he was. Good damn thing too or he might've actually considered what Cap had said at their exit ceremony: *"Is this the best you can do?"* Mac might like to act all tough and gruff. Hell, he *was* when the situation called for it, badass-take-you-out-machine, even. But it was no secret Mac was a pile of mushy love-struck goo when it came to Gunny.

"So I was thinking," Mac continued without commenting on Gunny's concern. "We go to DC, give our"—Gunny raised a single brow—"okay, *my* little speech, then we take us a little vacation."

Gunny grabbed a cold bottle of water out of the minifridge and held it up. When Mac nodded, Gunny tossed it to him and then grabbed one for himself. "I don't want to vacation in DC. It's not really what I'd call a relaxing, fun kind of town." Gunny leaned against the wall and opened his water.

Mac found himself distracted from the conversation again when Gunny tipped the bottle up, his throat working as he gulped the water down. Gunny swallowing down other things flashed in Mac's head, and his cock twitched. Unable to resist such a temptation, Mac went after that sexy throat, nipping it and then swiping his tongue from Gunny's Adam's apple up to just below his ear, tasting the salt of his skin. Gunny groaned, the deep husky sound going straight to Mac's groin.

"I had this idea," Mac murmured against Gunny's warm flesh.

"Let me guess, it involves lube and me sweating even more."

"Yes, that's the immediate plan," Mac agreed. He grabbed Gunny's hips, pulling him toward the weight bench. Mac sat and encouraged Gunny to straddle him while Mac continued to lick and taste, hands roaming over Gunny's muscular back. "But I was talking about our vacation. After DC, I think we should finally take our honeymoon. What do you think of New York City?"

"Crowded and smelly," Gunny moaned, tipping his head to the side to give Mac more room to explore.

"True, but they also have a few of those clubs you've wanted to check out, and I've been dying to see you in those leathers I bought you."

"I think I like both your ideas." Gunny thrust hard against Mac's groin, emphasizing his meaning.

Mac responded in kind, rubbing and rutting, loving the way Gunny's hard body and equally hard cock felt against his. Twenty-two-plus years he and Gunny had been together, and it still amazed Mac that Gunny could rev him up like a teenager with just one look. Even more astonishing, each time with Gunny seemed to be better than the last.

Mac slid his hand between their bodies, past the waistband of Gunny's shorts and wrapped his fist around Gunny's cock. "Gonna work you out now," Mac told him. He didn't give Gunny a chance to respond, taking his mouth in a deep kiss while he set a hard, fast pace along Gunny's length. Mac kissed Gunny until he was forced to break for a breath, but the rhythm of their bodies never slowed. Gunny picked up the same pace, thrusting into Mac's fist.

Mac reluctantly released Gunny long enough to pull off his T-shirt, but took Gunny back in hand as soon as he was free from the material.

"Fuck yeah, that's better," Gunny commented as he ran his callused hands over Mac's chest. Mac yelped when Gunny leaned down and bit his right nipple at the same time he pinched the left. The spark of pain shot a jolt straight to his cock, causing it to throb. The pleasure intensified when Gunny shoved the front of Mac's shorts down and ran his rough hand along Mac's heated flesh.

The shrill sound of the phone distracted Mac for a second, but it wasn't enough to hold his attention long. Gunny didn't seem to notice it at all, his free hand landing on Mac's neck and holding him close as he sucked and licked at Mac's flesh while continuing to work Mac's cock.

The sound of his mom's voice on the answering machine was like a bucket of cold water poured on them, and they both froze. "Macalister, it's Mom. Just wanted you to know Dad and I will be there shortly."

"Fuck me," Mac cursed and jumped up, dumping Gunny on his ass.

"I was trying to," Gunny grumbled.

Mac jerked his shorts up. "What day is it?"

"Saturday, why?"

"Damn! Damn! Damn!" Mac ran a hand over his head as panic began to surge through him. The house was a mess, and he was pretty sure they'd left out evidence of their late-night fuck fest.

Gunny didn't seem to be concerned about the situation; rather, he lay back with a slight grin and began stroking himself. "C'mere and let's finish this. Will only take a second."

"Go ahead, but the thought of my mom and dad walking in while I have my dick"—Mac tilted his head, taking in the sight before him—"or your dick in my hand, makes me a little less than turned-on, ya know?"

"Bullshit! Your shorts are tented like a goddamn big top, now get over here."

Gunny's voice was demanding, seductive, but Mac could tell he was barely containing his laughter. Mac, on the other hand, was completely freaked-out. He was in his forties, for fuck's sake; he shouldn't be worried about being caught by Mommy and Daddy.

"You are just too adorable for words," Gunny chuckled.

"Fuck you and put that thing away," Mac grumbled. "Now go shower."

"Ooh, good idea. Water sports," Gunny purred teasingly and pushed to his feet.

Mac spun and stabbed a finger at Gunny. "No! You're going to shower—alone—and I'm going to go make sure there are no dirty drawers on the living room floor."

"Aww. C'mon, you started this," Gunny mumbled.

"Oh shit. There's a sink full of breakfast dishes." Mac grunted and swatted Gunny's hand away when he tried to grab Mac's shorts. He then shoved Gunny into the bathroom and closed the door before Gunny could try anything else.

"Oh good Lord, you do realize you're over twenty-one, don't you? Then again, even at your age, you probably don't want your parents finding what's lying on the coffee table," Gunny called out before Mac heard the distinctive sound of a shower coming on.

Mac's chin nearly hit the floor. The thought of his parents finding the toy had him rushing up the stairs. "Why in the hell didn't you remind me they were coming!" There were certain things a man shouldn't have to explain to his mother—*oh shit*—or his father. Mac picked up the pace, taking the steps two at a time. As he cleared the last step, the doorbell rang; seconds later, the front door squeaked open.

"Macalister, Gunther?" Mom called out.

Mac dove toward the table. "Ow!" he yelped as his knee came in contact with the corner of the end table. Ignoring the throbbing pain, Mac grabbed the dildo and shoved it under the cushion of the couch just as his mom and dad walked in.

"The door was open," his mom said in way of greeting.

Mac scrambled to his feet and sat on the couch. "Hi," he responded and waved, breathing harshly. His eyes went wide in panic when the toy began to vibrate. "Uh, umm… c'mon in," he sputtered and shifted again, hoping the damn thing would turn off. To his horror, the vibration intensified.

"What's that vibrating?" his dad asked as he took a seat in the recliner at the end of the couch.

A double-headed shlong. "New back massager," he lied. Unable to meet his dad's eyes, Mac grabbed the remote and clicked on the television, turning the volume up. "Gunny's in the shower, and I was just about to watch the game."

"What game?" Dad asked, eyeing him with suspicion.

"Umm… well…. One I recorded," he sputtered.

"I brought you two some zucchini bread," his mom commented and held up a brown paper bag. "I'll just take it to the kitchen."

Bless you for the save. Mac smiled. "Thanks and don't mind the mess. I haven't had a chance to do the breakfast dishes yet." He shifted again, but the damn thing wouldn't turn off. Sweat dampened his brow, his belly flip-flopping nervously as he looked back and forth between his parents who were staring at him with odd expressions.

"Everything okay?" Mom asked, sounding concerned.

"Never better. Hey, Dad, I gotta show you the… ummm…. The new greenhouse." Mac jumped up, praying the schlong vibrating beneath the cushion stayed hidden.

"I saw it the last time I was here."

"Oh yeah… but… I got some new plants." Mac stood near his dad's chair, blocking the view of the couch, just in case.

"Right now? I just got here, and you said you had a game to watch."

"No time like the present, and I'm sure you've seen it."

"Oh, Theodore, go look at Mac's greenhouse. He's obviously very proud of it," Mom said with a wink toward Mac before she headed to the kitchen. Mac was so going to kiss her for that.

Dad grumbled something incoherent, but he got up and followed his wife, Mac trailing along behind them.

Once Mom was at the counter and Dad was heading out the back door, Mac called out, "Go ahead and check it out, I'll meet you out there. Just going to call down and let Gunny know you're here." *And hide my rubber dicky.*

Dad tossed a wave in acknowledgment over his shoulder, and while Mom took care of her treats, Mac rushed to the living room, grabbed the hidden toy, and ran to the stairs. "Gunny, my mom and dad are here," he yelled out and tossed the dildo, then cringed when the thing hit Gunny in the chest as he suddenly appeared.

"What the hell, man!"

"Serves you right," Mac hissed, completely unapologetic. He left Gunny to take care of the damn thing. After all, a little rubber rash was nothing compared to the severe case of embarrassment Mac was dealing with.

"Hi, Clare," Gunny said happily as he entered the kitchen.

"Hi, sweetie," Clare replied over her shoulder as she ran water into the sink. "There's fresh zucchini bread in the breadbox."

"Oh yum, I do love your bread. You don't have to do those." Gunny pecked her on the cheek.

"Mac forgot we were coming, didn't he?" Clare ignored Gunny's protest and started washing dishes.

"What makes you think that?"

"Dirty drawers on the floor, breakfast dishes in the sink, and if that wasn't enough of a hint, then the fact your husband was hiding sex toys in the couch was a dead giveaway."

"Clare!"

"Yes, dear?"

"He was not," Gunny lied. He turned his back to her to hide his warm cheeks. He opened the fridge, contemplated a beer—he damn sure could use one—but took a soda instead. "Where is he anyway?" If he was going to beat Mac for dropping him in this hornets' nest, he at least had to know where the bastard was.

"He took Theodore out to show him his new plants."

"Mac hasn't gotten any new plants," Gunny said, confused, as he leaned against the counter, keeping his face averted.

"Yes, dear, I know. You might want to go check and make sure everything is in order in the living room, and while you're there, could you turn that television down?"

Gunny could not believe he was having this conversation with Mac's mom. The fact that she was so blasé about it was even scarier, or hell, maybe it was cool that she wasn't bothered about it. Nope, it was scary, and he was thankful to get the hell out of the kitchen and end this freaky conversation.

Chapter 2

MAC HAD offered to take his parents out to dinner, but Mom insisted on making him and Gunny a home-cooked meal. As Mac shoved in another large bite of honey-glazed ham, he could easily admit her idea was a hell of a lot better than his.

"Any more mashed potatoes?" Mac asked as he eyed the bowl hopefully.

"Don't talk with your mouth full," his mom chastised. "You already cleaned the bowl, but I can make more if you like."

"That would be great!"

"Don't trouble yourself, Clare. He's had plenty," Gunny piped in and then kicked Mac under the table.

"Ow! What the hell was that for?" Mac grumbled.

"For being greedy. Now finish your supper like a good boy and you can have dessert."

Mac stuck his tongue out at Gunny like a petulant two-year-old, just for show. He really wasn't all that upset, not with Mom's chocolate cake in the kitchen with his name on it.

"Have there been any issues with your retirement or pension, you know, with what happened at the exit ceremony?" his dad suddenly asked.

Mac knew his dad was still a little uncomfortable with Mac's sexuality, but he was trying. It was all Mac could ask for.

"No, sir. No problems at all. In fact, I was telling Gunny right before you got here that I received a call from Captain Walker. He wants us to go to DC and speak at a convention."

"How exciting," Mom exclaimed. "You're a great public speaker, Macalister."

"I've been following a bit of it in the news. Quite a few military personnel don't seem to be real happy with the repeal." Dad wiped his mouth on a napkin, then tossed it on his empty plate and pushed it aside.

"I'll grab the coffee and dessert," Mom offered. "Come help me, will you, Gunther?"

"Yes, ma'am."

Mac waited until Mom and Gunny left before responding to his dad's statement. "It's going to take some time before people are comfortable with it. I suppose there are plenty that won't ever get used to it, but seeing as it's the law, they're just going to have to deal with it."

Dad was quiet, staring out the window. Mac knew he was thinking about what he'd heard by the thoughtful expression on his face. Mac was all kinds of curious, but he didn't push. Dad didn't make him wait long.

"I think I would have agreed with those opposing it," he finally said.

"Would have?" Mac asked when Dad didn't say anything further.

"I never knew any gay men, and the ones I saw on TV weren't real—" He thrummed his fingers on the table as if trying to find the correct word. He shrugged one shoulder, then settled on "Manly. I don't know that I'd want that Red Paul guy—"

"RuPaul," Mac corrected.

"Whatever his name is. He, in those heels and wigs, wouldn't make me feel all that safe if he were the one I was depending on to protect this country. But you," his dad said, turning his head and looking Mac in the eye. "I slept peacefully knowing men like you and Gunther were keeping watch."

A lump of emotion formed in Mac's throat, and he had to force it down before he could respond. "Thank you, that means a lot to me."

"You proved me wrong and changed my opinion about gays in the military. You're a damn fine Marine, son."

Mac didn't know what else to say. Hell, he didn't know if he could, not with a steady voice anyway. He simply smiled and nodded and tried his damnedest not to start bawling. It meant the world to him that his parents accepted him and Gunny, but it was especially important to him that he make his dad proud.

Gunny came in carrying a tray with coffee mugs and dessert, Mom right behind him. Mac could tell from the concerned expression on Gunny's face that he noticed Mac's mental state. All Mac could do to reassure Gunny was, once again, nod and smile, the emotions swirling through him not allowing him to do anything more.

No one said a word until the coffee and cake was handed out and Gunny and Mom had once again taken their seats. Gunny laid a hand on Mac's thigh and squeezed, silently letting him know he was there for him.

"How are you feeling about giving the speech in DC, Gunther?" Dad asked.

Gunny washed down his cake with a sip of coffee and then said, "I'm not worried at all, sir, since I won't be speaking. It's going to be a repeat of the speech at the exit ceremony. I'll just be there for moral support."

"It's what he does best," Mac said with a wink. It really wasn't what Gunny did best, but it was the best thing he did that could be admitted to in present company.

"I'm sure that's not true. Gunther can handle himself just fine; he's simply a man of few words," Mom piped in.

"Ha! You don't know him like I do. He can outtalk me."

Dad raised a brow, his expression disbelieving.

"What? He can," Mac insisted.

"Mmm-hmm," Dad hummed, not looking the least bit convinced.

"Macalister Jones, you stop telling fibs. Ain't no man nor woman alive that can get a word in edgewise when you get on a roll," Mom said, calling him out on his bullshit.

Gunny snorted, then choked on his cake and began laughing along with his parents.

"Whatever," Mac grumbled and took a big bite. He could be quiet—sometimes—when he wanted to. He just rarely wanted to.

Once the laughter died down, Mom turned to Gunny and asked, "How are your parents?"

"They're doing well, thank you. Mom and I have been talking quite a bit. It's still a little awkward, but she's trying."

"That's good," Mom responded with a gentle smile. "It's hard letting go of old hurts sometimes, but as long as you're both willing to try and are honest, it will work out."

"Yes, ma'am."

"And if it doesn't, you got this old mama to turn to," she added and patted Gunny's arm. "I'll pray for you both."

"Thank you," Gunny muttered, sounding nearly as choked up as Mac felt earlier.

"You're welcome. Now, have you two decided what you're going to do for the holidays? Dad and I would love it if you came home."

"Gunny and I haven't really talked about it yet, but I'm not so sure it's a good idea."

Dad started to respond, but Mac held up a hand to stop him. "You know I love you both, but I don't want to ruin your holiday, because quite honestly, I don't know if I can spend an hour, let alone a full two days with Ted." *Not without punching the fucker in the mouth.* A trip to the ER for Ted, blood on Mom's carpet, and Dad having to break up his sons certainly would put a damper on the holiday festivities. There was no love lost between him and the hypocritical, homophobic asshole.

"He's still your brother," Dad pointed out.

"Don't remind me," Mac sniffed.

"Macalister, Ted is trying. He's been clean and sober for thirty-eight days."

"Wow, Mom, really, a whole thirty-eight days? Did he tell you that?" He didn't trust Ted as far as he could throw the fat bastard.

"As a matter of fact, he did."

"Pfft, I don't—"

"Macalister," Mom said harshly and shot him a look that made him feel like he was five and just caught being naughty. He snapped his mouth shut.

"Dad and I went to his thirty-day celebration. He really is working hard this time and already looks so much better. He plans on staying in rehab for however long it takes to heal and get healthy."

"That's because he has nowhere else to go," Mac muttered under his breath.

"What was that?" Mom asked.

"Nothing. I hope for your sake he does stay clean and sober, but you'll have to forgive me if I don't share your faith in his recovery." Mac leaned close to Gunny's ear and whispered, "Then he'd be a clean asshole."

Gunny elbowed him and bit his lip to keep from laughing. He and Gunny had discussed Mac's relationship with Ted. While Gunny understood Mac's distaste for his brother—Gunny felt the same way—he thought Mac should try to forgive Ted for their mom's sake.

Mac would rather have his left nut ripped from his body than have to deal with Ted again. The man was a waste of breath.

"At least consider coming home," Dad offered, successfully ending the conversation on Ted for now. "Clare, we better get this mess cleaned up and get going."

"Going? Going where? You're more than welcome to stay in our spare room," Gunny suggested.

"Dad and I got ourselves a honeymoon suite down at the Econo Lodge."

"Seriously?" Mac chuckled. "Mom, that old place doesn't have a suite, let alone one suitable for newlyweds."

"Anytime your dad and I get us a hotel, we act like newlyweds. Ain't that right, Tiger," she purred, waggling her brows at her husband.

Mac pointed a finger at her warningly. "We are so not going there."

Mom laughed and began gathering up the dirty dishes. "Well, son, we're old, not dead. Your dad still has a little pep."

Mac covered his ears. "Dad, make her stop."

Dad shrugged and sat back in his chair with a cheeky grin.

"Mac, grab them dishes," Gunny blurted out and jumped to his feet. Apparently he was done with the conversation too. "We'll clean up and let these two honeymooners get to their suite."

"I honestly hope you two will consider coming for Christmas," Mom repeated.

"I promise we will try," Mac said as he and Gunny walked his parents to the door.

She then hit Mac with a low blow to his heartstrings when she added, "Dad and I are getting up there in years, don't know how many more we have left."

"Way to go, Mom. You want to stomp on the heart you just stabbed while you're at it?" Mac grumbled.

"Nope. I'll save that for if you don't show up. Love you." She pecked his cheek and then Gunny's before walking out with a grin.

Mac patted his dad's back. "That's a wicked woman you got there."

"Don't I know it. See you two at Christmas." He chuckled and followed his wife out the door.

"Looks like we'll be doing a bit of traveling over the next few weeks," Gunny pointed out. "I better check with Tom and see if he can keep an eye on the place while we're gone."

Mac grabbed Gunny's arm and stopped him before he could walk away. Gunny gave Mac a questioning look. Mac's response was to spin Gunny and shove him against the door, then use his body to pin him against it.

"Then you better wear me out on our honeymoon. Make sure I'm good and relaxed before I have to deal with Ted."

"I thought it was about my fantasy, not yours," Gunny responded. He grabbed Mac's hips and pulled him closer still.

"What's yours is mine, as the saying goes."

Gunny thrust hard against Mac, causing him to hiss. "And what's yours is mine. Now where were we before your parents interrupted us?"

"Right here," Mac growled and took Gunny's mouth in a deep kiss.

Chapter 3

"THIS IS Blake Henderson. How can I help you?"

"Hi, my name is Macalister Jones, and I'm calling about possibly visiting your club."

"The club is open to the public. Doors open Monday through Sunday at seven pm."

Mac shifted the phone to his other ear. "No, sir. I'm not interested in the dance club. I'd like to bring my partner to your exclusive club while we're on our honeymoon."

"Ah, we don't normally allow day passes," Blake chuckled. "Would kind of negate the exclusive part, now wouldn't it? Plus, we do a very extensive background check, require references, and you would need to be sponsored by a current member."

"Oh," Mac responded dejectedly as he ran a hand over his head. "I hadn't realized there was such a thorough process. This would be our first time at a club such as yours."

"There are other clubs in the area that are open to the public," Blake informed him.

"Great. Gunny and I live in Riverview and aren't familiar with the area. Could you perhaps recommend a place?"

"I can try. What exactly are you looking for?"

"To be honest, I'm not actually sure. Gunny and I haven't ever been to a club. We basically started playing with the whole power exchange thing for fun and learned it helped Gunny deal with the stresses of combat."

"Combat?"

"Yes, sir. Gunny and I were Marines for over twenty years. He sometimes needs to give up control to ground him. But we just retired, and he's got this fantasy about visiting a club. I want to make it come true on our honeymoon."

"Wow," Blake replied. "How long have you been together?"

"We met in boot camp."

"You stayed together the entire time? In the military?"

"Yes, sir."

"That had to be hard, considering the attitudes toward gay men." Blake sounded awed.

"Well, it's not like anyone knew we were gay."

"Even more impressive. I'll tell you what, I'd still require the background check on both of you. The safety of our members is of the utmost importance here, but…."

Mac heard a tapping sound, as if Blake was thrumming his fingers on a hard surface. "Sir?"

"I'd love to help you fulfill your husband's fantasy here at the Guards of Folsom."

"Great! Thank you, I truly appreciate it."

"You're welcome. I'm going to transfer you to my partner since I have no idea what my fax number is. Ty will be able to take your information and answer any other questions you have. And Mr. Jones?"

"Yes, sir?"

"Thank you for your service."

"My pleasure."

Ty, as promised, was able to get the process rolling and was completely professional. Mac still wasn't totally comfortable with the idea of Gunny dressed in leather and men gawking at him. Mac's inner jealous madman hated the idea. However, there wasn't much he wouldn't do for Gunny, and Ty and Blake's professionalism and security process did set Mac's mind a little at ease.

WITH THE rescheduling of the conference in DC until after the New Year, it freed up a little time for Mac to focus on their honeymoon. All the documents had been faxed to Ty and Blake, and they'd been approved for a day pass to the club. Ty had sent Mac a contract along with the club rules. Most of them were pretty basic, common-sense kinds of things like respecting others and being nonjudgmental and discreet. Blah, blah, blah. What they didn't include were the rules of how a Dom should behave while at the club. He didn't know what was expected of him, how he was supposed to behave, and he hated not having all the facts before walking into a situation new to him.

Now, here he was in New York City feeling like a fish out of water, flopping around and gasping for breath.

Mac stepped out of the elevator, a pocket full of aspirin for the throb in his head, which had settled there as his nerves began to fray. *Dammit, it's your honeymoon, for fuck's sake, enjoy it.* One last deep breath and he slid the card into the slot, then entered the hotel room.

Gunny stood in the middle of their room dressed in nothing but the tight leather pants Mac had bought him. Gunny's hands were clasped behind his back, bare feet shoulder-width apart, impressive chest pushed out and head held high. He was a sight to behold.

All worries fled as Mac took a moment to appreciate Gunny's magnificent form. The pelt of dark hair on his chest and belly was now sprinkled with silver, as was the hair on his face and head, but his muscles were still thick and taut. Gunny worked hard to stay fit and keep his body powerful, and it showed. In Mac's opinion, Gunny was sexier now than he was the first time he'd laid eyes on him. The years, maturity, and wisdom looked damn good on his man. Mmm, and on his boy. And tonight that's what Gunny was, his boy and all Mac's.

Mac noticed the way Gunny's breathing sped ever so slightly, the only outward appearance of Gunny's excitement and anticipation. As Mac continued to stare, he knew Gunny would stand there, perfectly still, for however long Mac asked him to. Having control of such a powerful creature was a major turn-on. The fact Gunny handed the control over to him willingly and with complete trust made it all the more intense.

Although Gunny would wait, Mac was greedy and impatient. He needed to touch, explore, lick, and taste. He stood behind Gunny and ran the tip of his index finger down Gunny's spine, enjoying the way the skin flushed from his touch. He then followed the same path with his tongue, the flush turning into a full-body shudder.

Mac grinned against Gunny's warm flesh. "You seem to be anticipating something, boy," Mac teased.

"Anything you want to give me, Sir."

Mac continued to kiss and lick Gunny's back as he spoke. "I'm not sure I want to share you with anyone."

"I'm all yours, Sir."

"Yes, you are," Mac said adamantly. "Every luscious inch of you is mine. I don't know how well I'm going to handle having every man in the club drooling over you," he admitted.

Gunny was silent for a moment, allowing Mac to explore. Mac swirled his tongue around the boney prominent at Gunny's neck, causing him to shudder again. "We don't have to go," Gunny finally responded.

It was true. If Mac called it off and kept Gunny all to himself, Gunny wouldn't complain. However, Mac had heard the hint of regret in Gunny's voice and seen the way his shoulders slumped ever so slightly. Mac would not deny him this fantasy. The jealousy and possessiveness was his issue, not Gunny's. As much as he'd prefer to lock Gunny in the hotel room and have him all to himself, it was selfish.

He was supposed to be proud to show off such a beautiful man as his sub, and he was. Damn proud. If he were more secure in his role as Dom, surely it wouldn't bother him as much. But he wasn't a Dom, and Gunny wasn't his sub. They didn't live the lifestyle, nor did either of them want to. At least they had never talked about it. Their lives before retirement hadn't really allowed for them to explore the possibilities. It had always been something that was private between them, something Gunny needed when his head got all wonky, as he called it, and his need to give up control and just be still became overwhelming. But in a club setting, around strangers, Mac didn't feel in control one bit. To say he was nervous about giving Gunny what he needed, to be what he needed, was an understatement.

He needed a distraction, something to calm his frazzled nerves, and he knew exactly who and what could do that. It wasn't the pills in his pocket he needed. Sighing internally, Mac pushed down his apprehension. His first priority and concern had to be Gunny. He needed to help Gunny find his headspace. What he had planned to get Gunny there, their preclub hors d'oeuvres so to speak, would help calm his nerves and relax them both. Win-win.

Mac moved to stand in front of Gunny. "Look at me, boy."

Gunny raised his eyes and met Mac's gaze.

"Don't I always give you what you need?"

"Yes, Sir," Gunny replied without hesitation.

"Do I ever deny you anything?"

"You deny me orgasms," Gunny said and then bit his lip trying to hide his grin.

"Let me rephrase that," Mac chuckled. "Don't I only deny you when it's for your own good?"

"Yes, Sir," Gunny said soberly, the look of regret back in Gunny's eyes as he must be thinking Mac was going to deny him his fantasy.

"Stop worrying and trust me. I'm going to show you off tonight, but first a little appetizer is in order. Take out your cock."

"Yes, Sir." Gunny instantly began untying his leathers, but when he started to push them down his hips, Mac stopped him.

"Leave them on. I had a hell of a time getting them on you."

"Sir?" Gunny asked, tilting his head in confusion.

Mac pushed Gunny's hands out of the way and carefully adjusted Gunny's cock till the head was exposed just above the leather laces, the strands crossing the length of his shaft. The black ties looked obscene against Gunny's ruddy flesh, causing Mac's mouth to water.

Once he had Gunny exactly as he wanted him, he leaned in and nipped Gunny's chin. "You're not to come until I tell you."

"Yes, Sir."

Mac licked and nipped his way down Gunny's furred chest and belly and then went to his knees as he placed a soft kiss to the head of Gunny's cock. "You're not to move from your display position," Mac informed him, then swiped the tip of his tongue over the slit, Gunny's delicious flavor exploding across his taste buds. He licked it again, dipping his tongue into the slit, searching out more until Gunny moaned.

"You're not to move, will not interfere in any way until I've had my fill, but I want your voice. I want to hear what you're thinking, feeling." Mac scraped his teeth gently over the swollen head. "Want to hear you beg."

"Yes, Sir," Gunny groaned, twitching as he fought not to pull away from the tickling sensation of Mac's teeth and tongue.

Mac took the flared head into his mouth, sucking hard until he pulled another deep, husky moan from Gunny. "You taste good, boy."

"Thank you, Sir, feels good too."

"Describe it," Mac demanded and then sucked Gunny back into his mouth.

"Oh God! I can feel you sucking it, your tongue swirling in and out of my slit. Sends a jolt right down to my nuts." Mac sucked harder. "Damn, more intense now, the head is tingling, balls a little achy."

Mac pulled off with a pop, licking his lips for flair. "You are a true feast, boy." He then ran his tongue around the rim of Gunny's cock head, feeling and exploring each little bump and ridge while he deeply inhaled Gunny's musky scent.

"Tickles," Gunny moaned.

"You think you could come from me doing this?" Mac asked as he continued to tease Gunny.

"Don't know. It feels good, but I think I need more… more…." Gunny blew out a heavy breath. "Fuck, that's nice, but I need more friction."

"Like this?" Mac asked as he cupped Gunny's cock and squeezed slightly.

"Fuck yeah, just like that." Gunny thrust hard against Mac's hand.

Mac instantly withdrew. "Boy," he warned.

Gunny went still. "Sorry, Sir."

"I probably should punish you for your disobedience." Mac eyed Gunny's cock and licked his lips. "Perhaps I will later."

Gunny cried out when Mac squeezed his balls roughly and sucked the head of his cock back into his mouth, greedily taking Gunny's flavor in.

"I like it when you squeeze them. Like the edge of pain it's creating, like…. Oh fuck." Gunny groaned harshly when Mac tightened his grip. "Like the way my body reacts. Not sure if I want to pull away or beg for more. Frustrating. Not sure. It's like… I… ah."

The trembling in Gunny's body increased as if he were having a hard time staying in position. The urge to thrust had to be maddening. "Keep talking, boy," Mac ordered when Gunny grew silent.

"There's this coiling at the base of my spine, tightening, hardening with each suck, swirl of your tongue. Like a knot forming."

Mac swiped his tongue down Gunny's cock, teasing each bit of exposed flesh between the ties. "If I allowed you to move, what would you be doing right now?" Mac asked as he moved back up to the head of Gunny's cock and took it into his mouth again.

"Take my pants off—"

Mac sat back and smirked up at Gunny as he continued to roughly massage his balls. "But you couldn't wait to get into them. Don't you like my gift?" Mac teased.

"I love them, but what I'd really like to do is grab the back of your head and fuck your mouth. Make you take me deep—blow my load down your throat. Thrust. God, how I want to thrust and move and…. So goddamn frustrating."

Gunny's words became garbled, running together when Mac took him back into his mouth and began to suck in earnest. Gunny wouldn't last much longer. The shaking in his body had increased, and he was breathing harshly. Mac had no intentions of making Gunny suffer too long. This was about an immediate need, to take the edge off.

Mac popped the button on his jeans and unzipped, freeing his own throbbing cock. He wrapped his fist around it and began stroking hard and fast. It wouldn't take much for either of them. Gunny was too fucking sexy when he needed, the sound of his deep, husky voice revving Mac up.

Gunny's moaning and babbling increased, as did the shaking. Mac stroked faster until his balls drew up and his orgasm rushed through him.

"Come for me, boy," Mac demanded.

Gunny cried out, and Mac barely had time to take Gunny back into his mouth before Gunny was coming. Mac swallowed hungrily, drinking down his lover's seed. It was all he needed to push him over the edge, and he came hard, shooting his load just as he took in the last drop of Gunny's release.

Mac laid his cheek against Gunny's thigh as he caught his breath—the cool leather felt good against his heated skin. It took him a moment to compose himself before he could stand on weak legs.

"Well now," he murmured as he pressed his lips against Gunny's. "That's what I call one hell of an appetizer."

"I so agree, Sir. Whew, so, so good," Gunny mumbled.

Mac nuzzled the side of Gunny's neck, licking the salt from his skin and enjoying the closeness and postorgasm glow for a moment longer. "Okay, boy, we better get going," Mac said with one last kiss to Gunny's neck. "I cleaned up your mess. It's only fair you clean up mine."

Gunny followed Mac's gaze to the floor, a smile stretching across his handsome face. "Wow, you really did enjoy your appetizer, Sir."

"That I did, boy." Mac chuckled and popped Gunny on the ass. From the bathroom door he tossed Gunny a towel. "Now get busy, I've got a date to get ready for."

"Yes, Sir," Gunny responded, sounding happy and sated.

Mac knew the feeling well. He was no longer so nervous about taking Gunny to the club. He was sure the nerves would show themselves again, but he was now calm enough to handle the challenge and overcome it. He might be a little scared, but he had to admit, he was also feeling smug as hell. Gunny was his, all his, and the other men at the club could just eat their hearts out—literally, if they dared to touch what was his. Mac laughed at his insanity and flipped on the sink to wash the remnants of his pleasure from his hands.

Chapter 4

A COLD winter wind blew, causing Gunny to wrap his coat tighter around himself as he stepped out of the cab. He scanned the area as Mac paid the fare. The crowds on the busy streets of New York bustled by, their heads down as they tried to hide from the evening chill. New York City had never been one of Gunny's favorite places to visit. Actually, he disliked most big cities, and the older he got, the more he loathed them. He was excited about attending the club with Mac—hell, it was a fantasy come true. But the big city wasn't where he'd have chosen for his honeymoon. A secluded log cabin in the woods, a tent off grid—peace, quiet, and Mac. Now that they were retired, out, Gunny was much like his husband in that he didn't like to share his man. Unlike Mac, it wasn't jealousy that caused Gunny to feel this way, but rather after all the years of being apart, hiding, denying, each moment he spent with Mac was a gift.

The wind howled, a light snow swirling and with it a dampness that seeped into Gunny. He shifted from foot to foot in an attempt to keep warm, wrapping his arms around himself, irritated Mac was taking so long. But when Mac stepped out of the cab, laughing about something, it hit Gunny square in the chest how handsome Mac was when his face was lit up with happiness. Who cared about the crowds, the noise, the stink, or the cold? He was on his honeymoon, about to have a fantasy fulfilled, and he had the whole rest of his life to spend with Mac.

Mac slid an arm around Gunny's waist and led him to the door of the club. As they stepped into the foyer, they both shook the flakes from their hair and brushed them from their coats. Gunny wasn't sure what he had expected, but this wasn't it.

There weren't that many people in the club, which wasn't surprising for a Tuesday night, but the brightly flashing strobe lights, techno music, and gyrating dancers did shock him.

"Umm, Mac?" Gunny spoke against Mac's ear. "You sure this is the right place?"

"It's the right address," Mac responded, his eyes scanning the area, a confused expression contorting his features. "Doesn't look like much of a leather club, does it?"

"I appear to be the only one in leather," Gunny pointed out.

"ID please," said a man half leaning, half sitting on a barstool.

"Seriously?" Mac chuckled. "Dude, do I look under twenty-one?"

The guy shrugged. "House rules."

"Macalister Jones?" asked a large man—a few inches taller and even wider than he and Mac—with longish dirty-blond hair and matching beard.

"Yes, that's right," Mac replied, looking at the stranger suspiciously.

"I'm Tek Cain, head of security," the guy announced and held out his hand to Mac, ignoring Gunny completely. "If you and your boy would follow me, Mr. Henderson is waiting."

"Show time, boy," Mac said with a wink and laid a hand at the base of Gunny's back, encouraging him to follow Tek.

Gunny took a few deep breaths as they made their way across the club, trying to find some calm even while his heart sped and his body infused with heat. Although he'd never been a true sub, nor done this in public, Gunny knew enough about the lifestyle to know his role and what would be expected of him. His priority was to make Mac, his Dom for the night, proud. He straightened his posture, and even as he kept his head held high, he lowered his eyes but took in his surroundings critically.

Tek nodded to another man who rivaled him in size and held back a curtain leading to a hallway as they approached. Gunny's heart picked up the pace when he heard the other man's heavy footfalls behind them. His training kicked in, and he had to fight the urge to turn and face the possible threat of a stranger behind him. It took effort to stay in role, but he managed. Tek punched in a code on a keypad next to a heavy wooden door at the end of the hallway and held the door open for them.

Now this *is what I'm talking about.* The room was decorated in black, red, and chrome. The low lighting and color palette should have made the room feel dark, but it was anything but. It was a mix of old and modern, light and dark, each complementing rather than overpowering the other. The balance gave the club a warm, inviting vibe.

Gunny jerked his head around when the door slammed shut behind him.

"I'll take your coats," Tek offered.

He and Mac handed him their coats, Tek hung them on a hook, and then he and the other man stood on either side of the door, arms crossed over their massive chests. Their sheer size should have put Gunny on edge, but they both sported big grins and laughing eyes, making them seem less imposing.

Gunny pulled at the neck of his long-sleeved leather shirt. He'd thought Mac was kidding about having it buttoned to the top when he'd given it to him, but no. Mac had insisted adamantly. Gunny argued buttoning it up wouldn't allow him to wear the leather collar that had also been part of his gift. Mac's response was to take the collar and toss it back into the suitcase.

"Stop messing with it, you look amazing," Mac whispered and ran his hand down Gunny's back.

Who needs to breathe anyway? "Yes, Sir," he responded as he dropped his arms and rolled his neck.

"Mr. Jones, so glad to finally meet you," greeted a short, stocky man with blond hair, hand stretched out. "I'm Ty Callahan. Welcome to the Guards of Folsom."

"Thank you." Mac accepted the offered hand. "Nice to meet you as well. Please call me Mac, sir. This is my hus—boy, Gunther Duchene."

"Only if you promise not to call me sir, that's my husband's title," Ty said with a wink and then turned to Gunny. "Mr. Duchene, welcome."

"Please, call me Gunny, sir."

"Wow you two are really polite, aren't ya?" Ty drawled with a hint of a Southern accent noticeable.

"Hard habit to kick. Years under Uncle Sam's thumb will do that to you." Mac smiled.

"I had the damnedest time with it, so the years in the military will serve your boy well." Ty chuckled. "Save him many strokes, I'm sure. C'mon, I'll introduce you to Blake."

Mac leaned in and brushed his lips against Gunny's ear. "If only he knew how much my boy likes being stroked," Mac muttered, his tickling breath causing Gunny to shudder just as much as the thought did.

They were led to the bar where a thin, dark-haired, and ridiculously handsome man sat. He had a warm smile on his face as they approached, but Gunny could tell from the intense look in his dark eyes he was sizing him and Mac up.

"Sir, this is Macalister Jones and his boy," Ty told the man and then went to a display position next to him, Ty's role instantly clear.

"Nice to finally meet you, Mr. Jones, please have a seat. Can I get you anything to drink?"

"Likewise," Mac responded and sat on the stool next to Blake. "Water or soda, either is fine."

"Micah," Blake called to the curly-haired man with his elbows on the bar, talking to an older gentleman with salt and pepper hair, and waved him over.

Micah hurried to them, the swish and sway of his lean hips exaggerated. "Yes, sir?" He then gave a little wave toward Gunny and mouthed, *Hi.*

"Micah, could you please get Mr. Jones a…." He turned to Mac.

"I'll just have water."

"Yes, sir, and shall I fetch something for your totally delicious boy there?" Micah asked.

Mac tensed, and Gunny held his breath as he waited to see how his jealous lover would handle the obviously flirtatious remark.

"Micah," Blake warned harshly, then turned to Mac. "You'll have to forgive our Micah. He's a bit outspoken and an extremely naughty pup. I do believe he's trying to provoke his Master into beating him." Blake then waved the older gentleman over.

"Aww, are you seriously going to tattle on me?" Micah asked with a pout, but it didn't work. Gunny saw the glint of mischief in Micah's eyes, and he was sure everyone else witnessed it too. A muffled snort had Gunny glancing at Ty, who had his head down and was biting his bottom lip in an apparent attempt to hold in his laughter.

"Mr. Jones—"

"Please, call me Mac," Mac interrupted Blake.

"Very well. Mac, this is my dear friend and the frustrated master of the naughty pup, Tackett Austen."

"Nice to meet you," Mac responded.

"You too," Tackett replied, a slight grin on his face. "What has the pup done now?"

"Absolutely nothing," Blake told him. "He's been unusually polite and focused. Your heavy hand has apparently done some good with him. I only wanted you to meet our guests."

Micah's eyes went comically wide, and he gawked at Blake in disbelief with his mouth hanging open.

"Damn, and I was so looking forward to trying out my new paddle."

Ty lost the battle and began snickering. Obviously knowing when he'd been played, Micah sighed heavily. "One bottle of water coming up," he muttered and walked away, but not before sticking his tongue out at a still laughing Ty. Both Tackett and Blake joined in.

Gunny had no clue what the hell was going on. It was strange to be excluded. First Tek ignored him, and now he was being left out of this conversation, neither Blake nor Tackett even acknowledging his presence. Yet, it was somewhat comforting, as strange as that seemed. He never knew what to say to strangers, never felt comfortable striking up or keeping a conversation going unless he was talking about the military. Mac, on the other hand, thrived on it. Gunny liked being able to take everything in that was happening around him without being expected to participate.

"Blake has told me you served for over twenty years in the Marines. Hell of a tough job," Tackett commented.

Mac, Tackett, and Blake began making small talk, but Gunny kind of tuned them out as he surveyed the club. There weren't a lot of men, but Gunny could easily distinguish the Dominants from the submissives. At a small table close to the stage sat three men. Two larger middle-aged men sat on either side of a younger, petite man dressed in black leather pants and a black fishnet shirt. The way the two large men touched him, surrounding him, protecting, Gunny concluded they were Doms, and it appeared the small guy belonged to both of them from the intimate way the three of them spoke and touched.

Two tables over from the trio was a no-brainer. A man dressed in a charcoal gray suit chatted on his cell while sipping a glass of wine, a man in nothing but black micro-shorts kneeled at his feet with his head hanging down and his hands clasped in his lap. If the attire and positions weren't enough of a clue, then the leash around business guy's wrist, which was attached to a collar on the kneeling man's neck, was a dead giveaway.

"Boy."

In fact, many men had collars on, but it was Ty's that had caught Gunny's attention. It was the only one made of what looked like forged steel, and rather than a buckle or padlock, it was secured with rivets as if it were permanent, as impossible as it sounded.

"Boy."

Tek and the other man at the door were the only ones Gunny couldn't get a read on. They were undoubtedly security, but the way they looked at each other while they talked screamed lovers, yet both men cast a vibe that was completely dominant. Perhaps they were like he and Mac, dominant in their everyday life and played in the lifestyle. Gunny tried to picture either of them as submissive but was unable to imagine it. He shook his head at the irony. He was sure most would have the same difficulty if they looked at him and tried to fit him into a kneeling, submissive role.

Gunny made a loud *oomph* sound when an elbow connected with his gut. "Gunny!"

"What!" Gunny growled in irritation and then realized where he was and who had elbowed him. "Oh shit, I'm sorry, Ma—Sir. I got distracted," he admitted lamely, his cheeks heating as all eyes were on him.

"Your boy and mine would be dangerous together," Tackett laughed.

"Apparently." Mac smirked.

Micah giggled from behind the bar, looking not the least bit apologetic. "You and I would rule the world."

"World domination would only last until he saw something shiny," Ty muttered quietly to Gunny.

"I heard that. Unfortunately it's sad but true," Micah admitted. "But we'd still have fun and look damn good while it lasted. I gotta take care of my customers. You sure you don't want something to drink before I go?"

"No, I'm good," Gunny replied, still looking at Mac apologetically.

Mac slid his arm around Gunny's waist, rubbing his lower back. "It's okay, you can make it up to me later." Mac's voice went lower, seductive, when he added, "When you're naked and bound."

Gunny's cock twitched and began to fill. "Yes, Sir."

"There's a show starting in an hour, and Tackett has been gracious enough to offer to introduce us to some of the other members beforehand. Come along, boy, and pay attention," Mac instructed. He then stood and followed Tackett.

"Yes, Sir." Gunny fell in behind his lover, keeping his focus on the back of Mac's neck.

MAC HAD been wrong on both accounts. He hadn't had to worry about knowing the rules. Beyond being respectful of others, what he and Gunny chose to do or not do was totally up to them as was the case with the other members. He'd also been wrong in worrying about the green-eyed monster of jealousy rearing its ugly head. In fact he found great pride, walked with his chest a little pushed out, so fucking proud that he had the best-looking man in the club, at least in his opinion, and that was all that mattered. Oh, and he'd been wrong about one other thing too. He and Gunny should have done this years ago. The members were discreet and totally fucking cool.

"Mac, this is Bobby, Rig, and their beautiful boy, Mason," Tackett said, pointing to each one as he said their names.

"Nice to meet you, and this is my beautiful boy, Gunny," Mac greeted, puffing up even further.

The three stood in unison, Bobby and Rig still surrounding Mason, who seemed to shrink into them, and offered their free hands. "Welcome to the Guards of Folsom," Bobby said. "Blake has told us about you, and we've been looking forward to meeting you."

"You have me at a disadvantage, then," Mac admitted.

"Well, sit a spell, and we'll rectify that problem. Bobby and I are open books." Rig sat and pulled his boy onto his lap. Mason instantly buried his face in Rig's chest. Rig stroked a hand soothingly down Mason's back and leaned in, whispering something in his ear. Mac couldn't make out what was being said, but whatever it was had Mason nodding and he seemed to calm, snuggling further into Rig.

"Mason doesn't do well with strangers," Bobby said in way of explanation.

"Understandable. There aren't too many stranger than me." Mac chuckled and took a seat next to Bobby.

"Hang out here long enough, and you'll be proven wrong," Tackett laughed.

"Do you mind if I address your boy," Rig asked respectfully.

Mac hesitated for a moment, shocked by the question, then caught up and remembered where he was. "No, no, go right ahead."

"Blake has told us you served also." Gunny nodded. "Thank you for your service as well."

"Thank you, sir."

Mac felt Gunny's eyes on him and turned to see Gunny staring at him with a questioning expression. Mac wasn't about to allow Gunny to snuggle up on his lap—they'd break the damn chair—but he was beginning to relax into his role and needed to step up his game and get Gunny into it.

"You can kneel next to me, boy," Mac instructed.

"Yes, Sir." Gunny eased down next to Mac, hands still clasped behind his back as he hung his head respectfully low.

Mac petted the short stubble on Gunny's head, enjoying the way it felt against his palm and the way Gunny's submission caused Mac's pride and cock to swell.

Chapter 5

As he kneeled at Mac's feet, once again excluded from conversation, it struck Gunny how odd everything was, but not in a bad way. Years of always having to be in the forefront with recruits, the leader, Gunny was thoroughly enjoying letting all that go and just being. No struggling to keep the conversation going and interesting, no worrying about what he said. In this place, he completely belonged to Mac, allowed him to make all the decisions and gab away. Yet everyone in the club knew they were together, and that in itself was freeing.

Gunny pushed into Mac's touch as he slid his hand down Gunny's head, along his neck, and farther down his spine. Though Mac was chatting with the men at the table, Gunny knew Mac was constantly aware of his presence, the soothing touch conveying the message loud and clear.

Gunny closed his eyes and cleared his mind of everything but Mac's touch. Even though he was in an unfamiliar place, surrounded by strangers, he was calmer than he had been in days.

He didn't know how long they sat there—time wasn't important. Gunny had found his headspace without the aid of binds or strokes, completely aware of only Mac.

So he knew it was time to move when Mac patted his back and said, "Come along, boy, Tackett is going to show us the private rooms."

"Yes, Sir," Gunny responded sedately and pushed himself to his feet, following close behind Mac.

Although he kept his eyes low and on Mac, Gunny could feel the gazes of others watching him, and damn if he didn't like it. He straightened his back, adjusted his posture, walked a little prouder, and did his best to keep his features neutral, even though the silly grin was dying to get out. He really, really liked knowing others were watching him, not out of vanity, but pride. *That's right, boys, he's mine and I'm his.*

"Normally the rooms are occupied by members. Especially on the weekends, it's tough to get a room," Tackett pointed out. "But Blake cleared the books for tonight to allow you and your boy to tour them. You have your choice of any room you wish to use."

"That's very kind of him, I'll have to thank him," Mac said as Tackett opened the first door.

"This is the suspension room. You can do anything from a fun fuck in one of the swings all the way up to complete sensory deprivation in here."

The walls were painted black, no windows or doors other than the one they entered. Recessed lighting was used to highlight swings hanging from the ceilings as well as nylon cuffs. There appeared little in the way of anything that would make a noise. A large water-filled tank, full-grown-man size, was situated against the back wall with some kind of hoisting mechanism above it.

Mac noticed it too. "Human fish tank?"

"Sort of," Tackett chuckled. "Floating gives the sensation of weightlessness. As I mentioned, complete deprivation can be achieved here. Want to try?"

"Does it spark your interest, boy?" Mac asked.

Gunny shook his head. "No, Sir."

"Good, me neither. This would be torture for both of us," Mac told Tackett. "I have a hard time keeping my hands off Gunny."

"And you've been together over twenty years but still can't go without touching him?"

Mac shrugged. "What can I say? He's got a very touchable bod."

"I hope Micah and I are that way in twenty years."

Mac winked at Gunny. "It takes lots of work and even more ass whippings," Mac teased.

Gunny barely contained the eye roll.

"Then I have a damn good chance of achieving longevity. Micah earns plenty every day," Tackett laughed. From only the few moments Gunny had been around Micah, he would bet Tackett's arm got one hell of a workout.

They followed Tackett to the next room. Like the previous one, the walls were painted black and had recessed lighting, but that was where the similarities ended.

"This room is the dungeon. If you and your boy get off on the heavy hand or like to use floggers, crops, paddles"—Tackett swiped his hand toward the wall where such implements hung—"this room is for you."

Mac whistled. "Now we're talking. Whatcha think, boy? Can you imagine yourself bound to the St. Andrew's cross or hanging from the shackles while I make you fly?"

The half-hard cock Gunny had been sporting all night filled to a full throbbing erection as he took in the room, imagining himself and Mac here, feeling the sting of Mac's belt or the thud of his heavy flogger.

Mac cupped Gunny's cock. "No need to reply. I got your answer right here."

Gunny moaned, eyes threatening to close as the pressure on his dick increased. The urge to thrust into Mac's hand was strong, but he fought it and held his position.

"We may just have to come back to this room," Mac told Tackett and then released Gunny's cock, much to Gunny's disappointment.

"It's all yours, but let me show you the rest. Blake has thought out each room carefully and spared no expense on providing safe, fun play. You won't find another club like it."

They didn't spend much time in the next room. It was plain with a large king-size bed, armoire, and several large trunks on the floor. Tackett explained it was for role-playing and various costumes, props, and toys could be found within the trunks.

The fourth room had Gunny vehemently shaking his head. There was no fucking way he wanted any kind of electrical volts going through him. It wasn't his kink.

The tour ended in a room complete with a large bed dressed in luxurious linens, a hot tub, and massage table.

"And here we have a room you can simply relax and pamper your boy, or he can pamper you," Tackett said with a wink. "Although it can also be used by those with medical kinks. The massage table can be used as a gurney or exam table, and the cabinets beneath it contain all kinds of Dr. Feel Good kind of goodies."

"Wanna play doctor, boy?" Mac asked, waggling his brows lewdly.

"If that's what pleases you, Sir," Gunny responded with a sly grin.

He knew Mac was bullshitting and was more than likely still thinking about the dungeon, just as Gunny was.

"Shit!" Tackett blurted as he checked his watch. "Show's going to start soon, and trust me, you're not going to want to miss it."

They headed back out into the main club and had just enough time to grab a couple bottles of water and find an empty table near the stage before the show started.

Mac pulled a chair close to his. "Have a seat, boy." Gunny slid into the seat and then jerked when Mac's hand unexpectedly landed on his cock. "Don't want to talk too much during the show so I'll just use this as a guide as to how much you're enjoying it."

Mac began massaging Gunny's cock with just the perfect amount of pressure, stroking him through the soft leather. Gunny's pulse sped as heat rushed through him. "Won't matter how much I like or dislike the show. You keep doing that, and I won't care about what's happening on the stage."

Mac leaned in and licked a path from Gunny's neck up to his ear. Gunny shuddered. "No coming in your retirement gift."

The curtain opened, and Gunny gasped. It was going to be hard enough not to come with Mac stroking him, but with the three men bound and naked on stage and a fourth man dressed in black leather from head to toe tapping a crop against his thigh, it was going to be almost impossible to keep from blowing his load and ruining Mac's gift.

Watching a bondage video was one thing; to witness it live took the hotness to a whole new level. The Dom on the stage began working in a circle, the slap of leather against flesh, the grunts of pleasurable pain loud in the otherwise silent club. The scent of arousal was so strong it was nearly palpable.

Gunny sat enthralled by the scene before him. His pulse raced, body thrumming. He was mesmerized, envisioning Mac as the one working the flogger and rather than an unknown man bound and naked, it was himself. The idea, the fantasy was hot as fuck, but Gunny would never in actuality share such an intimate act with strangers. It was still exciting being there, though, imagining it, considering the possibilities.

Mac leaned in, breath tickling Gunny's ear. "I don't know whether to be turned on by how hard you are or jealous," Mac murmured.

Gunny pushed into Mac's hand as Mac continued to rub him through the leather pants, the friction delicious. Although the room was dark and Mac's hand was beneath the table, being in public still intensified the eroticism of the act.

Gunny kept his eyes trained on the onstage Dom as the man found his rhythm, working the subs one at time until the slaps, moans, and groans were a steady melody of seductive noises. Still, Gunny was completely aware of Mac.

"Trust me, while I find what's happening on the stage extremely hot, your hand, your voice, your scent is way fucking hotter." Gunny groaned and then added, "Sir," when Mac nipped his ear.

"Good answer, boy," Mac praised. He then began assaulting Gunny's neck, licking, nipping, and sucking, all the while keeping the friction against Gunny's cock firm and steady. "Keep your eyes on the stage."

"Yes, Sir."

"Did you like kneeling at my feet? Did it feel like you hoped it would?"

"Yes," Gunny breathed.

"Do you care why you liked it?" Mac asked as he began to stroke his knuckles over Gunny's cock.

One of the reasons he'd wanted to come to a club, to explore this with Mac, hadn't only been for the kink, but to learn why he felt the way he did. Why a highly trained Marine needed to kneel at another man's feet, a position he'd thought should make him feel weak. After being there, seeing others, experiencing it, Gunny only knew it felt good, right, and here, in this setting, it all became crystal clear. He no longer cared about the why of it. He didn't need to understand, didn't need a club or the approval of others. None of it mattered, only that he and Mac enjoyed it and got what they needed from the other.

"No, Sir," he admitted.

"Men have been drooling over you tonight, wanting you, wishing you belonged to them. But you're mine, aren't you? Only mine?"

"All yours, Sir. Never wanted anyone but you," Gunny admitted honestly.

Mac skimmed his lips along Gunny's jaw, licked the corner of his mouth. Gunny tried to follow those warm, intoxicating lips, but he didn't dare turn away from the stage, disobey Mac's order. He lost contact with them when Mac followed the same path back to

Gunny's ear. Gunny groaned his frustration. Mac's mouth was better than any show.

"That's why it's not bothering me that they look," Mac whispered. "Because that's all they can do. And it will be all they can do when this show is over—watch me lead you to the back rooms." Fuck, Gunny would gladly forego watching the rest of the show.

"They'll know where we're going. They will be wishing it was them taking you to the back, watching you strip, binding you, beating you, fucking you," Mac growled, his voice husky and deep. "You'll be their fantasy."

The light glistened off the sweat-slick body of the sub to the right, highlighting the red marks from the flogger. Gunny didn't care about being anyone's fantasy except Mac's. But what he really wanted was to be his reality. Wanted nothing more than to be the one with a sweat-slick back, flesh heated, begging for more.

"I don't know how much longer I'm going to last," Gunny panted. "Want you so bad."

"Want to feel the kiss of my leather?"

"God yes," Gunny groaned and turned his pleading gaze toward Mac.

"Eyes straight ahead, boy," Mac demanded.

Gunny snapped his head back, his gaze returning to the scene, but his attention, his focus, stayed firmly on Mac's hand, his voice and his heat. "Sorry, Sir. You've got me so worked up. Don't care about what they are doing… only…. Fuck… only you."

Mac sucked aggressively on Gunny's neck as the pressure of his hand increased on Gunny's groin, a knot forming at the base of Gunny's spine, signaling his impending release.

"I… I'm…." Gunny gritted his teeth, breathing harshly through his nose as he tried to get his spiraling out-of-control need for release reined in, but it was a losing battle. "I can't hold back much longer. Sir. Fuck. Sir. I'm going to come."

Mac sat back instantly, pulled his hand away, denying Gunny the pressure, the heat, everything. "Deep breaths, boy. You are not to come. Not here," Mac ordered.

Gunny held his breath, every muscle tight, coiled, and ready. His entire body begged for release, even his toes curled in the confines of his heavy boots. He closed his eyes, focused on his hammering heart, the rush of blood in his ears. He blew out a long breath, inhaled deeply, and blew out again.

After a few seconds, the immediate danger passed, and he shook his head. "Whew! That was close."

Obviously, Gunny wasn't the only one close. Mac jumped to his feet and grabbed Gunny's hand, pulling him from his chair. "Let's go."

"Show's not over," Gunny pointed out, following easily.

Mac didn't respond, instead practically ran down the hall, threw open the door, and shoved Gunny in. "It's just about to start."

Chapter 6

"STRIP."

"Yes, Sir."

Mac watched as Gunny undid the ties on his pants and struggled to push the binding material down his hips, the effort all the more difficult due to the raging hard-on Gunny was sporting.

As he got them halfway down his ass, Mac stopped him. "Leave them there and remove your shirt."

Gunny instantly began unbuttoning it and let it slide down his muscular arms to pool at his feet. Mac traced the tribal tattoo on Gunny's bicep, grinning as he remembered the day they had gotten it inked. Mac had bitched and moaned while receiving his, but Gunny had lain silently with a blissed-out expression on his handsome face. He leaned in and kissed the tat, then traced it with his tongue as he slid a single finger down Gunny's spine to the top of his exposed ass crack. He then teased farther down beneath the tight leather until he was satisfied with the deep rumbling moan he pulled from Gunny.

"Arms over your head," Mac ordered and pulled his shirt off, tossing it behind him. He then pressed his chest against Gunny's back, enjoying the heat and hardness of Gunny's body. Mac ran his hands up Gunny's arms, massaging and kneading the taut muscles.

Grabbing one of the hanging shackles, Mac attached it to Gunny's wrist, the rattling of the chain causing Gunny's breath to hitch. "You like that, don't you, boy? The cold, hard steel binding you?" he asked against Gunny's ear as he secured the metal cuff.

"Yes, Sir. I like being at your mercy."

Mac repeated the action on the other wrist. "You sure it's my mercy you like being at or the fact that you know you're about to get fucked?"

"Both." Gunny smirked.

Mac grabbed Gunny's hips and thrust his hardness against Gunny's ass. "I heard the smugness in your voice, boy. You don't think I can resist you when you're like this, do you?"

"I hope not."

"Dammit, you know I can't," Mac responded huskily. He held on tightly to Gunny's right hip while he used his free hand to roam over Gunny's ribs and flat belly. He loved the way the soft hair on Gunny's torso felt against his palm. He moved up to Gunny's chest, curled his fingers in the thick pelt of hair. "You keep distracting me with this sexy-as-fuck body, I may not be willing to let go of it long enough to light it up."

"I'm so fucking turned-on right now, I don't care. I just need you," Gunny moaned.

Mac teased a finger over Gunny's mouth. His tongue flicked out, licking Mac's flesh, humming his pleasure as he did so. Mac allowed it for a moment, watching Gunny enthusiastically lap at Mac's finger. He'd had the pleasure of Gunny's mouth against him, warm and wet as he sucked Mac to orgasm, but he never tired of it.

"I thought we were here to fulfill your fantasy," Mac murmured.

"You already have, now stop teasing me, I'm about to fucking explode," Gunny growled.

Mac stepped back and swatted Gunny's ass hard. "Did you forget your place, boy?"

A groan filled the air, deeper, rougher than usual, the frustration in Gunny's tone obvious. "Sorry, Mac. I just…. Fuck, Sir," he amended. "You got me so out of my head crazy for you. Need you."

Mac moved around Gunny's body, teased his knuckles over his belly, and leaned in and brushed their lips together. "Don't I always give you what you need?"

"Yes."

"Then be patient," Mac murmured and stepped back. Gunny whimpered when Mac's closeness and touch was suddenly gone.

Mac began to pace around Gunny. *So perfect*. Every inch of his man was perfection. All muscles and strength. All that power was bound and waiting for Mac to drain it from him.

But not yet.

As badly as they both needed release, Mac wasn't ready for it to end.

He spun around and paced in a circle, touching randomly as he moved, all the while concentrating on his breathing, doing his best to calm the urgency racing through him. Gunny sucked in a ragged breath. His ribs expanded, the light sheen of perspiration highlighting his well-defined muscles. Mac's gaze drifted lower to Gunny's hard cock. Beautifully, gloriously hard and wanting, needing what only Mac could give him.

"I promised to fulfill your fantasy, and I won't disappoint you."

"You haven't."

Mac pressed his finger against Gunny's mouth. "Shh, no more talking." Mac held Gunny's gaze until he finally nodded in understanding and submitted.

Mac began pacing again as he unbuttoned his pants and eased down the zipper. Mac knew Gunny was watching his every move when he gasped as Mac freed his cock. Mac came to a halt in front of Gunny and began stroking himself, enjoying the way Gunny's eyes felt upon him as well as the heat of his own hand.

"You're not to talk, unless it's to beg me to allow you to come. Nod if you understand." Gunny nodded, his gaze never leaving Mac's groin as his hand sped, his thumb teasing over the head on each pass, an act he couldn't handle for too long. He was as desperate as Gunny was, and as his balls began to draw up tight against his body, he covered his cock head and squeezed just hard enough to hold back his orgasm.

Mac took a few deep breaths and wiped the sweat from his brow with his free hand. Once he was in better control, he released his dick and began to pace again. "So many options, so many ways to take my pleasure from this magnificent body."

Gunny shifted, the chains rattling, and the rise and fall of his chest increased.

"I'm not sure if I should take a paddle to this tight ass," Mac commented as he swatted the ass in question, continuing to circle Gunny. "Or just ram my cock up it."

Mac held off for a few more passes, but denying himself was agony. Not able to stand it for another second, he pressed his body against Gunny's back. He knew what he had to have. He shifted until his cock was pressed against the crease of Gunny's ass and wrapped his arms around Gunny's chest, holding him still as Mac began to rub and rut.

"Do you want my cock buried balls deep in your ass?"

Gunny's body tightened further, trembling, but he followed Mac's order not to speak, nodding instead.

"While I stroke you hard and fast?" he asked as he slid his right hand down and wrapped his fingers around Gunny's cock.

Gunny nodded vigorously as he rocked between Mac's fist and body. The tight hold Mac had on him didn't allow for him to thrust. Instead, he wriggled helplessly, moaning and whimpering his frustration and pleasure. The sound of his need and the rattling chains echoed off the walls, inflaming Mac further.

Mac pressed a kiss to Gunny's shoulder and tightened his fist, squeezing Gunny's shaft, knowing exactly how Gunny liked it.

"I'm going to let you come tonight, but not until I tell you. Is that understood?"

Gunny nodded.

Suddenly Mac felt like his orgasm was crashing down on him, the urgency overwhelming, his need painful. He'd been hard most of the night, and his control was shredding fast. He had to… needed to be inside Gunny—right fucking now.

Mac fumbled, struggling to pull the lube from his front pocket at the same time he was pushing down his pants. All-consuming desire spurred him on, stripping him of reason and restraint.

Mac's hands trembled as he popped the top on the lube and dripped a good amount onto his cock, wincing as the cool fluid made contact with his heated flesh. He slid his fingers through the lube, coating them and his cock. With his clean hand, he inched the tight leather pants down to Gunny's thighs and then laid his hand between Gunny's shoulders. Gunny couldn't bend too far, the chains not allowing it, but Mac encouraged him to move as far as he could, tapping Gunny's boot with his own until Gunny took a step back into the perfect position.

Gunny's ass was always tight, but in this position with his legs bound together by the leather pants, it would make him even tighter. The thought egged Mac on. Mac slid his fingers between Gunny's ass cheeks. Mac's need was pushing him hard, demanding release, but he forced himself to slow down. Although Gunny wouldn't protest, Mac would never intentionally cause his lover unnecessary pain.

Gunny tensed for a second, clenching his ass as Mac's fingers pressed against his hole. "Relax and let me in," Mac murmured.

He laid his free hand on Gunny's belly, fingers splayed. Gunny took a deep breath, blew it out, and stilled, relaxing and letting Mac do as he pleased.

Mac slid a finger inside, spreading the lube, slowly rotating the digit until the tight muscle eased and allowed Mac to push deeper. "That's it," Mac praised. "Take it for me." He added a second finger. Although difficult with Gunny's legs pressed together, he managed. He worked quickly until Gunny was lubed up and whimpering, begging with his body for more. Mac withdrew his fingers and pressed his erection against Gunny's hole.

Gunny pushed back against Mac, forgetting his directions and his role. "Please, Mac."

The please went straight to Mac's cock, and it throbbed with each thump of his rapidly beating heart. Steadying Gunny's hips, Mac thrust into him in one perfect motion until he was buried to the hilt within Gunny's body.

Gunny gasped at the sudden invasion but struggled against Mac's restrictive hold on him, trying to force Mac to move inside him.

The control for slow, measured thrusts had been stripped from him. They'd both waited too long, been deprived the pleasure long enough. Mac pounded into Gunny, hard and fast, holding on to his lover with a powerful grasp, strong enough to leave bruises, in order to keep him close.

Gunny pulled against his restraints, rattling chains, moaning, begging for more. The sound raced down Mac's spine, merging with the tight heat around his cock, and he nearly came but somehow managed to hold it off long enough to wrap his fist tightly around Gunny's dick and jerk him off in fast, hard pulls.

Every muscle in Gunny's body knotted tighter and tighter, and Mac knew there would be no stopping Gunny's orgasm this time.

"Come!"

Gunny jerked in his restraints, throwing his head back as he screamed. The deep, husky sound bounced off the walls of the small room and slammed into Mac when Gunny's hole clenched even tighter as he came, ripping the orgasm out of Mac.

Mac half collapsed, panting for breath, buried deep inside Gunny. He stared down over Gunny's shoulder to where he still held Gunny's cock in his hand and watched the last drop of seed drip from the end and land in the pool of his release.

Mac basked in the heat of Gunny's body, held his cock till he softened, and breathed in the heavy aroma of sweat and arousal. It was several minutes before Mac finally summoned up the will to release Gunny from his restraints and step away from him, both moaning as Mac slipped from Gunny's body. Mac grabbed a white towel from a shelf and, after swiping it down his wet dick, pressed it against Gunny's groin.

"Ow… oh… shit, that's sensitive," Gunny stammered as he squirmed, trying to pull away from the rough terry cloth, too abrasive for overly sensitive flesh.

"Hey, I was trying to help clean my boy up," Mac chuckled. Gunny spun away, taking the cloth with him, and nearly fell on his ass when his bound legs betrayed him. Mac caught him just in time. "Easy there."

Gunny grabbed Mac's shoulders and then leaned in and buried his face in Mac's neck, holding on as he breathed harshly. "Help a guy out here, will ya?"

Mac let Gunny cling to him while he pulled up Gunny's pants and carefully tucked his soft cock back in before tying them up. "I bet you wish we would have picked a room with a soft bed right about now," Mac pointed out.

"Nope, I'm good. At least I will be until we get back to our own room." Gunny took a step back. He met Mac's gaze, his expression serious, sated, but with a slight grin curling his lip. "Thank you, this was—" He leaned in and pressed his lips to Mac's, kissing him softly. "—a dream come true." He kissed Mac again.

Mac's chest tightened as he was struck speechless. He quickly straightened up his clothes. "We can stay longer if you like," Mac said reluctantly. He wished they were already back at their hotel room, showered and cuddled up beneath the soft sheets. But he'd stay.

"Nope. I wonder if they'd think we were rude if we snuck out the back door?"

"I don't think there is a back door, unfortunately. However this will be the fastest good-bye ever." He grabbed the towel from Gunny, quickly cleaned up the remnants from their lovemaking, and tossed the towel in a hamper before grabbing Gunny's hand and heading for the door.

Maybe he could get away with a wave as they rushed to the exit. He'd shared his lover long enough—it was time for cuddling.

Chapter 7

A CHILL ran down Mac's spine, and he blindly reached out for Gunny's warmth, frowning when he came in contact with nothing but cold sheets. Throwing the covers off his head, Mac sat up in bed, blinking rapidly until his vision came into focus and settled on Gunny. He was standing naked, looking in the mirror, and poking at a dark spot on his hip.

"What the hell are you doing?" Mac growled and crossed his arms over his chest.

Gunny glanced back at him over his shoulder and then poked at another bruise. "I look like I got mauled by a bear."

"You did, and he's a great big growly bear, because someone forgot rule number one. Now get your ass back in this bed before I maul you again and not in a good way."

"I didn't think I was your boy this morning," Gunny teased with a sly grin as he slowly turned.

"You're always my boy, but I was talking about retirement rule number one. No one—"

"—is allowed out of this bed in the morning before cuddles and blowjobs," Gunny finished for him.

"If you knew, then why in the hell am I over here cold with a hard-on and you're waaay over there?" Mac grumbled.

"You're not the only one who can deny orgasms, ya know."

Mac grabbed the sheet, ready to throw it off, and started inching toward the edge of the bed. "Don't make me beat you."

Instead of taking the threat seriously, Gunny grabbed his cock and shook it. "Come and get it. Or do I need to dip it in honey first?" Mac saw the glint of mischief in Gunny's eyes just before he spun and made a play for the bathroom.

Anticipating Gunny's movement, Mac sprang from the bed and in a blink of an eye had Gunny wrapped in a strong hold. Then they were falling back onto the bed, only Mac hadn't planned for a protruding hipbone to slam into his morning wood, and he howled in pain.

Gunny instantly twisted off Mac and stared down at him with concern. "You okay?"

Mac's hand flew to his abused dick, and he rocked as he fought to keep down the bile that had shot up into his throat.

"Hold on. I'll get you an ice pack." Gunny started to scramble from the bed, but Mac grabbed his arm.

"No," he breathed harshly. "The last thing I need is for you to freeze them off. Jesus, that fucking hurt."

"Guess the blowjob is out," Gunny said sympathetically. He lay on his side, pushed close, and rubbed Mac's belly gently.

"Cuddles it is." Mac pushed up closer still, burying his face in Gunny's neck, enjoying his man's scent and heat.

"My poor little cuddle whore."

The searing pain in Mac's groin began to ease, and he relaxed against his lover. Gunny pulled the covers up over them and held Mac. This was how his morning was supposed to begin, not cold sheets and broken balls. Obviously, he and Gunny were going to have to go over the retirement rules again, but not right now. Now he was content to let Gunny hold him and listen to the steady beat of Gunny's heart beneath his ear.

They lay there enjoying the lazy quiet morning, Mac tracing random patterns through the hair on Gunny's chest and belly. Gunny in turn, soothed a hand up and down Mac's back.

"I was just thinking," Gunny murmured, breaking the long comfortable silence.

"Don't hurt yourself," Mac teased sleepily. He jerked, then chuckled when Gunny swatted his ass. "Sorry, do share."

"Last night was really great, and everyone at the Guards of Folsom was so cool and interesting, but I think visiting once was enough for me."

Mac propped himself up on his elbow and stared down at Gunny in shock. "Really? It's not something you'd want to do again?"

"Nope."

"Wow, I hadn't seen that one coming. I would have thought for sure after your reaction to the show, you'd have already been planning our next visit."

"Well, it was a hell of a show," Gunny said slyly. "But, nope. As I was sitting there watching what was happening on stage—the Dom was very talented, by the way—I kept thinking of us, not up on stage, mind you, but in private. It was a great experience; however it also made me realize I wouldn't ever want to share those kinds of intimacies with others, and I sure in the hell can't imagine us doing it full-time like Ty and Blake or Tackett and Micah." Gunny shrugged. "I like what we have."

"So you're saying it's okay once in a while when your head gets all wonky, but you're not going to take up permanent residence kneeling at my feet?" Mac clarified.

"No, I'm totally cool with the occasional thing, you know, when I get crazy. It's a great stress reliever."

"And don't forget hot." Mac leered and waggled his brows.

"Definitely," Gunny agreed. "But the majority of the time I like it to be just Mac and Gunny, old retired married folks."

"Me too," Mac said and kissed Gunny soundly. "But never old, retired, and boring."

Gunny grabbed Mac's ass and squeezed. "Never boring."

Mac groaned, his abused dick trying to fill as Gunny continued to massage Mac's ass. Mac slapped his hand away and laid his head back down on Gunny's chest. "But recovery mode is a must once in a while."

"Totally," Gunny laughed. "My hips and ass seriously need some recovery time."

Mac grinned and kissed the soft spot over Gunny's heart. Damn but they were compatible in nearly everything they enjoyed and did. Crazy he'd ever worried what retirement would be like. It—just like his relationship with Gunny—was damn near perfect. He closed his eyes, enjoying the moment.

Recovery mode activated.

A KNOCK on the hotel door roused Gunny from sleep. "Housekeeping."

"Shit," he grumbled and extricated himself from beneath Mac.

"I thought we put the Do Not Disturb sign out?" Mac pulled the covers over his head.

He glanced at the clock. "We did, but they probably thought we left it on the door when we left since it's past check-out time."

Gunny snatched a damp towel from the floor and wrapped it around his waist as he heard a key card slide into the lock. He rushed to the door and blocked it before it could be opened all the way.

"Oops, sorry. No one responded to my knock."

"It's okay," Gunny assured the young girl as he peeked his head out. "If you'll give us a few more minutes, the room will be all yours."

"Of course, sir. Sorry to have bothered you."

"It's okay, just running a few minutes late. We'll hurry."

"Take your time, I've got plenty of other rooms to keep me busy," she replied as she pushed her cart down the hall.

Gunny shut the door and flipped the bar across the lock. "All right, Mac, time to rise and shine. We've got places to go, people to see, and I want food before our journey begins."

"Don't remind me," Mac groaned.

Gunny wasn't all that thrilled either at the prospect of having to see Ted again, but they'd promised Mac's mom and dad. He was, however, looking forward to Clare's cooking and exchanging gifts with his husband—God, he'd never tire of saying that—and his family.

Gunny hesitated at the bathroom door, hand gripping the towel. "Mac?"

"What?" Mac asked, his voice muffled from his face being buried in the mattress.

"Mac?"

"Dammit, Gunny, I said what." Mac popped his head out, and Gunny dropped the towel.

"Recovery time is over." He turned and shook his ass before disappearing into the bathroom. He smiled knowingly when he heard covers rustle seconds before Mac came rushing into the room. Gunny set the taps, and Mac shoved him beneath the warm flow, crowding him.

"Part two of rule one about to commence," Mac whooped.

Gunny smiled into the kiss Mac laid on him. He'd be damn smart to never forget the rules or what a truly amazing man he'd married. Gunny's grin grew as the kiss deepened. Nor would he ever forget the night his fantasy came to life. The night he spent in a club being mauled by a big burly bear would forever be etched in his mind and his heart.

Guards of Folsom: Book One

Micah "Pup" Slayde knows he wants Tackett Austin the moment he lays eyes on him in the Guards of Folsom. Micah wants to have purpose, to be taken care of, and to take care of his Dom—wants to trust him completely, live for him, belong to him. To become his everything. Micah is sure Tackett is the one. The problem is, in order to be the perfect sub, he needs to stay focused, and that's not easy for Micah, who suffers from what he refers to as a "broken brain." Focus and adult attention deficit disorder rarely coexist.

Ever since Ty Callahan and Blake Henderson's collaring ceremony, Tackett's been thinking too much about his own loneliness. Even though Ty introduces Micah and urges Tackett to give him a try, Tackett isn't so easily convinced. He's spent his life pursuing a successful business career, and the subs he dominates almost never enjoy the kiss of his leather twice. Twenty years Micah's senior, Tackett has no interest in taking on and taming such a young and naughty sub—but it's difficult to resist such an adorable pup when he begs.

www.dreamspinnerpress.com

Guards of Folsom: Book Two

Following the death of their sub, the former owners of the Guards of Folsom, Robert "Bobby" Alcott and Rig Beckworth, were left to pick up the pieces as best they could. After seven years, these two Doms are ready to move on and find the boy who will complete them. Their painful past comes crashing back when they meet Mason Howard, a submissive who just weeks ago lost his Doms in a car accident.

Reeling from overwhelming grief that's complicated by a severe social anxiety disorder, Mason can barely leave his home. When Rig and Bobby find him, he's hit rock bottom, believing life is no longer worth living. Bobby and Rig set out to prove the younger man wrong. Fate has brought the three men together, but they'll have to face the pain of fear and loss head-on before they can all truly live again.

www.dreamspinnerpress.com

Guards of Folsom: Book Three

Grant Maxwell, aka Max, wakes to find his coffeepot has died in the night. Not one who can start his day without his favorite brew, he heads to the local coffee shop. Max finds something even more appealing than caffeine in the form of twenty-six-year-old hottie Aiden James. For the first time in his life, well-established, confident and respected Dom Max finds himself sputtering and unsure in the face of Aiden's charms.

Aiden lives with three roommates, works a dead-end job, and isn't sure where his life is heading. That is until he meets Max. Max introduces him to a foreign yet intriguing lifestyle, and they soon discover they have something more than mutual attraction in common.

A shared kink is one thing, but Aiden's past vanilla sexual experiences as well as his fear of losing himself in Max may keep Aiden from experiencing his fantasy. Max has an obstacle of his own to overcome. He must somehow figure out how to help Aiden explore his submissive side when, for the first time in his life, he's head over heels in love.

www.dreamspinnerpress.com

ROPED

A GUARDS OF FOLSOM NOVEL

SJD PETERSON

Guards of Folsom: Book Four

Life has been known by a series of constants. Violence, anger, drugs, sex, death, heartbreak, pain, fear and the most common, hunger. Always hunger. Not the kind that can be satisfied with food, but the kind born of circumstance. The kind that not only claws within a gut, but settles into a heart, consumes a mind. Deeper. Encircles, penetrates the soul. Hunger for something more, something better, safer. Always just out of grasp.

Craving. Starved.

It's part of me.

Who I am.

Born of blood and violence, hunger is my fate.

Yet, the slightest things can change the directions of a life. An unplanned circumstance, random act—a connection—a chance event, like a lightning strike, fate trumped.

Jamie is my lightning strike.

Tek Cain

Tek Cain was cultivated from birth to lead the motorcycle gang, Crimson Eight. Jamie Ryan, his best friend, is destined to be his second. But forbidden desires have them questioning everything they know, and an undeniable bond makes them want more than their supposed brotherhood can provide. Their love could get them killed, but they are bound to each other—from the cradle to the grave.

www.dreamspinnerpress.com

SJD PETERSON, better known as Jo, is a bestselling and award-winning author of gay romance. She lives in Michigan with her Itty Bitty Kitty and Little Man. She does her best writing when under pressure of deadlines and at 3:00 a.m. when the world is quiet. Jo loves to tell stories about real people with real flaws. The happily ever after isn't guaranteed unless it's earned through hard work and growth. Oh, but when it's comes, the rewards are all the better!

Facebook: www.facebook.com/SJD.Peterson

Blog: sjdpeterson.blogspot.com
Twitter: @SJDPeterson
Goodreads: www.goodreads.com/author/show/4563849.S_J_D_ Peterson
E-mail: sjdpeterson@gmail.com